In the Lies
of the
Beholder

PATRICK CLEVELAND

CHAPTER ONE

The tall figure passed under a street light and continued down the sidewalk at a brisk pace. At first glance, he could've easily been mistaken for a late night exerciser -- his head down and his arms pumping with each long stride. But in the middle of the block, where the glow of the light waned, he glanced over his shoulder in both directions before darting between two houses.

Concealed in the darkness, he sprinted behind the houses, ducked under a clothes line and then dodged a bird bath, before meeting the fence beyond that. Without slowing, his gloved hands slammed against the rail of the chain link fence, easily vaulting over it. Landing on both feet, he crouched and hid behind a hydrangea bush.

His heart pounded furiously, fueled by the rush of adrenalin and crack cocaine that coursed through his veins. He felt everything at hyper human levels: the cold steel of the gun barrel in his waistband; the edges of the lock-blade in his pocket; the individual fibers of his black stocking cap. And across the yard through the darkness, he could see his destination.

To an outsider, it was no different than all of the other houses on the block. They were all two bedroom, one story bungalows -- neatly lined up, one after the other. But he was no outsider. He was intimately familiar with what was inside, which according to his plan, would soon include him.

So far so good . . . no barking dogs . . . no motion activated lights. The only sound he could hear was his heart hammering in his chest.

But then came the crickets. One chirp first, close to him -- most likely from their leader. He knew his thumping heart had alerted them. The lead cricket picked up the vibrations on his tiny antennae and now he was warning the others. A second cricket quickly responded, followed by another, and then another. His first reaction was to befriend them with a lie; tell them that everything was all right. But it was too late. The crickets had turned against him with a wave of chirps that spread across the yard in a deafening noise.

Angry, he sprang from the bush toward the house. He had to get to the house, but he also had to kill the crickets before they warned the people inside. Firmly in the grip of drug-induced paranoia, he stomped his way forward in a hop-scotch pattern. Guttural grunts escaped through his clenched teeth as he slammed each foot to the ground, zigzagging across the lawn.

They're everywhere. They must stop. They must die.

Four, five six -- crunch, crunch, crunch. Seven, eight, nine -- it was an impossible task. Halfway to the house, he realized there were just too many -- he couldn't get them all. But he knew that if he killed enough of them, the others would be scared into silence. That's how things worked in his world.

In reality, there were only three crickets in the yard, none of which were trained in home security. Oblivious to his presence they chirped away in their efforts to attract a mate, and despite his wild stomping, they were never in any danger.

When he reached the rear of the small bungalow, he froze with his back pressed against the white clapboard. Panting heavily, he sucked in the night air, trying to catch his breath and slow his heart. Just for a moment, he thought about making another run across the yard to make sure they got the message, "You chirp . . . you die." But as the stillness of the night settled in around him, he realized he had defeated the crickets. He had stomped the little bastards into silence before they could ruin his plan.

Shuffling sideways, but being careful not to lean against the house, he made his way to the back door. When he was close, his gloved hand reached out and grasped the knob. It was locked, but he wasn't surprised. His plan would not change.

Continuing past the door, he eased his way with careful steps, until he reached the edge of the house. He knew there was a window just around the corner, only a few feet away. And that would be the point of no return.

In that moment, the thought of what he was about to do startled him. *What if the fucking crickets woke them up? It's not too late. Go back to the car.*

His eyes flashed wildly across the back yard, as if looking for a way to escape. But then he remembered -- it had to be done.

Fearful that his high was beginning to wear off, as well as his courage, he crouched down at the corner of the house and fumbled for his glass pipe and lighter. Just one more hit. Then he would see it through.

With some difficulty he retrieved the items from his back pocket and then slipped the glass tube into his mouth. His hand trembling, he cupped the end of the pipe to hide the flame of the lighter. After three clicks, the blue jet finally appeared. Touching the flame to the cylinder, the contents crackled as he sucked the powerful smoke deep into his lungs.

When the hot smoke entered his chest, a fresh wave of euphoria flooded his brain, numbing his senses. He dropped to both knees and slumped forward -- completely surrendering his mind, body, and spirit to his master. He had an intimate relationship with the little white rocks -- more intense than the pleasure of sex, more fulfilling than love, and more rewarding than the other God that he had never been able to feel. This master was part of him -- enveloping him in a hot, fiery embrace that massaged his entire soul.

His eyelids heavy, he stared into the darkness as the warm goodness cascaded over his body and radiated out to his extremities. He didn't know it, but the receiving neurons in his brain were crackling like tendrils of dry grass in a fire, causing an overload of the chemical messenger associated with pleasure. All he knew was that it felt good . . . real good.

That's it. That's my baby. All fucking better now.

After his brain adjusted to the initial blast of chemicals, the wave of euphoria subsided into a steadier stream of pleasure that buzzed within him. Filled with new confidence, he stood up and shoved the paraphernalia back into his pocket.

Do it. Get inside. Finish the job.

Feeling invincible now, he retrieved the folding knife from his front pocket and opened the blade with a flip of his thumb. Then he reached under his t-shirt and pulled the semi-automatic pistol from his waistband. With the knife in his left hand and the gun in his right, he was ready.

Sliding around the corner, he walked with slow and deliberate steps, cautiously approaching the window only a few feet away. When he was next to it, he discovered that it was open, and there was only a screen between him and his pay day.

He could clearly see the room which was glowing from the light of a television on the floor, between two small beds. The far bed was empty, but the bed closest to the window held his victim. He could see the slender, black male stretched out on the bed, wearing only sweatpants, snoring loudly.

Although the television screen was facing away from him, he could hear the voice of his favorite artist, Phelony H.O., dropping down his rhyme.

He call me H.O. -- I'm a habitual offender

He take my life -- put me down -- give me a Public Defender

Eyeing his prey from the shadows, his apprehension faded away. His confidence was bolstered by the television rapper, whose lyrics seemed to legitimize his plan. They were a team now. Phelony H.O. was telling him what to do.

Now I got a nine in my pants, check it out, bling bling.

Pop, pop goes my nine, you gonna die when it sing.

His heart held no emotion. There was no guilt; no conscience; no shame in what he would do. He was completely consumed by his drug-induced euphoria, the madness of his plan, and the angry rapper urging him on.

He slipped the knife through the screen at the highest point he could reach. Moving his arm in a quick motion, the blade whispered quietly across its width and down the side until it reached the bottom, where he twisted the blade one more time and then ran it across the entire width again. The feint sound of the blade slipping through the nylon screen was easily covered up by his accomplice, Phelony H.O.

You can fly really high, ridin' dirty, havin' fun

All you need is a nine, make it pop, watch 'em run.

In his mind, he had always pictured himself climbing through the window. But as he finished cutting the screen, he noticed the window was just high enough to cause a problem. Realizing it would take too long to enter by climbing, he quickly thought of another method.

You can fly really high . . . . That's what his boy said.

He pushed the lock on the knife and folded the blade before shoving it back into his pocket. With the gun in his hand, he backed up to the fence on the side of the house and then without hesitation, he coiled and sprang ahead. One, two, three -- he pumped his arms and legs forward. On the fourth step, he funneled all of his energy into his legs and launched himself into the air, flying head first through the flapped screen.

The sound of a body hitting the floor was unmistakable, even to the young man who was sound asleep on the bed.

"What the hell?" the man jerked upright. He saw someone scrambling near the foot of the bed, but his brain was unable to process the impending danger. Instead of jumping up to defend himself, he reached for his bed lamp. But by that time, the swiftly moving figure was almost on him.

The young man abandoned the lamp and stuck his hands up to protect himself. And through his splayed fingers, he saw the intruder's face in the glow of the television -- a face that he instantly recognized.

"Yo! What the hell you doing?" he screamed.

CHAPTER TWO

With no light bar or markings, the white Ford Crown Victoria didn't stand out in the stream of cars cruising down the main thoroughfare of Big Shanty, Virginia.   Just like other traffic in the southern town, it matriculated down its path at a steady pace, cautiously navigating each turn with signal lights, and of course, traveling the speed limit at all times. Perhaps in a another city, a driver in the same situation would've honked his horn and flashed his high beams to get the slower cars to move over, but he didn't. After all, he was a Southerner himself, and in no particular hurry.   Besides, he was responding to a homicide, which by definition meant there was no rush to save anyone.

According to the call, the scene was a private residence on Astor Street. Due to the location, John Keene already suspected drug involvement. Astor Street was just on the edge of Old Town, where most of the city's drug activity occurred, as well as four murders in the previous two years. But Keene knew those were just hoodlums killing each other on street corners. This thing -- this violent intrusion into the private sanctity of a home seemed different.

Keene turned his car onto Astor Street and saw the flashing police lights reflecting against the rows of houses. As he drove closer, he could see numerous cruisers in the street, as well as two ambulances, a fire truck, and several small groups of onlookers. A thin yellow band of police tape surrounded the entire perimeter of the house, including sections of the sidewalk and street.

From experience, Keene knew the onlookers would stay as long as the lights were flashing. Like moths to flame, they couldn't help themselves. It was human nature to want to be involved -- to be affected by tragedy. If they stayed long enough, they could tell the reporters that they knew the family and that they were personally impacted by the crime. If nothing else, each of them had a good story to tell their friends and coworkers the next day.

Keene parked his car and walked past the crowd. Without slowing, he ducked under the police tape. One officer looked his way, but didn't say anything.

"Where's Lieutenant Childress?" Keene asked.

The officer pointed to the house.

Keene continued past other officers, making his way to the porch. As he approached the small bungalow, Lieutenant Childress stepped out the front door.

The lieutenant was in his mid-fifties, nearing the end of his career in the Big Shanty Police Department, and he showed it. Ever since Keene had known him, he'd had a perpetually bored look, like an adult on a kiddy ride at the carnival. His white hair appeared to be styled by a hard night's sleep and his bushy white eyebrows stood up at the ends like a Great Horned Owl. He could've also used a diet, as his belly pushed tightly against the disposable protective suit that he was wearing.

"Good evening, Lieutenant," Keene said.

"Mornin'," Childress nodded.

"Sounds like you have a good one in there," Keene quipped.

"Oh, it's real good." Childress unzipped the front of his protective suit and retrieved a pack of cigarettes from his shirt pocket. He shook one into his mouth. "You really want to go in there?" he cupped his hands, lighting the cigarette.

Keene knew that Childress didn't want him in there so early, but he didn't care what Childress thought. Childress was a decent person and an adequate cop, but he was also stubborn and had a problem with authority, especially the authority that emanated from Keene's position as the Chief Commonwealth's Attorney. On more than one occasion, Keene had had to use that authority to put him in his place.

The last time Childress refused to allow him access to a fresh homicide, Keene called the Chief of Police, who gave Childress orders to cooperate fully with the Commonwealth's Attorney's office. In order to save face with his fellow officers, Childress's apology was ripe with sarcasm, but Keene accepted it anyway, knowing that his power over Childress and the police department had been fully validated.

"Yeah, I better go in," Keene answered. "I didn't get out of bed in the middle of the night to read reports."

"Put a bunny suit on and stay close to me; the evidence tech isn't done yet," Childress gestured with his cigarette to a box of plasticized paper suits.

Keene reached into the box and pulled out a disposable white jumpsuit. Unfolding it, he found the legs and stepped into it. As he finished zipping it up, Childress took one last drag from his smoke, spit in his hand, and dashed it out in his palm. Slipping the butt into his shirt pocket, Childress zipped up his suit and pushed open the door. "Let's do this then."

The familiar smell of death filled Keene's nostrils. Like opening an old trunk in a forgotten attic corner, the scent released a host of images from his past; graphic images of murder, blood and rotting flesh. But with a conscious effort, he quickly chased the demons back into their hidden corner and prepared himself for new ones as he continued inside.

A small vestibule opened up into the living room which was on Keene's left as he entered. There was a couch against one wall and a glass coffee table in front of it. Opposite the couch there was an entertainment center with a television and various photos and knickknacks on the shelves. Although untidy, the room didn't appear to be disturbed by violence.

Keene caught up with Childress who was standing in the hallway just off the living room. He pointed into the first doorway on the left. "Our first victim is a nineteen-year-old black male, shot once in the chest, point blank. Looks like the bad guy came through the window."

Keene looked inside the bedroom just as a camera flashed. The evidence tech was standing in the corner taking pictures of the body that was sprawled on the floor between two small beds.

The young man was shirtless and lying on his back with his eyes open. There was a dark hole in his chest, about the size of a dime, with streaks jetting outward, which appeared to be from the muzzle blast of the weapon. Obviously the killer had pressed the gun into the kid's chest and pulled the trigger. Keene couldn't see it, but he knew the exit hole in his back would be larger, as evidenced by the mat of dried blood that had formed around him.

Glancing about the room, Keene saw that it had been ransacked. The nightstand between the beds was upended and a lamp was broken on the floor. The closet doors were open and the clothes were strewn across the bedroom. Keene noted that whoever had killed the boy had gone through the closet afterwards, because the pile of clothes strewn from the closet continued across the room, partially covering the lower half of the deceased. Most importantly, Keene knew the killer had likely found what he had been looking for, because the living room had not been disturbed.

"Who found them?"

"The twin brother of this guy," Childress pointed to the bloody body. "Apparently he'd been out of town since yesterday, and returned home to find this nightmare. He's out on the street with other officers right now."

"How long have they been dead?"

"Anywhere from twenty-four to thirty-six hours. We'll know more once the M.E. digs into them. Watch out for those," he pointed to the floor.

Keene looked down and saw two empty shell casings circled with a fluorescent marking.

"What's the caliber?" Keene asked.

"Nine millimeter," Childress stopped near the end of the hall. "This is the father, who must've heard the commotion and got up to check it out. It looks like he was shot in the spine as he was running back to his room, and then once again in the back of the head when he was down."

Keene stepped past Childress and bent over the body for a closer look. The African-American male was facing down with his chin slightly tucked, so his face was not visible. One arm was bent upwards past his head and the other was down by his side, as if he had been swimming laps in the hallway. There was a hole in the back of his head. Another hole was present near the base of his spine. Blood from the spine hole had spilled into his boxer shorts, which had soaked it up like a sponge.

Childress pointed to the door at the end of the hallway. "The mother is in there . . . still in bed. You can look if you want. The tech's done in there." Then he added, "Excuse me for a second," as he keyed the microphone on his handheld radio Whether he was answering a call or making one, Keene couldn't tell. Either way, it was clear the bedroom was not a part of the crime scene Childress wanted to see again.

Keene took three steps to the end of the hallway and looked into the doorway on the right. Inside, there was a queen-size bed, which took up much of the small room. Although there was obviously a body lying on the bed, it was completely covered by a blood soaked sheet. Stepping into the room, Keene made his way to the side of the bed.

On the nightstand, he noticed an eight by ten framed photo of a man and woman holding each other. The woman was dressed in white and the man was wearing a tuxedo. Their cheeks were pressed together and they were both grinning at the camera, exuding pure, unabashed joy with the excitement of a new life together.

Staring at the photo, Keene imagined their life and the trials and tribulations they must have faced. Their lives, like that of any family, must have ticked by deceivingly slowly, but in definable stages. They fell in love, they married, they forged careers and then raised a family. Just when they seemed to have made it; when the boys they had raised had become men and were ready to take on the world by themselves, and when the middle aged couple began to look back and reflect upon the fruits of their labor, it suddenly ended. What they had accomplished in their lives and more importantly, what they had overcome, meant nothing to the person who had killed them.

But their lives meant something to Keene. Looking at the photo -- that snapshot in time from long ago, Keene knew that they were good people with good intentions. The woman's expression told him that.

She was beautiful then. Her full velvet-glossy lips were turned up in a wide smile, revealing bright white teeth with a small gap in the front. She had flawless ebony skin, stretched tight over high cheek bones, which gave her an exotic, almost model-like appearance. Her shiny black hair trailed down from a white veil and swept across her forehead, just above her eyes. Those eyes . . . .

It was her eyes that spoke to him. They were large, dark-brown pools of life, brimming with compassion. They were reflections of innocence, yet they held a certain, uncanny wisdom evincing knowledge of the future, as if she somehow knew that someday her life would end in tragedy. It was a secret she had kept to herself. But now, Keene could see it clearly, as if she was bearing her soul to him. Her eyes were pleading with him . . . begging him to act.

Look at me. See what he did to me.

Slowly turning to the bed, Keene's eyes fell upon the covered body.

Yes. It is me. I am with you.

He fought her advances at first, trying desperately to keep her at bay. But his senses betrayed him -- the smell of blood; the gaping wounds; the bedroom violence; the sight of death.

Mother.

With his senses sufficiently marinated, Déjà vu sunk her talons deep into his psyche. Surrendering his grip on reality, he melted into a time and place far away from the Lawson home, but strangely similar.

He was in *her* bedroom now. And *she* was there. He saw her body completely covered by the sheet. Out of breath, he stopped at the doorway, afraid to enter the room. Silence.

He was her only hope. He had to do something, but his legs were so heavy. Unable to lift them, he shuffled one foot in front of the other, slowly moving closer. Left . . . right . . . left. Pushing forward, he entered the beam of light escaping from the bathroom door. Almost to her now. His vision tapered into a narrow tunnel. There at the edge of the bed, he saw her hand protruding from the sheet -- dangling in the air. He tried to tell himself that it was all a bad dream. Maybe she was sleeping.

But then he saw the bloody sheets, which sent a wave of panic cascading through his body.

"Mother?"

He heard her groan and saw her hand twitch. She's alive! He could still help her! His heart racing, he ran to her side, grabbed the corner of the sheet and flung it back.

"Stop it," he whispered, chasing the memory of his mother away.

Death's putrid breath wafted into his face as he pulled back the sheet, unveiling the obscene corpse of Cleo Lawson. She was lying on her back with her head turned to him, as if she had been waiting for him. Her eyes swollen and bulging out of their sockets, she stared directly into his soul -- screaming in terror.

Although the woman's mouth appeared to be open in the form of a shriek, there was no sound. In fact, her mouth was not open at all. Looking closer, Keene realized that a bullet had gone through her face, right below her nose, creating a large hole through her upper lip, teeth, and gums.

He pulled the bloody sheet back farther to reveal her naked body. There were two other bullet holes in her torso, one in her abdomen and another in her shoulder. Blood had spilled from the holes, soaking the sheets around her.

"Son of a bitch," Keene said under his breath. A wave of nausea crept through him as he replaced the sheet, covering her face again. He turned to the photograph, hoping to replace the ghastly image of death with one of life. But he knew that it was too late. Her image would stay with him, just like the others.

He felt the anger building up within him as he stared at the photograph. This killer was no different than the others. He was an evil, merciless pig, who ignored the pleas of the innocent. He was a heartless coward who shot and killed a defenseless woman hiding beneath her sheets.

Keene also knew that when it came time for his punishment, the killer would be like the others, begging for mercy and crying for forgiveness. But he would get neither. Keene was going to take great pleasure in bringing this killer to justice and taking away his life and freedom as he had done to this family.

Taking one last glance about the room, he turned and went back into the hallway where Childress was busy writing on a pad of paper.

"What are their names?" Keene asked.

"The kid out front is Tommy Lawson. His dead brother in the other room is Timmy Lawson. And these are his parents, Frank and Cleo."

"Any suspects?"

"Yep," Childress answered. "Let's go outside."

They retraced their steps to the front door. Once outside, Keene drew in the fresh night air. He was glad to be out of the house. As a prosecutor, he knew he had it much easier than the detectives and evidence techs who had to wallow around in the blood and stench for hours. He wondered how many sleepless nights they would have, haunted by the grotesque images burned into their minds.

"Do you remember a guy named Larice Jones?" Childress asked as they were removing their bunny suits on the front porch.

"Of course." Although he had assigned one of his assistants to handle the case, he still knew the details, especially the outcome.

Larice Jones had been charged with distribution of crack cocaine approximately three months earlier. The narcotics division caught him making an exchange in a car behind a local convenience store. After the exchange, the jump team converged. They found a couple of rocks on the buyer and a pocket full of cash on Larice Jones.

When it came time for trial, the defense attorney for Jones came up with the theory that the buyer was working as a paid informant for the police and that his client was coerced into selling him crack cocaine. The defense attorney demanded to know the details of the set up and how much the informant had been paid for his work. Since the police didn't want to reveal the fact that the buyer was a paid snitch, especially considering the small amount of illegal drugs involved, Keene's office dropped the charges, and Larice was released.

"What does Jones have to do with this?" Keene asked.

"That dead kid in there was the snitch who set him up. We didn't realize it at first, but when the twin gave us the names, it kind of rang a bell with me. I called narcotics and they confirmed it."

"And where's Jones now?" Keene asked.

"We're not sure, but I have an unmarked unit sitting tight at his last known address, just keeping an eye out for him while we sort this thing out. We'll try to get those shell casings dusted and get as much as we can from the scene before we get a warrant."

"What's his address?"

"It's listed as Second Street. He apparently lives with his mother over there."

Childress placed his bunny suit in a bag and held it for Keene to dispose of his. "There's more," he added. "The twin knows Larice Jones -- he calls him Ice. And he's got some interesting information about him."

Childress waved his arm for Keene to follow as he turned and walked towards the street.

The nineteen year old twin was sitting on the trunk of a patrol car with his heels on the back bumper. Slender and athletically built, he was dressed in baggy jeans and a basketball jersey. Leaning forward with his chin in his hands and his elbows resting on his knees, his eyes were distant and pensive.

As they approached, Keene recognized that he was an identical twin to the corpse inside the house. Staring at the boy, Keene was struck with an eerie feeling, as if the dead body inside the house had stood up, wiped away the blood and then walked out and sat on the patrol car.

"How are you doing, Tommy?" Childress asked.

The young man looked down and shrugged his shoulders.

Keene saw that his body was suffering from tremors. No doubt due to the shock of seeing his family dead.

"I want you to meet someone. This is John Keene and he is the Commonwealth's Attorney. He's the guy that will prosecute whoever did this."

The young man looked up again, tilting his head and focusing his eyes on Keene.

"Hello son," Keene held out his hand. The kid extended his free hand from the blanket and Keene shook it. His hand was wet with perspiration.

"I'm sorry about your family," Keene dropped his hand to his pant leg and wiped it off. "This has to be a very difficult time for you."

The kid did not respond.

There was a moment of silence before Detective Childress continued. "I know you've told the officers all you know, but would you mind telling Mr. Keene about who you think did this?"

The kid glanced at Keene again before returning his stare to that distant place. His eyebrows furrowed into a hawk-like expression and his eyes began to blink and shift rapidly. "Allz I know is that Timmy's been messin' with drugs for awhile now. He got hooked up with a dealer named Ice, who was making him sell drugs. He wanted me to help, but I told him no way."

"Tell Mr. Keene about what happened lately," Childress interrupted. "About what you told me."

The young man shook his head. "A few weeks ago Timmy told me that he heard from another guy that Ice was out to get him. Ice thought Timmy set him up with the police and he was going to kill him for it. Timmy told me to watch out for Ice because he heard he was out of jail and if I ever saw him in the neighborhood, he told me I better run the other way . . . you know, cuz if Ice thought I was Timmy he might try to kill me by mistake." Tommy dropped his head and said more to himself than anyone, "I should've called the police. I should've done something."

"Have you ever seen this Ice guy?" Keene asked.

"Yeah, Timmy was hangin' with him for awhile. I saw him come and pick up Timmy a few times."

"What about recently, have you seen him recently near your house?" Keene pressed.

"Not for a few months."

"When's the last time you were home?"

"I haven't been home since yesterday morning," the kid answered. "I was in Richmond at a concert."

"Someone must be looking out for you. If you were home, you could be dead right now too," Childress stated.

The kid nodded without responding as his eyes slipped back into that faraway place.

"Hang in there," Childress said. He turned and nodded to Keene, and they both began walking back toward the house.

When they were a safe distance away from the kid, Keene asked, "How long is it going to take for the fingerprints?"

"Probably twenty four hours, but hopefully we'll know something before the sun comes up."

"All right. I'd just sit tight until you get something else. I don't think we have enough for an arrest yet, but you're doing the right thing by trying to keep an eye out for this Ice guy."

Childress seemed to ruffle. "Thanks for your input, but I think I can handle my job. You just take care of business when I catch him."

There's the attitude again, Keene thought. But he would let it go this time.

"I've got court in the morning, so I'm going home, but let me know if anything else comes up."

"As you wish," Childress answered.

CHAPTER THREE

Like many small towns along Virginia's Roanoke River, Big Shanty was spawned by a single ferry boat in the second half of the seventeenth century. After the ferry boat began its operations between the muddy banks, it didn't take long for other entrepreneurs to congregate along the river and construct buildings from which to sell goods to travelers. Eventually, as time passed, more buildings sprang up and the community of Big Shanty, Virginia, came into existence.

Although it was a ferry boat that gave birth to Big Shanty, it was tobacco and cotton that made it thrive. Throughout the eighteenth century, tobacco and cotton were the kings of agriculture, and Big Shanty prospered nicely with the help of slaves who toiled to produce the golden crops. But after the Civil War, the cotton and tobacco trades eventually faded away and manufacturing became the driving force of Big Shanty's economy.

The largest manufacturer, Gibbon Textile Company, had taken over many of the old tobacco warehouses and had been the city's largest employer for twenty-five years. But even its economic reign ended in the late 1980s and the warehouses in the downtown area were soon abandoned, like most of Main Street.

At the time of the Lawson family murder, there were no more tobacco fields. They had been replaced by numerous housing developments with paved streets, block curbs, and concrete sidewalks that curved in an out of a seemingly endless number of cul-de-sacs. In select corridors between these developments, shopping malls, super sized grocery stores, and big box department stores flourished, which caused the once bustling downtown area to slip into an economic coma. After all, most of the community's 100,000 residents had no reason to go downtown when there were major retail franchises offering them discounted Chinese goods in the suburbs.

Economics and landscape aside, there were some things in Big Shanty that hadn't changed much over the years. The city still prided itself as a Christian community with traditional southern values. For the most part, the people of Big Shanty enjoyed a clean lifestyle and they didn't tolerate those who strayed from the law. That's why John Keene did so well there.

Keene understood the culture of Big Shanty and the people who lived there. Although he grew up in Richmond, which was almost two hours away, he was sent to the Christian Boys Academy in Big Shanty when he was just twelve years old. If his mother had not died, his knowledge of Big Shanty would've ended in his grade school geography class, but such was not the case.

His Aunt, who had married a wealthy man from Baltimore, took custody of him after his mom died. Shortly thereafter, her well-to-do husband demanded that he be given a proper education; one that was far enough away so that he wouldn't interfere in their lives. For five years he stayed at the boarding school in Big Shanty, returning to visit his Aunt and Uncle in Baltimore only on holidays and three weeks during each summer.

After he graduated, they sent him to the University of Virginia in Charlottesville. By then, he knew that he wanted to eventually become a lawyer -- not because he thought he could make a lot of money, but because he knew it was the only way he could find purpose in his life.

With a degree in political science and the pull of his Auntie's rich husband, he went on to law school at Harvard. Three years later, he had his law degree and was ready to fulfill his destiny. And his destiny, which was spawned from the tragic loss of his mother, was to return to Big Shanty to serve the community. After all, the community and the Academy were the closest things that he ever had to a real family.

As a prosecuting attorney, John Keene's mission was to stop bad guys from hurting innocent people. That was his first and most important responsibility in life. In fact, it *was* his life and he had no problem admitting it. Unlike others, he never pretended that God and family came first. For him, justice came first. That's why he had never married. He didn't have time for a woman in his life, let alone children.

The people of Big Shanty appreciated his devotion, electing him as the community's chief prosecutor at the tender age of twenty-eight, with just four years of legal experience under his belt. But his swift rise to power had more to do with the unfortunate circumstances of his predecessor and a local degenerate named Marvin Lester, rather than his own legal acumen.

Marvin Lester owned and operated the only toy store on Main Street for as long as anyone could remember. But he wasn't just a business owner. He was also a city council member, as well as a member of the Chamber of Commerce. In addition, he served as one of the deacons in his church. Because of this, just about everyone in Big Shanty knew his name and many knew him personally.

Everyone knew about Marvin Lester's personal tragedy as well. Less than a year after he was married, his wife and unborn child had died in a horrible car accident. That's what Marvin Lester claimed, anyway. He had told everyone that he and his newlywed lived in Nashville, Tennessee and that after the horrible tragedy, he just wanted to move far away. He told everyone that he never got a chance to spoil his own child, so he opened his toy store in Big Shanty in order to devote his life to spoiling the children of others.

No one knew, at least for many years, that Marvin's love for children was an unnatural one. It started as a rumor, as such things always do. But for too many years, the rumors failed to grow into anything of substance. Perhaps it was because he was such a respected, upstanding member of the community. But more likely it was because he chose his victims very carefully.

It was always the troubled children who Marvin preyed upon. Marvin's victims, and there were allegedly many over the years, all fit a distinct profile. They were all just old enough to visit his store without their parents, they were all poor, and they all had few or no friends. Most importantly, every single victim had been caught trying to steal something in Marvin's toy store.

When he caught them, he would take them to his back room and lecture them about the evils of stealing. Then he would mention the police and the bad things that happen to children in jail. Finally, when he had them at their weakest moment, he would suggest a way out, an alternative form of punishment in which neither the police, nor the parents would have to get involved. Unfortunately for the children, the alternative punishment always involved touching Marvin's private parts.

After two different complaints, Marvin was arrested and faced trial. Fortunately for Marvin, the alleged victim had several larceny convictions on his juvenile record. Always the smooth talker, Marvin somehow convinced the jury that he was the victim and that it was the boy who was trying to capitalize on his falsely rumored past.

When the jury acquitted Marvin, the people of Big Shanty blamed the verdict on the inadequacies of the chief prosecutor. It didn't help that the major newspapers in the state picked up on the story, portraying the chief prosecutor of Big Shanty as a backwoods hillbilly, too ignorant to stop a child molester from hurting innocent children. And if a certain assistant prosecutor hadn't stirred the pot by contacting the newspapers with the story, perhaps there never would have been a change in the prosecutor's office.

But John Keene, who was that assistant prosecutor, saw his window of opportunity and capitalized on it. Just three months before the fall election, he resigned from the Commonwealth Attorney's office and ran against his former boss as an independent. During his campaign, he told the people of the community their chief prosecutor was soft on crime and that it was time for change. Without mentioning any specific names, he vowed to bring criminals to justice, including those that had escaped prosecution in the past.

His timing could not have been better. The community *was* ready for change. And they showed it by electing John Keene as their Commonwealth's Attorney.

Shortly after he took office, Keene began his investigation into the affairs of Marvin Lester. He was able to make contact with some of the victims who had previously failed to come forward, one of whom had since moved out of town. With Keene's prodding, the father and his boy agreed to cooperate in Marvin's prosecution. Keene reopened the old case and convinced the grand jury to indict Marvin Lester for numerous felonies.

When the case finally went to trial, the jury convicted Marvin Lester of taking indecent liberties with a child and John Keene became a local hero. True to his word, Keene finally obtained justice for the people of his community, putting Marvin Lester in prison for twenty years. He was their savior and he knew it. And in the final year of his third term, he continued to take his responsibilities as the town savior very seriously.

In the years following Marvin Lester's conviction, the leaders of Big Shanty tried hard to forget about the entire affair. They didn't like the blemish that Marvin Lester had made on their community and they were desperate to move on. In their efforts to attract new industry to town, they wanted to focus on Big Shanty's Christian values, southern hospitality, and low crime rate, rather than the aberration of Marvin Lester.

That's not to say that Big Shanty was free of crime. Like most medium sized communities, there were plenty of sexual assaults, larcenies and burglaries occurring on a weekly basis, not to mention the steady stream of intoxicated drivers and wife beaters. But those crimes hardly made the news in Big Shanty. For the most part, such crimes were buried in the back pages of the newspaper and all but ignored by the community. They didn't want to face the reality that crime was on the rise and that drugs were the primary cause of it.

But all that changed when the people of Big Shanty read about the slaughter of an innocent family in their home at 21 Astor Street. Once again, they were forced to admit that even Big Shanty had its share of evil.

The *Big Shanty Gazette* was all over it. "Family Murdered in Their Sleep," the headlines proclaimed. There was a full color photo of the house just below the headlines and photos of each of the family members offset to the right. In the large photo of the house, two men could be seen on the front porch, wearing white disposable suits.

Everyone was talking about it; at the coffee shops where people stopped for five dollar coffee on their way to work; in the breakfast diners where the elderly gathered to gossip about their neighbors; and at office buildings, where workers discussed it over the tops of cubicles. Throughout the day, the horrible crimes remained on the mind of just about everyone. They all wanted to know who did it and when they would get caught.

John Keene and the police department already knew who was responsible for the crimes. They just didn't have any hard evidence to prove it. The problem was that all of the crime scene evidence had to be shipped to the state lab in Richmond. The fingerprints would be the first to come back, perhaps within a day, but the blood, fiber, and hair analysis usually took months. And John Keene knew that he didn't have months to take action on this one.

He knew that the citizens of Big Shanty would not feel at ease until an arrest was made. Besides that, the Mayor and two city council members had already called, wanting to know what was being done.

What was being done was all that could be done. There was a "be on the lookout" for Larice Jones on the computer and unmarked police units continued their surveillance at his last known address. In addition, narcotics officers were busy contacting all of their snitches and other sources for any information that would lead to the whereabouts of the prime suspect.

But by the end of the first day after discovering the bodies, despite all of the efforts of the police department, Larice Jones had still not been found. Not that they could've arrested him at that point anyway. Keene knew that they didn't have enough to charge him with anything. Nonetheless, it would have been nice to know where he was in order to keep him contained until the results came back from the lab.

Whether it was luck or fate, or a little of both, the question of Larice Jones' whereabouts was answered at approximately 6:30 p.m. the next evening, just as the people of Big Shanty were discussing the murders over dinner.

John Keene was still at his desk, reviewing the following day's court cases when his cell phone rang. It was Lieutenant Childress.

"9-1-1 just received a call from a male, claiming to know where Larice Jones is," he said.

"Who called?" Keene asked.

"They don't know. All they could tell me was that it was a male voice and it sounded like he was African-American."

"What'd he say?"

"He said that he knew who did it. He said the guy's name was Ice and that he was hiding in the yellow house on the corner of 3rd Avenue and Sherman Street."

"Interesting."

"I've already sent an unmarked unit over there. I'm on my way to get a search warrant right now," Childress added.

"Can they trace the call? We need to find the caller," Keene said.

"They tried. The call came in from a prepaid cell phone. That's all they have."

"All right," Keene said. "I'll need the tape of the call. Can you have them send it over?"

"Sure thing."

"Good luck," Keene said before hanging up.

To Keene, the call seemed legitimate, but only because he knew that they had not released any suspect names to the media. Unfortunately, the caller didn't say how he knew such information. This bothered Keene because it meant that the caller could've been involved in the crime. The only other possibility was that the caller either witnessed the crime or Larice Jones told him about it. Perhaps the recording of the call would give him a better clue, he thought. It would be nice to hear the caller's voice to see if it could be identified.

There was something else that bothered Keene. Even though the caller had identified Larice Jones as the killer, his anonymity could pose a problem. Keene spun in his chair and pulled his home-made handbook regarding search and seizure law from the shelf behind his desk. He paged to the cases that he had collected regarding snitches, tipsters, and anonymous callers.

It didn't take him long to find the case that was "on all fours" as they say. After reading the case, he pushed the manual aside and quickly dialed Childress's cell phone. When Childress didn't answer, Keene left a message.

"Lieutenant, it's John. I've done some quick research. The anonymous caller isn't enough. Don't even try to get the search warrant yet -- it's not going to pass muster in court. Call me as soon as you can."

* * * * * * *

The yellow house on the corner appeared to be dark and unoccupied, which is why the narcotics officers were focusing their attention on the street and sidewalk, waiting for Ice's return. They both knew who they were looking for -- a twenty year old African-American male, five feet-eleven inches tall and 200 pounds with multiple felony and misdemeanor convictions, including cocaine possession, cocaine distribution, firearms charges and assault. With that record, neither of the officers was surprised when he was named as the primary suspect in the year's first multiple homicide.

"When's the last time you had contact with him?" Officer James Huber asked his partner.

"Three months ago. An informant made a buy from him and we got him for distribution. I put a pretty good knot on his head, too. But I guess after three months, he forgot his lesson and now he's back. Only this time he's turned it up a notch."

Seconds later a light came on in the house. Both of them jerked to attention as Officer Huber grabbed the radio. "Fourteen three . . . we have activity in the house."

A shadow moved across the window and then disappeared.

"We know you're in there," Huber whispered. "And there's only one way out."

Their orders were to conduct surveillance and report any activity while they waited for Detective Childress to get the search warrant. Once they identified the suspect, they were to maintain visual contact and report his actions and whereabouts.

Over the next few minutes, the officers watched the shadow re-appear in the window several times as they sat in their unmarked van across the street. But then the light went out, which put them on immediate alert. A moment later, the suspect opened the front door. And that's when the surveillance plan fell apart.

"Fourteen three," Officer Huber quietly announced over the radio. "We have a visual on the suspect. He's exited the front door of the house. You may want to send backup units to the area in case he runs."

The suspect appeared lost at first, standing in the middle of his driveway. The officers watched him as he looked up and then down the street. When his eyes fell upon the unmarked police van, both officers instinctively slouched, but it was too late. A second later, Ice bolted in the opposite direction, towards the side of the yellow house.

"Fourteen three, 10-80! He's on the run, north side of the house, on foot!" Huber screamed into his radio. Both officers scrambled from the van and ran towards the house. "Stop . . . police!" they yelled, but the suspect had already rounded the rear corner of the building. Huber trailed him while the other officer peeled away and ran around the other end of the house.

"He's coming around!" Huber yelled.

As his partner rounded the opposite corner of the house, his legs pumping at full speed, he ran head on into Ice, who was trying to double back. The impact caused both of them to reel backwards and fall. But before Ice could regain his feet, Huber was on him.

"Show me your hands!" he screamed, pointing his flashlight in one hand and his weapon in the other. "Put 'em on your head or I'm gonna shoot!" he yelled again. The young man complied, raising his hands to the back of his head, as he lay face first on the ground. Huber's partner scrambled to his feet and with all of his weight behind him, dropped down onto the suspects back with his knee. Ice bellowed as the air was forced from his lungs. The officer grabbed one of his hands, cracked a cuff against his wrist, twisted his arms down and cuffed both hands behind his back. After patting him down and searching his pockets, the officer stood up to catch his breath.

"Dumb, dumb, dumb," he said between quick breaths. "Don't ever fucking run. Don't you know that?"

Ice writhed on the ground, gasping for air, unable to respond.

"Stop moving around!" the officer screamed, giving him a solid kick to the buttocks with his steel toed work shoe.

"Oww!" Ice yelled. "That ain't necessary!"

After Huber holstered his weapon, he reached down and grabbed Ice by the arm, jerking him to his feet. "Larice Jones," he said, grabbing his hair and pulling him close to his face. "You're under arrest for murder."

"What you talking about?" Ice whined.

"You know what I'm talking about," the officer answered.

"You got the wrong guy. I got nothin' to do with it!"

"Nothing to do with what?"

"Nothin' to do with nothing'!"

"We'll see about that," Huber keyed his hand held radio. "Fourteen three, suspect is in custody."

When Lieutenant Childress arrived, there were three marked units on the street in front of the yellow house with lights flashing. He pulled his car in behind the units and the narcotics officers met him as he was getting out.

"Where's Ice?" Childress asked.

"He's in the cruiser there," Huber pointed.

As they were speaking, Special Agent Calhoun, the supervising officer of the narcotics division arrived. Standing well over six feet with a heavy muscular build, he looked more like a professional wrestler than a cop. Although he was dressed in jeans and a t-shirt, with a baseball cap twisted backwards, it was only a cover. He was all cop -- ruling the streets of Old Town with an iron fist. Despite the occasional complaint from a disgruntled citizen who cried abuse, Calhoun was one of the most valuable assets of the police department. He knew the streets, he knew the inner workings of the drug community, and he knew Ice.

Calhoun went directly to Childress. "That the search warrant?"

"Yep," Lieutenant Childress answered. "You want the honors?"

"Of course." Calhoun took the paper Childress offered. Calhoun was the officer who supervised the buy between Timmy Lawson and Larice

Jones three months earlier. And everyone in the department knew that Calhoun resented the outcome.

"Anyone Mirandize him yet?" Calhoun asked.

"I did," Officer Huber answered.

Calhoun eyed the house and then looked up and down the street before approaching the cruiser. He opened the rear door and leaned in.

"Well, hello there," Calhoun greeted him in a sarcastic tone. "You look familiar."

Ice glanced at Calhoun and then turned away.

"It seems like we just put you in jail not more than a few months ago, and now, here you are in trouble again. You don't learn too well, do you?"

Ice did not respond.

"I was over at the house last night. And what you did to that family is a horrible thing."

Ice's eyes widened. "I didn't do nothin' to nobody!"

"Where's the gun? Is it in the house?"

Ice looked away and shook his head. "I don't own no gun."

"Is anyone else in the house?"

"I ain't gonna talk to you," Ice hissed.

"Don't be stupid, Ice. You're in one big heap of shit here and you're the only one that can help yourself now. If you cooperate, I may be able to help you. If you don't, I'm gonna come down on you hard . . . real hard."

"You gonna do nuthin' but try to put me in jail," Ice glared. "Like you tried to do the last time."

Calhoun shook his head. "You just don't get it do you? I've got a search warrant right here!" he slapped Ice in the face with the judge signed paper. "And this time, no fancy lawyer's gonna save your ass!" Calhoun slammed the door before Ice could respond.

"I've got this, Lieutenant," Calhoun smiled at Childress.

CHAPTER FOUR

At 9:03 p.m. John Keene was still in his office, waiting for Lieutenant Childress to return his call. He was hoping Childress had received his messages and hadn't attempted to get a search warrant. But he feared the worst.

When Childress's number flashed on his cell, he was quick to answer the call.

"What's going on?" Keene barked.

"We've got him in custody," Childress answered. "And we're taking him in for an interview."

"Didn't you get my message?"

"What message?" Childress sounded somewhat sincere.

"My message that you should wait on the search warrant."

"Too late. The magistrate already issued the warrant and his house is being searched as I speak. Why would you want us to wait?"

Keene shook his head. There was no point in continuing the argument.

"Never mind. Where are you taking him?"

"To the interview room at the station."

"I'll meet you there," Keene said. "Don't start without me."

When Keene arrived at the police station a few minutes later, Childress was standing at the rear door smoking a cigarette.

"We've got him chilling out," Childress took one last drag from his cigarette, put the butt in a tall cylinder beside the door, and waved his badge across the electronic pad. The lock clicked open and Keene followed him in.

Childress led Keene through a large room filled with desks, some of which were occupied by narcotics officers. In a corridor on the other side they passed two metal doors with small windows. At the third door, Childress paused to glance in the window. "He's in this one."

Keene stepped up. A young black male was sitting in a chair next to a small table in the corner of the room. He was wearing a blue track suit with white stripes on the sleeves and pant legs. The top was unzipped halfway, exposing a thick gold chain on his bare chest.

"Come on, let's go to the control room," Childress beckoned.

They entered the control room at the end of the hall, which was nothing more than a room with two folding tables. There was a digital recording machine on the table to the left and three large monitors occupying the table on the right. Keene took a seat in one of the empty chairs in front of the monitor table as Childress powered up the recorder and flicked on the middle monitor, which was a live feed from the interview room where Ice was sitting.

The bird's eye view of Ice gave Keene a detached feeling of power, as if he was God looking down upon a lowly sinner. Although Ice appeared puny and powerless with his hands cuffed behind his back, Keene knew the evil secrets that lay in his heart and what he had done.

There will be no mercy for you, Keene thought, as the words from Ezekiel came to him.

I will treat you in accordance with the anger and jealousy you showed in your hatred of them and I will make myself known among them when I judge you.

A knock on the door interrupted his thoughts. The door opened and an officer leaned in. "Tommy Lawson is here," he announced.

"Bring him in," Lieutenant Childress waved.

The door opened wider and an officer escorted the surviving twin into the room.

"Take a look at the monitor," Childress pointed. "Is that the guy your brother's been hanging with?"

The kid leaned forward and then answered. "That's him. That's Ice."

"You sure, now?"

"Absolutely positive," Lawson nodded.

"Thanks for coming down here, son," Detective Childress said to the boy. "I don't think we'll need anything else from you, tonight. Did you find a place to stay?"

"Yes sir. I'm staying with a friend."

"Just let one of the officers know where you'll be so we can contact you if we have to."

"All right."

The officer escorted Lawson from the control room as another plain clothed, but younger-looking officer entered. "You want me to stay on this end?" he asked Childress.

"Yeah, that would be best. You know John Keene, don't you?"

The officer looked at Keene and stuck out his hand. "Nice to see you Mr. Keene."

"Likewise," Keene shook his hand. Although the officer looked familiar, Keene didn't know his name and he really didn't care to know it, either.

Childress finished keying information into the machine and started the recording process before standing up. "Let me know if Calhoun shows up with anything from the search warrant."

"Will do," the officer took a seat beside Keene in front of the monitors.

Keene watched the monitor as Childress entered the interview room.

"Hello, Mr. Jones," Childress pulled a chair up to the table. "My name is Lieutenant Childress and I'm going to be working with you tonight. I'm sorry this is taking so long," he added. "If I take those cuffs off, you're not gonna run or do anything stupid, are you?"

"No, man. I ain't about that," Ice answered.

Not that he had the choice, Keene thought as he stared at the monitor. He probably knew the door to the interview room automatically locked when shut.

"I wanna make a report," Ice rubbed his wrists where the cuffs had left ridges. "For police brutality."

"I can help you with that," Childress took a pen from his pocket and clicked it. "We can talk about it and I can get you a complaint form to fill out. But right now, we need to go over a few formalities before we can do anything else," Childress placed a form on the table and slid his chair closer. With the pen in his hand, he began writing at the top of the paper. "Is it Larice or Lareese?" he asked.

"Larice . . . as in Ice."

"Is that what you go by, Ice?" Childress asked.

"Some people call me that," he shrugged.

"Let me explain something, Ice . . . may I call you Ice?"

"Yeah, whatever."

"We haven't taken out any formal charges on you yet because we want to find out if you're willing to cooperate with us first. Your level of cooperation may be important when we decide if and what to charge you with. Now, what we're talking about is the death of three people over on Astor Street. But before I ask you any questions, I need to go over a few things with you."

Childress showed him the advice of rights form and then went through each paragraph, reading all of the Miranda rights. Childress then asked him to initial each paragraph and sign the bottom statement that he read and understood everything.

Childress retrieved the form and continued. "Now that we got the formalities out of the way, let's talk about this case here and see if we can't figure out how this happened."

"I don't know nothin' about it," Ice interrupted.

"Well, maybe you don't. But then again, maybe you do know something that could help us and you just don't realize it yet," Childress explained. "You'd want to help us if you could, wouldn't you?"

"Sure, man. Sure," Ice nodded.

"Let me tell you this. It's a bad scene over there at that house. There's three people dead and they were definitely murdered. You know what street I'm talking about don't you?"

"What street is it?"

"Astor street."

"Yeah, I know where it is," Ice shrugged. "But I don't know anybody there."

"Did you hear anything about the incident? You know, like on the news or on the street?"

"Never heard nothin' about it," Ice leaned back and folded his arms.

"One of them is a teenager. His name is Timmy Lawson. Do you remember him?"

Ice blinked rapidly and looked away. "Nope."

"Are you sure? He's the kid that bought crack cocaine from you that night a few months ago when you were last arrested. You remember that, don't you?"

Ice squinted and looked away before his eyes widened. "Oh yeah," he said as if he had forgotten about it.

"And I heard that you were pretty good friends with him, that is until he set you up with the police," Childress said.

"I don't know nothin' about that," Ice flinched. "We wasn't even friends."

"You know what I heard? I heard that you knew him real well and that you had been hanging out with him for over a year. You knew where he lived, right?"

Ice blinked rapidly again. "Man, you got it all wrong. The only thing I know is that the guy's name was T, but that's all. I sure as hell don't know where he lives."

Someone knocked on the interview room door. Childress looked over his shoulder and then turned back to Ice. "I've got to talk to somebody for a second. Can I get you something to drink? Water or a soda?"

"I'll have a soda," Ice wiped the corners of his mouth with his fingers.

"No problem, I'll be right back." Childress walked to the door and leaned ahead, passing the fob on his badge across the electronic pad and unlocking the door. He stepped through the door and off the video screen which Keene was watching intently.

From the control room, Keene couldn't see who had knocked on the door, but he figured it was an officer involved in the search of Ice's house. Not wanting to take the chance that he would miss any information, Keene exited the control room and made his way towards the interview room. As he approached the interview room, he heard Childress' voice down the opposite corridor. He followed the sound of the voice until he found Childress and Calhoun in the break room at the end of the hall.

Childress was searching his pockets for coins in front of the soda machine.

"You got any quarters?" he asked, looking up at Keene.

Keene reached into his own pockets and retrieved two quarters. "Anything from the search warrant?" he asked, looking at Calhoun.

"They're still there," Calhoun answered. They haven't found a weapon yet, but we found a gold Armani watch with the letters T L engraved on the back. I called Tommy Lawson and he confirmed that it's Timmy's watch. He said that his grandmother had given them the watches for high school graduation."

"Nice."

"There's more," Calhoun continued. "We found an owe list in a Bible that he kept in his nightstand. Timmy Lawson was on that list."

"Was it his full name and address, or just the letter T for Timmy," Childress asked.

"It said 'Timmy, Astor Street' and there were several numbers behind the name."

"He lied about knowing him," Childress said. "He told me that he only knew the kid as T and he didn't know where he lived."

"He say anything else?" Calhoun asked.

"He's denying everything. But the brother has identified him as the guy who Timmy had been involved with. He said he saw Ice come by on occasion to pick Timmy up. But we haven't confronted him with any of that information yet."

"May I?" Calhoun asked.

"Sure," Childress answered, "you're the one who knows him best." Childress pushed the button on the machine and a can of soda pop rattled down into the dispenser. "Let's go turn him over."

Keene returned to the control room and watched the monitor as Childress and Calhoun entered the interview room. Ice seemed happy to see Detective Childress again, who opened the can and handed it to him. But his expression changed when Calhoun stepped into the room behind him.

Calhoun didn't bother with a greeting. "I think I know why they call you Ice . . . Ice. Only someone named Ice could kill a teenager, his father, and his defenseless mother, and then sit here and sip a soda like nothing happened."

"I didn't do nothin'!" Ice yelled, choking on the drink.

"Yeah, I know. You didn't do nothin'. You don't know anybody over there on Astor Street. You never heard anything about this. But I know you're lying."

"I've told the detective here everything I know," Ice exclaimed.

"Oh?" Calhoun asked. "Did you tell him that you deal drugs for a living and that you keep an owe list in your Bible with Timmy's name in it?" Calhoun asked. "T-I-M-M-Y, Timmy. And did you tell him that you also knew Timmy lived on Astor Street like you wrote in your Bible? Did you tell the Lieutenant that, or did you lie to him and say you only knew him as T?" Calhoun asked sarcastically.

Ice dropped his head, not wanting to make eye contact with him.

"Let me tell you something," Calhoun leaned forward. "When someone kills three people over drugs, do you know what they do to you? That's a capital murder charge right there. That means they will kill you with electricity. The chair, Ice. That's what they're going to do to you when you're found guilty of capital murder. And let me tell you, I've been really busy tonight and I know a lot more about you than you think I know. So you better decide right now what direction you want to go with this. If you cooperate, that may go a long way towards convincing us that you don't deserve to be electrocuted. If you don't cooperate and you want to keep lying to us, you're only hurting yourself in the end."

"Man, I'm telling you, I didn't do this thing," Ice pleaded.

"Yes you did," Calhoun answered quickly. "I suppose next you're going to tell me that you don't own a nine millimeter gun and you don't deal drugs. Go on . . . Ice! Look me in the face and tell me you don't have a gun and you don't deal drugs."

"I don't!" Ice stammered. "I ain't got no gun. So if you found one, you planted it," Ice countered.

"We found lots of good stuff in your house," Calhoun ignored him. "I already told you about the owe list in the Bible, but there was other stuff -- the drug scale, the cash in the sugar tin, the cash in the hole in the wall behind the picture, and the baggies you use for packaging the stuff. We found other things too, Ice. The kinds of things that prove you were the murderer. But I'm not going to bother talking about it unless you decide to cooperate." Calhoun paused. "Now, Lieutenant Childress is a patient guy. He could probably sit here and listen to you lie about things all night. But I'm not so patient. And I'm going to give you one last chance to come clean on this and take a step towards saving your own life."

Calhoun leaned closer and stuck out his muscled arm, jabbing his finger in Larice's chest. "If the next words that come out of your mouth are a lie, it's all over. I'm going down to the magistrate to get capital murder warrants. And you'll have nobody to blame but yourself."

Keene smiled as he watched from the control room. Calhoun was bluffing. Only a Commonwealth Attorney could take out capital murder warrants.

Ice looked around the room, as if he wanted to escape. "I want to talk to my mama," he said. "I want Mama here before I say anything."

Calhoun laughed. "You want your mama?" He looked over to Lieutenant Childress and continued to laugh. "The bad ass killer is just a poor baby who wants his mama, Lieutenant. Can you believe that?" Calhoun forced another laugh, then leaned into Ice again. "Let me tell you something," he breathed. "You're not a juvenile anymore, Ice.

You're in the big time now and you don't have a right to have your mama here during questioning."

"But I didn't kill them people!" Ice whined.

Agent Calhoun lost his cool. "If you didn't kill them, then how did Timmy Lawson's watch end up in your bedroom!" he yelled, slamming his fist onto the table.

Ice jumped and his eyes widened. His mouth started moving and he began to stutter something, but Calhoun cut him off. "That's right . . . the gold watch with the letters "TL" on the back. Timmy Lawson's watch. We found it on your nightstand. You stole it after you killed him."

Ice stammered again, but Calhoun held up his hand.

"Not a word," he said, "unless you really want to save your life and tell us the truth."

"Listen," Childress cut in, playing the nice cop. "I don't think you really went over to that house wanting to kill those people. That's why we're giving you this chance to cooperate, to tell your side of what happened. You probably just wanted to get some money back or some crack cocaine, or whatever he was dealing for you. And then things got crazy once you got into the house. Maybe the kid attacked you and you didn't have a choice. Maybe you got scared and he got shot and then things spiraled out of control. It's okay," Childress said softly. "Believe me. We see things like this happen all the time. Don't we?" he turned to Calhoun.

Calhoun nodded. "All the time."

"That's right, all the time," Childress continued. "One person intends to get something back from someone that owes him and the next thing you know, all hell's breaking loose. And the guy never meant to harm anyone. And that's the kind of scenario that can save your life. If you meant to go over there and kill them . . . well that's one thing. But if it was something different . . . like it happened on the spur of the moment . . . well, then that's different. If this was some sort of accident, then they probably won't put you in the electric chair. So just do yourself a favor and let us know what happened. Now's your chance." Without skipping a beat, Childress continued. "How long ago did you first meet this Timmy Lawson kid?"

Ice looked at Childress, and then at Calhoun. It appeared that he was thinking very hard, wringing his hands together and slightly rocking in his chair. After a few moments, he spoke.

"What if I tell you that I did it?" he asked. "Will that keep me from going to the electric chair?"

Calhoun grinned. "I can promise you one thing. I will personally talk to the prosecutor and let him know that you cooperated. And I will recommend that he give you a prison sentence, instead of the electric chair. A prison sentence would be better for you than the electric chair, wouldn't it?" Calhoun asked.

Ice nodded. "Yes sir. I don't want no electric chair."

"Very good then," Calhoun said reassuringly. "We have ourselves a deal. Tell us what you did."

Ice stared at the table. It appeared that he was looking at the advice of rights form that he had signed. He reached out and picked up the form, examining it closer. After a few moments, he turned to Calhoun.

"I'll tell you," Ice said. "But first I better do what this paper says and talk to a lawyer."

John Keene sighed in the control room. The kid had just unequivocally requested an attorney. And the law was clear. Once a defendant asked for an attorney, the police couldn't question him any further. It's all over, Keene thought. There will be no confession.

The control room door opened and an officer leaned in. "Is Childress here?" he asked.

Keene looked at the officer, recognizing him as a tech who had been at the crime scene. He slid his chair to the side and pointed at the monitor. "He's in the interview room. What's up?"

"We just got the lab results on the shell casing fingerprints. They're a match for Larice Jones."

Keene smiled and turned to the monitor. "You stupid son of a bitch," he said to the monitor. "Lawyer or not . . . you're going down."

CHAPTER FIVE

On Thursday morning, Big Shanty's Chief Public Defender unfolded his newspaper and read the headlines: "Suspect Nabbed in Murder Case." The article relayed all of the typical information that a reporter could retrieve from the arrest warrants. The suspect's name was Larice Jones, he was a twenty-year-old black male and a resident of the city. He was charged with a host of crimes, including breaking and entering, three counts of robbery, six counts of using a firearm in the commission of a felony, possession of a firearm by a convicted felon, and of course, three counts of murder in the first degree. The reporter also noted that he was a convicted felon. Next to the article, there was a booking photo of Larice Jones. He looked very scared.

The reporter who wrote the article also had an inside connection. According to unnamed sources, the reporter claimed the suspect's fingerprints were identified on the shell casings left at the scene and that the crime involved illegal narcotics.

When he finished reading the article, Nolan Getty spun in his chair and typed the suspect's name into his client database. Numerous entries appeared on the screen. His office had previously represented him on several misdemeanors, including trespassing, driving suspended, marijuana possession, and assault; some as a juvenile, others after he was eighteen. And then there was his first felony at age eighteen: possession of a controlled substance, followed by possession of a firearm by a convicted felon when he was nineteen years old. The firearm charge had been reduced to a misdemeanor attempted possession.

As Nolan paged through the database entries, he heard a knock on his door. He looked up to see Vicki, his secretary, enter his office. She was dressed in a white blouse and a black skirt. As usual, her blouse was unbuttoned just enough to expose her cleavage, which was always a problem for Nolan to ignore. Rising to the challenge, Nolan pulled his eyes from her chest and saw that she was carrying a stack of manila folders in her hands, which he knew were new clients the court had appointed his office to represent.

"Let me guess," Nolan said. "Does one of those files have the name Larice Jones on it?"

Vicki smiled. "You're a real genius."

Nolan shrugged. "There goes my summer vacation at the beach. And this year I was going to take the whole office."

"I'm allergic to the sun, anyway," Vicki dropped the stack of files on Nolan's desk. "I've already checked -- there's no conflict."

Nolan grimaced. He had been hoping there would be some sort of client conflict which would prevent his office from representing the murder defendant. Sometimes, the victims or the victim's family were current or former clients, which would create such a conflict. But according to Vicki, he had no such luck, which meant that he would have a long, busy summer preparing for one of the biggest cases in recent history.

Without hesitation, Vicki turned and walked away. Nolan watched as her hips danced rhythmically to each step, until she had turned the corner and disappeared out of sight. She had a great figure for her age, which was ten years older than him. She was also smart enough to handle three lawyers, as well as the scheduling of their entire case load, which was the main reason that she had been the office manager long before he had become the Chief Public Defender.

Reaching for the stack of files, Nolan spread them apart until he found the Larice Jones folder. He opened it and immediately saw the stamp from the court on the advisement papers: "Defendant Requested Bond Hearing." In the blank next to the stamp was a hand written date for the hearing, which was the next morning. Although Nolan usually liked to stay out of the courts on Fridays, he knew that he wouldn't be able to wait for this one. He'd have to show up in the morning so that his new client wouldn't start freaking out, even though the bail hearing was a complete waste of time.

The truth of the matter was that if the magistrate hadn't given the defendant a bond when he was arrested, the judge sure as hell was not going to be inclined to give one either. And when it came to something serious, like murder, no one in Big Shanty had ever been given bail.

But Nolan would go through the motions of a bail hearing anyway. After all, that was what he was paid to do.

Picking up the phone, he dialed the Commonwealth's Attorney's Office. Once connected, he punched in the extension of the scheduler, who answered on the first ring.

"Hello Elizabeth, it's Nolan. "How are you this fine morning?"

"I'm doing well, considering," she answered.

"Considering what?" Nolan asked. "That you work for an obsessive maniac?"

She laughed. "Now you know I can't comment on that. What can I do for you?"

Nolan always liked to tease her. She seemed to be the only person in the entire Commonwealth's Attorney's Office who had a sense of humor and a lick of common sense.

"I was just calling to see who the attorney is in the big murder case -- Larice Jones is the defendant's name.

"Let's see here," she said. Nolan heard clicking sounds from a keyboard. "Oh," she exclaimed. "It's Mr. Keene."

Nolan winced again. It was the last name he wanted to hear. "I thought we had a silent agreement -- you keep him pushing papers at the office and I whip up on his assistants in the courtroom. It's been working just fine so far."

Elizabeth laughed. "I know one thing. He sure does have his shorts in a bunch over this one."

"I'll bet he does," Nolan commented. "They're tighty whities, aren't they?"

Elizabeth laughed again. "Goodbye Mr. Getty."

CHAPTER SIX

August 18th, Big Shanty Circuit Court

In late August, the Big Shanty Valley becomes a reservoir of oppressing heat and stifling humidity. The puffy clouds that drift across the sky provide only temporary relief from the blazing sun. It was that way when the ferry boat operation began, even so when the Union blue soldiers made their way across the Roanoke River in the Battle of Big Shanty, and so it was in the new millennium.

On a particularly hot summer day in August, as the high clouds drifted over the Blue Ridge Mountains and across the valley, one cast its shadow upon the dome of the Big Shanty Circuit Courthouse. Once it had passed, a beam of sunlight penetrated the small windows located high on the east wall of the court room, creating a natural spotlight that fell onto the floor just in front of the jury box. Inside the jury box, twelve citizens sat quietly, absorbing the smell of old wood and leather which permeated the air of the ancient building.

The timing of the passing cloud could not have been better for John Keene, who buttoned his suit jacket, preparing to address the jury. This was his shining moment. After working so hard for so many months, the time had finally come for justice. The jury had been chosen; the gallery was filled to capacity; and he was ready to show the people of Big Shanty that he was still their savior.

Leaving his notes on the table, Keene slowly approached the jury and positioned himself directly under the beam of sunshine. Before he began to speak, his eyes fell upon his new best friend, a retired school teacher who spent her time gardening and volunteering at her church.

Keene had always thought that school teachers made the best jurors. This one would be no different. She understood the importance of rules and social order. She was someone who valued justice. And Keene knew that she would have no problem convicting the defendant and sending him to prison for life. That's why he looked directly at her when he began his opening statement.

"Ladies and gentleman, I feel compelled to thank you in advance for what you are doing today. Not because you're here performing your duty as citizens of this city, but because of the horrible and gruesome facts that you will be exposed to during this trial."

Keene moved closer to the jury before continuing.

"On April 11th of this year, which was a Sunday evening . . . an unusually warm Sunday evening, an intruder entered the home of Frank and Cleo Lawson, who lived at 21 Astor Street, right here in Big Shanty. The intruder cut the screen of an open window in the bedroom where their son, Timmy was asleep. When nineteen-year old Timmy Lawson awoke, a violent struggle ensued. The clatter woke up the young man's father, who ran down the hall to investigate."

Keene walked to the corner of the jury box as he continued.

"When Frank Lawson reached his son's bedroom, he saw the man struggling with Timmy," Keene explained in a calm voice. "But before he could do anything, the intruder shot Timmy in the chest, killing him instantly. Timmy's Dad turned and tried to run back to his own bedroom -- no doubt in an effort to protect his wife. But he was not fast enough. The killer ran after him and shot him in the back as he tried to escape. And as Frank Lawson lay on the floor at the end of the hallway, paralyzed and motionless, the sick predator calmly walked up behind him and put another bullet into the back of his head."

The school teacher grimaced as Keene made his way to the other end of the jury box.

"But the killing did not end there, folks," he continued. "The merciless predator entered Frank and Cleo's bedroom, the private sanctity which they had shared for over twenty years of marriage. And there, hiding under the covers of the bed, was Cleo Lawson -- a faithful wife . . . a loving mother. With senseless brutality, he raised his gun and shot through the blankets into her body. One bullet pierced her shoulder. She screamed. Another bullet ripped through her abdomen. She screamed again. And finally, she was silenced by the third bullet, which shattered her teeth and ricocheted up through the roof of her mouth and into her brain."

Juror number four, an elderly man with a balding head and gray hair closely cropped above his ears, shook his head in disgust as Keene continued.

"Who could have done such a thing? What man on this earth could be so despicable?" Keene asked.

"Well, I'll tell you. This was no random act of violence. This was an act of vengeance." Keene began slowly backing up as he spoke. "And this act of vengeance was perpetrated by the only person in the world who had the sick motivation to do such a thing." Keene elevated his voice as he moved closer to the defense table.

"During the course of this trial, I will prove to you, beyond a reasonable doubt, that THIS man is the predator!" he shouted, pointing his finger at the defendant. "This is the man who shot down an innocent family in cold blood!"

Using his finger as an instrument of accusation, Keene held it firmly upon the defendant for several seconds as he stared the killer in the eyes. Unwavering, the defendant returned Keene's stare with his chin held high, as if he wasn't even ashamed of his crimes.

* * * * * * *

Long before the trial of Larice Jones, Nolan Getty had warned his client that Keene would approach the defense table during his opening statement and point a finger in his face. The Big Shanty prosecutors were all so predictable. They had obviously all been to the same trial seminar, where some genius had told them that pointing and shouting at the defendant was the best way to get the jury's attention. But to Nolan, it all seemed so childish.

More than anything, Nolan was embarrassed when the prosecutors stomped their feet and pointed their fingers like spoiled children. But his clients usually had a different reaction -- one that could best be described as unbridled rage. That's why Nolan made a special point to give Larice Jones an advanced warning of Keene's finger-pointing attack. He didn't want Larice to jump across the defense table and break Keene's finger off.

After the finger pointing, Keene told the jury about the drug deal between Timmy Lawson and Larice Jones and how Timmy had helped put Larice in jail, which, according to his theory, was why Larice had broken into the Lawson home and killed everyone. Keene also explained to the jury that there was one family member who escaped the tragedy -- Tommy Lawson. According to Keene, Tommy had been out of town on the night of the murders and when he returned home, he found his family massacred.

"And now, after months of investigation, we are here today for justice; justice for the Lawson family and justice for Tommy, the only surviving member," Keene's voice echoed.

Nolan kept his head bent to the table, focused on a law book. Although he appeared indifferent, he was actually listening intently to every word of Keene's statement. He just didn't want the jury to know that he cared.

"Today, I will show you all of the evidence against Mr. Larice Jones -- circumstantial evidence, scientific evidence, and yes, even the so called smoking gun. And when I'm done, I am certain that you will have absolutely no trouble finding beyond a reasonable doubt that the defendant is a cold blooded murderer and guilty of these crimes. Beyond a reasonable doubt . . . beyond *any* doubt . . . Larice Jones must pay for these despicable acts." Keene finished with a long hard stare at the defendant.

As Keene and the jury stared at the defense table, Nolan pulled his coat sleeve back and looked at his watch. Tapping the crystal, he then held the watch to his ear, as if he was concerned that it wasn't working. The watch was fine. The problem was that Nolan couldn't help being a smart ass.

"Thank you," Keene finished, whirling his coat-tails and returning to his seat.

"Mr. Getty?" the judge nodded.

Nolan gave his client a pat on the back as he stood up. Buttoning his suit coat, he pushed his chair in and then stepped towards the prosecution table.

Standing in front of the prosecution table, he slowly raised his arm and then extended his finger, pointing it directly at Keene's face. "This man is wrong!" he shouted, staring at the jury. His words seemed to reverberate off the marble floors and dissipate into the high ceiling.

"During the course of this trial, I'm going to show you that Larice Jones had nothing to do with the murder of the Lawson family."

Turning to face Keene, Nolan winked at him with his left eye so that the jury couldn't see him. Keene folded his arms and grunted.

"You heard me right, folks," Nolan continued as he stepped toward the jury. "The evidence will show that my client, Larice Jones, had nothing to do with this horrible crime. Put another way, he is completely innocent of all charges."

"Your duty," Nolan said raising his finger in the air, "prescribed by law and reaffirmed by your own oaths today . . . is to presume this very fact -- that the defendant is completely innocent. If you start at that point, which the law demands, then you will be able to see the evidence for what it is."

"You see, Mr. Keene is going to help me with my case today," Nolan smiled, glancing back at the prosecutor's table again. "He doesn't know it yet, but his own evidence -- the evidence that he has had in his possession for several months now, and the evidence that he will present to you in an attempt to gain a conviction, will actually help exonerate my client."

"I just wish I could tell you all about it right now," Nolan added, shaking his head. "Unfortunately, I am forced to wait until Mr. Keene has presented his case. Only then will I be able to reveal the truth -- the truth that has escaped Mr. Keene from the beginning."

"All that I ask from you is to keep an open mind as the prosecution presents its case," Nolan continued. "Please don't jump to any conclusions until all of the evidence is in. Only then will you find the truth. Only then will you discover that Larice Jones is innocent."

Nolan turned his back to the jury and returned to the defense table. It was a brief opening statement, much shorter than the prosecution's. But it had to be that way. After all, he couldn't afford to tip off the prosecution at that point. He still needed Keene to call a certain witness. And then he needed to somehow convince the jury that Keene's own witness was the murderer.

CHAPTER SEVEN

John Keene arrived at Big Shanty General District Court just a few minutes before nine a.m. General District Court was the first formal venue in which all criminal defendants appeared. Two days earlier, the defendant had made his first appearance to be advised of his rights and to get an attorney appointed to represent him. Now, it was time for his bond hearing in the same court.

After breezing past the security gate, Keene entered the double doors of the courtroom and walked down the middle aisle of the gallery, passing through the small swinging gates that separated the general public from the players involved in the day's docket.

Unlike Circuit Court, the trial court in which the defendant's path to justice would eventually end, General District Court was a small claims court; the home of advisements, misdemeanors, traffic infractions, and of course, initial bond hearings. Much like the courts on daytime television, the litigants testified from a podium, rather than a witness box beside the judge.

There was one free-standing podium in front of the judge's bench, which was reserved for witnesses. The defense and prosecution tables were placed on each side of the podium, each with their own table-top podium and microphone. By requiring witnesses to stand at the middle podium, the Court was able to progress through cases more quickly. Justice was swift in Big Shanty General District Court; delivered with the conveyor-like efficiency of a kill line in a slaughterhouse.

To the left of the witness podium, beyond the prosecution table, were side benches where several police officers waited, as well as two of Keene's assistant prosecutors. On the right side of the podium area, the defense attorneys were gathered on their benches. On both sides, the players were either chatting or rattling through newspapers, as if everyone was sitting on the judge's front porch waiting for lemonade to be served.

But back in the gallery, the non-incarcerated criminal defendants were mostly quiet, wondering what was going to happen to them when the lemonade came out.

Keene nodded to one of his assistant prosecutors as he made his way to the left and sat down on the front bench. He turned his attention to the gallery and scanned the crowd. He expected the local newspaper reporter to be there, but he wasn't. Neither was the television reporter from Roanoke. The lack of interest surprised him.

Maybe the reporters were a little more savvy than he thought. After all, the chances of the bond hearing actually taking place were slim. Keene knew that Larice Jones had been appointed a Public Defender and that Public Defenders were notorious for requesting a continuance at the first hearing, which was set up automatically by the court. He had no reason to think that this hearing would be any different. Still it bothered him that no reporters would be present if the Public Defender was actually ready to go.

Keene stood up and walked back through the swinging gates, exited the main doors of the courtroom, and entered the first small conference room on the left, closing the door behind him.

Looking through his cell phone list he eventually found the number he was looking for and dialed it. The person on the other end answered after two rings.

"Scotty. John Keene here. How are you?" he asked.

"Good, sir. How are you today?"

"I'm doing just fine. Look, I'm down here at General District Court for a bond hearing in the triple murders we had last week. I didn't see anybody here to cover it and I just wanted to let you know that this thing was scheduled this morning. I think the community may be interested in whether the defendant in this case is going to bond out or not," he added.

"Absolutely," Scotty answered. "I had no idea. It must have slipped through the cracks on us."

"Well, that's what I was thinking," Keene said.

"Thanks for the call. I'll be there in a few minutes."

Keene flipped his cell phone shut. For the most part, he and Scotty had a good relationship, somewhat like a shark and a pilot fish. As the criminal reporter for the *Big Shanty Gazette*, Scotty was the conduit between Keene and the citizens. Keene needed him to let the people know that he was constantly working on their behalf, and Scotty needed him for a good story. There were times when Scotty didn't paint the best picture, but those times were rare.

Keene opened the door and stepped into the lobby. As he was about to return to the courtroom, he glanced towards the front entrance, surprised to see Tommy Lawson coming through the security gate. Tommy looked up just in time to see him. He had a worried look on his face.

"Mr. Keene," Tommy waved. He picked up his things from the tray at the security desk and hurried over to Keene. "I just heard from the lady at your office that there was a bond hearing today. That son of a bitch killed my family! How can they let him bond out?" he asked.

"Let's step into this conference room," Keene suggested. He didn't know which one of his victim witness advocates had given the information to the boy, but he was going to make a point to correct her when he returned to the office.

When they were behind the closed door, Keene explained. "This is a routine procedure for everyone that is arrested. The court sets up a bond hearing, because everyone has a right to a bond hearing. But chances are, the guy's attorney will request a continuance and this hearing will not even happen today. Even if it does, I'm prepared to convince the judge that he shouldn't get a bond. Okay?"

"Oh, I didn't know. They just told me there was a bond hearing this morning."

"That's true," Keene said. "But I don't want you here anyway. The less you're around these preliminary proceedings, the better it will be. The last thing you want is this guy's defense attorney harassing you for information that you're not required to disclose."

"What do you mean?" Lawson asked.

"I'm saying that his defense attorney will probably want to ask you a lot of questions in an effort to obtain information that will help his client. You don't want to help him with his case, do you?" Keene asked.

"Hell no," Lawson answered. "I want him to pay for what he did."

"Well, all right, then. The best thing for you to do is to go back home and let me handle everything. I don't want you ever appearing in court unless you're with one of our victim witness advocates. They'll tell you when it's appropriate to be here and they'll also be with you when you do appear," Keene explained.

"All right," Lawson answered. "You'll let me know what happens, won't you?"

"I'll let you know right now. The guy is not getting a bond," Keene reassured him. "In the future, call your victim witness advocate and she will keep you informed."

Keene opened the door and ushered the boy out to the security gate. This kid may turn into a problem, Keene thought as he watched him leave. During a time when most people would be incapacitated by grief, this kid was running around town demanding retribution.

Keene turned and entered the courtroom. Once inside, he looked for a Public Defender, but he didn't see any of them. He paused on the other side of the swinging gates and asked the nearest deputy if he had seen one.

"There's one coming in right now," the deputy nodded.

Keene turned around and saw Nolan Getty coming through the double doors. He was wearing a shiny blue suit with a red tie. With his slicked back hair, he looked like he was trying to be the cover boy of an Italian fashion magazine. As he got closer, he lifted a hand to wave to the deputy and his gold cuff links flashed.

Who does this guy think he is, some big shot lawyer?

Keene had no idea where Getty got the money to buy designer suits, but it probably wasn't from his Public Defender salary. Unless, that is, he spent his paycheck on clothes instead of rent and food.

Keene didn't bother with a greeting. "Do you have Larice Jones?" he asked as Getty came through the swinging gates.

"Yup," Getty answered.

"Are you ready to go, or do you want a continuance?" he asked.

"I'll be ready as soon as I talk to him," Getty answered. Without slowing, Getty continued to the door in the corner of the courtroom. Keene watched as Getty spoke to a deputy, who opened the door and escorted him to the back lockup, where they kept the incarcerated defendants.

You cocky bastard, you have no idea who you're dealing with.

Keene's animosity towards Nolan Getty was both obvious and well founded. His first and only run in with Getty occurred in the Marvin Lester case. Getty was an Assistant Public Defender at the time and the attorney appointed to defend Marvin Lester. After Keene won the case, Getty seemed to take the loss personally. On appeal, Getty resorted to personal attacks against him, claiming that he withheld exculpatory evidence and that Lester was not given a fair trial. In the end, the Appellate Court refused to hear the appeal and nothing more was made of it.

Two years later, when Getty took over as the Chief Public Defender after the previous Chief committed suicide, Keene tried to bury the hatchet. He sent a note over to the Public Defender Office with his condolences and wishing Getty good luck in his new position. A few days later, he received the note back with the words, "Fuck You," scrawled in large letters across it. But that was just the start of Keene's problems with Getty.

At about the same time that Getty became the Chief Public Defender, Keene noticed that his assistant prosecutors began to lose a significant number of cases. At first, he thought the losses were due to the inexperience of many of his assistants. But after awhile, he began to recognize a pattern. Looking through the losing case files, Keene saw only one common factor, one that affected even his most tenured lawyers. In most of them, the defending attorney was Nolan Getty.

Keene heard the grumblings from his assistants when he assigned cases in which Getty was listed as the defense attorney. He saw them return to the office after trials with their tails between their legs in defeat. He read the headlines of the local paper and saw that Getty was getting more press than himself. Worse yet, the indigent defendants were even starting to ask for Getty at their advisement hearings. And Keene knew there was a problem when defendants began begging for a Public Defender.

But all that talk was going to end soon. Keene knew that he was finally going to get his opportunity to rectify the situation. He relished the idea of slapping Getty down in court, like he had in the Marvin Lester case, and showing everyone that good always wins over bad; at least when he was on the prosecuting end.

A few minutes later, Keene heard the judge's chamber door open and the deputy banged his gavel.

"All rise for the Honorable Judge Yancey R. Hadley, the Third," the deputy announced.

Judge Hadley appeared, standing behind his chair on the bench. With his long white hair and flowing black robe, he was a story-book vision of justice. From all accounts, he had been dispensing southern justice in General District Court for over forty years. Although he could be very cranky and bitter at times, often lashing out at the prosecution or defense for no apparent reason, Keene knew that there was no better judge to have for a bond hearing.

Wearing his signature, black rimmed glasses, which had come in and out of style at least twice during his career, Judge Hadley eyed the gallery closely before taking his seat.

"Larice Jones," Judge Hadley immediately called out.

Keene approached the prosecution table as the deputy went to the lockup to retrieve the defendant. At the same time, Nolan Getty appeared from the lockup door in the corner of the courtroom and approached the defense table.

Judge Hadley ignored Getty. "Good morning Mr. Keene, is this the murder case?"

"Yes sir."

Judge Hadley put his pen down and leaned back in his chair.

"Good morning, your Honor," Getty cut in.

"Morning," Hadley nodded as he crossed his arms. "Do you have any witnesses, besides the defendant?"

"No witnesses, sir."

Larice Jones appeared from the side door, escorted by a deputy. Jones was wearing orange coveralls and flip flops. Keene watched as he shuffled across the court room in leg irons. He was eager to cross-examine him. Even though he knew that Judge Hadley wouldn't give him a bond, Keene wanted to set the correct tone for this case, right out of the gate. There was no way this animal was going to get by with half-truths and lies about having a job or ties to the community, Keene thought. He was going to show everyone, including Scotty the newspaper reporter, how worthless and despicable this killer was.

As Larice Jones took his position beside his lawyer at the defense table, Judge Hadley addressed him.

"Are you Larice Jones?" he asked.

"Yes sir," Larice answered.

"Raise your right hand to be sworn in," Hadley directed.

Getty interrupted the judge. "Actually, your Honor, Mr. Jones will not be testifying today. I would like to proffer his information to the court for the purposes of this bond hearing."

The move surprised Keene. But before Judge Hadley could respond, Keene interrupted.

"Your Honor," Keene said. "This is an important case for the Commonwealth and I think it would be appropriate for this court to be able to judge the defendant's request for a bond based on the defendant's own testimony and demeanor, not the second hand information proffered by the defense attorney."

Judge Hadley thought for a second. "I agree. I want to hear it from the horse's mouth."

Getty shrugged. "Well, if you're not going to let me proffer the information, then I would object to allowing the Commonwealth Attorney to proffer his information. If Mr. Keene wants to talk about the facts of the case, then he must have a witness here to testify as to those facts. And if he wants to give information to the court regarding the defendant's criminal record, then he'll have to have someone here to testify to that also."

Judge Hadley turned to Keene. "What's good for the goose is good for the gander," he said. "Do you really want that?"

Keene wasn't ready for the turnabout. Even if he could arrange it, there was no way he was going to put officers on the stand at this stage and open them up for cross-examination by the defense.

"I'm just saying that if this defendant really thinks he deserves a bond, then his defense attorney should allow him to testify in order to show that he's sincere about his request and to give assurance to the court that he will abide by any terms of a bond," Keene answered.

The orange-clad defendant leaned into his attorney's ear and barked loud enough for everyone to hear, "Yeah, man. I want to tell the judge myself."

"Shut up," Getty shot back, before addressing the judge.

"Your honor, perhaps if Mr. Keene was the defense attorney, he would run this case differently. But I am the official counsel for Mr. Jones, and my objection stands."

"Sustained," Hadley grunted. "Go ahead with your proffer."

No matter, Keene thought. He would have liked to make the defendant squirm, but he knew there would be plenty of opportunities for that in the future. Besides, the end result of the bond hearing would not be affected.

Keene listened as Getty proffered the defendant's background information to the court. Getty talked of part-time jobs in the past and jobs that the defendant was going to report to in the future, but he never mentioned anything about present employment. Getty talked about the defendant's mother and sister who lived in the area and the close relationship that they had. He claimed that the defendant was a member of the Southern Baptist Church and attended regularly. He even claimed that the defendant had been spending time at the local Boys and Girls Club, telling children about the evils of drugs and alcohol.

What a crock of dung, Keene thought. When it was Keene's turn, he was ready. He went back to the night of the murders and described the horrible crime scene. He told the judge about the bodies and where they had been shot down in cold blood. He described the evidence that linked the defendant to the murders, the watch that belonged to the young victim, the owe list found in his Bible, the fingerprints on the shell casings, and the cash and drug paraphernalia found in the defendant's home. Finally he finished with the defendant's criminal record, which included previous acts of violence, weapons charges, drug charges, and at least two prior occasions in which the defendant failed to appear for scheduled court dates.

"This man is a violent, career criminal who represents a danger to everyone in this community. And it sickens me to stand hear and listen to his defense attorney tell the court that he helps boys and girls of this community, when the reality is that he is the biggest menace that this town has ever seen."

Judge Hadley didn't wait for an argument from the defense. "Bond is denied," he stated coldly, staring at the defendant.

"Thank you, your Honor," Nolan smiled.

CHAPTER EIGHT

August 18th, Big Shanty Circuit Court

Keene's first witness in the trial of Larice Jones was obvious. His plan was to work his way up to his star witness, but first, he wanted to set the stage with the officer in charge of the investigation.

"I call Lieutenant Jack Childress of the Big Shanty Police Department," Keene announced in a loud voice.

The deputy opened the side door of the courtroom and leaned into the corridor. "Lieutenant Childress!" he yelled. All of the jurors turned as Lieutenant Childress stepped through the doorway. Having never seen the man before, the jury couldn't appreciate how well he cleaned up. He was wearing a crisp, gray suit and his once disheveled hair was combed back, perfectly frozen in place by styling gel.

When he was seated, the judge made him raise his right hand. "Do you swear and affirm, under oath and penalty of law, that you shall tell the truth in all that you say?" he asked.

"Yes sir," Childress answered.

The twelve jurors sat quietly and fanned themselves with court-issued paper paddles as Keene extracted Childress's background information. But within a few minutes, when Childress began to describe the crime scene, the jurors forgot about the heat and stopped fanning as they listened to the graphic details.

"Please tell the jury in your own words what you found when you entered the Lawson house," Keene instructed, leaning on the podium next to the jury box.

Childress glanced at the judge, and then looked into the jury box as he leaned ahead to the microphone.

"Probably one of the most disturbing crime scenes I'd ever seen," he answered.

Keene glanced at the defense attorney, expecting him to object, but he didn't.

"In what way?"

"In every way . . . the blood . . . the fact that three people had been shot to death in their own home . . . the lack of any evidence to show that they had a chance to fight back . . ." Childress trailed off while shaking his head. "It was all real bad."

"I'm showing you a photo that I have marked as Commonwealth's Exhibit One. Do you recognize this photo?"

"Yes," Childress answered.

"Does this photo fairly and accurately represent what you saw on the night of April 12th?"

"Yes," Childress glanced at the jury again.

"Please tell the jury what this is."

"This is a photo of Timmy Lawson. We found him on the floor of the first bedroom on the left."

After the judge admitted the photo into evidence, Keene handed it to the jury and waited as they passed it from one to the other. Some jurors studied it closely, while others glanced at it briefly before passing it on.

What they saw in the first photo and others that followed would stay with the jurors forever. Most of them had at some point in life been to a funeral of a friend or a loved one. But none of them had seen death like this before -- the kind of death that hadn't been prettied up by an undertaker. None of them had seen the vacant eyes . . . the lifeless bodies frozen in awkward positions . . . the bullet holes torn into human flesh . . . and the black, coagulated pools of blood. Like a scar, these images would fade with time, but no juror would ever be completely free from them.

One after the other, Keene introduced the graphic photos. The jurors passed the photos to each other in silence. Some grimaced, while others hid their emotions with stone faces. It was an awkward several minutes, but it had to be done that way. Keene wanted them to see the deceased family as he had seen them -- violated, defiled, and dead.

After Keene finished the family photo show, he continued with other matters.

"How is it that the police were contacted in the first place?"

"We received a 9-1-1 call from Tommy Lawson," Childress answered.

"And for the record, who is Tommy Lawson?"

"He is the surviving twin of Frank and Cleo Lawson -- the brother of Timmy Lawson, who we found shot to death."

"Did Tommy Lawson identify the bodies?"

"Yes sir."

"Did you develop Larice Jones as a suspect on the night that you investigated these murders?"

"Yes we did."

"I don't want you to go into detail, but can you tell the jury where you got the information that led you to believe Larice Jones was the killer?" Keene asked.

"Well, it was based on statements I received from Tommy Lawson and also information from our narcotics officers who told me about the past connection between Timmy Lawson and Larice Jones."

"What did you do in response to this information?"

"We sent an unmarked unit to the last known address of Larice Jones in order to conduct surveillance," Childress explained.

"Did you find him at his last known address?"

"No we didn't," Childress shook his head.

"Without repeating any specific words that were said, how is it that you found Larice Jones?"

"The Big Shanty Communications Department -- that's our 9-1-1 system, received a telephone call from an anonymous person who told us where Larice Jones was hiding."

"Objection," Nolan Getty interrupted. "The witnesses' statement that my client was hiding is pure speculation and personal opinion."

"Sustained," the judge ruled. "Please disregard the officer's testimony that the defendant was hiding."

"Based on information in the telephone call, did you in fact find Larice Jones?" Keene continued.

"Yes. We found him at 17 Sherman Street."

"Is that where he was arrested?"

"Yes sir."

"When did the arrest take place?"

"That was the day after we found the bodies, on the evening of April 13th," Childress responded.

"After he was arrested, did you interview him?"

"Yes, after reading him his rights, he agreed to talk with us."

"What did Larice Jones tell you during that interview?"

Childress looked directly at the jury. "He said he didn't know Timmy Lawson. But when I reminded him that he was arrested for selling drugs to him three months earlier, he claimed that he only knew him as T."

"What else did he say?" Keene prodded.

"He said he had no idea where he lived and that he had never been to the Lawson house."

"And at the time of this interview, did you have knowledge that conflicted with those statements?"

"Yes sir, we certainly did," Childress answered.

"No further questions," Keene finished.

"Mr. Getty," the judge leaned ahead. "Do you have any questions for this witness?"

"Yes sir." As Nolan Getty stood and approached the podium, Keene turned to the jury and saw several of them cross their arms and lean back in their chairs, which was a good sign.

"Officer Childress, on the night that you investigated these deaths, who did you identify as possible suspects?" Getty began.

"Well, we didn't exclude Tommy Lawson as being a possible suspect, if that's what you're getting at. Not until later, anyway."

"Did Tommy Lawson ever give you an alibi regarding his whereabouts when his family was killed?"

"Yes, he said he had been at a music concert in Richmond and he had not been home," Childress answered.

"What steps did you take to verify this story?"

"The usual steps -- I checked to see if there had been a concert and there was. Other than that, there was nothing else to check -- he said that the friends that he was supposed to meet at the concert never showed up," Childress answered.

"So isn't it true that Tommy Lawson's alibi was never confirmed by a second person?"

"That's true," Childress answered.

"No more questions," Getty finished, returning to the defense table.

CHAPTER NINE

In the spectrum of lawyers, perhaps there are none more respected than prosecutors. They don't advertise, chase ambulances, or fleece people for money. Their only purpose is to protect the public by putting criminals behind bars. Therefore, to everyone but the accused, prosecutors are the good guys.

At the opposite end of that spectrum there is another lawyer: the Public Defender. The Public Defender's only purpose is to represent criminals -- poor criminals who can't afford an attorney. Therefore, to everyone but the accused, Public Defenders are the bad guys.

But Nolan Getty didn't see it that way. In his mind, there was only one clear bad guy in the justice system: the prosecutor. And for Nolan, his job was as his title implied -- to defend the public from him.

Nolan hadn't always been interested in the law. He was certainly smart enough, but his problem had been money, barely making it through college due to a lack thereof. Although his mother and father supported him in his quest for a degree, they couldn't help him financially. He scraped by with loans and part-time jobs. At one point, he took a two semester sabbatical in order to work full time, just so he could finish his senior year. But it was in the midst of that final year at Virginia Tech University when his luck changed forever, at least financially.

It was a cold day in January when a lawyer called from Florida with the good news. His Aunt Shirley had passed away, leaving behind a significant estate, which had been created by her third marriage to a Florida yacht maker. The specific bequest to Nolan was sizeable enough to change his life. Not only did he pay off his college loans, he also finally had enough money to finance a larger ambition -- a law degree.

After graduating from Richmond School of Law, Cum Laude, he decided to get a taste of the big city life, applying for first year law jobs at several large law firms in Washington, D.C. He eventually landed a job at Chatham, Steiner and Gold, a huge plaintiff tort firm in D.C.

The firm, or "factory" as he later called it, had thousands of clients, all of whom had allegedly taken some harmful drug. Whether it was Fen Phen, Redux, Vioxx, or Drug-X, it didn't matter. If it was manufactured by a pharmaceutical company with deep pockets, Chatham, Steiner and Gold went after it.

As a junior lawyer, he spent most of his time in the basement of the law firm, sifting through boxes of discovery documents that had been turned over by the defendant drug companies. Hour after hour, week after week, he searched for a smoking gun that would lead to a favorable verdict.

Occasionally, his supervising partner would allow him a reprieve from the search, but for the most part, he spent his entire first year after law school in the firm's basement with his friends, the boxes.

Luckily for Nolan, during his second year at the firm, the partners decided to give back to their community. Ira Steiner, one of the senior partners, started the initiative. Many thought that it was an effort to appease the Bar Association and pave his way to a leadership role in the organization, but whatever the reason, he had made a commitment to the Bar to take on more pro bono work. Of course, Mr. Steiner was too busy for such work himself, so he assigned it to his junior attorneys, one of which was Nolan Getty.

In his first real case as an attorney, Nolan was summoned from the basement to represent Reginald Jackson, an inner city youth charged with marijuana possession and assault on a police officer. Not familiar with criminal matters, Nolan spent every spare moment studying the criminal code and pouring over search and seizure cases, eventually concluding that his client had been illegally searched and arrested. When the case went to trial, Nolan was ready to mount a solid defense. At least that's what he thought, anyway.

At the trial, the prosecutor completely rolled over him, successfully objecting to key pieces of evidence and convincing the judge to exclude most of the testimony and exhibits. The judge scoffed at Nolan's Constitutional arguments, finding his client guilty of both charges. After it was all said and done, Nolan was left with a sick feeling in his stomach; a feeling that basic Constitutional rights were of no importance to the prosecutors and judges involved in the criminal justice system. And at that moment, he knew that he wanted to be at the front lines of this Constitutional war. He wanted to be a criminal defense attorney.

A month later, he responded to a job advertisement in the *Litigator's Weekly*. The job was for an Assistant Public Defender in Big Shanty, a smaller Virginia town that he had heard of, but never visited. Although the pay was pathetically low, he applied anyway. His small taste of courtroom drama had made him hungry for more, not to mention the prospect of never having to return to Steiner's basement. Besides, his inheritance spawned investment portfolio was still going strong and he knew that it would make a nice supplement to even the lowest state salary.

When he accepted the position, his only concern was that the town was too small for any substantial criminal work. But he was wrong. Much like what he had witnessed in D.C., the police and prosecutors had little regard for anyone's Constitutional rights. The only difference between them and their northern counterparts was that they spoke with a southern drawl and ate grits for breakfast.

After seven years as a Public Defender in Big Shanty, Virginia, Nolan had seen too many injustices to think anything else. There was the mentally retarded boy prosecuted for indecent exposure for pulling his pants down in the mall. There was the elderly man with Alzheimer's prosecuted for larceny because he forgot to pay for his coffee at the convenience store. There was the high school teenager prosecuted for felony assault with a weapon for using a rubber band to shoot a paper clip at a classmate. And there were many more like them, none of which should have ever been prosecuted at all.

As far as Nolan Getty was concerned, Keene was the one responsible for those injustices, even though he rarely ever appeared in court. He preferred to send his assistants to the courtroom to do his dirty work. And although they pretended to think for themselves, ultimately they were nothing more than puppets, dangling from strings that led right to Keene's office. But now, Keene had dropped the strings to make a personal appearance in the trial of Larice Jones. The reason, Nolan thought, was because Keene was in the last year of his reign, having to face the inconvenience of another election in the coming year.

After the bond hearing on that Friday morning in April, Nolan returned to his office on foot. As he walked, he thought of the Marvin Lester case: the first and only time that he had faced John Keene. It was his first year on the job as an Assistant Public Defender, and by everyone's account, Keene had taken advantage of him. By Nolan's account, Keene had outright cheated in order to get the conviction. But Larice Jones was a new case and Nolan was much more experienced. And this time, he would be the one taking advantage.

By the time Nolan reached the front porch of his office, he was done thinking about Keene and ready to enjoy the rest of the day at the chateau. Nolan and his assistants called their office "the chateau" because it was an old house that had been converted into office space. Built by a local tobacco farmer in 1812, it had passed hands several times over the years before ending up in the hands of the Public Defender Commission, who purchased it because it was within convenient walking distance between Big Shanty's two courthouses.

The security chime chirped as Nolan entered the foyer. Vicki looked up from her desk in the former dining room.

"About time," she said. "Your boys are waiting for you in the basement."

"Is it Friday already?"

"Ha, ha," Vicki said flatly as she typed at her computer.

Nolan hung his suit jacket on the coat rack, set his briefcase at the bottom of the staircase to the second floor, and went straight to the basement door.

"I want a tight rack, you friggin' cheaters!" he yelled as he carefully made his way down the old wooden steps to the basement.

The pool table came with the house when the Public Defender Commission purchased it, but only because they didn't want to pay for it to be removed. Right after Nolan had been appointed Chief, he paid a billiard company to install K-66 bumpers and a new felt surface with his own money. But the Commission didn't know any of that. As far as they knew, the basement was for file storage.

When the pool table wasn't in use, they covered it with a thin sheet of plywood that had empty file boxes on it, two high, so that it appeared as if it was just another surface to stack boxes. The pool cues and rack were stored on hooks underneath the table, out of sight.

They had other secrets too. At the south end of the basement, just beyond the pool table, there was a floor-to-ceiling metal filing rack stuffed with files. In the middle of the rack, invisible to the eye, a doorway had been cut with hidden hinges on the back side. To pass through the filing rack, one only had to push against the middle section, which swung open to allow access to the ten foot by twelve foot "conference" room on the other side. Inside the conference room there was a couch, a lounge chair, a card table, and a television with a PS3 game console. There was also a refrigerator and a cabinet stocked with booze.

As an added safety measure, Nolan had the security company install a speaker in the basement so they could hear the chime when the front door opened. He also added a telephone in the pool room which was connected to the office system. He had probably seen too many re-runs of Hogan's Heroes. But on rare occasions, when the Colonel Klink of the Public Defender Commission visited, he never suspected a thing.

As Nolan reached the bottom of the steps he saw Rick bending over the rack end of the table. Officially, Rick was second in command at the office, but at twenty-five years old, he was lacking a certain level of maturity. Not only was he known to have a quick temper, but Nolan suspected that he was borderline schizophrenic. Luckily, what Rick lacked in maturity and mental health, he made up for in loyalty.

Although he was short, Rick's massive biceps put a strain on even the largest off-the-rack suits, which is probably why he always seemed to be in his t-shirt when he was in the office.

"This one is tighter than my prom date," Rick said, lifting the wooden rack. Nolan glanced at the triangular assembly of balls as he walked by the table.

"Was she a member of AARP?"

"Nope," Rick answered without hesitation. Sally Hollis, bless her heart. She screamed my name out that night. That was eight years ago, but I bet she still thinks of me when her husband is on her. "Rick, oh Rick – you're the man!" he yelled out in a shrill voice.

"That's no way to talk about your mother," Danny chimed in as he chalked the end of his cue.

Nolan glanced at Rick to see if he would react to Danny's feeble attempt at an insult. He did not.

Danny was the newest addition to the Public Defender's Office, having been on the job less than six months. Tall and skinny, he had perfectly quaffed blonde hair with long bangs that swept to the side, almost covering his left eye. Perhaps his hairstyle worked in the hip culture of Charlottesville where he grew up, but in Big Shanty, he stood out like a *Ken* doll in a biker bar.

Nonetheless, Danny was a bright young lawyer. He was the editor-in-chief for his law review and he graduated near the top of his class at the University of Virginia. But because of his youth, his mouth sometimes said things his muscle couldn't back up; especially while interacting with Rick.

"You want to play cut throat, or you want the winner?" Rick asked, ignoring Danny's comment.

"I'll play the winner, and the loser buys lunch," Nolan answered as he passed the table and walked into the file rack lounge. "Anyone else need a drink?"

"We're covered," Danny said.

Nolan pulled a bottle of Jack Daniels from the cabinet and poured three fingers into a plastic glass, then plopped a handful of ice cubes on top. Swirling the glass in his hand, he walked back into the pool room area.

"What's new?" Danny thrust his cue stick forward, smashing the white ball into the rack.

"We've got the Astor Street murders," Nolan took a sip of his whiskey. "I just finished the bond denial hearing."

"Son of a bitch," Rick exclaimed. "Can't anyone in this town afford a real attorney?"

"Who wants second chair?" Nolan asked.

"Danny does," Rick answered. "It's time for him to cut his teeth."

Danny looked seriously worried. "I'm not sure I'm ready for that, boss."

"Oh yes, you are," Rick shot back. "I've got the robbery case and two different rapes open. It's time you learned to fly with us eagles. Bank in the side," he added, gently poking the cue ball.

"Rick's right," Nolan looked at Danny. "He's got too much going on. All you need to do during the trial is the sentencing phase. I'll handle the rest."

Danny shrugged. "You're the boss."

"That a boy," Rick said, hunching over the table to line up his next shot. But just as he was about to shoot, the front door chime rang. Rick postponed his shot and reached for his glass which was resting on a stack of boxes. "Who's the prosecutor?"

"Keene," Nolan answered.

"Keene?" Rick shook his head in disbelief. "He can't trust one of his minions with it?"

"I guess not," Nolan answered. "But that's not odd. He's always handled the big ones -- it's just that we haven't had a big one since you've been here."

Rick had been a Public Defender for almost two years. In that time there had been four murders in Big Shanty. Nolan was the appointed attorney on one of them, but one of Keene's assistant prosecutors had handled that case. The other three either hired their own private attorney or the court appointed a private attorney to represent them because of a conflict of interest with the Public Defender's Office.

The telephone intercom beeped and Vicki's voice came over the speaker. "A woman named Ester Jones is here. She wants to speak to Nolan about her son. She says you're his attorney."

Nolan picked up the telephone receiver and pushed a button. "Tell her to make an appointment with me. I'll see her next week."

A few moments later, the door chime beeped and Vicki's voice came back on the intercom. "It's all clear."

Rick placed his glass on the stack of boxes and leaned over the table with his stick to take another shot. "Fourteen in the corner," he announced.

"I've never seen Keene in court before," Danny said to no one in particular as Rick was shooting.

"You're not missing anything," Nolan said. "If you think his assistants are jerks, you ought to see him."

"Have you had cases with him?" Danny asked.

"Just one," Nolan answered.

"Lester the Molester," Rick shouted out.

Rick was in law school when the case went to trial, but he grew up in Big Shanty, so like everyone else in town, he knew about it. He just didn't know the gory details until Nolan had told him.

"Marvin Lester was a kid toucher who owned a toy store on Main Street when I grew up," Rick explained. "The first time he got caught with his pants down, he was acquitted. After that, Keene took over as the Commonwealth's Attorney and brought him to trial again. Our boss here defended him and would've got him off again, if Keene hadn't cheated." Rick leaned over the table and took his next shot.

"Oh yeah?" Danny asked. "How'd he cheat?"

"He conveniently forgot to let me know that the father of the victim had pending criminal charges at the time that the boy testified," Nolan answered.

"What did that have to do with it?" Danny asked.

"They were sexual assault charges. Apparently he had been molesting his own boy for years, including during the time that the boy was allegedly assaulted by Mr. Lester."

"How could've that helped you?" Danny asked.

"Unbelievable!" Rick cut in. "Maybe you're not ready to fly yet."

"Let me explain something about criminal defense," Nolan paused to take another sip of whiskey. "The police . . . they got it easy. They find the best person to pin the crime on. But we ain't got it so easy. We're defense lawyers, so our job is to find the *second* best person to pin the crime on. And in the Lester case, I could've pinned the whole thing on the boy's father," Nolan answered. "The father pressured his son into lying in an effort to get out of his own charges."

As Rick was aiming for the eight ball, he looked away and stared at Danny. "Hey Danny . . . you lose," he said, striking the cue ball without taking his eyes from Danny. The cue ball contacted the eight ball, which rattled between the points of the corner pocket. But then it hung there without falling.

"Ooh!" Danny yelled. "You suck at the look-away!"

"Yeah, yeah," Rick grumbled. "I just wanted to give you a chance."

He turned to Nolan who was pouring more bourbon into his mouth.

"What's your boy have to say?" Rick asked.

"Haven't really talked to him about the charges yet," Nolan crunched an ice cube in his teeth. "I've set him on the back burner to simmer over the weekend. I'll see what he has to say Monday morning."

CHAPTER 10

Keene took his time leaving the courtroom after the bond hearing. He wanted to give the newspaper reporter plenty of time to get out to the lobby, just in case he needed a quote to add to his article.

He wasn't disappointed. Scotty was near the security gate at the front entrance, talking with the deputies. That was his nature -- always interested, always cultivating the human landscape for tidbits of gossip -- anything that he could use to create a story and sell it. As a Northerner, he wasn't saddled by the politeness of his southern peers. He just kept asking questions until he got the right answers and he had absolutely no shame in doing it.

Scotty looked up as Keene approached the security gate. "Hello, sir," he flipped to a blank page in his notebook. "Do you have a second to comment on the bond hearing?"

"Certainly," Keene answered.

"Did I hear correctly? Did the judge deny bond altogether?"

"That's right," Keene answered. "The judge agreed with me that Larice Jones represents an extraordinary danger to the community and I commend him for his actions."

"I took a look at the arrest warrants in this case and I saw that Mr. Jones is charged with murder, but not capital murder. Are you not going to seek the death penalty in this case?" Scotty asked.

The question caught Keene by surprise. But he recovered quickly.

"That's something we are looking at right now. The problem is that death penalty cases can cost the tax payers more money than sending a defendant to jail for life, without the possibility of parole. But rest assured, either way, Larice Jones is going to be brought to justice and I am going to do everything in my power to make sure that he never hurts anyone again."

Satisfied that Scotty had an appropriate quote, Keene excused himself and exited the courthouse. Once he was at the bottom of the front steps, he rounded the corner and walked to his office, which was in the city government building directly behind the courthouse. He could have taken the back way, which was quicker, but then he would have missed Scotty.

On his way back to the office, Keene thought of Tommy Lawson's surprise appearance at the bond hearing. He decided that he would have to call a meeting when he returned. Sometimes his support staff got a little too comfortable and lazy with their positions. Although they would never fully understand the pressure associated with his position and the consequences of losing a case, he would take this opportunity to enlighten them as much as he could.

"Good morning Mr. Keene," the receptionist greeted him as he entered the lobby of the Commonwealth Attorney's Office. She was seated behind a panel of bullet proof glass, her voice crackling through a speaker.

Since he had been elected as the Chief Commonwealth's Attorney, he had made many changes, including the renovation of his office space. With a grant from the Homeland Security Department, he completely gutted the interior and installed a secure door between the lobby and the office area behind it. In addition, he created a secure reception area, separated from the lobby by a large panel of bullet proof glass that shielded the receptionist and his staff from the public. After all, he couldn't have some disgruntled citizen waltz in with a gun and open fire.

"Good morning," Keene responded.

From behind the glass, his young receptionist pushed a button, electronically unlocking the door that led into the inner bowels of his sanctum. After he was through the door, he nodded to her again and continued down the hallway to his corner office. Outside his office door, he stopped at his assistant's cubicle, which was separated from the corridor by a half wall with a narrow counter top. She was too busy with her telephone conversation to notice him.

"Rachel," Keene interrupted. Rachel looked up and then quickly excused herself from the conversation, holding her hand over the mouth piece.

"Yes sir?" she asked.

"I want an all-staff meeting in the conference room at ten o'clock. Everyone but the attorneys. And tell Fred Mutz to meet me in my office right now."

"Yes sir," Rachel turned to the phone. "I've got to go," she said and quickly hung up.

Keene entered his large corner office and placed the Larice Jones file on the conference table before hanging up his suit jacket in his closet. As he was returning to his desk, there was a knock at his door and Fred Mutz entered.

Mutz was not wearing a coat or a tie and the sleeves of his white dress shirt were rolled up past his elbows. The buttons on the front of his shirt strained to contain his belly, which created enough force to separate his shirt between the buttons, revealing an off-white t-shirt underneath. Mutz was far from the picture of professionalism that Keene wanted to see.

"What's up, boss?" the pudgy one asked.

Keene glared at him for second. "There's no such thing as casual Fridays -- where's your coat and tie?"

Mutz shrugged. "I just stepped out to grab some breakfast and I didn't have time to put them back on."

Keene glanced at his watch and frowned. "I want you to sit second chair on the triple murder case."

Fred's eyes lit up. "Awesome!"

Mutz obviously thought that he was being rewarded for his hard work, but Keene had no such intention. Fred Mutz had been with the Commonwealth's Attorney Office for three years. Although he was aggressive and meant well, Keene had not been satisfied with his progress.

Keene didn't expect new attorneys to come out of the gate winning every case, but time usually turned the curve around. In Mutz's case, time had not improved his performance. He was still losing just as many cases as when he started. And it was time for Mutz to sink or swim. For Keene, it was a win-win situation. By working closely with him, he would either be able to identify the inadequacies of Mutz and build a sound case for firing him, or he would ride him so hard that Mutz would just quit.

"The case file is on the table there. Make a copy of it and get yourself acquainted with the facts. Tomorrow afternoon let's get together and talk about what needs to be done."

"Yes sir," he picked up the file from the table and opened it. "Are we going for capital murder on this one?"

Keene grimaced as he walked behind Mutz towards his desk. "What would you do?" he asked as he turned and sat down.

"I'd fry the bastard," Mutz answered.

Yeah, right. Keene smiled. *You'd crap your pants if you had to pull the switch.*

He thought about telling Mutz that it was easier said than done. Anyone could say someone should fry, but it was another thing to be the one directly responsible for it. But he didn't want to waste his time. Instead, he picked up the phone and pushed his message light. "We'll see about that," he said to Mutz, who had enough common sense to know that their conversation was over.

Keene had been directly responsible for two capital murder convictions during his career. Neither of them had been easy. He knew what kind of determination that it took to ignore the pleas of another human being begging for his life, not to mention the difficulty of convincing twelve ordinary citizens to do the same.

From the beginning, he promised himself that he would never ask for the death penalty unless he was willing to see it through. That's why he had attended the executions of those he had convicted. That wasn't easy either. There were always crowds of dissenters with signs and placards denouncing the act. They yelled things like, "You're no better than him" or "You're a murderer too." Some signs contained messages for the governor, like "Reprieve Him Now." But there were also supporters who faced off against the dissenters, with signs like, "An Eye for an Eye," and "Kill the Murderer."

The lawyers, the reporters, the talking heads on television; everyone had something to say on execution day. The state-sanctioned killing of a Commonwealth citizen was always a circus.

But for those on the inside; for those who watched the actual act; it was far from a circus. There was nothing glamorous about a human body twisting and contorting under the strain of 2,000 volts of electricity or seeing smoke pour out from a hooded head, knowing that under the hood a man's face was melting.

Unlike Mutz, Keene knew intimately about that end result. And he had already decided that it wasn't going to be the result for Larice Jones. Not because he thought that Larice deserved a break. There was more to it than that.

Keene knew that only the Chief Public Defender in any given district was certified to represent defendants on capital murder charges. He also knew that since becoming the Chief Public Defender, Getty hadn't taken all of the Commonwealth required capital defense courses. If he filed capital murder charges, the Public Defender Commission would send in an outsider from Richmond or possibly Washington, D.C. And the last thing that he needed in an election year was some hot shot, big city defense attorneys coming into town and causing a big commotion. Besides, it was time for Getty to learn his lesson. And the Larice Jones case was going to be perfect for taking Getty to school.

Keene checked his messages and then glanced at his watch, making sure that he would be fashionably late for his impromptu conference with the staff.

They were all present when he entered the conference room; the secretaries, the paralegals, the victim witness advocates. He could have limited the meeting to the victim witness advocates, after all, it was one of them who screwed up. But he wanted everyone to hear the message. He wanted everyone to know that lazy mistakes would not be tolerated.

"This morning I was in General District Court for a bond hearing in the triple murder case," he began. "Some of you may have heard of it," he added sarcastically, eyeing the three female victim witness advocates sitting together at the end of the conference table. They smiled nervously as he continued. "It's the one where the family was murdered in their own home in the middle of the night. The one that the media has gotten the entire community riled up about, including the mayor, city counsel, church leaders, and everyone else who has a heartbeat. And in case you didn't notice -- maybe y'all have been too busy with your personal calls and extended lunches -- the one that has turned a spotlight on this office -- a shining light that will reveal every little mistake that we may make," Keene explained. His voice became louder as he spoke, evaporating the nervous smiles and creating a room full of bowed heads.

"And for the life of me," Keene's voice rose, "I can't figure out how the most important witness in this case -- the only surviving member of the murdered family -- comes waltzing into the court house all alone!" he yelled, slapping his hand on the table. Rachel, his secretary, visibly flinched.

With a clenched jaw and veins bulging in his forehead, Keene stared at each of his employees in silence. Not a single person had the courage to lift their head and look him in the eye.

Finally, his gaze landed on Jill, who was the assigned advocate for Tommy Lawson. She was very petite and pretty, always dressed well, with perfect blonde hair and manicured nails. But obviously, she was more concerned about her looks than doing her job.

"Will somebody please tell me how that happened?" Keene shouted, flailing his arms as he paced at the head of the table.

Jill raised her perfectly manicured hand as if she was in school. "He called me and wanted to know if it was true there was going to be a bond hearing. All I told him was that it was on the schedule -- I didn't know he would show up there."

Keene shook his head, disgusted. "Do you have any idea what kind of field day the reporters would have had if they had spotted him?" He paused to glare.

"More importantly, do you know what would've happened if the defense lawyer had cornered him?" Keene asked in an overly pleasant tone, but he didn't wait for Jill to respond.

"He would have cut his fucking heart out and ate it for lunch!" Keene shouted, banging his fist on the table again. This time, everyone flinched.

"From now on," Keene said, staring at the three female advocates, "when there is a hearing and you are assigned to the victim, you will make sure that that person never even gets *near* the courthouse without you. And even if you think the victim will not be present, you better make sure you lift your asses and march down there in case the witness does show up. Got it?" Keene yelled.

They nodded.

"And as for everyone else," Keene continued. "Y'all better straighten up and fly right because we are in for a storm here, folks." The rest of the support staff appeared surprised, unable to understand why Keene had turned on them, too.

"All of our jobs are in jeopardy if we don't get a conviction. That means you better not be gossiping about this case around town. I don't want a word spoken about this outside the office -- not to your little Bunko mates, your yoga buddies, or your church group -- not even during pillow talk with your spouses. Got it?" he asked.

Everyone nodded their heads.

"Thank you," Keene finished. "Together, if we work hard and we don't make any stupid mistakes, we'll bring the man who killed this family to justice."

CHAPTER 11

August 19th, Big Shanty Circuit Court

For his first witness on the second day of Larice Jones's murder trial, John Keene called Special Agent Calhoun of the Big Shanty Police Department, Narcotics Division. A large man with hair down to his shoulders appeared through the side door. He was wearing a sport coat, khaki pants, and a white shirt, with a blue tie. He took the stand and swore to tell the truth. After Keene asked him the appropriate background questions involving his personal history and occupation, Keene turned to the topic of Larice Jones.

"Do you know Larice Jones?" he asked.

"Yes, I've known him for a few years now," Calhoun answered.

"Does he have any nicknames?"

Calhoun turned to the jury, "On the street, they call him Ice."

"Now, I'd like to take you to April 13th of this year. Were you at the scene where Larice Jones was arrested on these charges?"

"Yes I was."

"And on the night that he was arrested, did you execute a search warrant at the house where he was staying?"

"Yes I did."

"May I approach, your Honor," Keene asked.

The judge nodded and Keene approached his witness with the search warrant in his hand. "For the record, I'm showing the witness an item marked for identification as Commonwealth's Exhibit Eleven. Do you recognize this document?"

"Yes sir. This is the search warrant and the inventory of items that we found pursuant to the search warrant."

"Your Honor, I'd ask that Commonwealth's Exhibit Eleven be admitted into evidence."

"Any objection?" the judge turned and asked the defense.

"No objection," Getty answered.

"Very well," the judge shrugged. "Exhibit Eleven is admitted without objection."

"Tell me, Agent Calhoun, did you find any items in the house that are relevant to this case?"

"Yes sir."

Keene approached his witness holding a plastic bag with a Bible inside of it. After setting the foundation with appropriate questions, Keene successfully had the Bible admitted into evidence.

"Where did you find this Bible?" Keene asked.

"In the night stand, next to the bed."

And what relevance does this Bible have?"

"At the end of Jude, I found a list of names," Calhoun said, paging to the appropriate page. "Beside each name there is a numerical note. And on this list is the name Timmy Lawson - Astor Street, and beside his name there were several numbers, all of them crossed out but one."

"And what meaning does that have for you?" Keene asked.

"What this looks like is something called an owe list. In the illegal drug market, dealers keep lists of what each of their lower distributors owe them -- usually it denotes money that is owed for fronting drugs," Calhoun stated.

"Thank you," Keene returned to the prosecution table and retrieved another plastic bag. He opened the bag and showed the contents to the defense attorney, who nodded. Keene then returned to the witness stand and handed the bag to Calhoun.

"Your honor, let the record reflect that I'm handing the witness an item marked for identification as Commonwealth Exhibit 13. Special Agent Calhoun, do you recognized this item?"

Calhoun looked into the bag and nodded. "Yes sir.'

"How do you recognize this item?"

"It's another item that I seized from the Jones house while executing the search warrant."

"And where did you find it?"

"Right on his nightstand beside his bed."

"Please take the item out of the bag and tell the jury what it is."

Calhoun reached into the opaque bag and pulled out a gold watch. "It's a gold watch," he held it up, showing the jury.

"Your honor, I ask that this gold watch be admitted into evidence as Commonwealth's Exhibit 13."

The judge glanced at the defense table. "Any objection?"

"No objection."

"And what is the significance of this gold watch?" Keene prodded.

Calhoun turned the watch over. "It has the letters TL engraved on the back."

Keene spun around to face the jury. "Not LJ for Larice Jones?"

"No sir. TL as in Timmy Lawson."

"How do you know the letters stand for Timmy Lawson?" Keene continued.

"Because I showed Tommy Lawson the watch and he positively identified it as his brother's watch."

"Agent Calhoun, did you have an opportunity to confront Mr. Jones about the Bible and the watch?"

"Yes I did," Calhoun nodded to the jury. "Right after we found these items, I went to the police station where Mr. Jones was being held and I joined Lieutenant Childress at the interview."

"Now, Agent Calhoun, I'd like to take you back a few months before the time of these murders. Was there a time that you had contact with the defendant, Mr. Jones?"

"Yes."

"And what was the nature of that contact?" Keene asked.

"Well, my office got a call from Timmy Lawson about a drug deal. Timmy had been working as an informant for us for quite awhile at the time. He told us that Ice, um, I mean Mr. Jones, was going to sell him two hundred dollars of crack cocaine."

"What did you do then?" Keene asked.

"We set up surveillance in the parking lot of Shaker's Market . . . the one on Shanty Town Road. As per our previous plan with Timmy, he was carrying marked bills which totaled two hundred dollars. Once everything was ready and at the appropriate time, Timmy drove his own car into the back lot, behind the store building, where we anticipated the drug transaction was going to take place. After approximately twenty minutes, I personally observed Larice Jones enter the parking lot on foot. He immediately approached Timmy Lawson's car and entered it via the passenger side door."

"Then what happened?"

"At that time, I personally observed Timmy Lawson hand Larice Jones the money. Mr. Jones counted the money and then placed it in his left front, inside jacket pocket. I then observed Larice Jones reach into his right front, inside jacket pocket and make a hand to hand transaction with Timmy Lawson. At that time, Mr. Lawson stated the code words that we had agreed upon, which let us know that the drug transaction had taken place."

"What happened then?" Keene asked.

"At that time, Mr. Jones exited the car and began to walk across the parking lot. Before he was able to get away, we sent our jump team in for the arrest."

"What's a jump team?"

"That's our team of officers who are called in to make the arrest after sting operations such as this," Calhoun answered. "In this case, they were waiting in an unmarked van across the street from the parking lot."

"What happened then?"

"After the jump team had Mr. Jones in custody, I searched him and retrieved the marked bills from his inside jacket pocket At that time he was charged with distribution of controlled narcotics."

"What about Timmy Lawson?"

"We took him into custody as well in an effort to maintain his integrity as an informant. He was placed in handcuffs and searched in the same manner as Mr. Jones, which resulted in the confiscation of two rocks of crack cocaine from his pocket."

"Did there come a time when Mr. Jones faced trial on those charges?" Keene asked.

"It never did go to trial," Calhoun answered.

"And why is that?"

"Because Mr. Jones, through his attorney, alleged that he was entrapped and coerced into selling narcotics by an undercover informant. There was a hearing scheduled on the matter, but we didn't want to reveal that Timmy Lawson was actually working as an informant, so the charges against Mr. Jones were dropped."

"Thank you Agent Calhoun," Keene concluded. "I have no further questions."

CHAPTER 12

On Monday morning, Nolan Getty turned into the parking lot of the Big Shanty Adult Detention Facility and found an empty parking space near the front. A sign labeled, "Lawyers Only," was prominently displayed on a post in front of the empty space.

Unlike the other government buildings in town, the detention facility was fairly new. Due to overcrowding and dangerous disrepair, the old jail had been demolished at the turn of the new century. In its place, the city erected a jail with three foot thick concrete walls, state of the art monitoring systems, magnetically locking doors, and lots of thick glass instead of steel bars.

Just inside the front door, a large group of people formed a line that led to the main desk, which was elevated above the floor like a sales tower in a car dealership. A strong odor of pine hung heavy in the air, caused by an inmate who was busy mopping the floor. Nolan stepped around the mopper and cut to the front of the line.

"Hello, Mr. Getty," the desk corporal greeted him. "Who you seeing?"

"Larice Jones."

The corporal handed Nolan a temporary badge and called for an escort. Within a few minutes, a jailor appeared and led him down a long corridor to a steel door, which opened automatically. Once inside, the first door closed and a second door opened, which allowed them to continue into the controlled area. The jailor led Nolan down another long corridor, stopped near the end, and inserted a key into a door on the right. He gave a quick look inside, and then stepped aside for Nolan to enter.

"Thanks," Nolan entered the booth and closed the door behind him.

The booth was no more than five feet wide by five feet deep. A thick glass window with reinforced mesh imbedded within it separated the visitor side from the prisoner side. At the bottom of the glass was a narrow slot, which allowed the transfer of documents between an inmate and his attorney. Just above the slot, there was a round metal speaker with a button. The speaker system was useless, however. Not only was it difficult to take turns pushing the button and talking, but any attempt to speak into the thing resulted in a garbled, crackling mess.

Nolan put his folder on the counter and waited for the door on the opposite side to open. Within a few minutes, the door opened and Larice Jones appeared.

He was wearing bright orange coveralls that appeared to be at least one size too big. Swaggering to the glass, he flipped the plastic chair around and swung his leg over it to sit down. His sleeves were rolled up, revealing a series of crude tattoos on his forearms. One was a dagger with blood dripping from it.

His eyes narrowed as he brought his face close to the glass.

"How you doing?" Nolan asked, leaning near the pass through slot.

"How come you didn't come see me before the bond hearing?" Larice asked.

"I ran out of time. But I'm here now."

"Why wouldn't you let me talk at the bond hearing? Even the prosecutor knew that I had to talk to get a bond."

"That was all bullshit," Nolan answered. "The fact that you didn't testify had nothing to do with the judge denying your bond. The only reason the prosecutor wanted you to testify was to get information that he could use against you."

Larice tilted his head and stared at Nolan through the corners of his eyes, as if he was being scammed. Nolan changed the subject.

"First things first," Nolan said. "You probably know this, but don't talk to anybody in this jail about your case. Don't talk about it to inmates or visitors. And don't talk about it on the telephone or through letters. Everything you say or write is intercepted by the jail and it could be used against you later. Understand?"

"I know," Larice answered, brushing something invisible off his orange sleeve.

"Second. Before you tell me what happened, I want you to know that everything you tell me is completely confidential, and so I don't want you to hold anything back when you tell me about it. I need to know everything, just the way it happened and without any fabrications. Only then can I find the best way to help you out of this jam."

"I ain't gonna lie," Larice interrupted. "I didn't have nothin' to do with this!"

"Let's go over the evidence against you, then. And maybe you can explain it all to me. First, they say that you denied knowing the dead kid, Timmy Lawson. But then they found a list in your house with his name on it. Not only that, but they say that they found the kid's wrist watch in your house. Tell me about that."

"Yeah, I knew the guy," Larice answered. "But it's not what they think. I didn't kill him or anybody else. He owed me some money from gambling. That's why I had his name in my drawer."

Nolan stared at Larice through the glass, watching his eyes and his demeanor. He immediately knew that he was lying. "Why did you lie about that to the police? Why did you tell them that you didn't know the kid?" Nolan asked.

"Man, they had me scared, talking about all that electric chair stuff. I just thought it would be better to say what I said."

"And the watch?" Nolan asked. "How did the kid's watch get in your house?"

"I got that from him for the gambling money he owed me. And that goes all the way back to last summer."

Nolan moved on. "The prosecutor said that your fingerprints were found on the shell casings inside the house. What about that?"

"It's the fucking cops," Larice answered. "They're trying to set me up with false evidence because I walked on a drug charge a while back. There's no way my fingerprints can be on those bullets."

Nolan shook his head. He wasn't getting much traction with his client, and he didn't have time to put up with lies or chase down idiotic theories.

"Let me tell you something," Nolan said. "The kid had a twin brother. Did you know that he had a twin brother?"

Larice shook his head.

"Well, he did. And that twin brother is telling the cops that his dead brother was mixed up with you selling drugs. That twin brother is going to testify that Timmy was afraid of you, that you were going to kill him for setting him up with the police. But that's not all." Nolan paused for Larice to digest the information. "The cops also found that owe list in your house, a bunch of cash, a scale and some baggies. And all that together can only mean one thing. All this is about drugs. Now you can sit here and tell me this and that about gambling and dirty cops planting evidence, but we both know that no jury in this town is going to buy that. The only thing that story's going to get you is a ticket to a life sentence."

Larice shook his head. "Man, I need a lawyer that's going to work for me. You can't be telling me what happened or didn't happen. How you know what happened?"

"Oh, I know," Nolan continued. "You were involved with Timmy Lawson, your fingerprints are really on the shell casings, and you were really involved in drugs. That's what the jury is going to believe, so you better start from there. The only way to save your life is to give me an explanation as to how all that happened. And the gambling story isn't going to cut it."

Larice shook his head, refusing to fold. "Man, you talk just like them. Everyone wants to put me away."

"Look," Nolan added. "I believe you when you say you didn't do this." In reality, Nolan didn't have an opinion, one way or the other, but he needed to get the kid on board. "But give me something better than that," Nolan continued. "Help me help you. I've beaten murder charges before and there's no reason why I can't do the same for you. But if you don't tell me what really happened, you're going to go down. There's just too much evidence the gambling story doesn't cover."

Larice looked away and stared at the wall for a few seconds. "Awe, to hell with it!" he yelled. Then he looked back at Nolan, and with a look of resignation, or perhaps relief, he began again.

"I'm sorry, man. They just got me so scared. I don't know what to do."

Nolan sat quietly, waiting for a better story.

"You're right. It ain't about gambling. I just thought I could make it all better by saying that. That's what I told the cops and I didn't want to tell you something different. I was afraid you wouldn't believe me anyway." Larice covered his face with his hands and rubbed them up and down.

"That's okay," Nolan reassured him. "Just tell me what happened."

"All right," Larice sighed, removing his hands from his face. "Here's what really happened . . . ."

CHAPTER 13

Keene paged directly to the local news section of the paper and eyed the headline. "Suspect in Lawson Murders Denied Bond," it read. He scanned the article and was pleased that Scotty had included his quote.

He was eager to begin the construction of his case against Larice Jones. Although he hadn't personally handled a case in over a year, to him it was like riding a bicycle. You either know how or you don't. And he definitely knew how to put bad guys behind bars.

As with all of the other cases in his past, he would follow a ritual. His assistant, Rachel, had been instructed not to disturb him. His desk had been cleared of all things extraneous to the case. The conference table was bare with all chairs neatly placed around it. The books on his shelves were in perfect order, like soldiers in formation, ready for service. His desk lamp and floor lamp were glowing, adding contemporaneous light to the room. In short, his office could have been the set of a Hollywood movie. That was his ritual -- to start clean and perfect, without any distractions.

He opened the only file on his desk, which was also in perfect order. The warrants, bond information, and criminal history report of Larice Jones had been hole punched and bound by metal fingers at the top of the left side of the file. Everything else -- the police reports, warrants, crime scene data, interviews, and photos, were all bound in sequential order, from back to front, on the right side of the file.

Keene started from the back on the right side, folding the documents until he came to the photographs of the murdered family -- first the son, then the father, then the mother. Then he turned to the other photos -- the cut screen, the disheveled room, and the shell casings. After studying all of the photos of the crime scene, his eyes returned to the photo of Mrs. Lawson.

The bloody sheets were turned down to her waist, exposing a naked torso spotted with black holes. Her arms were frozen upward, with palms facing out, as if she was a mime trapped in some nightmarish, invisible box. Her breasts were limp, sagging outward and pointing into the bed on each side. Then Keene looked at the face in the photograph: a contorted mass with bulging eyes and a ghastly black hole where her mouth and lips should have been.

As Keene stared at the grim picture with its lifeless, mangled face, his eyes slowly lost focus and his thoughts began to drift to another place and time. His peripheral vision narrowed, as if he was entering a tunnel, and his eyes fell dead. The oculatory signals that should have been relaying the light spectrum associated with the photograph of Mrs. Lawson became blurred and were replaced by the vision of someone else; a vision formed long ago and entombed deep within his memory, but just as clear and detailed as the photo displayed before him.

In life she was a picture of beauty. He could still see her long, auburn hair, gracefully flowing to her shoulders and framing her elegant face. She had a long narrow nose and a prominent jaw line, which created a distinctive, aristocratic look. Her green eyes were playful and laughing, as if she never had a care in the world.

The vision that always came to him was that of her in the flowered dress which she sometimes wore to church. Tucked in her auburn hair and behind her ear was a small, white carnation. He could smell the fresh scent of the carnation and see her beautiful face as if she was right in front of him.

But the real beauty was within her. She was a strong person with unflagging morals and a keen dedication to the ones she loved. She was a protector, a caregiver, and the only person that ever loved him without conditions, without any terms, and without reserve. She was a beautiful woman, a wonderful human being, and a perfect mother . . . in life.

In death, she was left with the same ghastly grimace as Mrs. Lawson.

At a young age, way too young for a boy to have such thoughts, John Keene recognized that his stepfather did not deserve such a wife. And he did not deserve such a stepfather. But that was how things were. His real dad left his mother and Richard Keene stepped into the picture at what must have been her weakest moment. And although his mother married him and they both took his name, John knew from the beginning that Richard Keene was not his real dad.

Richard Keene was the antithesis of all the good things that his mother represented. Where there was love from her, there was criticism from Richard. Where there was forgiveness in her, there was retribution from him. Richard was all things that his mother wasn't -- a hater, a punisher, a coward.

Richard only gave to his family the minimum that every man had a duty to provide -- food and shelter. But even that was far from a constant. He was a welder by trade, but he could never keep a full time job. Instead, he worked on a temporary basis, floating from project to project, with long layoffs in between. During the layoffs, Richard pursued his true love, which was tinkering with his car and drinking in his garage behind the house. But mostly drinking.

Those were the worst of times, during the layoffs. When Richard was working and sober, he was at best, apathetic towards his family. But when Richard was layed off and drinking, his apathy turned to pure evil.

During those times, John Keene learned to stay under his stepfather's radar. Even for a young boy, it only took a few times to learn his lesson. The first was when he and a friend were playing baseball in the yard. His friend hit the ball and it accidentally flew through the open window of the garage.

"Goddamn it!" Richard's voice boomed from within. A second later, he appeared from the doorway with such a look of rage on his face that John's friend ran away. John, on the other hand, was frozen with fear.

In a drunken rage, his stepfather stomped across the lawn until he was only a few feet from him. Winding his arm back, he threw the ball as hard as he could at John's head. Luckily, despite the fear that had frozen him, John instinctively ducked and the ball whizzed by, missing by a fraction of an inch.

"I'm sorry!" John yelled, covering his head and falling to the ground.

With his eyes bulging and veins popping out of his neck, Richard leaned over the cowering boy and pointed his finger, jabbing it into John's face as he yelled each word. "Don't you ever hit a ball into my shop again!"

"I'm sorry," John muttered again, still covering his head.

The second time, the one that first got Richard into trouble, was when John had borrowed Richard's chrome plated 9/16 inch wrench in order to change his bike tire. Although he tried, he was just too young to complete the project. In his disappointment, he forgot to take the wrench back to the shop. Instead he left it lying in the grass in the back yard.

Three days later, when Richard was looking for his wrench, he called him to the shop for questioning. John admitted to using it, but he was so afraid of the severe punishment that he would get for not putting it back, that he convinced himself of an untruth. "I put it back," he told his stepfather, "I swear."

After further questioning, he was forced to lead Richard to the location where he had attempted to change the bicycle tire. Stepping from side to side and sweeping the grass with his boot, Richard eventually kicked the wrench.

"You took it back, huh?" Richard reached down, retrieving the wrench from the grass.

John's eyes widened. "I was sure that I did!"

"Do you know what would happen if I had run over this wrench with the lawn mower?" he asked loudly, the veins beginning to pop in his neck.

John blinked, unconscious of the fact that his feet were taking backward steps away from his stepfather.

"This!" he screamed, hurling the wrench at young John. Before he could duck, the wrench struck him in the forehead. John's world turned black and his legs collapsed beneath him. A few seconds later he felt a tugging at his arm and heard his stepfather's voice.

"Goddamn you!" he yelled. "Look what you made me do."

As he was pulled to his feet, John could feel a warm wetness on his head and down the side of his face. He lifted his hand to his head and then looked at it. Seeing his crimson filled palm, he screamed in terror.

"Stop crying!" his stepfather yelled. "You'll be all right."

Evidently the neighbors didn't think so, because one of them called the police. By the time the police arrived, Richard had taken his boy into the house and put him on the couch with a cold dish rag on his head.

When Richard saw the police cruiser pull into the driveway he knelt down beside the boy and gave him instructions.

"Listen to me Johnny," he said close to his face, his breath heavy with the stench of alcohol. "We're going to tell the police that this was an accident. The wrench slipped from my hand while we were changing the bicycle tire. You say anything else, and we're all going to get in trouble."

John nodded.

When the police officers came into the house, Richard told them what had happened as he led them to his son on the couch. One of the police officers took Richard into the kitchen, while a second stayed with John. Once Richard was taken to the kitchen, the officer leaned down and lifted the rag to look at the wound.

"How you doing, son?" the officer asked.

"Fine," John answered.

"How did this happen?" he asked.

John repeated the story as his stepfather had instructed.

Satisfied that the bleeding was under control, the officer left the house. After taking a statement from the neighbor, who had seen the entire incident, the officer returned and arrested Richard for child abuse. The police called John's mother, who came home from work early to take John to the hospital. She cried when she saw him.

When they returned from the hospital, John's mom made his favorite meal -- tacos. After dinner, she baked a batch of chocolate chip cookies and they ate them in between rounds of Slap Jack. She made John laugh every time that she slapped the Queen, instead of the Jack. And when the Jack did appear, her hand was deliberately slow so that John could slap it first.

That night, she let John sleep in her bed and following doctor's orders, she woke him every two hours, just to make sure that he didn't slip into a coma.

Despite the head wound, John had never felt better. Richard was gone and it was just his mother and him. No yelling, no fighting -- just love and compassion. During the night, as his mother stroked his hair and hummed songs to him, he wished that Richard would never come back. He prayed that they would keep him in jail forever.

But they didn't.

The knock at Keene's office door evaporated the vision of his mother. He looked up to see Fred Mutz standing in the open doorway.

"Come in," Keene said. He waved him to the open chair on the opposite side of his desk.

"Are you caught up on the details?" he questioned Mutz.

"Yes sir," Mutz answered taking the open chair.

"We've got some work to do here," Keene paged through the file. "Let me ask you something. If you were in charge of this prosecution, what would your highest priority be at this point?"

Mutz thought for a second. "I guess I'd follow up on the DNA results and other laboratory analysis," he answered.

Keene stared at Mutz. He didn't like his answer. The results would come in whether they were followed up on or not. He thought about prodding Mutz some more, but he knew that the possibility of him coming up with the answer was as unlikely as a June snow. He began to wonder how a young man could be so cocky, yet so ignorant. Confidence was one thing, he thought, but at some point, it breeds complacency, and complacency leads to trial losses.

"Listen," Keene said. "Let me tell you something about prosecuting a case. And this is something that I don't think you've learned yet." He paused as Mutz shifted in his chair. "If you want to be a prosecutor you have to think like a defense attorney. Now, if you were the defense attorney, who would you try to blame this on?"

Mutz thought to himself for a moment but couldn't come up with an answer. "I don't know," he finally said. "Larice Jones obviously did it, so who could he possibly blame?"

Keene sighed. "Well, there are only two possible people mentioned in the file, besides the police officers."

Mutz appeared as if he wanted to open his file, but instead, he just continued to stare blankly at Keene. And then his eyes lit up.

"Is one of them Tommy Lawson?" he asked.

"Yes!" Keene yelled out. Mutz smiled and appeared more relaxed. But Keene continued. "That is a person in the file who is not a police officer, but that's not who I'm talking about!"

Mutz's smile disappeared.

"Did you ever think that the defense might want to point the finger at the anonymous caller?" Keene asked sarcastically.

Mutz nodded. "That's possible," he admitted.

"Possible?" Keene asked incredulously. "If I was a defense attorney, I would claim that the caller was the one who killed that family and I would hope to hell that the caller was never found."

Mutz cocked his head, seemingly confused. But Keene wasn't going to give him a chance to ask stupid questions.

"If we can't find the caller, then we can't disprove such a theory, and that is exactly what criminal defense attorneys prey on," Keene explained. "Just in case you haven't figured this out yet, Nolan Getty isn't just another lazy Public Defender collecting a check and clocking out at five o'clock. He takes every case personally, as if he is the one on trial, and he wants to win every case, whether his client is stone cold guilty or not. That's the kind of zealot we're working against here. He doesn't care about right and wrong. He only cares about winning. Therefore, we need to identify the caller. And if we do that, when it comes time for trial, we'll be able to crush any attempt by the defense to put the finger on him."

"How are we supposed to find an anonymous caller?" Mutz asked.

Keene answered quickly. "If I were you, I would talk to Lieutenant Childress and have him contact the Big Shanty Communications Center to find out if there's any electronic information from the call. And I mean any information, like the service used, the manufacturer of the phone, anything that could help us track down the owner."

"Okay," Mutz answered. "I can do that."

"I know you can," Keene cut in. "And you will."

There was a moment of silence as Keene stared at Mutz, who finally glanced down at his own file.

"What about any other problems?" Keene asked. "Do you see any other red flags with the evidence?"

"Not really," Mutz muttered, "it looks pretty cut and dry."

Although Mutz didn't have all of the information, he should have seen from his copied file that key pieces of evidence were missing. Keene continued to stare at Mutz, who was slouched in the chair with his legs spread apart, chewing gum. The sight of him was beginning to anger Keene. In fact, he began to feel an overwhelming desire to kick him like a dog. The gum smacking, the slouching, the ignorance -- it was all too much. Keene couldn't suppress the rage that suddenly exploded within him.

"It's all in the fucking file!" Keene yelled out, slapping his hand loudly on the file in front of him. Mutz visibly flinched and immediately bolted upright. He opened his own file, which was on his lap, but Keene didn't give him time to page through it.

"Do you think it will be important to find the murder weapon?"

"I guess that would be nice," Mutz answered defensively, his voice turning to a higher pitch. "But he could have ditched the gun anywhere and we'll probably never find it. Besides, we have the fingerprints from the shell casings and we have Timmy Lawson's watch in his possession."

Keene shook his head. "Let me tell you a secret. The minute you start thinking that you don't need something or that you've got enough evidence, that's the moment that you've lost the trial. We need absolutely everything. Every piece of evidence that is out there is critical. And if you don't find *every* piece of evidence -- if you think that you can cut corners and do a half-ass job, you're not going to be able to continue working here," Keene told him without bothering to yell. "I can't afford to have attorneys on my staff who think that *some* evidence is enough."

"I understand," Mutz reacted defensively. "I was just thinking about what we have."

"Well it's time you started thinking about what we don't have. I'd like you to contact the PD and find out what kind of search they've done. If they haven't drawn a line between the defendant's house and the crime scene and searched every possible hiding spot, including every storm sewer and garbage can, I want it done."

Mutz nodded his head.

"Thank you," Keene replied. "And one more thing. Don't count on the wrist watch to be our smoking gun. It may not do us any good."

Mutz looked confused. "Why not?"

"Because Nolan Getty has won six motions to suppress evidence this year, two of which were against you," he answered.

CHAPTER 14

Nolan Getty sat quietly as Larice prepared to tell him what really happened.

"Where do you want me to start?"

"Let's start with the night of your arrest. Why did you run from the police when you saw them parked outside your house?"

"I thought my girlfriend called them," he answered.

"Why would your girlfriend call the police?"

"We got in a little fight the day before. She said she was leaving me. But I didn't want her to leave, so I took her car keys. And then she got mad and just walked away. I figured she'd gone to stay with her mother, 'cause she never came back. Then, the next night I came out of the house and saw the five-o van parked there, so I figured she called them on me. And I didn't want to get arrested, so I ran."

"What's your girlfriend's name?" Nolan asked.

"Monica . . . Monica Lee."

"How can I get a hold of her?"

"She ain't gonna help none," Larice shot back. "She's done with me."

"I'll be the judge of that," Nolan countered. "I like to be thorough."

"She's with her mother now. Over on Jackson Street. I don't know the address."

"How about a telephone number?" Nolan pressed.

"I don't know it!" Larice said, bobbing his head in exasperation. "Like I said, she ain't gonna help none anyway."

"Tell me about Timmy Lawson," Nolan changed the subject.

"Man, he's just a dude on the street I knew."

"They say he set you up on a drug deal a few months ago," Nolan prodded.

"I didn't know none of that," Larice cried. "Alls I know is that I got arrested for distribution and I thought he got arrested too."

"You didn't know he was working for the police?"

"Nope," Larice said. "The cops are saying I was after him for it, but I never knew he was a narc. Besides, it was just a couple rocks and I beat the charge anyway, so why would I want to kill anyone?" he asked in that same exasperated tone.

"I don't know, why would you want to kill someone?" Nolan shot back, tiring of the game.

"I didn't!" Larice yelled. "Man, ain't you listening to me?"

"Yeah, I'm listening," Nolan answered. "What about the list with Timmy's name on it? What was that about?"

"He owed me money for some stuff that I fronted him," Larice answered.

"Drugs?" Nolan asked.

"Yeah, drugs, what the hell you think?" Larice shouted, as if Nolan should've magically known everything about him.

"When did this happen?"

"Last year," Larice answered.

"So he was dealing drugs for you?"

"Not really. He was just helping me move some stuff from time to time."

"What about the watch?"

"I didn't steal it from him like they say. He put up that watch for some stuff I fronted him a long time ago."

"Do you know anyone who could verify that you've had that watch since before the murders?" Nolan asked.

Larice seemed to think for a moment, scratching his chin and then finally shaking his head. "Maybe my mama."

"What about Monica Lee?"

"Like I said, she aint' gonna do nuthin' to help me," Larice replied. "Maybe she seen it, but she'd probably lie and say she didn't."

"They find anything else?"

Larice paused for a moment and then looked at Nolan with a quizzical expression. "Man, you're my lawyer and you don't even know what they found? What you been doing?" he asked.

"Look," Nolan said, losing his patience. "This is going to go a whole lot smoother if you just answer my questions and stop pulling my chain.

The first step is for you to tell me everything you know. Then I can go from there. I'll get the search warrants and see for myself, but right now I want to know everything you know, got it?"

"Whatever, man," Larice looked away.

"Do you know if they found anything else important?" Nolan repeated.

"Just bullshit that don't mean nuthin'," Larice answered.

"Okay, fine. I'll get copies of the search warrants and I'll be able to look at the inventory they made of the things they found. What about the gun that was used. How do you explain the fact that your fingerprints are on the shell casings left at the scene?"

"I don't know," Larice answered, slowly articulating each word and slapping his hand on the countertop as he said them.

"Do you have a gun?" Nolan asked.

"Yeah, I *had* a gun," Larice answered. "But it was stolen a little while ago, when I was in jail on that drug charge."

Nolan played along. "So that's how your fingerprints got on the shell casings. You loaded the gun, it was later stolen, and then someone used it to kill that family."

"Yeah," Larice said. "That's gotta be how it happened."

"Who would want to do that?" Nolan asked. "Can you think of any suspects?"

Larice shook his head. "I don't have no idea."

Nolan didn't have any idea either, except the most obvious one -- that Larice did it. But Nolan wasn't looking for a confession. He simply wanted a story that he could sell to the jury.

"Look," Nolan explained. "We're going to have to point to someone other than yourself if you want to win this case. That's just how it is."

"That's your job," Larice cut in. "Can't you find someone?"

"Well, my first instinct is to look at the surviving twin," Nolan answered. "That's obvious. But I need to know if you know of any other suspects that might've had a reason to kill this family."

"None that I can think of," Larice answered.

"All right, I'll work on that," Nolan said. "Where were you on the night of April Eleventh?"

"Man, how am I supposed to know that?" Larice asked incredulously.

"Well, you know that you were home on the night you were arrested, and that was April Thirteenth. So think back and remember where you were the two nights before that night," Nolan helped him, doing his best to hide his frustration. "It was a Sunday night."

Larice scratched his chin again and looked up. "Hmm," he hummed, trying to at least give the impression that he was thinking hard. "I'm pretty sure I was home both of those nights."

"Anyone with you?"

"Nope," Larice answered with a hard stare, as if he was proud not to have an alibi.

Nolan had enough of the attitude. Larice was starting to piss him off and he was about to lose his temper. But instead of yelling at him again, Nolan decided to end the interview.

"I'll be back in touch with you," he finished.

"When?"

"When it's time," Nolan answered. "In the meantime, keep your mouth shut about this whole thing."

Larice didn't say goodbye. He stood up and slammed his fist on the door. "Get me out of here!"

A jailor opened the door and Larice disappeared into the bowels of the jail without looking back.

Nolan shook his head and closed his case file. The kid was obviously not going to plead guilty to the crimes. That meant a jury trial ahead of him. But with such a bad attitude, he knew the kid wouldn't make a good witness. He learned long ago that bad attitudes never went over well with juries, regardless of guilt. Unfortunately, he also realized that juries were always suspicious when a defendant refused to testify, and despite all of the instructions and warnings not to, they always held it against the defendant.

* * * * * * *

When Nolan returned to his office, Mrs. Ester Jones and another young lady were waiting for him in the former dining room. Mrs. Jones was a large woman who appeared to be in her forties. She was wearing a bright orange, African-looking dress that flowed over her body. Just below the flowing dress, her legs, which were thick stumps, stuck out at almost right angles to her body.

The young girl sitting beside her appeared to be in her twenties and although she was African-American, her skin was lighter. Her hair was short and spiky, with just a hint of orange coloring in it, which perhaps made her skin appear lighter. She was wearing tight jeans and one of those blouses -- the kind that forms tightly around the breasts, but hangs loosely in the lower half. Nolan never did like the style -- it reminded him of maternity clothes.

Nolan nodded to both of them as he approached Vicki's desk.

"Mrs. Jones has an appointment to see you," Vicki said.

"Fine," Nolan turned and smiled at his visitors. "Why don't we go into the conference room so we can talk?"

Nolan led them across the hall. Closing the door behind them, he pulled two chairs away from the conference table for the ladies to sit, then sat down on the opposite side of the table.

"Have you seen my son yet?" Mrs. Jones asked.

"Yes ma'am," Nolan answered. "I was just at the jail with him."

"Is he all right? How's he doing?"

"He's doing fine."

"How come you wouldn't let him talk at the bond hearing? He needs to get out."

"That was for his protection. Unfortunately, he's not going to get a bond. He's charged with murdering three people and nobody gets a bond on murder charges in this town."

"He didn't kill nobody," the younger female interjected.

"What's your name?" Nolan asked.

"I'm his sister, Laronda."

"Listen," Nolan explained. "I'm his attorney and I'll do anything to help him. But they have some pretty solid evidence against him and he doesn't seem to have a very good alibi. So how do you know he didn't do it -- were you with him on the night of the murders?"

"No, but I know he didn't do it," Laronda answered.

"Did you see him on a regular basis before he was arrested?"

"Yeah, pretty regularly," the mother answered and the sister nodded.

"Did you ever see him wearing a gold Armani watch in the last year?"

"A gold watch?" the mother asked. "He ain't got no money for no gold watch!"

It was not exactly the answer that Nolan was looking for. And based on her response, there was no need to ask any more questions about it.

"You say that he didn't do it, but I need more than that -- I need evidence that will help him," Nolan explained.

"You don't understand," Mrs. Jones cut in. "Larice isn't normal. He never has been."

"What do you mean?"

"He's slow," Mrs. Jones answered. "He's always been slow, ever since he was born. He's not retarded or anything . . . but he can't think like a normal person."

"Did he go to school?" Nolan asked.

"Yeah, I always sent him to school. But he never made it past the tenth grade."

"He didn't seem that slow to me. I mean, he had a girlfriend he was living with over on Sherman Street, didn't he?"

"He's gotten good at fooling people into thinking he's normal," Mrs. Jones explained. "He tells people what he thinks they want to hear, but if you spent enough time with him, you'd know. Besides, it ain't what you think about that girl. She was using him. And I should've never let him move in with her, but the boy thought he was in love and just wouldn't listen to me."

"What do you mean?" Nolan asked. "How was she using him?"

"She just wanted his money, that's all," Mrs. Jones answered.

"What money?"

"He's been getting a social security check ever since his Daddy died when he was young. And then a few years ago that lady from social services had him tested and when they found out he was learning disabled, they started giving him another check every month. It wasn't much, but it was a steady check."

Nolan thought about what they were telling him. He thought about his interview with Larice and how he seemed to be very normal. Very angry, albeit, but normal.

"Did you ever suspect that he was involved with drugs?" Nolan tested their knowledge.

"You darn right," Mrs. Jones answered. "That's the thing about Larice. He was always wanting to be normal and he'd do anything to please people. That's how he got involved in drugs in the first place. Those boys at the car wash started pushing them on him until he got hooked. And then when they got him hooked, the drug dealers started using him and making him sell drugs for them."

Nolan nodded. Larice's mother was very convincing. Perhaps she would be an asset when it came time for the trial, he thought. Perhaps that could be a viable defense theory -- Larice was too dumb to pull off a triple homicide. At the very least, it would be decent mitigating evidence if the jury found him guilty.

"He tried to quit using those drugs," she continued. "When I couldn't talk any sense into him, I got our pastor to help out and he got him into that drug rehab place. He even had him giving talks to the kids down at the Center on how bad drugs are and all that. But then he got sent to jail and when he got out, he couldn't get back into the rehab."

"Can you get me all of his records, like the testing that the social services worker did and maybe his school records?" Nolan asked. "It may be important."

"Yes sir," Mrs. Jones answered. "I saved everything. It's all at home."

"Can you please help him?" Laronda begged. "If you knew him like we do, you'd know he'd never kill anyone."

"I'll do my best," Nolan answered. He wasn't lying about that. He always did his best. But it would take more than a loving mother and sister to convince a jury that Larice was too dumb to kill. After all, none of his clients were too bright. That's why they got in trouble with the law in the first place.

CHAPTER 15

On the second Monday in June, approximately two months after the Astor Street murders, Nolan Getty passed through the security gate of the Big Shanty General District Court just minutes before the Larice Jones preliminary hearing.

Just inside the entrance, he passed three doors on the left side of the hallway, each with a small window located at eye level. He paused at each window to glance into the conference rooms. The first room was empty. In the second room, John Keene, Fred Mutz and several police officers were sitting around a table, obviously discussing the upcoming hearing. Before any of them noticed his face in the window, he continued to the third window, where a young black male was sitting with a pretty blonde who he recognized as one of the victim witness advocates. The young man had to be the surviving twin of the Lawson family.

It was the first time that Nolan had actually seen him. Both he and his investigator had been trying to track the kid down, but they couldn't find him. The kid hadn't returned to the house on Astor Street and no forwarding address could be found. It was almost as if the kid existed only as a rumor, mentioned in newspapers and referred to by the police. But now here he was, in the flesh, and ready to testify.

Getty knocked on the door and opened it without waiting for an answer. "Good morning," he said as he leaned his head into the room. "Are you Tommy Lawson?"

The kid looked up. "Yes," he answered.

"Can I have a word with you?" Nolan asked.

The victim witness advocate turned to the kid and whispered, "That's the defendant's attorney -- you don't have to talk to him."

The kid nodded at her and then turned back to Nolan. "I'm not talking to no one without my attorney."

"Your attorney?" Nolan asked. "Who's your attorney?"

The kid glanced at the advocate before answering. "Mr. Keene."

"I've got news for you," Nolan shot back. "Mr. Keene is not your attorney. He represents the Commonwealth of Virginia. Has he instructed you not to talk to me?"

The advocate jumped from her seat and yelled out, "I am in a private meeting with a victim and you have no right to interrupt us. Now please shut the door and leave us alone!"

Nolan wasn't ready to back down. "Yes or no. Are you refusing to talk to me?" he asked the kid.

"That's right," the kid nodded.

"Have it your way," Nolan smiled. "I'll see you inside."

Nolan let the door shut and proceeded to the courtroom. There were a handful of lawyers milling around the back of the court room and a few people in the gallery, but the judge was not yet on the bench. Nolan made his way to the front and approached one of the deputies, who was paging through a docket.

"You got anyone in the back yet?" he asked the deputy.

"Who you looking for?" the deputy asked.

"Larice Jones," Nolan answered.

"Yeah, he's here. "I'll take you back."

Nolan followed as the deputy passed his badge across the electronic pad next to the corner door to unlock it. They proceeded down a corridor to a second door. The deputy passed his badge again at the second door and they entered the holding area. "I think he's in the second cell," the deputy said.

The holding area was just another corridor with five cells lined along the right side. At the end of the corridor there was a small desk, where another deputy sat with a newspaper in front of him. The deputy folded back one side of the newspaper to look at Nolan. "You gonna need to get in a cell?" the deputy asked.

"That's all right," Nolan answered. He really didn't feel like emptying his pockets. Besides, he didn't have anything confidential to say to his client.

Nolan peered into the second window and saw Larice sitting on a bench next to two other inmates.

"Mr. Jones," Nolan yelled into the glass.

Larice looked up and nodded to Nolan.

"Come up to the window so you can hear me."

Larice stood up and approached the window. Once they were face to face, Nolan continued. "How are you?"

Larice shrugged on the other side of the window. "I'm in jail," he said as a matter of fact.

"This is your preliminary hearing this morning," Nolan continued. "As I told you earlier, you will not be testifying today. The only purpose of this hearing is for the court to see if the prosecutor has a case against you. They'll put on evidence and try to show the court that you probably did this. They don't have to prove their case beyond a reasonable doubt at this stage -- only probable cause. If they establish probable cause, your case will be sent on to Circuit Court, where we will have a trial in a few months. You're not going to testify today and we won't present any evidence. We're just going to listen to their evidence and I'll be able to question their witnesses. Understand?"

"Yeah," Larice nodded.

"Very good," Nolan said. "I'll see you out in the courtroom."

* * * * * * *

At 9:45 a.m. the deputy banged a gavel against a wooden block at the front of the courtroom and announced loudly, "All rise. Oyez, Oyez, the Big Shanty General District Court is now in session, with the Honorable Judge Yancey R. Hadley, the Third presiding."

Nolan entered the courtroom from the lockup just as the deputy was making his announcement. Judge Hadley appeared from the door behind the bench and took his rightful place on the throne of justice. After he was seated, the deputy spoke one more time, "Be seated."

Nolan Getty sat down in the first row of the two church-like pews on the side of the courtroom. He saw John Keene, Fred Mutz, and several police officers seated in the two pews on the opposite side of the courtroom. The gallery, which was now full, was on his left, separated by small swinging gates.

Judge Hadley retrieved a stack of folders from the clerk who was positioned on his right, and then turned to the audience. "When I call your case, please come forward."

He pulled the top file from the stack and then nodded to John Keene. "Larice Jones," he yelled out.

John Keene and his entourage stood up and approached the prosecution table on their side of the courtroom. Nolan also stood up and walked to the defense table.

"Is he in custody?" the judge asked Nolan.

"Yes sir," Nolan answered. Evidently the good judge had forgotten that he had denied him bond two months earlier.

The door to the lockup made an electronic buzzing sound before it opened. Larice Jones stepped into the courtroom with a deputy at his side. He was wearing orange coveralls and flat, canvas shoes. The deputy escorted him to the defense table and instructed him to stand beside Nolan at the table.

"Are you Larice Jones?" Judge Hadley asked.

"Yes sir," Larice answered.

"Mr. Jones, this is a preliminary hearing in your case. Do you want me to read the charges?"

Nolan cut in before Larice could respond. "No sir, Mr. Jones understands what he's charged with."

"Very well. Is the Commonwealth ready to proceed?"

"Yes sir," John Keene responded.

"Is the defense ready to proceed?"

"Yes sir."

After the prosecution witnesses were sworn in, Judge Hadley turned to the defense. "Do you have any witnesses?" he asked.

"No sir," Nolan responded.

"Who's your first witness?" Hadley turned to Keene.

"Tommy Lawson," John Keene answered.

The court room deputy gestured to the young man to approach the middle podium. As he stood, his victim witness advocate patted him on the shoulder for support.

Once he was in front of the podium, the deputy adjusted the microphone to his level and instructed the witness to speak into the microphone when testifying. The deputy then returned to his position at the corner of the judge's bench and crossed his arms.

"Please tell the court your name," Keene instructed.

The young man leaned into the microphone. "My name is Tommy Lawson."

As the young man spoke, Larice Jones leaned forward in his chair, as if he was trying to get closer to the witness. Nolan glanced at Larice, who appeared to have a dumbfounded expression on his face.

"Where do you live?" Keene asked the witness.

"I used to live at 21 Astor Street, but now I'm staying in an apartment here in Big Shanty," the young man responded.

Larice moved his legs under the table and slid up to the edge of his seat, as if he was getting ready to stand up. The deputy unfolded his arms and moved a few steps closer to the defense table, obviously getting himself in position to react if the defendant tried to do anything stupid.

Nolan watched his client from the corner of his eye. Larice appeared very agitated, leaning ahead in his chair even further to stare at the witness. Only Nolan was close enough to hear the words that came out under his breath. "What the fuck is going on here?" Larice whispered.

Nolan reached over and placed a hand on his arm. "Calm down," he whispered.

Larice didn't seem to hear Nolan. Just as the witness was about to answer another of Keene's background questions, Larice jumped to his feet.

"You bitch!" he yelled out.

The deputy was the first to react, as he had seen it coming before any of the others. He quickly stepped over to the defense table and yelled, "Sit down and shut up!"

Judge Hadley banged his gavel and also yelled at the defense table. "Mr. Getty, control your client!"

Larice Jones didn't appear to be listening to either the deputy or the judge. He pointed his finger to the witness and yelled out again, "You're a lying bitch!"

The deputy reached out and grabbed Larice's arm as another deputy rushed in from the side of the courtroom. Larice struggled to free his arm, but with the help of the second deputy, they managed to get both of his arms behind his back. Larice kicked the defense table, knocking the pitcher of water to the floor. Instinctively, Nolan stood up and took two steps away from the table, out of harm's way.

A woman screamed as Larice kicked again, this time like a mule, which sent his chair flying backwards into the low partition that separated the front of the courtroom from the gallery.

"Order in this court!" Hadley yelled, banging his gavel furiously.

As the two deputies struggled with Larice, a third deputy stepped forward and pulled a taser gun from his holster. He pointed it directly at Larice and quickly pulled the trigger, blasting two prongs into his chest. The clicking of electricity followed and Larice let out a high pitched scream before collapsing to the floor. The clicking and screaming continued as Larice convulsed wildly on the floor beside the defense table.

After several seconds, the deputy finally released the trigger. One of the deputies placed his knee on the back of Larice's neck as the other deputy twisted his arms behind his back and cuffed him.

"This court is in recess for ten minutes!" Judge Hadley yelled. "Clear the courtroom and take the defendant to lock up," he instructed. Hadley banged his gavel one more time before standing up and exiting the door behind the bench.

A deputy ran through the swinging gates and pointed to the door. "Everyone out, now!" he yelled. The people in the gallery stood up and rushed to the door. As the courtroom was emptying, John Keene approached his witness and made a motion for the young man to follow him through the side door. Fred Mutz exited close behind them.

The deputies lifted Larice Jones to his feet and dragged him across the courtroom towards the door in the corner that led to the lock up.

"This is a set up!" he screamed as they pulled him. Just as they were getting him through the door, he turned over his shoulder and with wild eyes yelled directly to Nolan, "You gotta do something! You're my fucking lawyer . . . ." But he was cut off by the slamming door.

Once the deputies and Larice had disappeared, only Nolan, the clerk, and a slight odor of singed flesh remained in the courtroom.

"Oh my God!" the clerk exclaimed. "That was crazy."

"No kidding," Nolan said. He pulled the table back into its original position and then reached down to pick up the water pitcher.

"What's the matter with him?" the clerk asked.

"I have no idea," Nolan answered as he picked up the chair and pushed it up to the defense table. "But I guess I better go find out."

After everything was back in place, Nolan walked to the corner door and knocked on it. A few moments later, the deputy opened the door.

"Can I talk with him now?" Nolan asked.

"Knock yourself out," the deputy opened the door wider for Nolan to enter. "We've got him in his own cell at the end."

Once they reached the end cell, Nolan began emptying his pockets. "I guess I better have a private conversation with him."

"Suit yourself," the deputy said.

After Nolan emptied his pockets into a plastic tray, the deputy unlocked the cell door for him.

Larice was chained to the bench in the corner of the cell, with his hands and feet cuffed. Nolan sat down on the bench beside him.

"Are you okay?" he asked.

"No I'm not okay!" Larice yelled. "They fucking shocked me!"

"Why did you freak out in there?" Nolan asked.

"That's not who they say it is," Larice answered.

"What? What are you talking about?"

"That guy is not who he says he is," Larice repeated. "That guy is Timmy Lawson."

Nolan shook his head. "That was Tommy Lawson out there. He is the identical twin of Timmy Lawson. Timmy Lawson was murdered."

"Like hell he was," Larice shot back. "That was Timmy Lawson right there in that courtroom."

Nolan shook his head again. "Come on, now," he said. "How could that be? You just think he's Timmy because they're identical twins. You see this kid and your mind tells you that it's Timmy."

"I'm telling you that he's Timmy Lawson!" Larice shouted. "He's the guy that calls himself T and he's the guy that's a narc for the cops, and he's the guy that I've been dealing with for years. I know T and that guy in there is definitely T. Did you see his face when I called him out?"

Nolan stared blankly at Larice.

"Well, did you?"

"No," Nolan answered.

"He's lying. He's pretending to be someone he ain't."

"But that doesn't even make sense," Nolan said. "Why would he lie about something like that?"

"I don't know," Larice shot back. "Maybe he's the one that killed his own family."

Nolan sat back and thought about what Larice was telling him. Could the surviving twin actually be Timmy Lawson pretending to be Tommy Lawson? The police or the medical examiner would have had to identify the body somehow. Wouldn't they know for sure if the dead person was

Timmy or Tommy? They must be able to verify something like that, he thought. Unless they just took the surviving twin's word for it.

Nolan's mind raced through the evidence, trying to piece together a puzzle in which the final picture revealed Timmy as the surviving twin, instead of Tommy. If Tommy is really Timmy, he thought, then Timmy must have been involved in the murders. But why would someone want to kill his own family? It still didn't make sense to him, but the idea was exciting.

"How can you be so sure that it was Timmy in there if you've never seen his twin?" Nolan asked.

"I've seen his brother," Larice answered. "He was always at the house when I went to see T. He even hung out with us a few times."

"I thought you told me that you didn't know that Timmy had a twin?"

Larice shook his head. "I lied. And that's because I didn't know if you were gonna be on my side or theirs."

Nolan ignored the confession. "How can you tell them apart?"

"I just can," Larice answered. "T is always blinking and moving his eyes back and forth when he talks, just like he was in the courtroom."

"That's it?" Nolan asked. "He blinks his eyes?"

"No man, there's other stuff you can check about him. For one, T smokes cigarettes and his brother smokes those little cigars."

There was a knock on the cell door and the sound of keys in the lock. The door opened and the deputy leaned in. "The judge is ready for us to bring him out," he said.

"All right," Nolan nodded. And then he turned to Larice. "You've got to control yourself in there. I'll be thinking about what you just told me, and I'll find a way to handle it, but you can't act up anymore."

"Don't worry about it," Larice answered.

When they entered the courtroom, only the judge, the deputies, and the prosecutors were present. Larice shuffled alongside Nolan, still in handcuffs and leg shackles.

Judge Hadley didn't wait for them to be seated. "Mr. Jones, I'm not going to allow you to disrupt my courtroom like you just did. Now you have two choices. You can either sit quietly like a gentleman and listen to the evidence, or I can have you bound and gagged throughout this process. Do you want me to have the deputies restrain you like that?"

"No sir," Larice lowered his eyes.

"Then you better keep your mouth shut for the rest of this hearing, or that's what will happen, understand?"

"Yes sir," he looked back up.

The judge instructed the deputies to open the courtroom. As the people returned, he instructed the deputy at the side door to bring the witness back to the podium. The deputy opened the door and called for Tommy Lawson. A moment later, the deputy escorted him to the middle podium, between the defense and prosecution tables.

For the first time, Nolan began to pay particular attention to the boy. He was of slight build, standing just under six feet in height. His face was narrow with a sharp jaw line which led to a slightly pointed chin. He appeared to be well groomed with closely cropped hair and a naturally accentuated part on the side. He was wearing a white, short sleeved shirt and slightly baggy kaki pants with a wide black belt.

As he walked to the podium, he carried himself with confidence, but he didn't make eye contact with anyone. After he positioned himself, he finally glanced in Nolan's direction. When he did, Nolan noticed for the first time that the young man's eyes were closely set together underneath sharply lined eyebrows that pointed down to the bridge of his nose, which gave him a hawk-like appearance.

When everyone was settled, the deputy announced loudly, "This court is now in session, remain seated."

"You may proceed Mr. Keene," the judge nodded.

John Keene stood up to address his witness.

"Let's try this again," he stated. "Please tell the court your name."

The young man leaned ahead and blinked his eyes rapidly as he cleared his throat. "Tommy Lawson," he said.

"And I think we already established that you lived at 21 Astor Street, correct?" Keene asked.

The witness darted his eyes and blinked again. "That's correct."

Larice nudged Nolan in the side and leaned into him. Nolan bent his ear closer to Larice, who whispered, "Watch him, you see what I mean?"

Nolan nodded. "I'm watching, just take it easy."

Through his direct examination, John Keene established that on the night of April Eleventh, Tommy Lawson had been in Richmond at a concert. According to the young man, he was supposed to meet some friends there, but they never showed. He attended the concert anyway. Afterwards, he was too tired to drive back home, so he pulled into a rest stop and slept there overnight. When he returned to town, he did not go home. Instead, he spent the day at a friend's house. Finally, in the early evening he returned home.

When Keene asked him about what he found when he returned home, the young man choked up, squeezed his eyes with his fingers, then began to cry. With a trembling voice, he managed to tell the judge how he had found his twin brother, his father, and his mother shot to death. He remembered running around the house, crying and screaming as he came across each body. He said he touched each of his family members and knew that they were dead. He didn't know how long he had been in the house before he called 9-1-1, but he thought it had been several minutes.

"Can you tell the judge what your brother told you about the defendant in the days leading up to his death?" John Keene asked.

Nolan didn't bother to object to the hearsay. After all, it was just a preliminary hearing and he wanted to know as much information as possible.

"Timmy was afraid of him," the witness answered. "He told me that Ice was after him and that if I saw Ice near the house that he was probably coming to try to kill him."

"At that time, did you know who Ice was?" Keene asked.

"Yes sir. I had seen him come to our house on a few different occasions."

"And what was your brother's relationship with Ice," Keene put special emphasis on the word Ice.

"Ice was making Timmy sell drugs for him. At first, Timmy wanted me to do it too, but I wouldn't. Later, he tried to stop selling the drugs, but Ice wouldn't let him."

"That's a lie," Larice whispered to Nolan. "That dude was always begging me to get a piece of my action."

"Do you know of any reason why Ice would want to kill Timmy?" Keene asked.

"Well, probably because Timmy helped the cops bust him. Timmy told me that it was the only way he could get out of his jam with selling drugs and everything. He told me that he had to set Ice up so that he would go to prison and leave him alone."

"And do you see this guy that you call Ice in the courtroom?" Keene asked.

Without making eye contact, Tommy pointed to the defense table to his right and said, "He's sitting right there in the orange jail suit."

"That's all the questions I have," Keene finished.

Judge Hadley nodded to Nolan. "Your witness, Mr. Getty."

Nolan never liked to waste too much time beating around the bush when it came to cross-examinations.

"Mr. Lawson, who was it that you saw in concert at Richmond?" Nolan asked.

Tommy leaned into the microphone and looked towards Nolan. "A group called Jiggernaut."

"And where did they play?" Nolan asked.

"At the National, downtown," he answered.

"What are the names of your friends that didn't show up?"

Tommy thought for a minute and then blinked rapidly as he darted his eyes back and forth. "Jackie and Shawn," he said.

"What about last names?"

"I really don't know Jackie's last name, but it's Shawn Henderson."

"Where does Shawn Henderson live?" Nolan asked.

"He lives on Baker Street. I could point you to the house, but I don't know the number."

"What's the nearest cross street?"

"It's across the street from the park," he answered.

"And who is the friend that you were with when you returned from the concert, the one that you spent the day with?"

John Keene stood up and intervened. "I'm going to object to this line of questioning, your Honor. This hearing is not intended to be a discovery session for the defense, it's solely meant to establish probable cause that the defendant committed these crimes. And the questions from Mr. Getty have nothing to do with probable cause."

"He's right, Mr. Getty. This isn't discovery, it's a preliminary hearing," Judge Hadley said.

"I have a right to cross-examine this witness regarding those matters that he testified about on direct examination. He already testified that he spent the day with a friend and now I want to know who it was," Nolan responded.

Judge Hadley thought for a second before ruling. "All right, you can ask his name, but I don't want you twisting this hearing into some discovery tool for the defendant."

"What's your friend's name," Nolan pressed.

"Johnny Randolph," Lawson answered.

"Where's he live?" Nolan asked.

"Objection," Keene yelled out.

"Sustained," Judge Hadley ruled, without hesitation. "Get on with your cross-examination."

Nolan shook his head. He knew that he had every right to ask such questions, but Hadley wasn't going to give him much more leeway on cross-examination, so he decided to initiate the plan that he developed between the lock up and the courtroom. He reached into his briefcase and retrieved the fattest marker that he could find. Without trying to be too obvious, he placed the marker in his front pocket and quickly manipulated it with his hand from the outside of his pocket, wiping it clean of any previous fingerprints.

"Where in the house did you find your brother," Nolan asked.

"He was in his room," Tommy answered.

"And as I understand it, there is a hallway in your house and his room is the first on the left, correct?"

"Actually, we both share that room," Tommy answered.

"And your father?"

"He was on the floor at the end of the hallway."

"And your mother and father's room is at the end of the hallway on the right?"

"That's right."

Nolan pulled out a sheet of blank paper and quickly sketched out the perimeter of a rectangle on it. He drew two lines in front of the rectangle. Between the lines he wrote the words "Astor Street".

"Just so I'm sure about where these bodies were in relation to each other, could you please show me on this sketch that I made?" Nolan asked as he approached.

John Keene stood up and met Nolan at the witness podium.

When he was next to the witness, Nolan pulled out the marker from his pocket and handed it to the boy.

"I don't care about walls and hallways, I just want to know the general area of each body in the house. If you could, please place an X where you found your brother, a Y for your father, and a Z for your mother."

The boy grasped the marker and studied the sketch. "Right about in here," he said, placing the letters within the rectangular outline of the house. When he was done, Nolan retrieved the marker from the boy, being careful to grasp it from the tip only. He replaced the cap and placed the marker in his jacket pocket.

"Thank you, Mr. Lawson," he said. "I don't have any further questions."

John Keene's next witness was Lieutenant Childress, who went over the details of the crime scene, including how many times each of the victims was shot, where they were shot, and what they were shot with. He told the judge that it appeared that the killer entered the boy's room through the window screen, which had been cut.

After he described the details of the crime scene, Lieutenant Childress told the judge about the anonymous call that came in the next day and what they did in response to the call. Finally, he finished his testimony by describing the interview with Larice Jones and how he initially denied knowing anyone who lived on Astor Street, including Timmy Lawson.

After Lieutenant Childress, Keene called the officer who collected evidence at the scene. The officer told the judge that he found several shell casings throughout the house and that he sent them to the state laboratory for fingerprinting. Once Keene had established the chain of custody involving the shell casings, he produced the fingerprint results which the judge admitted into evidence. According to the laboratory, the fingerprints matched those of Larice Jones.

Keene rested his case there and asked the judge to certify the charges to the grand jury. Knowing that Judge Hadley would never dismiss the charges, Nolan waived argument on the matter.

Judge Hadley didn't hesitate with his ruling. "Based on the evidence presented, I find probable cause that the defendant has committed the crimes charged, and I am certifying the charges to the grand jury." He stamped the warrants before closing the file and handing it to the clerk.

CHAPTER 16

When he returned to the chateau the next morning, Nolan stopped to chat with Vicki before going to his office. "Is Eric here yet?"

Eric was a retired detective of the Big Shanty Police Department, who worked part time as an investigator for the Public Defender's Office. Nolan called him after Larice Jones's preliminary hearing and had asked him to meet him in the office that morning.

"He's upstairs with the boys," Vicki answered.

Nolan first met Eric at a "Friends of the NRA" fundraiser shortly after he became an Assistant Public Defender. They were the two primary bidders on a battle-used, M1 Garand rifle from World War II. In the end, Eric obviously wanted the gun more than Nolan, as he shelled out 1,200 clams for it. After the auction, Nolan met up with Eric to congratulate him on his winning bid. It turned out that Eric's father and Nolan's grandfather had both been in the Battle of Okinawa during the war. Because of their shared interest in the war and the rifle, Eric invited Nolan to try out the gun with him at the shooting range the next day. What started with a day at the range, turned into a lasting friendship. They not only worked together, but they also fished, hunted, and drank together.

Nolan climbed the old staircase with its creaking steps and worn carpet. When he reached the top, he could hear Eric's deep voice and laughter coming from his office. And he knew Eric was holding court with his assistants.

"What's up, boys?" Nolan said as he entered the office.

"Jesus Christ, you sure do like your sleep," Eric said, swiveling in the chair opposite of Nolan's desk. "We've already knocked down a pot of coffee."

Nolan reached out and shook his hand. Eric was dressed in his familiar blue sport coat and khakis, looking every bit like the retired cop he was. He was a large man and slightly overweight, which made the chair that he was in appear unreasonably small. Beside him in the other chair, Danny also looked unreasonably small.

"Hey boss," Rick said. He was lying on Nolan's couch with his feet propped up on the arm rest and a newspaper in his hands. "I was just reading the article about your murderer's preliminary hearing. Sounds like your boy freaked out."

"Yeah, it got a bit ugly," Nolan said. "They tasered him right in the courtroom."

"That's awesome!" Rick exclaimed. "Why'd they do that?"

"He started yelling at the witness and then he kicked the table and knocked the chair over."

Rick laughed out loud. "Don't taser me, dude!" he yelled.

They all laughed as Rick gyrated on the couch and yelled again, "Ouch, ouch, ouch . . . don't taser me dude!"

Eric shook his head. "These boys have some real issues," he said with a grin. "Are you sure they have law degrees?"

"I took their word for it," Nolan answered. He grabbed the coffee pot on the file cabinet and drained the last bit into his cup. "We may have us an interesting case here, Danny."

"How's that?" Danny asked.

"Well, for one, our client seems to think that the surviving twin is not who he says he is."

Rick stopped gyrating and sat up. "What?"

"You got your twin brothers," Nolan explained. "The dead one is supposed to be Timmy Lawson and the living one is supposed to be Tommy Lawson. And our client says that the person who testified yesterday is actually Timmy Lawson pretending to be Tommy Lawson."

"Whoa!" Rick exclaimed. "That does sound good. Any chance he may be right?"

"I don't know, but I'm going to find out," Nolan said, reaching into his pocket and pulling out a plastic baggie with a fat marker in it. He held up the baggie so that everyone could take a look.

"What's that?" Danny asked.

"You sneaky son of a bitch!" Rick exclaimed. "You have his fingerprints?"

"I'm pretty sure I do," Nolan answered.

"Wait . . . aren't they identical twins?" Danny asked. "Do twins have different fingerprints?"

"Do they Eric?" Nolan asked.

"Yes they do," Eric answered, shifting his large frame to face Danny. "Back when I was on the force, we had a robbery case where one of you sneaky defense attorneys tried to claim the defendant's identical twin was the real perp. We brought in an expert and showed that although identical twins have virtually indistinguishable DNA, their fingerprints are different."

"But was that just one expert's opinion?" Danny asked. "I mean, was this guy some fringe mad scientist that you flew in from the Ukraine, or is it common scientific knowledge?"

"Are all you defense attorneys paranoid conspiracy theorists?" Eric asked, shaking his head. "No, it's not junk science. Apparently fingerprints are more a product of environment than genetics -- you know, one twin might be in a different position in the womb or get different nutrition as a fetus, and because of that, although the whorl patterns may have similarities, there's gonna be differences that standard fingerprinting can easily identify."

"How are you going to find out whose fingerprints are on that?" Danny asked Nolan.

"I'm not," Nolan answered. "You are."

"I am?" Danny asked.

"Yes. You're going to find me an expert in fingerprinting. Jump on the internet -- there should be plenty to choose from. Once you find one, let Eric know who it is and he can send this marker to him with a recorded chain of custody."

"But what about the comparison?" Rick asked. "What will he compare them with?"

Nolan turned to Eric. "Any way for you to dig up fingerprint cards for either Timmy or Tommy Lawson?" he asked.

Eric thought for a moment. "I could check with the DMV or maybe one of them has an arrest record and I can find something at the PD," he answered.

"If or when you find any official print cards, send it all together under the same chain of custody to the expert that Danny finds," Nolan instructed.

Nolan put the baggie on the desk and sat back in his chair with his cup of coffee. "Why would this kid lie about who he is?" Nolan asked.

"Because he's the one who did it," Rick answered.

"Yeah, but why would the dude kill his twin brother and his parents? How am I going to get a jury to believe that?"

"Maybe it's the good old fashioned money motive," Eric answered. "Maybe his parents had life insurance."

"Good point," Nolan answered. "Is there any way you can find that out?"

Eric squinted. "That may be a tough one. They like to keep those records very private. But I guess you could subpoena the kid's bank records to see if he's made any large deposits."

"That would be nice, but the kid's not talking to me. I don't even know where he's living, let alone where he banks. Besides, I want to keep this on the down-low. If this is true, we don't want to tip off the prosecution by sending out subpoenas to everyone."

"I'll try to figure something out," Eric offered. "There's got to be some way we can see if the family had money, whether it's in life insurance or maybe in a will. You got anything else for me?"

Nolan described the details of the case. He gave Eric the name of Larice's girlfriend and the vague contact information for her. He also gave him all of the information that he had garnered from the witness who claimed to be Tommy Lawson, including the names of his friends and his alleged alibi about being in Richmond overnight. He knew that even with such vague information, Eric could probably track everyone down.

"I'll check his alibi," Eric said. "What concert did he say he was at?"

Nolan opened up his case folder and looked through his notes. "It sounds like some hip-hop band, someone I've never heard of," Nolan read through his notes. "Here it is. Jiggernaut."

"Jiggernaut?" Rick asked. "You never heard of Kool Karjak and Jiggernaut? Come on man, how old are you?" Without waiting for Nolan's answer, he began singing and slapping the arm of the couch with his hand.

"My bitches in the club droppin' down drinkin' bubs. Flash my grill, throwin' stacks, pay it all, movin' dubs. I said I'm movin' dubs. What? I said I'm movin' dubs. Yah."

Eric shook his head again and looked over at Nolan. "What the hell is that boy saying?"

"That's my man, Kool Karjak," Rick answered. "He's a local artist from Richmond."

"That's what you call an artist?" Eric asked.

"Furillaz, my gorillaz," Rick said, getting off the couch. "Now if you'll excuse me, I have to take a shizzle."

"What'd he say?" Eric asked.

CHAPTER 17

John Keene was relieved that Judge Hadley had certified the charges against Larice Jones, but he was concerned about his evidence. He knew that Getty was eventually going to file a motion to suppress the evidence, which meant that they wouldn't be able to use the watch and the Bible. From his own research, he knew that an anonymous tip wasn't enough to create probable cause for a search warrant. The plain and simple fact was that they needed more evidence. They needed to have some positive DNA analysis and they also needed the murder weapon.

On the morning after the hearing, Keene called Mutz into his office to discuss the case. Mutz probably didn't know it, but he had a lot of work to do before the trial.

"Do you think Mr. Getty's going to file any motions to suppress in this case?" he asked Mutz.

Mutz rubbed his chin and looked away. "Umm, I doubt it. What would be the basis?"

Keene shook his head. "You think the search warrant is good?"

Mutz grunted. "Sure, why not?"

Keene's veins bulged in his forehead as he fought to control his temper. "What's it take to get a search warrant?" he gritted his teeth.

Evidently Mutz sensed the impending explosion, because he sat up straight. "Probable cause. So you're saying there might not be probable cause?"

"That's exactly what I'm saying. This search warrant was based on an anonymous tip, which usually isn't enough to support probable cause, so I need you to research the matter and find a case that can over rule Getty's motion to suppress, which I know he will file in Circuit Court."

"Okay, no problem," Mutz nodded.

"That's not all you have to do," Keene said. "We can't go into this trial with nothing but fingerprints and conjecture. We must . . . and I mean *must*, obtain more evidence, whether it's the murder weapon, DNA analysis, or anything else. We're missing too much," Keene told him. "Can you think of anything else we can do to further that goal?"

Mutz appeared to ponder the question, but nothing came from his mouth. Keene stared blankly at him until his patience ran out.

"You and the others seem to forget about one of the most useful tools a prosecutor has to obtain information," Keene explained. "The defendant has been in jail for approximately two months now. During that time he has been in constant contact with at least a dozen other inmates, if not more. Perhaps he bragged about his deeds, or maybe he inadvertently let some information slip out. Therefore, I want you to contact the jail and find out which inmates he's been in contact with. And then I want you to set up interviews with those inmates and find out if he's said anything."

"What if those inmates have attorneys?" Mutz asked. "Don't we have to get their permission to talk to them?"

"Do we?" Keene asked contemptuously. "Not if we are discussing matters that are unrelated to their pending charges. We'll wait and see if anyone has any information. If we find such a person, then we'll contact their attorney and discuss a plea bargain in exchange for their testimony, understand?"

Mutz smiled and nodded.

"I also want you to talk to Captain Danforth at the jail and see about getting the recordings of any telephone calls the defendant has made, as well as copies of any letters he has sent or received."

"We can do that?" Mutz asked. "Isn't that some sort of privacy violation?"

Keene finally erupted. "I don't give a damn!" he shouted, slamming his hand on the desk. "Let me tell you something about rights. That murdered family had a right to live. And as far as I'm concerned, inmates don't have rights. So unless you're aware of some other law, I suggest you get this done."

"Sure, no problem. I was just asking," Mutz grumbled.

"Every collect call from the jail is recorded. The inmates have an identity number that they punch in before making a call, so it should be easy to pull up every one of his phone calls. As for the letters, you'll have to ask the Captain to intercept them and either copy them or notify you when one is sent or received so that you can copy them."

"Okay," Mutz answered. "I'll get right on it."

I'll get right on it. The stupid bastard needed a good hard kick in the ass, Keene thought.

"Anything else?" Mutz asked.

Keene pointed towards the door. "Start getting on it."

CHAPTER 18

On the Friday afternoon two weeks after Larice's preliminary hearing, Nolan sent Vicki home early, locked the door behind her and then buzzed Rick on the intercom. "It's time to stop working. Meet me in the lounge."

"Ten four, boss," Rick answered.

Nolan went to the basement, pushed on the file rack at the back of the room, and entered the hidden area. He made two drinks – bourbon on the rocks, and held one of the cups out for Rick as he entered the lounge.

"Thanks," Rick grabbed the cup.

"To Fridays," Nolan held his plastic glass up.

"To fucking Fridays!" Rick joined him.

They each took a sip from their cups before sitting down on the old wingback chairs in front of the television. Nolan picked up the remote and clicked the power button. Even with rabbit ears, they could only pick up one station, and that was just down the road in Roanoke. The television came to life and a rerun of the Jerry Springer Show appeared before them. Nolan turned the volume down just as the crowd began to chant, "JERRY! JERRY!"

"I just heard something very interesting from a client of mine at the jail," Rick said. "And I think you'll find it interesting, too."

"Oh yeah? What's that?" Nolan asked.

"It seems that our friend, Mutz the Putz has been sticking his nose where it doesn't belong. Apparently, yesterday the jailors came and got my client from his cell and took him to an interview room. He thought that I was there to see him, but when he got to the visiting room, it was Mutz."

"Mutz?" Nolan asked. "What the hell is he doing at the jail?"

"My guy says Mutz asked him about Larice Jones. He wanted to know if he had been saying anything about the murders."

"Really," Nolan exclaimed.

"Can they do that?" Rick asked. "I mean, they can't be talking to my client without my permission, can they?"

Nolan tapped his glass as he thought about the Constitutional implications. He knew that once a defendant obtained an attorney, he was supposed to be off limits to the prosecution and the police. But talking to Rick's client wasn't the real issue. After all, they weren't questioning him about his own charges. The real issue was that they were actively trying to find inmates to snitch on his client. And Nolan knew that such actions were unconstitutional because not only are prosecutors barred from direct contact with a defendant, but so too are their agents. And from what Rick was telling him, Mutz was trying to find an agent to help him get information from Larice Jones.

"Did your guy tell him anything about Larice?" Nolan asked.

"He said he didn't have anything to tell them."

"Did Mutz ask your client to try and get information from Larice?"

"Yeah. Mutz gave him his card and asked him to call if he heard anything. Why do you ask?"

"Because if he gave him a card and asked him to call him with information, then Mutz has turned him into an agent, and that is clearly unconstitutional," Nolan explained.

"Hmmm," Rick said. "I never thought of that. Can you bring that up to the court?"

"I could. But right now it's not going to help us because your client didn't know anything. The only way it will matter is if your client obtains information and calls him back. Otherwise, you know the deal -- no harm, no foul."

"But what if they find some other jailhouse snitch?" Rick asked. "Can't we show the court that they were actively seeking agents?"

"Maybe," Nolan answered. "But unless the snitch is honest and admits to it, we'll have no way to prove our point. It's just going to be another example of them cheating and us not being able to prove it."

The chime from the front door chirped, interrupting their conversation. Rick quickly reached for the remote control and pressed the mute button.

"It should be Danny, I locked the front door before I came down here," Nolan said.

They heard footsteps bounding across the floor, and then Danny's voice upstairs. "Anyone home?"

"Down here!" Rick yelled. "Lock the fucking door!"

They heard Danny run across the main floor back to the front door, then more running back to the basement door, followed by heavy footsteps bounding down the stairs, as if he was running for his life. Rick shook his head as Danny appeared in the file rack doorway holding a piece of paper in his hand.

"Danny, Danny, Danny," Rick said as he continued to shake his head. "Here at the Public Defender's Office we walk down and nail them all."

Danny looked at Rick, confused. "What are you talking about?" he asked, out of breath from all of his running.

"It's an old joke. Two bulls are standing at the top of a hill looking down at a valley full of heifers that are just old enough to breed. The young bull says to the old bull, "We should run down there and nail one of those cows." The old bull shakes his head and says, "I've got a better idea . . . let's *walk* down and nail them *all*."

"Funny," Danny said without laughing. He turned to Nolan and the excitement returned to his face. "We got it!" he yelled. "The fingerprints match Timmy Lawson!"

Nolan blinked and shook his head. "Really? Where did Eric get the comparison prints?"

"He got a copy of a print card at the police department -- Timmy had a prior arrest," Danny explained.

Until then, Nolan hadn't really bought into Larice's speculation that Timmy was alive. He was just going through the motions to cover the file. When the trial was all said and done, and his client was serving life in prison, he didn't want his name on any appeal papers that contained the words, "ineffective assistance of counsel". That's mostly what he did as a Public Defender -- he covered the file with all sorts of meaningless investigations which usually resulted in dead ends. But this result was not the usual dead end. This result was truly shocking.

"Amazing," Nolan grinned at Rick.

Rick turned to Danny. "You lucky bastard," he said. "Your first trial and you get the Perry fucking Mason case. Meanwhile, I'm representing a gas station robber who dropped his wallet on the way out the door."

"This is going to be one hell of a trial, Danny boy," Nolan said. "Pour yourself a drink."

Danny opened the fridge and retrieved a can of soda. He popped the top and they all held their drinks for another toast. "To Danny P.

Mason," Nolan said. Rick and Nolan took a big gulp of their bourbon and then settled back into their chairs.

"There's something else we need to check," Nolan said.

"What's that?" Danny asked.

"The anonymous call that was made to the police the day after the murders," Nolan answered. "Now that we know that Tommy is really Timmy, I'd bet my pay check that the anonymous caller is Timmy."

"Good point, boss," Rick said.

"How do we find that out?" Danny asked.

Rick answered the question for Nolan. "You send a request letter to the Big Shanty Communications Department. They keep recordings of every 9-1-1 call and they have to give you a tape upon request."

"Once you have the tape, jump on the internet and find us a guru on voice analysis," Nolan instructed. "I taped the preliminary hearing, so we have Timmy's voice to compare with the 9-1-1 call."

"Sounds like a good plan to me," Danny said. "When are we going to tell Keene about the fingerprints?"

Nolan and Rick looked at each other, each raising their eyebrows, as if they couldn't believe the question. Then Rick shook his head and took the honors.

"Danny, Danny," he said condescendingly. "I don't know what they're teaching you kids in law school now days, but here in good ol' Virginny, we have trial by surprise. Do you know what that means?"

Danny shook his head. "Isn't there a hearing before the trial where each side discloses their witnesses and evidence? I mean, that's what they told us in law school."

"That may happen in other places, but not here in Big Shanty," Rick explained. "In Big Shanty, we hold our cards until all bets are in."

"Does that mean we're not going to tell him?" Danny asked.

Rick looked to Nolan. "What's your plan, chief?"

Rick wasn't completely accurate in his description of Virginia jury trials. In any criminal case, Nolan could file a motion for discovery which would require the prosecution to disclose all scientific evidence against his client and any inculpatory statements that his client had made to the police or anyone else. But if he filed such a motion, the discovery rules required him to disclose his own scientific evidence, as well as any alibi that the defendant planned to use at trial. Usually, filing a discovery motion was the smart thing to do, but on rare occasions, when his client had an alibi or there was significant scientific evidence that could prove his clients' innocence, Nolan didn't like to file for discovery, simply because he didn't want to disclose his evidence to the prosecution.

"Let me tell you my theory about prosecutors," Nolan said. "I think the successful ones usually have one thing in common. Sometime in their lives, they've been abused, cheated, or bullied by someone. And to deal with it, either to make sure that it doesn't happen to anyone else, or to rationalize why it happened to them, they become ruthless crusaders. And John Keene is one of those crusaders who doesn't care if someone is guilty or not. If the police think someone did it, then he will stop at nothing to send them to prison, including cheating and lying, and whatever else it takes to match the evidence to the facts."

"So what are you saying?" Danny asked.

"I'm saying that Keene can't be trusted to do the right thing," Nolan explained. "And if we play our cards right, Keene will have no idea that his star witness is Timmy Lawson pretending to be Tommy Lawson -- until it's too late."

Rick clamped his hand on Danny's neck and squeezed -- perhaps a little too hard. "And that's how you win a jury trial, my boy."

Danny winced and knocked his hand away. "But even if we show that he's lying about his identity, how is that going to prove Larice's innocence?"

"It's not," Nolan answered. "But it's most of the battle. You have to understand something about jury trials. This brief window of time that we have in front of the jury; this whole exercise of criminal defense is not about proving your client's innocence. And it's not even about finding the truth. It's about knocking holes in the prosecution's case and planting a little seed of doubt in the jury. Once the seed is there, all you have to do is fertilize it with an alternative theory or two, and presto -- the seed has a chance to grow into an acquittal."

Danny nodded. "And I guess our alternative theory is that Timmy is lying because he killed his own family, right?"

"That's what we have so far. But who knows, maybe that will change. In the end, it all depends upon the prosecution's evidence. Whatever they have at the time of trial will dictate our defense. The key is to find out what they have as evidence and then create an alternative theory that fits within that evidence -- something that they cannot disprove."

121

"The truth," Rick added, pointing his finger into the air, "is in the lies of the beholder."

CHAPTER 19

"I knew it!" Larice yelled, slamming his hand on the counter. "I knew he was Timmy."

Nolan smiled. "But now we still have to convince the jury that he killed his own family. I have my investigator trying to figure out if they had any insurance policies, but he's not so sure that he can find such a thing."

"Have you filed for discovery in my case, yet?" Larice asked.

"Discovery?" Nolan asked. Obviously, he was somewhat knowledgeable about criminal defense matters. And if he knew things about discovery, then he couldn't be that slow, Nolan thought.

"That's just what the guys in here are telling me. That you should file for discovery," Larice said.

"That's something we have to think about," Nolan answered. "If we ask for discovery, we have to reveal our little fingerprint secret, and I don't think that's a very good idea at this stage."

"But if they knew it was Timmy, wouldn't they drop the charges?" he asked.

Nolan shook his head. He knew from past experience that it wasn't going to be that easy. "You don't understand," he explained. "I wouldn't trust them to make that decision. They're out to get you; not Timmy, not Tommy, not anyone, but you. So unless we can come up with some specific evidence that Timmy killed his own family, nothing's going to change. And even if we did find such a thing, the better course is to spring it on them at your trial. That way they're not going to have the chance to explain away the evidence or twist it against you."

"Yeah, you're probably right," Larice said. He looked away and bit his lip, as if he was thinking about something specific. And then he looked back at Nolan.

"Listen," he said. "There's something I haven't told you."

Nolan raised one eyebrow. He hoped that Larice wasn't planning on telling him that he did it. There was nothing like a confession to screw up a good defense.

"What's that?" Nolan sighed.

"It's about Timmy," Larice continued. "I didn't want to say anything before I knew that it was really Timmy who's alive. But now that I know that for sure, I think you need to know about us."

Nolan felt slightly relieved, but he still wasn't sure where Larice was going with his revelation. "Go ahead," he nodded.

"You know that drug deal where Timmy set me up?"

"Yes, of course," Nolan answered.

"Well, it didn't go down exactly like the police say it went down."

"Just how did it go down, then?" Nolan frowned.

"I can't tell you that unless I tell you about the mess I was in with J," Larice explained.

"Who the hell is J?"

"I'll tell you straight up," Larice said. "I got a crack problem and I can't shake it. And J is the dude that's been supplying me. And when I didn't have the coin to buy it, he started making deals with me. It started out with just a few rocks. He'd give me a twenty if I sold a forty for him. But then it just kept going up from there. After awhile, he had me selling crack twenty-four seven. And since I was always behind, he kept giving me bigger and bigger batches I had to sell. I tried to stop a few times. But even when I quit using the crack, J just kept making me sell it anyway."

"What do you mean he made you sell it?" Nolan interjected. "How could he make you sell it?"

"He told me that he was connected with some real players and that he would tell those people that I wasn't doing my job and they would break my fucking legs or kill me if I didn't do my job."

Nolan nodded sympathetically, but only for show. After Larice's previous lies, he wasn't going to believe anything that came out of his mouth. But it was turning into an interesting story and Nolan was always open to something believable that he could relay to a jury.

"So then I had to get someone to help me, because I couldn't sell as much as J was giving me. So that's how T got involved. He started helping me sell all the shit that J was pushing on me. And when I called him and told him that J gave me two Big Eights, he told me he could sell one of them. So that night, I met him in the parking lot and I gave him one of them . . . ."

"Hold on," Nolan interrupted. "A Big Eight? As in an eighth of a kilo?"

"Yeah, a big ball of crack. And I mean a really big ball. Like this," Larice said, holding his hands in the shape of a baseball.

Nolan had represented many drug dealers in his time, but in Big Shanty they were mostly small timers. His all time record for the most crack that any of his clients had ever been caught distributing was 60 grams, and that one went to prison for twelve years. But according to Larice, he was supposed to sell two Big Eights, which were 125 grams each. And that was enough to put someone away for the maximum -- forty years.

"All right, so what went down with T?" Nolan asked.

"T fucked me over, that's what went down," Larice answered.

"How so?"

"After I gave him the Big Eight, I got out of his car and he started pulling away. But then a bunch of cops rolled in and busted us. They said they saw the whole thing and they were busting me for distribution."

Nolan nodded.

"But here's the thing," Larice continued. "They didn't charge me for selling a Big Eight -- they charged me for selling two little rocks. And so then I figured out that T must've busted off a few small rocks and hid the rest. And then he told the cops that I sold him the small rocks that he busted off."

"But what about the money?" Nolan asked. "For that much crack, he must've given you a pretty big wad."

"That's the other thing," Larice explained. "He didn't give me any money for the Big Eight. What he gave me was two hundred, and that was for the stuff that I fronted him the time before. He wasn't going to pay me for the Big Eight until after he sold it."

"So what made you think that Timmy set you up?" Nolan asked.

"First of all, there's no way the cops saw anything. And if they did . . . *which they didn't* . . . then they would've seen that big rock I gave him. So that tells me that he was in on it. That bitch stole my Big Eight and then he set me up to get busted. Second of all, I talked to my girlfriend from jail and she told me that T came to the house and told her that she was supposed to give him the other half. But she didn't give him anything. She told him she didn't know nothin' about no drugs. And then the very next night, the house is broken into and somebody takes the other Big Eight and my gun. So guess who that somebody is?" Larice asked.

Nolan quickly processed the details of his story, looking for any inconsistencies or other problems. The puzzle finally made sense, at least with respect to the stolen gun. It wasn't some random person that broke into Larice's house and stole his gun. It was Timmy who broke into the house to steal drugs. And it was believable that he also stole the gun while he was there. Regardless of whether it was true or not, the story not only made sense, but it was one that he could sell to a jury.

"Why didn't you just tell me that from the beginning?" Nolan asked.

"Cause I didn't know that Timmy was still alive in the beginning!" Larice whelped. "And if Timmy was the one that got killed, that whole thing just points to me as the murderer. Now if you were me, would you tell your lawyer that you had a shit-load of reasons to kill the dude?"

Nolan gave him the benefit of the doubt. "Probably not."

Nolan pondered the story a few more moments. "So that explains why Timmy broke into your house and how he got your gun. And of course your fingerprints are on the shell casings left at the murder scene because you had loaded the gun. It was loaded when it was stolen, right?" Nolan asked, making sure they were on the same page.

"Yeah, man . . . I kept it loaded," Larice bobbed his head.

"All right, but we're still going to need a reason why Timmy killed his own family."

"You ain't listening, man!" Larice yelled. "That guy stole two Big Eights from me. That's worth a lot of money -- probably more than what most people make in a year. Now, he thinks I'm going to be in jail for a long time, but then my lawyer pulls the get out of jail free card and he has to come up with some plan before I catch up with him. So he kills his family, and at the same time, he sets me up for a life sentence. How's that for a reason?"

Nolan shrugged. "That actually sounds like a pretty good one to me."

"Damn right!" Larice slapped his hand on the counter. "That's why he did it."

Nolan realized that Larice's girlfriend would be an important witness.

"Did your girlfriend file a police report on the burglary?" Nolan asked.

"I don't know, you'd have to ask her," Larice answered.

"Well let me ask you this," Nolan queried. "Did your girlfriend know that you had a Big Eight and a gun in the house?"

"Yeah, she knew," he said. "I don't know about the gun, but she knew about the drugs. That's the first thing she told me when I called her from the jail. She told me that someone stole the stuff."

"Where did you keep it?" Nolan asked.

"It was in a tampon box in her closet. But she ain't gonna want to tell anyone that she knew about it, cause she'd get a charge herself."

"We'll see about that," Nolan answered. He was already developing a plan in which he could force her to testify and at the same time, immunize her from future prosecution.

CHAPTER 20

August 19ᵗʰ, Big Shanty Circuit Court

Nolan sat patiently listening to Keene's direct examination of Special Agent Calhoun. When he had finished questioning Calhoun about the drug transaction between Timmy Lawson and Larice, Keene relinquished the floor. But before he did, he tapped the defense table and smiled, "Your witness, Mr. Getty."

"Mr. Getty, do you have any cross?" the judge asked.

"Yes sir," he said, rising from his chair.

Walking behind John Keene and Fred Mutz at the prosecution table, Nolan approached the podium, which was between the jury box and the prosecutor's table. He buttoned his suit coat as he walked and then nodded to the jury as he stepped up to the podium.

The members of the jury sat quietly, with all their attention trained on Nolan as he prepared for his cross examination. With Agent Calhoun being the first witness of the day, they hadn't yet settled into the legally induced lethargy that was common to all jurors in a lengthy trial. And at that early hour on the second day of the trial, they eyed Nolan carefully, especially the women of the jury, who saw that he was wearing an expensive blue suit, with matching suspenders and gold cuff links. They also didn't miss the small American flag pin on his lapel, which was a perfect complement to his red tie.

"Let me take you back to when Timmy Lawson set up my client to be arrested," Nolan began. "Where were you when you were observing the transaction in the parking lot?"

"I was on the roof of the market," Calhoun answered.

"Did you observe this transaction with your naked eye?"

"No. I had binoculars."

"Isn't it true that at the time of the transaction, it was dark?"

"That's true, but there was a street light that was providing some lighting."

"Isn't it also true that although you saw a hand to hand transaction between Mr. Jones and Mr. Lawson, you couldn't identify what was being passed."

"I couldn't specifically see it, but I saw Timmy Lawson put his hand into his right jacket pocket after the exchange, and that's where I found the two rocks of crack cocaine after he was taken into custody," Calhoun answered.

"Isn't it true that Mr. Jones walked all the way to the edge of the parking lot before the jump team dropped in to arrest him?" Nolan asked.

"Yes," Calhoun answered bluntly.

"And that is a fairly large parking lot, isn't it?"

"Yes, I suppose."

"So after Mr. Jones exited the car, how much time had passed before he was arrested by the jump team?"

"I'd say about twenty seconds."

"So during that long walk to the edge of the parking lot, which could have taken up to twenty seconds, isn't it possible that Mr. Jones met up with a second person who could have given him the two hundred dollars?" It was a trick question designed to set up Calhoun on a more important point.

Calhoun gave Nolan a puzzled look, as if he couldn't follow the logic of the question. A few jurors looked at each other and shook their heads, thinking that that they had just heard the dumbest question in the world.

"No, that's not possible."

"Why not?"

"Because I was watching him and there was no one else in the parking lot. Besides, I told you, the bills were marked and they were the same bills that I personally marked."

"You watched him the entire time he was walking across the parking lot?"

Calhoun nodded. "Yeah, the entire time."

So if you were watching Mr. Jones the whole time as he walked through the parking lot, then you wouldn't have had your eyes on Mr. Lawson the entire time, correct?"

Calhoun shrugged. "That's correct."

"And if you didn't have your eyes on Mr. Lawson, isn't it true that he could've had an opportunity to separate drugs from the transaction, keeping two rocks in his pocket and hiding the rest from you?"

Calhoun paused for a few seconds. "I suppose that would be possible, but I told you, I searched him after the arrest and there were only two rocks on him."

"But you didn't search the car, did you?" Nolan asked.

Calhoun paused again. "I have no personal recollection of searching the car, but I'm sure another officer must have. We typically search everything."

"I'll ask you again. You did not search the car yourself, did you?"

"No, I don't believe so," Calhoun answered.

"And you can't tell me with a hundred percent certainty that some other officer searched the car either, can you?"

"Not with certainty, no."

Nolan looked at the jury and raised one eyebrow before continuing the cross-examination. He had just introduced the idea that Timmy had stolen drugs from Larice. Now he had to shore it up with corroborating evidence.

"Let me ask you something else," Nolan began. "You said there was a list of numbers beside Timmy Lawson's name in the Bible. And you said that it appeared to be an owe list. So according to what you found, isn't it true that it appears that Larice Jones and Timmy Lawson had a drug dealing relationship?"

"Yes, that's how it appears."

"And what you're saying is that the list represents a relationship where Larice fronted drugs to Timmy Lawson and he wrote down the value of the drugs, to make sure that Timmy paid him back, correct?"

"That's correct."

"Isn't it also true that when it comes to fronting drugs to lower level dealers, sometimes the lower level dealer will provide something of value as collateral when the drugs are fronted to him?"

"Yes, that happens," Calhoun answered.

"So knowing that there was an owe list with Timmy Lawson's name and there was a watch that apparently belonged to Timmy Lawson, isn't it possible that the watch was actually something of value that Timmy gave to my client for drugs that were fronted to him, long before the murders occurred?"

Calhoun shrugged. "I suppose anything's possible, but it's also possible that he stole it from Timmy Lawson after he killed him."

"Let me ask you something else, Detective Calhoun," Nolan continued. "You said that on this owe list, all of the numbers were crossed out but one. What was the number that was not crossed out?"

"It was ten thousand," Calhoun responded. "I remember that because it was such a large number."

"Ten thousand?" Nolan asked, pretending to be surprised. "So according to your testimony that this is an owe list, wouldn't it be true then that at the time of Larice Jones's arrest, Timmy owed Larice ten thousand dollars worth of drugs that were fronted him?"

"That would be correct," Calhoun answered.

"And with respect to the setup, you can't say for sure whether the two hundred dollars that you gave Mr. Lawson to give to Mr. Jones was intended to be payment for that particular transaction or whether it was a payment for a previous transaction, correct?"

"Well, Mr. Lawson told us that he was going to buy drugs from Mr. Jones and he was going to pay two-hundred dollars for it, and so I assumed that it was for that particular transaction," Calhoun answered.

"But what if at the time Mr. Lawson spoke to you, he knew that he was going to pay Larice Jones for previously fronted drugs, and the exact amount of those drugs was two hundred dollars -- isn't it true that Mr. Lawson could've hid that fact from you and you wouldn't have any way of knowing any different?" Nolan asked.

Calhoun thought for a moment. "I suppose."

"Are you sure that the rocks you found on Mr. Lawson are even crack cocaine?" Nolan asked.

Calhoun smiled. "Yes of course, we had them analyzed by the state lab."

"And when the state lab analyzes suspect drugs, isn't it true that they also weigh the material?"

"Yes," Calhoun answered.

"And what did the rocks weigh in this case?"

Calhoun shrugged, "I'd have to look at my report for that."

"Go ahead," Nolan said. "We'll wait."

Calhoun opened a manila folder and paged through it. After sorting through the papers he finally said, "Here it is. One rock weighed 0.08 grams and the other was 0.12 grams."

"And could you please tell the jury what the street value for those rocks would be?"

"Street values vary between sellers," Calhoun answered.

Obviously, Calhoun was being evasive, so Nolan drilled a bit deeper for the truth.

"If you hear a person ask for a twenty rock, what is the amount of crack cocaine that he typically gets?" Nolan asked.

"Usually a rock that is a tenth of a gram," Calhoun finally relented.

"And so the street value for a tenth of a gram of crack cocaine is usually twenty dollars, correct?"

"That's usually the case, but it varies."

"And so the street value of these two rocks would be about forty dollars, correct?"

"I suppose, but maybe Larice Jones was trying to short him on the material," Calhoun offered.

"Oh, come on Agent Calhoun," Nolan scoffed. "You can't be serious, can you? Anybody who knows anything about drugs would see that one of these rocks was about twice the size of the other and that both of them put together could not possibly be worth two-hundred dollars, now wouldn't they?" Nolan asked.

"I can't speculate on what drug buyers know and what they don't know," Calhoun answered.

"But isn't that fact -- the fact that the amount of money exchanged was about five times more money than what the drugs were worth -- isn't that fact consistent with the theory that the two hundred dollars was for previously fronted drugs?" Nolan asked.

"It doesn't necessarily mean that," Calhoun asked.

"I didn't ask you if it necessarily meant that," Nolan raised his voice. "I asked you if it was consistent with such a theory. And it's true that those set of facts are consistent with the theory that the money was exchanged for previously fronted drugs, correct?" Nolan asked again.

"Yes, I suppose that the facts would be consistent with such a theory," Calhoun finally gave in.

"Thank you," Nolan said. "Now, one more question about the owe list in the Bible. You said that the last number was ten thousand and that it was not crossed out. But what was the number just before ten thousand; the last number that *was* crossed out?" Nolan asked.

"I'm not sure, I can't remember," Calhoun answered.

"Well let's look," Nolan responded. He approached the prosecutor's table. "May I?"

Nolan knew at that point Keene had no choice but to hand him the Bible. Keene couldn't very well act like he was trying to hide something. Besides, with the Bible already admitted into evidence, it was fair game for both sides.

Keene nodded and handed him the Bible.

Nolan immediately paged to the end of Jude and handed the Bible to Calhoun.

"What's the number, Detective Calhoun?" he asked.

Calhoun glanced at the list and then looked up. "It's two hundred."

"It's two hundred," Nolan repeated to the jury. "So doesn't that make my theory more probable -- that on the night of the setup, Timmy Lawson paid Larice Jones two hundred dollars for previously fronted drugs and at the same time, he received a new batch of drugs worth ten thousand dollars?"

"I don't know," Calhoun answered quickly.

Nolan didn't really care about Calhoun's answer. He just wanted to shore up his theory in front of the jury. "And isn't that also consistent with the idea that Timmy Lawson broke off a small amount of the drugs and hid the rest from you, in effect, stealing almost ten thousand dollars worth of drugs and setting up Larice Jones to go to prison at the same time?"

Calhoun thought for a moment and then smiled. "Even if that's what happened it doesn't change anything. It would be just another reason for Larice Jones to kill Timmy and his family."

"Let me ask you one more question, Detective Calhoun," Nolan continued, ignoring Calhoun's inappropriate statement. "Since the night of the murders, have you spoken with the surviving twin brother?"

Calhoun nodded his head. "Just briefly. I showed him the watch and he said it was his brother's. But that was it."

"And he looked just like Timmy, right?"

"Yeah. They're identical twins, what do you expect?" Calhoun asked, before grinning at the jury and shaking his head. A few jurors chuckled.

"Thank you," Nolan concluded. "No further questions."

Nolan had extracted all of the favorable information from Agent Calhoun that was possible. Later, he would tell the jury that Timmy stole about 250 grams of crack from Larice and that's the reason he framed him for the murders.

CHAPTER 21

Four weeks before the trial of Larice Jones, Nolan met Eric for breakfast at the Country Skillet, a restaurant they chose due to its location, more than anything else. It was only a few blocks from Jackson Street, where they expected to find Larice's girlfriend, Monica Lee. Although there were no Lee's listed in the phonebook for Jackson Street, Eric had easily tracked her down by simply looking in the township property records and finding a Georgia Lee at 24 Jackson Street. He could only assume that Georgia was Monica's mother. Their plan was to interview Monica Lee after breakfast.

After getting their coffee, they got down to business.

"Any luck finding the people that Lawson mentioned at the preliminary hearing?" Nolan asked.

"Well, the only thing I can confirm is that this Jiggernaut band was in fact playing at The National in Richmond on the night that Lawson says he went to see them. But I can't track down either of the kids that he was supposed to meet there. I've knocked on every door on Baker Street across from the park and nobody seems to know of a Shawn Henderson."

"What about the kid, John Randolph?" Nolan asked. "The one that Lawson says he was with the day after the concert?"

"There are six Randolphs in the phone book. None of them have a son named John. I'm still trying to check other sources, but so far nothing's coming up."

"What about motive?" Nolan asked. "Any luck on finding life insurance or anything else?"

"Well, I found out where the Lawson kid is staying -- he's in an apartment over in Wedgewood. And I've spent some time following him around. Did you know that he's driving a brand new Chrysler 300?" Eric asked.

Nolan raised an eyebrow. "Really. Do you have photos?"

"I've got photos," Eric answered. "And he uses the ATM at Southern Bank, so I assume that's his bank, if you want to subpoena any records."

"Has he been working anywhere?" Nolan asked.

"Nope," Eric answered. "But what I found out is that up until the day of the murders, Tommy Lawson had been working as an assistant manager at Patty's Platter -- that buffet restaurant out on the strip. And according to the manager, Tommy never showed up again after the murders. No calls, nothing," Eric said. "In fact, they're still holding a check for him, but they don't know where to send it."

"Nice," Nolan said. "More proof that Tommy is actually dead. I'll subpoena the manager for the trial."

"Who's got the corned beef hash?" the waitress hovered two plates above the table.

"That's me, sweetheart," Eric answered, rubbing his hands together. "One more minute and I would've starved to death."

"Yeah, you look a little thin," the waitress smiled as she put the plate in front of him.

On his plate were three eggs, over easy, plopped on top of a huge pile of hash, along with toast, a side of bacon, and a side of sausage. After tucking in his tie, Eric splayed open the eggs, releasing the runny orange liquid over the mound of hash and then stuffed a full fork of the mess into his mouth.

"That's pretty nasty," Nolan said. "I can't eat them any other way than scrambled."

"Did I ever tell you about my Uncle Larry?" Eric asked with a mouthful of breakfast and orange goo on his moustache.

"Do I want to know?"

"He lived on a farm south of town and raised chickens. Of course, he was eating eggs twice a day, so as they wouldn't go to waste. Well, his favorite thing was soft boiled eggs," Eric paused to slurp his coffee. "And one day, after he made his soft boiled eggs, he cracked one open. Now, this egg must've got lost in the straw for awhile, because a gangly little chicken fetus fell out of that shell and landed on his plate. And the damned thing was still half alive, flopping around! Can you believe that shit?" he asked. "Now that's what I call nasty."

Nolan shook his head. "That's friggin' disgusting. But how could the chicken fetus be alive if he boiled the eggs?"

"I told you," Eric said, waving another fork full of mush at him, "he soft boiled them -- it wasn't cooked all the way."

Nolan wasn't buying it. "Did I ever tell you about my grandfather who raised butchering chickens?"

"Nope," Eric took a bite of toast.

"One time I was visiting when he was butchering and he made me hold the chickens down while he chopped off their heads with a hatchet. But chickens don't like to die very easy and so even after they get their heads chopped off, they always flop around quite a bit. But there was this one chicken, who really took it to another level. After my grandpa chopped his head off, the damned thing jumped up and started running across the chicken yard."

"I heard of that happening before," Eric said.

"Yeah, but not like this," Nolan continued. "The chicken didn't have a head, but yet it kept running and running. Grandpa ran after it, but each time he got close to it, the darn thing would take off running again, as if it knew he was coming after him. And this went on for about ten minutes."

"Ten minutes?" Eric asked incredulously. "How can a chicken run around without his head for ten minutes?"

Nolan shrugged. "I tell you what. You kill the fetus in your chicken story and I'll take nine minutes of running time off mine."

Eric stared blankly at Nolan. "Smart ass."

"You have to admit, I had you going," Nolan grinned.

"Yeah, yeah," Eric said. "But my story really happened."

Nolan pointed to Eric's moustache. "You got some egg, there."

Eric wiped his upper lip before taking another slurp of coffee. They ate in silence until their plates were almost empty.

"What are you doing this weekend?" Eric shoved the last bit of toast in his mouth.

"Probably working on the Jones case," Nolan answered. "Why?"

"Me and Lieutenant Childress are going out to Happy Valley Saturday morning to shoot some skeet. And you're coming with."

Nolan knew that Eric was still friends with a lot of police officers, but he didn't know that he and Childress were close.

"Childress is involved in our case," Nolan stated. "I don't think he's gonna want to hang out with me."

Eric drained his coffee. "You're wrong. He's the one that wants you to come with us."

Eric caught Nolan by surprise. "Why would he want me to go with?"

"I think he wants to talk to you about the case," Eric wiped his mouth with a napkin.

"Really," Nolan responded. "What about it?"

"He wouldn't say," Eric answered. "But it must have something to do with the Jones case. Why else would he ask me to get you to come with?"

Nolan shrugged. "Maybe he wants to accidentally kill me."

"Maybe," Eric answered nonchalantly. "But then he'd lose his gun club privileges, and I don't think he'd want that. You got the check?" he asked, throwing his napkin on his plate.

Nolan nodded.

After Nolan paid the breakfast bill, they drove in separate cars to Jackson Street. Nolan didn't want to go alone for several reasons, but mostly because he would need Eric to testify about their conversation with Monica if she was unable or unwilling to testify later.

After traveling two and a half blocks on Jackson Street, Eric eased his car over to the curb and Nolan pulled in directly behind him. They got out and stood on the sidewalk in front of a row of houses. Except for different colored paint in various stages of wear, the houses were very similar. But none of the houses were in good condition, especially the one in front of them.

It was a two story house with fading yellow paint, most of which had peeled free, exposing the bare clapboard beneath it. A white porch extended across the entire front, but because it was sagging in the middle and had several missing balusters, it appeared as if the porch was the house's mouth, upturned into a gnarled smile that exposed several missing teeth.

To the right of the house was a detached, single car garage that was leaning to one side. In front of the garage there was an old blue T-bird with missing hubcaps and a rusted out rear panel. Between the garage and the house, there was a pile of junk that included a rusty bed spring with weeds growing through it. If there was such a magazine called *Butt Ugly Homes and Garbage*, Monica Lee's house would be in it.

Nolan and Eric climbed the steps on the leaning porch and knocked on the front door. They waited a few moments, then Eric knocked again as Nolan stepped over to a window and tried to look in.

"I hear you. Hold on!" a female voice yelled.

A moment later, a young black girl opened the front door a few inches and looked through.

"Are you Monica Lee?" Eric asked.

"Who wants to know?"

Eric pulled out his badge and held it up for her. It was his police-issued badge; but most people usually didn't notice the word "Retired" near the bottom of it. Although the badge had nothing to do with his current employment, it sure did make him look official.

"I'm a special investigator with the Public Defender's Office," he stated. "And this is the Chief Public Defender."

Nolan pulled out a business card and held it up to the crack. "I'm Nolan Getty, the attorney for Larice Jones, and we would just like to ask you a few questions about him."

"I got nothin' to do with him anymore," she said, not bothering to look at Nolan's business card. "And I'm not gonna lie for him."

"I'm not asking you to lie for him," Nolan said. "I just want to ask you a few questions."

What about?"

"Can we talk to you inside?" Eric glanced over his shoulder. "In private?"

"My mama's in here and she don't wanna be bothered," she opened the door and stepped forward. "I'll talk to you on the porch."

Eric and Nolan moved aside as she stepped out, closing the door quickly behind her. The girl appeared very young, perhaps eighteen or nineteen. She was no more than five feet tall and just about as round as she was high. In her loose fitting t-shirt, there was no distinction between her breasts and her belly -- it was all one round mass that bulged out in front.

Once the door was shut, she turned and waddled towards an upholstered chair to the left of the front door. As she was making her way to the chair, Nolan noticed that she was wearing black spandex pants, which accentuated every bulge in her large bottom.

Plopping into the chair, she reached behind her ear and retrieved a cigarette. "I don't know why you want to be hasslin' me," she said as she lit the cigarette with a mini disposable lighter. "Cause I ain't got nothin' to say that's gonna help y'all."

"Are you Larice's girlfriend?" Nolan asked, stepping closer to the chair.

"*Was* his girlfriend," she said, taking a deep drag. "But like I said, I'm done with him now. And you can tell him to stop trying to call me collect, cause I ain't never gonna accept the charges," she added, blowing smoke from her mouth.

Nolan noticed a lisp and saw for the first time that she was missing a front tooth.

"How long had you been with him?" he asked.

"Too damn long," she said, looking away. "More than a year. And that was one year too many."

"And when did it end between you two?"

"Right before he got arrested on those murder charges," Monica answered, flicking the end of her cigarette into a rusted iron frying pan on the porch floor. "Like the day or two before."

"Well I guess you know about the charges, then," Nolan said. "Do you remember whether you were with him on the night the family was murdered? It was Sunday, April Eleventh."

"I most definitely was not with him. Why? Is that liar saying I was?"

"I don't mean that you were with him and helped him commit murder. I'm assuming that Larice didn't do this. I was just looking for a possible alibi. Perhaps you were watching television with him at the time?" Nolan asked.

"I wasn't around him at all that night. I know, because I remember when I first heard about it, I thought, man, he could have done it and I wouldn't even know it because I was staying with my mother here at the house on the night it happened."

"I see," Nolan said. "Do you know Timmy Lawson?"

"Yeah, I knew him," she said, taking another drag from her cigarette. "He hung out with Larice quite a bit."

"Did you know that he was working for the police as an undercover informant and that he set Larice up on that drug charge?"

"That's what Larice told me," she said. "But he had lied to me so much that I didn't know whether to believe him or not."

"Well it's true," Nolan said. "He really did set him up with the police. Do you remember when Timmy came over to your house after Larice was arrested?"

"Yeah," Monica answered. "He was asking about some drugs. I told him that I didn't know nothin' about any drugs and that he better get his ass off my property."

"And then, as I understand it, shortly after that is when your house was broken into?"

"Yeah, that's right."

"And did the burglar steal the drugs that were in the house?"

"I told you. I don't know nothin' about no drugs. I wasn't involved in that junk."

"Listen," Nolan said. "They can't charge you with anything because of those drugs. Just because you knew they were there, doesn't mean that you did anything illegal. You see, there's a law in Virginia that says if you testify at a trial, the cops can't use any of your statements against you in a subsequent trial. That means that if you were to testify that Larice had drugs in the house and then they were stolen, they can't use your statements to prosecute you. And since they have no physical evidence of drugs on your property, there's no way they can convict you of anything. I just want you to know that up front. And I also want you to know that Larice could use your help on this one. I really believe that he didn't commit these murders and so far, you're the only one that can stop them from sending an innocent man to prison for the rest of his life."

Nolan was lying about his belief in Larice's innocence, but not about needing Monica's help.

Monica appeared to think for a few seconds, but she didn't falter. "Like I said, I don't know nothing about no drugs."

"What about Larice's gun?" Nolan asked. "You knew that was stolen, right?"

"I don't know nothing about no gun neither," she looked down the street as she took another deep drag from the cigarette.

Nolan thought that she could be lying, but he knew that if she wasn't willing to tell him about the drugs and the gun, then she surely didn't tell the police about such things when she reported the burglary.

"Did you file a police report after the burglary?" Nolan asked.

"Yeah, I called the police and they came out."

"Was anything stolen?"

"They took some money that I had in a jar and they busted up my things," she answered. "That's all."

Nolan knew that she wasn't going to be very helpful to the defense, but that wasn't going to stop him from sending a subpoena to her. Perhaps later down the road, she would have a change of heart and suddenly remember that drugs and a gun were stolen from her home. At the very least, she could testify that Timmy Lawson came to her house asking about drugs and then shortly thereafter, the burglary occurred. The jury would just have to fill in the blanks about the drugs and the gun.

"One more thing, Ms. Lee," Nolan said. "When's the last time you saw Larice's gold watch?"

Monica appeared confused. "What gold watch?"

"The gold Armani watch he's been wearing for the last year," Nolan said.

Monica shook her head. "I don't remember no gold watch."

"Thank you Ms. Lee, we'll be in touch," Nolan said, now almost certain that Larice had made up the watch story. He stuck out his business card again and she took it. "I'd appreciate a call if you can think of anything that can help him."

She looked away and flicked her cigarette into the frying pan. "Yeah, whatever."

CHAPTER 22

On Saturday morning, Nolan woke up early so that he could meet Eric and Lieutenant Childress by 9:00 a.m. at the gun club. After a shower, he put on a pair of jeans and a t-shirt, and then made a pot of coffee. When the coffee was done, he poured a cup and went outside to his front patio, just as the sun was beginning to evaporate the morning's dew.

His house was a two-story, Federal style brick manor, located just on the edge of Old Town. Originally constructed in 1897, the house was one of many homes built in the city's first major expansion after the Civil War. Back then, with its new cobblestone streets and gas lights on every corner, Old Town represented a period of great prosperity in the city's history. But more than a century later, as Big Shanty continued to grow outward into the tobacco fields, Old Town was eventually left behind. By the time that Nolan bought his home, many of the surrounding mansions were abandoned and the neighborhood had become an open air drug market.

The decaying neighborhood didn't bother Nolan. He just wanted a cheap house close to the courthouses. Besides, the drug dealers and gang bangers pretty much left him alone -- probably because they saw him as an ally. After all, he had represented many of them at one time or another.

Sitting on the front porch with his laptop in front of him, he searched "skeet shooting" to refresh his memory on the rules and format. After he had read all that was necessary, he finished his cup of coffee and retreated to the house. In his bedroom on the second floor, he retrieved two guns from the closet -- an over and under Berretta Silver Pigeon, and his favorite semi-automatic bird hunting gun -- a Model 50 Winchester Featherweight. He wasn't exactly sure how serious Eric and Childress were going to take their competition. If they shot skeet for fun, he'd use the Silver Pigeon, which was an elegant showpiece with fine, detailed engravings. If it was for money, he'd have to bring out the Winchester, which he'd grown up with and used so much that it was like a second extension of his own arm.

After casing the guns and pouring another cup of coffee for the road, he set the security alarm and exited the front door. He placed the gun case in the bed of his old pickup, then climbed in and fired it up. Driving slowly through the neighborhood, he took a right turn and followed the street down the hill until it intersected with Main Street. At that early hour, there were no drug dealers loitering on the corners -- their work shift didn't get going until early evening.

Taking a left, he drove down Main Street, which was mostly empty due to the early hour. But even during business hours, the small shops that lined the main thoroughfare were never too busy, as most people did their shopping in the strip malls and discount shopping centers in the suburbs.

Like every time that he drove down Main Street, he glanced at the store where Marvin's Toy Kingdom had been located. The two large windows that made up the store front were yellowed and dusty, barely revealing the empty blackness inside. Vacant since the trial, it stood only as a reminder of Big Shanty's embarrassing past and Nolan's first moral conflict as a new attorney.

Back then, he didn't exactly embrace the idea of representing a child molester. Although he did his best to represent Marvin Lester, he really didn't understand at the time what being a Public Defender had taught him since.

It was John Keene who had laid the stones for Nolan's moral foundation. Because of Keene's obsessive drive for convictions, it was easy for Nolan to focus on something infinitely more important than guilt, which was defending the Constitution and everyone's right to a fair trial. And from Nolan's point of view, both were under constant attack from Keene and his assistants.

After driving the eight blocks that made up Main Street, Nolan turned left onto the bridge that spanned the Roanoke River. Once over the bridge, he merged onto the highway that led out of town to the south.

As he drove, Nolan tried to figure out why Childress would want to meet him at the range. Maybe he had some information about the Jones case, he thought. Or maybe, it had nothing to do with criminals. Maybe Childress just wanted better competition at skeet shooting.

After five miles, Nolan saw a small sign nailed to a fence post near the road. The sign read, "Happy Valley Gun Club" and below it was an arrow.

Nolan turned his pickup onto the gravel road and drove another mile, leaving a plume of dust behind him. After cresting a ridge, he drove into a valley which was not visible from the highway. As he approached the gun club, he could see Eric's car parked in front of the small shack which served as the club house.

Eric and Childress were standing beyond the shack on the skeet range, less than thirty yards away, with their backs to him. With a silhouette very similar to Burt and Ernie, Eric was the taller Burt, while Childress was the shorter and more round Ernie. They were in the middle of the range, which was formed by small concrete pads arranged in a perfect, half-circle. Childress was holding the electronic control unit that released the clays, while Eric held a shotgun. They were both wearing ear protection, which made Nolan think that they probably didn't hear him drive up.

Climbing out of the pickup, Nolan grabbed his gear and began to walk towards the shooters. As he approached, Eric shouldered his shotgun and yelled, "Pull!" Childress pushed the button on the control unit and a clay suddenly appeared from the high house, flying left to right in front of them. Eric followed the clay with his shotgun barrel. A second later he jerked, but the gun didn't fire. The clay kept flying until it landed in the grass beyond the knoll.

"Damn it!" Eric yelled. "I had the safety on."

Nolan laughed loudly.

Eric and Childress turned, surprised to see him.

"Nice flinch!" Nolan said, still chuckling. "Let's shoot for money."

Childress grinned and stuck out his hand to shake Nolan's. "He's probably trying to sucker us into a big bet."

"No doubt," Nolan shook Childress's hand. By his friendly demeanor, Nolan already knew that Childress wasn't going to accidentally shoot him on purpose. "Thanks for inviting me out here," he added.

"Thanks for coming," Childress responded. "It ain't much of a facility, but we have a good time when we're here."

Nolan glanced around and saw that the skeet range was built to regulation. There were eight concrete pads, or stations, altogether -- seven pads made up the semi-circle, and the eighth pad was in the center. The clay pigeons were launched from two different houses, the first, or high house, was behind station one on the left, and the second, or low house, was behind station seven on the right.

"All right," Eric shouldered his gun. "I'm ready now. Pull!"

Childress pushed the button and a clay flew from the high house on the left side. Eric pointed and pulled the trigger, powdering the clay before it made the halfway point. "There we go!" he yelled. "How much you want to play for?" he asked, without even turning around.

Nolan twisted an ear plug between his finger and thumb, and then pushed it into his ear canal. "A dollar a clay -- and pay up today."

Eric shouldered his gun again. "Pull."

An orange clay appeared again, this time from the low house on the right and Eric blasted it, just as Nolan was getting his second ear plug in.

"I think you're warmed up enough there, chief," Childress commented. "You want a few warm ups?" he turned and asked Nolan.

"That's all right," Nolan answered. "I'll wing it."

Childress pulled the long cord connected to the button box as they walked over to the first station on the far left. "Who's going first?"

"Let Flinch here go first, since he's all warmed up," Nolan answered, as they lined up at the first station with the high house to their backs.

"All right, you sorry bastards, start digging in your pockets, 'cause I don't plan on missing," Eric announced, breaking the barrel of his shotgun and placing a single shell into the top chamber. "A little high, a little low," he closed the barrel. "Twenty five shots and you'll give me the dough."

Nolan laughed as Childress shook his head.

"Did it take you all morning to think up that little rhyme?" Childress asked.

Eric turned and winked. "Just an hour." Raising the gun to his shoulder, he yelled, "Pull!"

Eric pushed the button on the box and a motorized whir came from the high house behind them. The clay shot out over Eric's left shoulder, sailing away from them. Eric fired his shotgun and the clay split into two pieces.

"Well, you got at least one errant BB to hit it," Childress commented.

Eric reloaded and Childress released the second clay from the low house, which Eric shattered. Loading both barrels, Eric readied himself for his last attempt at the first station: simultaneous doubles -- one from the high house and one from the low house.

"Pull," he said with the shotgun at his shoulder. The clays came out in a criss-cross pattern. Eric shot the high house clay first, and then quickly adjusted his aim and blasted the low house clay as it trailed off to the left.

"Four for four," he said as he broke the barrel of his gun and ejected the empty shells. Lifting the gun near his mouth, Eric pursed his lips and blew on the wisp of smoke that was trailing from the open chamber.

"That's a nice touch," Childress commented. "We're really intimidated."

Eric chuckled as he backed away from the first station. Nolan stepped onto the concrete pad and loaded two shells in the magazine and one in the chamber of his Winchester. Without raising the gun to his shoulder, he said, "Pull." Childress pushed the button, sending the clay from the high house. Nolan raised his shotgun, taking only a second to put his bead on it and blast it from the air.

"Nice," Childress commented.

"Aren't you Mr. Skeet, starting with your gun down," Eric added.

"Hey," Nolan replied. "I don't walk around with the gun to my shoulder when I'm hunting birds, so I'm not going to start doing it here."

He turned to Childress. "Pull."

The second clay came from the low house, and in one fluid motion, Nolan raised his Winchester and locked on to the target. A second later, he pulled the trigger and the clay turned into a cloud of powder.

After loading one more shell into the magazine, the doubles flew and Nolan shattered them both.

"I see that I have my work cut out for me," Childress said, handing the button box to Eric.

Childress picked up his own shotgun and rose to the challenge, hitting all four targets at the first station as well.

From there, they made their way around the semi-circle, shooting at two clays from each of the concrete pads. As they took turns shooting, their conversations centered around guns and hunting. Not once did anyone mention police work or criminal defense. And not once did any of them miss their target.

After hitting the singles and then the doubles at station seven, they moved onto the final station in the middle. When Eric hit the first clay, he was allowed to shoot one more time, for his twenty fifth and final shot of the match. With the pressure on for a perfect score, Childress released the clay from the low house and Eric pointed and fired his shotgun, but the clay kept sailing.

"Damn it!" Eric shouted. "Almost a perfect score."

"The door's open," Childress nodded to Nolan. And then he turned to Eric. "You better get your dollar out."

"I can't believe I missed that son of a bitch," Eric said, popping his barrel and ejecting the shells. "I think it came out at a weird angle."

Childress laughed. "The only thing weird about that was your aim."

Stepping onto the pad, Nolan loaded two shells and turned to face the high house. "Pull."

He shouldered his gun and pulled the trigger quickly, vaporizing the clay.

"One more for the win," Childress said.

Turning to face the low house, Nolan winked at Eric. "One high, one low . . . one more shot and you'll give me the dough."

Eric grinned. "We'll see."

"Pull."

The clay came out of the low house fast and to the left. Nolan shouldered his gun and followed the clay longer than he should have. Just as it was about to pass him, he pulled the trigger and the clay exploded into a black cloud.

"You lucky son of a bitch!" Eric yelled.

Nolan shook his head. "I almost lost that one."

"Nice shot," Childress added. He turned to Eric and handed him the button box. "You may as well pull out two dollars."

After Childress hit both of his targets, Eric reached into his wallet and pulled out two singles. "I can't believe I missed that," he said again, handing each of them a dollar bill.

"You'll get us next time," Nolan grinned.

"Let's go to the shack," Childress said. "I've got some coffee in there."

With Childress leading them, they walked to the clubhouse and put their guns in the rack beside the front door.

Although it was starting to heat up outside, the air inside the one room shack was still cool. It was the first time that Nolan had been inside. The only other time that he had been at the range, the clubhouse was locked.

The room was about fifteen feet on each side. In the middle there was a pot belly stove sitting cold and dormant, with four large upholstered chairs arranged around it. There was a counter with cabinets along the back wall and a refrigerator in the corner. Above the counter there were two long shelves stocked with several bottles of liquor.

Childress walked to the counter, opened a cabinet and pulled out three paper cups. Placing the cups on the counter, he grabbed a metal thermos and filled the cups with coffee.

"Here you go, I hope you like it black," he said.

They all took a cup and Childress waved them to the seating area. Childress removed his shooting glasses and took a sip of coffee. "You guys don't shoot too bad -- considering the fact that one of you is old and retired and the other is a lawyer."

"You ain't that far behind me," Eric said, lowering his large frame into the chair opposite Childress. "I just started younger and got to retire earlier."

"How many years you guys work together?" Nolan asked.

"Well, I had been working three years before the Lieutenant came on, so I guess we spent about twenty seven years together," Eric said. "Back then, this guy had a full head of black hair and was skinny," he nodded to Childress.

Childress chuckled. "Look who's talking there with the gray moustache. Don't you think it's time to shave that thing off -- I mean now that you're retired and all."

"Yeah," Nolan added. "Isn't that what you're supposed to do when you leave the department -- turn in your gun and shave off your moustache?"

"This lip hasn't been bare since puberty, and I sure as hell ain't gonna cut it off now," Eric laughed. "Besides, the missus likes it," he added, pushing the hairs down with his thumb and index finger.

"Twenty seven years," Childress repeated. "And you got out just in time -- right before you had to start dealing with The Jackass."

"Who's that?" Nolan asked, thinking that he may have been talking about the Chief of Police.

"He's talking about your little buddy, the Commonwealth's Attorney," Eric said.

"Keene?" Nolan asked.

"Yeah, John Keene, the fucking spineless weasel who thinks he owns this town," Childress pulled a pack of cigarettes from his pocket shook one out. "You want one?" he asked.

"No thanks," Nolan said.

Childress shrugged and lit the cigarette.

"And here I thought I was the only one who couldn't stand him," Nolan smiled. He was surprised to hear such things from a veteran police officer who was supposed to be on the same side as the prosecutor

"Let me tell you something," Childress leaned ahead in his chair. "That guy is going off the deep end and he's trying to drag everybody with him. And that's one of the reasons I wanted you to come out here this morning," he looked at Nolan. "You need to know that he's trying to pull some shenanigans in the Larice Jones case."

"Oh yeah?" Nolan asked. "Like what?"

"Let's get one thing straight first," Childress said, shifting in his chair and flicking his cigarette in the ashtray next to him. "What I say doesn't leave this room. I'm only fourteen months from retirement and I don't want this coming back to bite me in the ass. That means I'm just giving you a friendly anonymous tip here, and you can't bring this up at the trial when I testify, agreed?"

Nolan nodded. He wasn't quite sure that he could uphold such an agreement because he didn't know what Childress was going to tell him, but he sure as hell wanted to find out.

"Now this is just my hunch, but I think you need to take a closer look at Tommy Lawson -- that surviving twin. There's something going on there that smells fishy to me."

Nolan glanced at Eric, who raised an eyebrow. Nolan knew that Eric would not have said anything to Childress about Tommy Lawson's identity and the fact that they were going to prove that he was really Timmy Lawson.

"What about him?" Nolan asked.

"Well, I was doing some research into his alibi and I was having problems verifying his story. So I called up Keene and told him that I wanted to interview the Lawson boy again -- this was a just a few weeks ago. And you know what he told me?"

"What?" Nolan responded.

"He said that the Lawson boy was unavailable and that I needed to focus my energy on Larice Jones. Well, we had a few words and he ended up hanging up on me. And wouldn't you know it, but the next day, the Chief calls me in and tells me to start cooperating with the CA or there was going to be trouble. Can you believe that?" he turned to Eric. "That fucking weasel went over my head again and the Chief just keeps sucking up to him."

"What a jackass," Eric commented.

"So I'm just saying -- there's something fishy there and you should do your own checking," Childress added.

"We'll do that," Nolan said.

"But that's not all," Childress said, taking a deep drag from the cigarette. "He's got his shorts in a bunch about that search warrant we got. He thinks you're going to file a motion to suppress. And he says the anonymous call was not enough for us to get the warrant. He also said that he needed something more . . . something that would've corroborated the anonymous tip before we got the warrant."

"He's right," Nolan nodded. "It takes more than an anonymous call to get a search warrant. If an anonymous tip is involved, you need some level of independent information that would tend to show that the tip was reliable."

"Yeah, that's what Keene was talking about. He wanted to know if I heard the radio call about Ice coming out of that house while I was at the magistrate's office getting the warrant. He said if the call came in while I was standing in front of the magistrate, it would be corroboration of the tip and it might be enough to create probable cause for the warrant."

Nolan sat back and smiled, realizing just how shrewd Keene could be. "So what did you tell him."

"Well, the truth is, I think that radio call did come in while I was at the magistrate, but then he showed me a log of the radio calls from the 9-1-1 center and the time of the radio call was about five minutes after the time that the warrant was signed. And you know how lawyers are -- he starts throwing out some scenarios, trying to get me to agree on some version that would help him. And he says, 'Could it be that the magistrate asked you for the time when he signed the warrant and you told him the time on your watch, but you later learned that your watch was five minutes slow?' He wanted me to make some bullshit story up like that, but I told him it didn't happen that way."

Nolan shook his head. "He's a cheater. I always knew that."

"Now I still think that your guy is guilty, but that ain't for me to decide -- that's for a jury. And I ain't gonna cheat to get him convicted. So I just wanted to let you know about that. Don't be surprised if he tries to call the magistrate to the stand and gets him to say that his watch was slow. Just be ready for something like that."

"I appreciate the info," Nolan said. "But I've been thinking about that whole search warrant thing and I'm not so sure that we'll be making an issue out of it at the trial," Nolan added, taking a sip of coffee. "But at any rate, I'm glad to know that us defense attorneys aren't the only ones who think Keene's a jackass."

"He's been a pain in my ass ever since he took over," Childress said, draining his coffee. "And for the life of me, I don't see how he's got everyone backing down to him, especially the Chief."

"I guess everyone's afraid of him," Eric added. "But if you ask me, the guy could use a good ass kicking."

"Anyway, that's all I had to tell you," Childress said, crushing his paper cup. "You guys want to go one more round?"

"I've got to go and get some work done for the trial. I'll let you two shoot it out." Nolan said. "But thanks for having me out here. Maybe we can do it again sometime."

"Absolutely," Childress stood up and held out his hand. "Good luck."

CHAPTER 23

"Boss!" Danny exclaimed as he hurried into Nolan's office. "We've got us a major problem!"

Nolan was standing near his window, staring at the street below. He turned to face Danny. "What's the problem?"

Danny held up a sheaf of papers. "We just got a ruling from Circuit Court on our Motion to Suppress. The judge dismissed it. He's not going to suppress the search warrant evidence!"

Nolan smiled as he walked behind the desk and sat in his chair. He leaned back and clasped his hands behind his head. "Let me guess. Is it because I filed it a day past the deadline?" Nolan asked.

Danny blinked, surprised at Nolan's reaction. "Yeah," he said. "That's right. Keene filed a response to our motion, asking the judge to dismiss it because we filed it late -- and the judge agreed with him."

"Mr. Keene pays close attention to detail, doesn't he?" Nolan said, still smiling.

Danny sat down in the chair in front of Nolan's desk. "What's so funny about that?"

"I meant to file the motion a day late. And I knew that Keene would catch it."

"I'm not following you," Danny said. "Why would you purposely file it late?"

"We don't really want the evidence collected from the search warrant suppressed," Nolan answered. "Think about it. The drug paraphernalia, the wrist watch, and the owe list -- it all fits neatly into our latest and best defense theory. We want the jury to know that Larice was involved in drugs and that he was fronting drugs to Timmy. It's all relevant to our theory that Timmy stole drugs from Larice and framed him for the murders. Therefore, there's no reason that we should have the evidence suppressed."

Danny nodded. "Yeah, I guess you're right. I never thought of it that way. But why even file the motion at all then?" Danny asked.

"Because if we didn't file the motion, then Keene would become suspicious and realize that the evidence is useful to us, and we don't want him to know that. We want him to think that it helps his case. And after he presents the evidence at trial, we'll use it to advance our own theory," Nolan explained. "It's an old trick. You tell the jury up front that the prosecution is so blind and biased that they can't even fairly process the evidence they have. And then you use the prosecution's evidence to prove your own case."

"That is tricky," Danny grinned.

"What the hell's going on in here," Rick said as he entered Nolan's office. As was his custom, he had shed his shirt and tie, and was wearing only a white t-shirt. "I heard Danny whining like a little girl all the way from my office." He slapped Danny on the back as he walked by him -- probably a little too hard. "What's the matter, Danny? Still trying to run down the hill and nail one?"

Danny turned in his chair and watched Rick plop down on Nolan's couch. "Where's your buckskin jacket, Gerry Spence?" Danny asked. "Why don't you close your eyes and fall back. I'll catch you . . . really," he added.

"Yeah, I just couldn't decide -- Gerry Spence's lawyer camp, or Clown School. In the end, it was Clown School, of course," Rick said as he leaned back and put his feet up on the arm of Nolan's couch. "Now what's all the hub-bub about?"

"The boss here has pulled another one over on John Keene," Danny said with a grin. As he was explaining, Nolan's telephone rang. Nolan checked the caller I.D. before answering. "Well, well, well . . . looks like we have the Commonwealth Attorney calling." Nolan reached over with his index finger. "Sit tight, gentlemen. We're going on speaker."

Nolan poked at the speaker button on the telephone. "Nolan Getty."

"Mr. Getty, this is Rachel at the Commonwealth Attorney's office. Mr. Keene wanted to speak with you. Are you available to talk with him right now?"

"Sure," Nolan said.

"All right, please hold while I patch you through."

Rick sprang from the couch. *"Please hold for Mr. Keene,"* he said in a high pitched voice. "What a fucking ego. I'll handle this."

Rick picked up Nolan's handset and cupped his hand over the mouth piece. "Two can play at this game," he winked.

Nolan shook his head and looked at Danny. "Don't try this at home."

When Keene picked up the line, Rick pinched his nose for effect. "Please hold for Nolan Getty," he said in a high nasally voice. Then he pushed the hold button on the telephone and hung it up. "He's waiting, whenever you're ready."

Nolan laughed as he reached to the phone. "Thanks for your secretarial support." He punched the speaker button and finally answered the call.

"This is Nolan."

"Nolan, this is John Keene. I'm calling about Commonwealth v. Larice Jones. Do you have a minute to discuss it?" he asked.

"Sure, what's up?"

"I'll get right to the point. As I'm sure you're aware, your Motion to Suppress was filed late and the judge has just dismissed it. And I'm more than a little concerned that you're not doing your job. The last thing we want is this thing coming back on appeal due to ineffective assistance of counsel after he gets convicted."

Nolan bristled from Keene's choice of the word, "we," as if they were somehow working together towards a common goal.

"Yeah, I guess I screwed that up," Nolan said into the speaker, smiling at Rick and Danny.

"Well, that can happen. But what worries me most is that you haven't even filed a Motion for Discovery. I mean, that's one of the most effective tools for a defense attorney and you haven't even used it. And I can't help but to think that your client is going to be very angry when he gets convicted, knowing that you didn't even do the bare minimum to help him," Keene said.

Nolan gave Rick and Danny a surprised look. "Did I miss the deadline on that too?" he asked. "I guess I need a better calendar system over here."

"Well, something's not working very well," Keene continued. "I tell you what. I wouldn't do this for everybody, but if you file your Discovery motion by tomorrow, I'll send you everything I have. If you do that, I'll feel a lot better about this and I shouldn't have to call the Bar Association."

"That's very nice of you," Nolan said, glancing at Rick and Danny again. "But if you're so concerned about helping me, why did you file a motion to dismiss my Motion to Suppress?"

Silence. "Look, I can't just ignore all of the rules -- I owe a duty to the people in this town," he finally said.

"I guess you do," Nolan said. "I'll see what I can do about that discovery motion."

Rick stood up and gave a double bird to the phone.

"I'll be looking for it," Keene said. "Have a nice day."

"One more thing, Mr. Keene," Nolan stopped him. "Are you interested in offering any plea agreement?"

There was a pause before he answered. "The only thing he's going to get is life in prison," Keene answered. "If you can talk him into pleading guilty for that, I'll send over the paper work."

"That's what I thought," Nolan said. "We'll see you at trial."

The phone clicked and went dead. Nolan reached over and pushed the speaker button to hang up.

"What a stupid son of a bitch!" Rick exclaimed. "Does he think we're that dumb that we can't see what he's up to?"

"Sounds like he's pretty desperate for reciprocal discovery," Nolan said.

"Now what are you going to do?" Danny asked.

"I'm going to pretend like he never called," Nolan answered. "Let him call the Bar on me."

"You know that sneaky bastard is going to call them," Rick said. "And then you'll have to deal with them while you're trying to get ready for this trial. That ain't right."

Nolan shrugged. "In the end, none of this will matter if we win. So all we have to do is win."

CHAPTER 24

Danny poked his head into Rick's office, but he wasn't at his desk. He had already looked in the basement and in the conference room. There were only a few rooms left in the chateau.

"Hello? Rick!" Danny yelled as he went from office to office on the second floor. "Are you up here somewhere?"

After the third shout, Danny finally heard an answer.

"What!" Rick's voice boomed from his office, though it sounded muffled.

Danny returned to Rick's office and peered in again. No Rick.

"Hello?" Danny queried.

"What the fuck!" he heard Rick's muffled voice again. It was coming from inside his closet.

Danny approached the closet door. He paused for a few moments to see if Rick would come out. He didn't.

Danny knocked on the door lightly. "Rick?"

"Yes?" Rick's voice answered in a sarcastic tone.

"Are you okay?" Danny asked.

"Yeeeees," Rick answered, drawing the word out. "Are you okay?"

Danny chuckled nervously. "I'm fine. I just wanted to ask you something."

After another moment, the door opened slightly. It was dark inside, but he could see Rick peering through the crack.

"What is it?" Rick asked.

"It's about discovery in a case of mine."

The door finally opened fully and Rick stepped out, blinking his eyes. "Fine," he said. "But I hope you know you've just interrupted a very important experiment I was conducting."

Danny politely chuckled again. He never knew when Rick was serious or joking. Obviously he was sleeping, but his delivery was completely serious. And it wouldn't have surprised Danny if Rick was slightly schizophrenic.

"What do you got?" Rick asked as he sat down at his desk.

"I've got my first solo felony -- it's a grand larceny and I just wanted to ask you some questions about discovery," Danny answered.

"Ask away," Rick said, yawning.

Should I file for discovery?" Danny asked.

"Yes," Rick answered quickly. "Always file for discovery."

"But the boss isn't filing for discovery in the murder case. So I was just thinking, maybe I shouldn't file for it in my grand larceny case."

"Listen," Rick said. "The boss is on a different level than you. He sees things that you can't even dream about. And until you reach that level, always file for discovery. Otherwise, the client will bite the hand that feeds him -- which would be yours. He'll file a complaint with the Bar saying that you didn't do your job."

Danny shrugged. "I guess that's a good enough reason for me. So when should I request it?" Danny asked.

"I always file for discovery after the preliminary hearing when the indictments come in from the grand jury. That way it's all automatic. Indictment comes in . . . I file for discovery. Dribble, dribble, shoot."

"So how do you get the information -- does the prosecutor send it in the mail?" Danny asked.

"Usually, they're too lazy for that," Rick answered. "What they've been doing lately is sending a letter telling us to set up an appointment to view the file in their office. Then you have to go over there and they give you the file to look at. Of course, it's a watered down file, containing only discoverable information."

Danny nodded. "All right, well that's what I'll do. The indictment just came in for the dude, so I'll file for discovery right now. But how will I know in the future whether to file or not? What are the reasons that you don't file?"

Rick smiled. "When you don't want to give them reciprocal discovery," he answered. "The statute says that if you file for discovery, then you have to also give the prosecution certain information, including scientific tests and any alibi."

"But if you have an alibi or other evidence that shows your guy is not guilty, then why wouldn't you show the prosecutor so that he drops the case?" Danny asked.

"They're cheaters," Rick answered. "If you give them something that shows your client's innocence, they twist it around or make up other evidence to refute it. You'll see," Rick added.

"How can that be?" Danny asked, not really believing him. "They can't do that or they'd get into trouble."

"Get in trouble with whom?" Rick asked. "With themselves? Who else is going to prosecute them?"

"Can't you complain to the Bar?" Danny asked.

"I suppose you could, if you had proof of their cheating. But there's never any proof," Rick answered. He walked over to the window, pulled up the shade and looked out. With his back to Danny, he continued to talk. "They're very sneaky, those prosecutors. Just once I'd like to catch them in the act."

Danny sat in silence as Rick stared out the window. After a few moments, Danny tried to engage him again. "What will . . . ."

"Shhh!" Rick cut him off. "I just thought of something," he turned to face Danny. He had a devious look about him. "How's that murder case going?"

"We're still just trying to get more evidence to prove that Timmy Lawson is the murderer," Danny answered. "Eric is working on that. Apparently, the dude is driving a new car around town, even though he doesn't have a job. So that's something Eric's trying to check into."

"You get anything else from the state lab, besides the fingerprints on the shell casings?" Rick asked.

"Nothing," Danny answered.

"Does our dude have an alibi or anything?"

"Not really. He says he was home alone, watching T.V., but of course, there's nobody to verify that," Danny answered.

"And still no murder weapon, huh?"

"Nope."

Rick smiled and began to pace behind his desk. "There's something I've always wanted to do," he said rubbing his chin. "And this may be the perfect case to do it," he added. "What if I told you that I have a way to prove that the prosecutors cheat?" he asked. "Would you help me?"

Danny shrugged. "I don't know. What are you talking about?"

"I've always had this idea floating in my head, and this is the perfect case for it -- it's high profile, they're desperate for evidence, and they'll do anything to get it."

"What is it?" Danny shifted in his chair.

Rick spun around with a crazed look. "What if we made a fake file on Larice Jones and put information in that file -- information that is completely false. And what if we put that file in a place where the prosecutors would have a chance to look at it. Wouldn't that be something?"

Danny wasn't completely following him. "What kind of information?"

"Anything we wanted," Rick exclaimed. "Maybe a false alibi, or maybe a false location for the murder weapon . . . anything that would make them react and show that they tried to cheat by looking through our file."

"But what's wrong if they look through our file? They could just say they were trying to find out who it belonged to."

"No, no, no." Rick exclaimed. "You put the name of the client in big letters on the file, and you stamp the outside of the file with the Public Defender stamp, and maybe you write the words, 'Confidential' or 'Lawyer-Client Privileged Material' -- something like that. And then you bury the false information in the back of the file in a place where they would have to dig for it."

"Where would we leave the file?"

"You could take it with you when you retrieve the discovery on your grand larceny case. You could leave the fake file on the table or floor in their conference room -- as if you were carrying it around and forgot it there." Rick was grinning madly. "Oh, man, this could be really good!" he slapped his hands together.

"I don't know," Danny said, shaking his head. "That sounds a little weird. We should run it by the boss before we do something like that."

Rick shook his head. "Trust me on this one -- the boss will love it. But if we tell him about it, he'll have to say no. He's the boss, and that's what boss's do. If we don't tell him and just do it, then he has no complaints because his hands are clean."

Danny shrugged. "I guess that makes sense. Are you sure he's not going to get mad?"

"Positive," Rick exclaimed, clapping his hands together. "You do this and he is going to have a whole new respect for you."

Danny grinned. "But couldn't we get in trouble by providing false information?"

"We're not providing anything -- they'll be trying to steal information. And we can put it in a way so that they can't use it against us," Rick explained.

Danny didn't know how to say no. So he just nodded.

"Now, let's think about this together," Rick continued. "What could we put in the file that would send them on a wild goose chase?"

CHAPTER 25

With less than a month to go before the trial, Keene had arranged for his star witness, Tommy Lawson, to come into the office for a meeting. As was the case with all victim witnesses before a trial, the victim witness advocate assigned to his case prepped him thoroughly about the upcoming proceedings, including what to wear for clothing, the "do's and don'ts" of testifying, and what to expect during cross examination. When she had finished her hour long meeting with Lawson, she called Keene as he had instructed.

Keene entered the conference room and nodded to the advocate. "You can go, now," he said. "I'll finish up with him."

"Yes sir," she said. But before she left, she stood up and gave the Lawson boy a big hug. "Everything's going to be all right. Mr. Keene will make sure of that."

"Thank you for your help," the boy nodded. "We'll see you next month."

Keene waited until she had left the room and closed the door behind her. "Have a seat," he waved. After Lawson sat back down, Keene took his seat at the head of the table and opened his case file.

"We've got some problems," he began. "Lieutenant Childress has told me he's having trouble verifying your story about where you were on the night of the murders."

"What kind of problems?" the kid shifted his eyes back and forth and blinked rapidly.

"He said that he contacted Shawn Henderson, who told him that the plan was for him to pick you up at your house. But when he went to your house, nobody answered the door and you didn't answer the telephone. On top of that, Henderson says that he never saw you at the concert."

Lawson shifted his eyes. "Naw man, that ain't the way I remember it. We was supposed to meet at the concert, at the front entrance. And I don't know if he was there or not 'cause there was a lot of people there and chances are, he didn't see me because of the big crowd. As far as me not answering the phone, I didn't have my cell phone on me that night. I forgot it at home."

Keene shook his head. "That may be, but it's still something that caught Childress's attention -- so I'm sure the defense attorney will be snooping around as well. If I were you, I'd get a hold of that Henderson boy and let him know that he doesn't have to answer any questions from any defense lawyers, if they track him down."

"They ain't gonna track him down," Lawson said. "He's already moved out of town."

Keene gave the Lawson boy a long, hard stare. "That's fine," he continued. "But there are other problems. Lieutenant Childress told me that he can't find the other kid that you were supposed to meet at the concert -- Jackie. Do you know where he is?"

"I have no idea," Lawson answered. "Like I said, I don't even know the dude's last name. I've seen him in our same circle of friends and I found out that he was a fan of Jiggernaut like me and so we just decided to meet at the concert. But he never showed up."

Keene wasn't buying it. "What about Johnny Randolph? You said that when you came back from the concert the next day, you stayed with that kid all day and didn't go home until that night."

"What about him?" Lawson asked.

"Childress told me that he couldn't find him either. The person who lives at the house that you described, told us that he has never even heard of Johnny Randolph. So what do you have to say about that?"

Lawson shrugged. "Maybe he moved."

"No sir, he didn't move," Keene raised his voice. "The owner of the home said that he had been there for ten years. There has never been a Johnny Randolph living there. And Childress checked all of the other houses on the street -- just in case you were mistaken about the exact location -- and not one person has ever heard of him."

Lawson shrugged. "I guess I don't know what to tell you."

Keene's anger flared. "Tell me the truth!" he yelled. "You're hiding something and I want to know what it is. Right now!" Keene slapped his hand on the table.

Lawson jumped in his chair. He shifted his eyes again and blurted out, "Come on man, you don't have to act all crazy."

Keene's eyes narrowed. "First of all, don't ever call me crazy," he hissed in a lower, more menacing tone. "Secondly, you need to listen very carefully to me. I am going to send you to jail if I don't get some straight answers. So start talking right now."

"Jail?" Lawson asked in a high pitched voice. "For what?"

"For making false statements to a law enforcement officer," Keene answered. "And I'll give you one more chance to tell the truth right now. Otherwise, I'll file charges and prosecute you myself."

Lawson fidgeted and looked away. He appeared to be thinking very intensely. After a few moments, he let out a big sigh. "I guess I better tell you." His eyes shifted and he paused before shrugging his shoulders. "I'll tell you. It's like this. Johnny Randolph is not a guy. It's a girl. And she doesn't live in Big Shanty -- she lives in Charlottesville. I gave you guys a fake address because I didn't want you knowing what I . . . well, me and Timmy . . . what we were doing."

Keene raised his eyebrows. "What were you doing?"

"Johnny was a girl that Timmy dated every now and then," Lawson began. "But once in awhile, just for kicks, I would go over to Charlottesville and go on a date with her and I would pretend that I was Timmy. And she never knew the difference," he explained. "That's where I was that day. Instead of driving back home the day after the concert, I drove over to Charlottesville. I called her on her cell phone and she met me at the mall over there. We hung out all day together. But I didn't want anyone to know about her because she thought she was with Timmy. And if anyone asked -- like you or the other lawyer, she would've told you that she was with Timmy, and I would've looked bad."

Keene knew that there was something not quite right about Lawson's original story. And now, he had an explanation that at least made sense. Keene also recalled that at the preliminary hearing, Lawson didn't answer Getty's question about where Johnny Randolph lived due to his objection. So he had not made any false statements under oath. That was a good thing -- otherwise he would have to disclose the false statement to the defense. And although Lawson had lied to him about Johnny Randolph and where he lived, that really didn't matter. The only thing that mattered was what he would say when Getty asked him the same question at the trial.

"The defense attorney might ask you about Johnny Randolph's whereabouts at the trial. An unlike at the preliminary hearing, you're going to have to answer him. So what are you going to tell him?"

"I'll tell him that she's a friend that lives in Charlottesville, but I don't know where, because every time I went up there, we met at some public place. And then we'd go to a motel."

"What if he asks you what her cell phone number is?" Keene asked. "He'll be able to track her down from that."

Lawson shrugged. "I'll tell him."

Keene frowned. "If he can track her down, he'll bring her into court and like you say, she'll tell everyone that it was Timmy Lawson that she was with. And although you might be able to explain your little trick to the jury -- they're not going to like the fact that you were fooling her. I mean, that's a little disturbing . . . and there's possibly something illegal in there, especially if you were having sex with her and she thought you were someone else."

Lawson's eyes widened.

"But on the other hand," Keene continued. "If you don't have her number memorized, you can't give it to the defense lawyer, can you?" Keene asked.

Lawson nodded. "That's right -- I don't have it memorized."

"And if your cell phone was accidentally damaged or got lost, you wouldn't be able to retrieve her telephone number from it, would you?"

Lawson nodded again and smiled. "I wish I could give you her number, but I can't. I lost my phone this morning."

Keene smiled and continued. "Has Lieutenant Childress or the defense contacted you in any way since you moved into that apartment?"

Lawson shook his head. "No sir."

"Good," Keene commented. "The rent is paid through my budget, not the police department's, so Childress shouldn't be able to track you down. And the defense attorney shouldn't be able to find you either. But if they do somehow find you, I want to remind you that you're under no obligation to answer any of their questions. In fact, you should not talk to them at all. But call me immediately if anyone approaches you, all right?"

Lawson nodded.

"And make sure you get your lost cell phone replaced immediately -- like today," Keene winked. "That way you can call me if anything comes up."

Lawson nodded again. "Can you pay for that?"

Keene shook his head. "Not a chance. I can pay for your apartment for witness protection purposes, but I'm not going to get you a cell phone. You'll just have to suck it up and pay for it yourself."

"All right," Lawson said. "No problem."

CHAPTER 26

Fred Mutz was the first person in the conference room for the Friday morning staff meeting, which Keene always held at ten o'clock sharp. Turning on the lights, he made his way around the large, rectangular shaped table to his favorite chair near the middle on the left side. He had several case files under his arm, some of which were ones that he had closed during the week; the others were cases scheduled for the next week. Placing the case files on the conference table, he walked over to the coffee pot, started a fresh brew, and headed back to his seat.

As he was approaching his chair, something on the floor near the end of the conference table caught his eye. Looking closer, he saw that it was a manila folder, but he also recognized that it was not a Commonwealth Attorney's file. Unlike their files, this one had small writing on it and no colored stickers which identified the type of case.

Mutz reached down and picked it up. In small letters near the top of the folder were the words, "Office of the Public Defender." He also noticed the name on the tab -- Larice Jones. It didn't take him long to realize that Danny Roberson had inadvertently left the file behind when he was there the day before to obtain discovery.

Mutz placed it on top of his own files and sat alone in the room, staring at the foreign file. Near the bottom he noticed a series of red words that looked like they had been stamped onto the folder, as they were slightly off-center and at an angle. They read, "This file contains confidential, lawyer-client privileged material. Do not open without specific authorization, under penalty of law."

Perhaps if he hadn't read the warnings, his interest level wouldn't have peaked. But instead of warning him, the stamped statement only fueled his curiosity. Right in front of him, within arm's reach, sat a folder containing confidential information on Larice Jones; interesting information that could possibly help their own case -- like the defendant's alibi, or a confession, or information about where he hid the gun.

If there had been a good angel sitting on his shoulder, it would have warned him not to open the file, but he probably wouldn't have heard it anyway due to the cacophony of noise in his present consciousness, most of which was in the form of Keene's angry voice echoing in his mind.

All of our jobs are in jeopardy if we don't get a conviction.

We need absolutely everything. And if you don't find every piece of evidence . . . you're not going to be able to continue working here.

At that moment, whether he knew it or not, Mutz was going to open that file. Like an alcoholic reaching for his first drink of the day, he knew better, but he couldn't stop himself.

Mutz glanced at the door before placing his hand at the edge of the folder and flipping it open. On the left side of the folder, there was a sheet of paper stapled to the inside of the front cover, labeled "Notes." There were several entries, listed by date, which described events in the case. The bond hearing was the first event listed, followed by several other events, which included visits with the client at the jail and interviews with various witnesses. Mutz read quickly through the list and then turned his attention to the right side of the folder, where numerous documents were clamped together.

Mutz paged through the papers. The arrest warrants were first, followed by the indictment papers and all of the other court documents associated with the case. Mutz quickly flipped through all of the official documents, until he came to a pad of yellow legal paper with hand writing. It looked like lawyer notes -- either from Nolan Getty or Danny Roberson.

The notes covered very general topics; Larice's address, his family's address, and his background information, which included his criminal history, as well as other inane facts. There was nothing interesting, until his eyes reached the bottom of the second page of the legal pad. And what he saw next made his jaw literally drop open.

Written in cursive at the bottom of the page were the words, *Client says they can't pin murders on him — no evidence. no gun found. Hid under bridge, Roanoke River.*

"Yes!" he said, pumping his fist in the air. Pushing his chair back, he stood up and began to pace near the table. "This is big," he said, running his hands through his hair and pacing back and forth beside the table.

After the first turn, he glanced at the open folder again. "I can't believe this," he said to himself. "This is really big."

After a few moments, during which Mutz appeared to be deep in thought, he returned to his seat and continued looking through the notes. But there was no other shocking information in the folder.

When he had finished reading everything, he closed the file and tucked it under his arm. Glancing at his watch, he hastily left the conference room on his way to Keene's office, just down the corridor.

He hurried toward Keene's door without even acknowledging Rachel, who was sitting in her cubicle just outside of his office.

"Hey," Rachel said, interrupting his charge to the door. "You can't go in there."

Mutz spun around. "Is Mr. Keene in his office?"

"Yeah, but he'll be out in a minute for the staff meeting."

"I need to see him now," Mutz explained. "It's very important."

Rachel shrugged. She pushed a button on the telephone and leaned into it. "Fred is here to see you. He says it's important."

"Send him in," Keene's voice responded over the speaker.

Mutz opened the office door.

Keene looked up from his desk. "What is it?"

"I found this file in the conference room," Mutz said, holding the manila folder in the air. But then without thinking, he betrayed himself by giving out too much information. "It was upside down, so I didn't see whose it was. But when I picked it up and opened it, I realized that it's a Public Defender file on Larice Jones. Danny Roberson from the PD's office must have left it behind when he was here for discovery on another case."

"So?" Keene frowned. "Call them up and have them come get it."

"You don't understand," Mutz continued. "There's a note in the file. And I think it reveals the location of the gun."

Keene dropped his pen. "Really?"

"Yeah, I think so," Mutz answered, stepping forward to show him the file. "See here . . ."

"I don't want to see it," Keene cut him off. "I want you to tell me what you saw."

Mutz stopped. "It said, 'no gun found. Hid under bridge Roanoake River.'"

Keene slightly smiled, but then he pushed his chair back and crossed his arms. Without saying anything he turned and looked at the books on the shelf behind him, as if he was thinking about something in particular that was in one of the books. After a few moments, he shook his head and turned back to Mutz.

"You're putting me in a very difficult situation here. On one hand, I can't ignore the fact that you've searched through a file of the Public Defender's office without their permission . . ."

"It was an accident!" Mutz exclaimed.

Keene held up his hand. "Save it," he said. "It's clear to me what happened. You looked through a confidential file that belongs to the defense attorney. Now that's a violation of the Code of Ethics if you ask me. But I'll have to do some research and check into it to see if I need to take further action."

Mutz's face turned red and his jaw dropped for the second time in less than ten minutes.

"On the other hand, even though you've probably violated the Code of Ethics, I can't very well ignore the public safety issue involved here. After all, I'd hate for some young child to find a gun. We'll have to make sure that it's not there," Keene stated.

Mutz continued to stand silent and motionless, as if Keene's words had frozen him in place.

"I should probably call Lieutenant Childress and get him involved," Keene continued. "But since I'm not sure what action I should take with you, I think maybe you should run down to the bridge and see if it's under there. If so, you can contact me and I'll call the Lieutenant. If not, then we may have to pursue other avenues."

Mutz closed his mouth and nodded, apparently satisfied that he was off the hook, at least temporarily. "I'll go right now," he stated.

Keene's tone and demeanor were not unlike that of a father telling his small child to complete a chore. If Keene had said, "I'll time you," Mutz would've probably run all the way to the bridge.

"Call me immediately either way. But if it's there, don't touch it," Keene ordered.

"Yes sir," Mutz said, turning to leave.

"And leave that file with Rachel before you leave. She'll call the Public Defender's office and have them come get it."

"Yes sir," Mutz said as he hurried out the door.

CHAPTER 27

"Danny, get your ass in here, it's happening," Rick squealed over the speaker phone.

Danny dropped his pen and ran down the hall to Rick's office, which faced south. Rick was at the window, staring out with binoculars.

"What's happening?"

"I told you it wouldn't take long!" Rick screamed. "The dumb bastard is down there . . . look," he handed the binoculars to Danny.

Danny grabbed them and pointed them at the bridge, which was several hundred yards away. After adjusting the focus, Fred Mutz came into view. He was climbing over the rail at the near end of the bridge. "Holy shit!" Danny exclaimed.

"Give me those," Rick snatched the binoculars. "This is too fucking much," he laughed as he stared out the window. "There he goes . . . under the bridge. Don't get dirty, Putz!"

Danny watched alongside Rick as Mutz disappeared under the bridge. Rick lowered the binoculars and turned with his hand up. Danny obliged by giving him a high five.

"What a stupid bastard, huh?" Rick laughed. "This is just too good."

"We're not going to get into any trouble, are we?" Danny smiled.

"Nooo," Rick groaned. "Are you kidding? How could we get into trouble? It's just Mutz putzing around under the bridge, that's all."

He turned back to the window and raised the binoculars. "Here he comes . . . oh . . . I told you not to get dirty, Putz!" Rick laughed. "Holy shit," Rick was laughing so hard he couldn't speak. "He's . . . oh my God . . . he's . . . he's absolutely covered in mud!" Rick doubled over, wheezing from laughter.

171

Danny grabbed the binoculars and focused in. "Oh my God . . . look at him." Even Danny had to laugh when he saw that Mutz appeared to be wearing knee high boots made of mud.

When Mutz had finished crawling under the near side of the bridge, he drove to the other side and crawled under the other end. All together, Rick and Danny were entertained for almost an hour.

CHAPTER 28

Nolan had been in his office on the second floor of the chateau for three straight days preparing for the trial of Larice Jones. The list of things to do before a jury trial seemed endless: submit subpoenas, review witness testimony, create jury instructions, track down experts, write up direct and cross examinations, label exhibits, conduct jury background checks . . . . Although he had done it numerous times, it was always a challenge.

He heard footsteps and looked up to see Vicki enter his office.

"Hello."

"Hello," she answered, then plopped down an envelope. "Thought you might want to see this immediately."

Nolan noticed the plastic window on the front of the envelope revealing the pink paper inside and the large words above his address, "Timely Reply Required," with the State seal beside it. He immediately knew it was a bar complaint.

"Nice," Nolan grasped the envelope, ripped open the end and blew into it before retrieving the contents. He held the paper to his head and closed his eyes. "John Keene, Fred Mutz, and the Virginia Bar Association." Nolan opened his eyes and unfolded the paper. "And the question is . . . name a liar, a crier, and who can put my feet to the fire."

Vicki chuckled. "Nice rhyme. Is it bad?"

"Nothing I didn't expect," Nolan reviewed the paper. "Looks like Fred Mutz has filed a complaint against a fellow bar member, which is me."

"Fred Mutz?" Vicki asked surprised. "This isn't from a client?"

"Nope. It says here I am accused of failing to properly represent a client, and the complainant is Fred Mutz."

"Unbelievable," Vicki shook her head.

"What's up?" Rick appeared, sauntering over to the couch and doing his best impression of a high jumper, flipping himself into the air and landing on the couch with his hands behind his head. Danny followed him in and sat down in the chair in front of Nolan's desk.

"I'll let you boys mull it over," Vicki turned and sashayed to the door.

Rick stared at Vicki as she walked away. Without turning his eyes to Nolan, he said loudly, "I came in to see if you think you can get your hands on that thing we were talking about."

Nolan played along as he also stared. "I did have it . . . right in my hands, but that was awhile ago – it's probably lost forever."

"What a shame," Rick replied, "to lose something like that."

By then Vicki was gone.

"What are you talking about?" Danny cut in.

"Nothing," Nolan turned his attention back to the letter. "Fred Mutz has filed a bar complaint against me."

"What the . . . ?" Rick jumped up. "Let me see that!"

Nolan handed him the letter.

"This is complete bullshit!" Rick yelled as he plopped back into the couch. "I should go kick his ass."

"Why would he do that?" Danny asked.

"They're trying to get me kicked off the case," Nolan answered. "They would like to see someone else representing Jones -- maybe a private lawyer who won't do shit because he'd be getting court appointed fees . . . or maybe you or Rick."

"Fuck them," Rick yelled. "They can't get away with this. You know Keene put him up to this, right?"

"Yup," Nolan stood up. After working at his desk all morning, it felt good to stretch his legs. He wandered over to the window behind his desk and gazed out upon the Big Shanty landscape with the Roanoke River snaking through it. Looking south, Nolan immediately noticed the buzz of activity down by the bridge that crossed the river, two blocks away. He could see a fire truck and several police cars with their lights flashing. He also saw a skiff in the water and what looked to be scuba divers.

"Looks like somebody jumped off the bridge down there or something."

"Oh yeah?" Danny joined him beside the window.

Danny's mouth fell open as he continued to stare. "Why would they go to all that trouble?" His voice trembled as he spoke.

Nolan turned to Danny, who appeared to lose color in his face. "You all right?"

"What?" Danny jerked his head towards Nolan. "Yeah, I'm fine. And then he changed the subject, stuttering, "I-I-I found an expert in voice analysis."

"Oh yeah?" Nolan turned from the window and sat down at his desk. "Tell me about him."

Danny returned to his seat. "He's a retired FBI guy who claims that he was a pioneer in the voice analysis field. Anyway, I sent him the tapes and he just called me this morning. Apparently, because the tapes are low quality, and because the 9-1-1 call was so short, he can't say for sure whether the voices match. But he did say that the voices were consistent in some of their patterns."

"Well, I guess that's better than nothing," Nolan said.

"The way he acted, it was good news," Danny explained. "He basically said that there was nothing in the voice patterns that would indicate they were made by two different people."

Nolan thought for a second and nodded. "He's right. That will work just fine. It's more scientific evidence that we can present to a jury and it supports our theory. Make sure he's available on the trial date and tell him to contact me for payment. I don't want to be going through the court on this one to get the funds."

"I already talked to him about that and he said he's available. I'll have him call you about the payment."

"Excellent," Nolan responded. "How's everything else going?"

"Oh, you know . . . busy, busy," Danny answered.

"Have we gotten anything else from the lab?" Nolan asked.

"Not that I know of," Danny answered.

"That's what I thought," Nolan said shaking his head. He spun in his chair and grabbed the murder file from the credenza. He paged through the file until he found the letter that Danny had sent to the lab. He wanted to make sure that Danny had requested all existing and future analyses. He reviewed the letter and saw that Danny had used the correct form letter.

"Something's not adding up," Nolan commented. "The only physical evidence they have is the fingerprint analysis on the shell casings. And I'm getting an uneasy feeling that we're missing something here -- something that they might be hiding."

"What else could they have?" Danny asked. "I sent the request letter to the lab, and they're required to send us everything related to the case."

"I want to see their subpoena list," Nolan said. "They have to send their subpoenas through the court just like we do. And the court will keep copies of them in the file. The file is in the clerk's office, so you'll have to ask her to see it."

"Will they have a problem with me looking at it?" Danny asked.

"Of course not, it's a public record," Nolan said. "You should be doing that in all of your felony cases anyway. And from now until the trial, I'd like you to check the file every day to make sure they don't sneak in a subpoena at the last minute."

"No problem," Danny said.

"Also, I want you to prepare for sentencing," Nolan instructed.

"What do I need to do for that?" Danny asked.

"You need to come up with some mitigating evidence for Mr. Jones. First, you'll need to interview him and get his life history. You can come with me to the jail the next time I visit him. Then you'll have to contact any relatives that he may have and see about getting them to testify on his behalf; especially his mother and sister. If he's found guilty, we want to get him something shorter than life. And to do that, we need to paint a picture to the jury that he's human."

"You just want me to get the information, right?" Danny asked. "I mean, you're going to present all of the evidence and make the argument for sentencing, right?"

"Wrong," Nolan said. "I need you to do everything for sentencing. That's the way it works. The jury will have heard me talk for the whole trial, and if they decide that Mr. Jones is guilty, they're not going to be so inclined to listen to me about sentencing. They need to hear it from someone else . . . from you."

"Time to fly!" Rick laughed.

Danny suddenly appeared very nervous. "But I've never been in front of a jury yet."

"You'll have to start somewhere. And sentencing is a good start," Nolan said. "You can do it, I have faith in you."

"I'll do my best."

Nolan smiled. Danny looked like he wanted to throw up and he wasn't even in the courtroom yet.

"You don't look so good."

Danny shifted in his chair and glanced over Nolan's shoulder to the window before turning to Rick. "I think we better tell him."

"Oh my God," Rick rolled his yes. "You're such a chicken shit. I knew you'd fucking fold."

"What?" Nolan was confused.

"Rick and I did something that I'm thinking you should probably know about," Danny confessed.

"What's that?" Nolan asked.

"Well . . . ." Danny glanced at Rick, unable to hold back. "Well . . . it's like this, we made this case file that was a replica of our Larice Jones file, except that we left out all of the confidential information and instead, we put in a note that gave the location of the murder weapon," Danny winced. "And I left that fake file in the Commonwealth's Attorney's Office when I was over there getting discovery in another case."

Nolan raised an eyebrow and turned to Rick.

Rick smiled sheepishly. "We were gonna tell you, but we thought it would be better if you were left out of the loop."

Nolan shrugged. "That was probably a good decision. And for the record, I'm still not involved." Nolan paused for a moment and then his eyes lit up. He pushed his chair back and stepped over to the window again. "And let me guess . . . you said the gun was in the river under the bridge."

"Well, we said under the bridge, but we didn't think they'd start searching in the river!" Danny squealed as he and Rick joined Nolan at the window.

"Look there. I wonder what's happening down there by the river?" Nolan's tone was sarcastic to say the least.

Rick stepped closer and stared a few moments. "It looks like they're dragging the damned river."

"Yes, it looks like they're dragging the damned river to me," Nolan turned to Danny. "How about you, Danny? Does it look like they're dragging the damned river to you?"

Danny shook his head in shame.

"Oops," Rick offered. "Looks like this has gone a little farther than we expected."

"Yeah, I'd say so," Nolan shook his head. But even he couldn't suppress a slight grin.

The three lawyers stood in a row, staring out the window as the team of emergency personnel toiled down at the river. After a few minutes, Nolan finally broke the silence. "Did they call to let you know that you left the file at their office?"

"Yup," Rick grinned. "And here's the best part. After they called, I went over there to get my own discovery on another case this morning. And you know how they call up the lawyers and they come to the front to escort you to the conference room, right?" Rick asked.

Nolan nodded.

"Well, I waited until Mutz had come up front, and then I said, 'Hey, by the way, Danny said you called about a file that he left over here -- he wanted me to pick it up.' And the receptionist hands me the file. As Mutz is standing there, I look at the file and act really surprised. 'Oh, this is the big murder case file,' I say out loud. 'I sure hope you guys didn't snoop through it. Otherwise Danny is going to get in real trouble for forgetting it here.' And Mutz's face turned bright red."

"Did he say anything?" Nolan asked.

"Not a damn thing."

"That's funny," Nolan said without laughing.

A few more moments of silence passed before Nolan spoke again. "Well, how are you planning to fix this?"

"Don't you worry, boss, I had a plan when I wrote the words . . . just in case it came back to haunt me . . . huh, I guess like it is now."

Rick stepped over to the telephone and dialed a number. After a moment, he said, "Fred Mutz, please." Rick looked up and winked. "Everything will be fine."

"Fred? Yeah, this is Rick at the Public Defender. You got a minute?" Good. Well, I wanted to talk to you about something. See, I was just going through that murder file that Danny left over there, you know, just making sure that there wasn't any confidential information in there or anything and I came across some notes that I made when I interviewed our client. And . . ." Rick paused and chuckled, "well, I also just looked out the window and I saw a boat and a bunch of scuba divers and lots of police down by the river, and I got to thinking about what was going on. Well, I'm sure it's just a coincidence but I hope you guys aren't searching that river because of something you may have accidentally seen in the file,

I mean, I've got to tell you, I wrote down the fact that our client hid under the bridge when he heard about the murders . . . he was afraid the same person that killed the family was going to kill him too, and anyway, I hope you didn't take that to mean that he hid any evidence under the bridge. I mean, I hate to see the city wasting their resources on such a misunderstanding."

"No? Well, that's good. Yeah, I didn't think you would've accidentally seen the notes, I mean, they were buried in the middle of the file and everything, but I just wanted to make sure of it. I know it's got to be awfully expensive for the city to drag the river and all that. Just forget I mentioned anything, okay?"

"All right, goodbye," Rick smiled as he hung up the phone. "Done!" he clapped his hands and waved his fingers, as if he was a magician.

Nolan finally chuckled.

"That's not very nice -- you don't play well with others."

"No," Rick chuckled, "that's what they said on my grade school report card too."

"I'm the same way," Nolan picked up the phone and punched the number pad. "Now it's my turn."

Rick raised an eyebrow and glanced at Danny.

"Fred Mutz, please," Nolan winked at Rick as he pushed the speaker button and leaned back in his chair. "This is going to be good."

A moment later, Fred's voice came on. "This is Fred Mutz."

"Hello Fred, Nolan Getty here. I just got the complaint you filed with the Bar Association and wanted to talk to you about it."

"What's to talk about?" Fred answered. "You should be talking to the Bar, not me."

"Well, that's the thing," Nolan continued. "I just thought you might want to know why I didn't file a discovery motion and all that legal mumbo jumbo stuff . . . I was hoping that you would call the Bar and tell them it was all a big mistake."

"Why would I do that?" Mutz asked.

"Well, because I have a very good reason for not filing that motion."

"And what's that?" Mutz asked.

"Jones is pleading guilty," Nolan glanced at Rick and Danny. "I didn't tell you because I was hoping Keene would give him some sort of plea offer at the last minute, but I guess that's not the case, so it's time I let the cat out of the bag."

Mutz was silent.

"Fred, you still there?"

"Yeah, I'm here," he sounded excited. "So there's not going to be a trial?"

"That's right," Nolan nodded. "I talked him into pleading guilty. He'd rather take his chances with the judge for sentencing rather than have a jury sentence him to life. He's already signed the "guilty plea" form, but I also told him we would keep it a secret in hopes that you would offer him a plea deal. Now, you can imagine what would happen if he finds out I told you our secret. He's not going to be a very happy camper, is he?"

"No, I don't suppose," Mutz agreed.

"That's why I need you to keep this a secret. When we get to the trial date, I'll just tell him that you didn't offer a deal and then he'll plead guilty and we'll all get on with our lives. Sound good to you?"

"Yeah, sure. That'll work for me," Mutz chuckled.

"But we have to work together on this," Nolan continued. "You have to contact the Bar and tell them you're withdrawing your complaint. Otherwise, I will have to respond and tell them I didn't file the motions because my client is pleading guilty. And when my client finds out I showed his cards, he's probably going to create a big stink . . . he might even get new counsel and force a trial."

"Yeah, I see what you mean," Fred responded.

"Now, I know that Keene probably put you up to this complaint, so I don't hold it against you. But he doesn't have to know about any of this. We can't afford to let this get out, otherwise the whole deal is down the drain."

"Uh-huh," Mutz grunted.

"So is it a deal? You withdraw the complaint and my client pleads guilty as planned?"

Mutz was silent for a moment. "Sure, you got yourself a deal."

"Very good. We'll see you at the guilty plea . . . uh, I mean the *trial*," Nolan heaped on the sarcasm, hoping Mutz would fall for it.

"Yes, we'll see you at the *trial*," Mutz chuckled.

Nolan clicked the speaker button and grinned.

"You're a dirty bastard!" Rick jumped from the couch and held his hand up. Nolan high-fived him.

"I can't believe it! You are one slick son of a bitch!"

"I told you I don't play well with others."

They both laughed.

"I didn't know he was going to plead guilty," Danny looked shocked.

Nolan and Rick paused to glance at each other, then they both broke into laughter again. Rick fell into the couch, convulsing and cackling like a maniac.

Nolan paused between his laughter just long enough to spurt out, "I didn't either," which led to another burst of hyena-like laughter.

Danny smiled and shook his head, "Oh, I think I get it."

CHAPTER 29

Keene was enraged when Mutz told him about the call from Rick. He knew immediately that the Public Defender office had planted the file and the notes. But in the few days following the river incident, Keene's raging inferno slowly waned into a burning determination that churned deep in his stomach. Putting everything else aside, he began to focus his entire energy on the Larice Jones trial. It wasn't about the conviction anymore. That was just going to be icing on the cake compared to the joy of humiliating Getty at trial.

His first reaction was to fire Fred Mutz on the spot. By snooping through Getty's file, Mutz had not only jeopardized the entire case, he had also come close to putting a stain on the entire Commonwealth's Attorney's Office. But for the time being, Keene knew that he had Mutz where he wanted him. Now all he had to do was light a fire under him to get him going. Mutz still hadn't found a snitch and he still hadn't produced any jail calls from the Defendant. Irritated, Keene dialed Mutz on the telephone.

"Yes, Mr. Keene," Mutz answered on the first ring. "What can I do for you?"

Keene paused. "What can you do for me? I'll tell you. Where in the hell are the telephone recordings I asked for?"

"Uh, I'm going to go up there next week to get them. I already talked to Captain Danforth at the jail and he's putting everything there is on a disk for us."

"Well, that's a start, I guess. What about the other thing . . . how many of the Defendant's inmates have you interviewed?"

Mutz paused. "Uh, I've talked to a few."

"A few?" Keene asked. "What do you mean a few? You should have talked to them all by now."

"Well, I actually talked to a guy who said he had some info, but then I got sidetracked."

"Jesus Christ, Mutz, what are you telling me?" Keene screamed. "I told you to get this done and I meant it! Now you're telling me you got sidetracked? What the hell are you doing?"

"Well, I guess I better tell you now," Mutz quickly folded. "I wasn't supposed to say anything, but Getty told me the defendant's pleading guilty."

Keene paused. "What do you mean he's pleading guilty?"

"That's what he said. He said that's the reason he never filed for discovery and all that. He said his client's pleading guilty. There's not going be a trial, Mr. Keene."

Keene was silent for a moment, but then he burst into laughter. "Are you kidding me?" he sputtered out between laughter. "Okay, that's a good one. That's a real fucking good one. And so why is it that you didn't tell me this?"

"Uh, because Getty said if the word got out, his client might make a big fuss and maybe get a new attorney and then force a trial. I wanted to tell you . . . I guess looking back now, I know I should've told you, but I just didn't want to ruin our deal."

Keene continued to chuckle. "Deal? What deal?"

"I withdrew the Bar complaint you made me file and he's going to make his client plead guilty."

Keene burst into laughter again, but this time, it was a haunting, maniacal rant that almost scared Mutz.

"What's so funny?" Mutz finally interrupted.

"Oh, I'm sorry," Keene collected himself before his tone changed. "I just had no idea how fucking ignorant you are!" he screamed.

"What do you mean?" Mutz squealed.

"Do you really believe that story? I mean, are you really that dumb to believe a tale like that?"

Mutz was silent.

"It's a ploy," Keene softened his voice. "It's a God-damned ploy, and you fell for it."

"A ploy?" Mutz asked.

"Yeah, it's a fucking ploy, open your eyes and wake up!" Keene raised his voice again. "He got you to withdraw the complaint and at the same

183

time, he gets you to slack up on trial preparation. Now isn't that a nice little stunt?"

Mutz stammered, "I had no idea."

"Yeah, well, I guess at least you told me before it was too late. What's this about an inmate with information?"

Mutz seemed glad to move on with the conversation. "Oh, his name's right here." Keene could hear Mutz rifling through papers. "Here it is, Gamond Edwards."

"What does he know?"

"He wouldn't say. He just told me that he has information about the murders and that the only person he will talk to is the Chief Prosecutor," Mutz answered.

Keene reached over and typed the name into his database. Edwards was in jail on pending charges of cocaine distribution. Clicking onto his criminal history, the defendant's convictions rolled by on the screen. Not seeing any perjury charges that would immediately eliminate him as a credible witness, Keene continued.

"Tell the jail that I want to see him at 9:00 a.m. sharp tomorrow morning. Meet me there at that time."

"Yes sir," Mutz said.

"What about letters?" Keene asked.

"Captain Danforth said he'd have a guy screen them for information."

"No, no, no!" Keene exploded. "A jailor isn't going to know what to look for. You need to get copies of every letter that is sent to and from him, and I want the copies kept in our file. And I want to personally read every one of them."

"Okay, okay," Mutz said defensively. "I'll talk to Danforth again."

Mutz's incompetence was driving Keene nuts. He just doesn't get it, Keene thought. No wonder Getty was always kicking his ass in the courtroom.

* * * * * * *

Early the next morning, before any visitors were allowed in the jail, Keene and Mutz arrived at the front desk. Keeping with standard operating procedure, Keene maintained a low profile when it came to interviewing jailhouse snitches. He didn't want any rumors floating around that certain defendants were snitching on other defendants. The jail had its own reasons to keep Keene's visits under the radar, as such rumors tended to incite violence amongst the inmates.

Keene and Mutz signed the log book at the front desk just as any visitor would, but from there, they were escorted to the visiting room in such a way so that no other inmates could possibly see or hear them. And when the cell block attendant retrieved Gamond Edwards, he would be informed that his lawyer was waiting to see him.

Keene and Mutz entered the small visiting booth, which was the same booth in which defense attorneys used to interview their clients. The booth was appropriately sized for one person, but two made it feel crowded. With only one chair, Mutz elected to stand next to Keene as they waited for their snitch to appear on the other side of the reinforced glass.

They already knew just about everything there was to know about Mr. Edwards. He was a twenty-eight year old African-American, being held without bond on pending charges of crack cocaine distribution, which carried five to forty years in prison. And in his case, he was caught with a huge package of crack, so he was looking at the higher end of the range.

They knew what he looked like from his booking photograph. They knew that he was six foot two inches tall and two hundred fifty pounds. They knew his criminal history, which included previous convictions for larceny, marijuana possession, cocaine possession, cocaine distribution, illegal firearms and several assault and battery charges, as well as several probation violations. From the previous probation violation reports, they also knew that he was born in Philadelphia, Pennsylvania and that he had been living in Big Shanty for the past five years. The probation reports also described his work history, which was at best, sporadic. From all reports, he appeared to be a career criminal with special emphasis on narcotics.

The door on the other side of the glass opened and a tall, thick man in orange coveralls entered the booth. The coveralls were zipped only halfway up in the front, exposing his bare chest. As the door shut behind him, he took both hands and pushed back his hair which was bunched into long dreadlocks that fell down to his shoulders. Swaggering the three steps to the counter, he looked first at Keene and then to Mutz, before his eyebrows furrowed and his lips parted in a snarl.

"Who the fuck are you?" he glared at Keene.

"I'm John Keene, the Chief Prosecutor. Are you Gamond Edwards?"

"That's me."

"You've already met my assistant, Fred Mutz," Keene nodded to his side. "We're here to see what you have to say regarding the murder case. Have a seat."

Mutz placed a small recorder on the counter in front of the glass and pushed the record button, but Keene reached over and shut it off. "Not yet," he said.

Edwards sat down in the plastic chair and leaned ahead with his face close to the glass. His eyes were not brown, like most African-American men. They were smoky-gray, cold and lifeless -- like they belonged in the head of a mannequin.

"I'll tell you what I know," he said, narrowing his eyes to gray slits. "But first I want to know what's in it for me."

"It depends upon what kind of information you have," Keene answered. "As you can imagine, we get these kinds of calls all the time and most of them don't amount to anything. Chances are, we already know what you're about to tell us. And if that's the case, it's not going to be worth much to you."

"You don't know what I got to say." He had a raspy voice that resonated in the small booth area. "So what do I get?"

"Let me explain how this works," Keene continued. "We're looking for someone with specific information that will help convict the defendant on these murder charges. And chances are that in order for such information to be effective, you would have to testify at the defendant's trial. Do you have such information and are you willing to testify at trial?"

"That depends on what's in it for me," he answered. "Can you drop my distribution charges?"

"I can't make any specific deals up front with anyone," Keene explained. "If I did, your testimony would be worthless because I'd have to disclose the agreement to the defense. But what I can tell you is that in the past, when someone has testified on behalf of the prosecution, and that testimony has been critical in obtaining a conviction, we've been able to help that person out significantly."

Gamond Edwards gave Keene a suspicious look out of the corner of his eye. He didn't appear to be very excited about the scenario. "Naw, man. I don't think so," he shook his head of dreadlocks. "I'm the one with the 4-1-1, so I give the terms. I want all my charges dropped . . . and

I want it *in writing!*" he poked the glass with his finger as he said the last two words.

With his tall, muscular stature, long dreadlocks and steel gray eyes, Gamond Edwards could have intimidated just about anyone. But he didn't scare John Keene. Turning to Mutz, Keene clenched his jaw and blinked slowly. "Would you excuse us, please?"

Mutz looked at Keene, confused. "You want me to leave?"

"Yes," Keene answered. "I'll meet you back at the office."

With a shrug, Mutz turned and exited the interview booth. When the door had closed behind him, Keene turned to the snitch behind the glass.

"Look you piece of shit," Keene said in a quiet and controlled voice. "I'm the one that runs this town, not you. You're the one facing a drug distribution charge that carries up to forty years in prison. But that doesn't matter, because you're going to do just fine . . . if you cooperate. On the other hand, if you want to withhold information and help a murderer escape conviction, then I'm going to do everything in my power to send you down for all forty of those years. And nobody . . . not even your attorney, will be able to stop me. So unless you want to spend most of your life in a ten by ten box, I suggest you start talking right now, before I walk out this door."

Edwards appeared worried. "Listen man, you don't have to be like that. I was just trying to get me the best deal . . ."

"Shut the fuck up!" Keene yelled. "And tell me what you know!"

"All right!" Edwards whined in a high raspy voice. Glancing quickly at the door behind him, he leaned ahead in his chair and lowered his tone. "I know the guy that killed that family. His name is Ice. And he told me . . . ."

"Hold on," Keene said. He reached across the counter and pushed a button on the recorder. "This is John Keene, Commonwealth's Attorney, and this is a recording of an interview with Mr. Gamond Edwards. Mr. Edwards, please tell me what you know about Larice Jones and his involvement in the murder of the Lawson family."

CHAPTER 30

August 19th, Big Shanty Circuit Court

"I call Tommy Lawson," Keene said in his loud, courtroom voice.

As the deputy retrieved Tommy, Keene stared at the jury. He knew they couldn't wait to hear the boy testify and tell them in his own words how he had found his family murdered. And although they couldn't change anything that had happened, they were all ready to do the right thing, for those that had died, and more importantly, for the one who had survived.

The young man entered the courtroom through the side door and the deputy escorted him to the stand. He was wearing what Keene had instructed him to wear; a white, short sleeved button shirt with a blue tie and tan dress pants. Keene wanted him to look nice, naïve, and innocent, but not overly formal.

As he took the stand, the jurors watched intently, and waited anxiously for him to speak. For Keene, this was the crowning moment of the trial. He had set the background with the previous witnesses. The jury already knew what, when and how it had all happened. They had seen the photographs of the crime scene, the lifeless bodies with bullet holes in them, and all of the blood that had been spilled throughout the home. Now, they would hear from the sole surviving member of the family.

"Please tell the jury your name," Keene instructed.

The young man leaned into the microphone and glanced at the jury. "My name is Tommy Lawson," he said, breaking the eerie silence of the packed courtroom.

"How old are you Tommy?"

"I'm nineteen."

"And where were you living in April of this year?"

Lawson shifted in his chair. "I was living with my mother and father, and twin brother at 21 Astor Street."

"How long had you lived there?"

"All my life," he answered. "That's where we all lived since I was born."

"Did you have a job at the time?"

"Yes sir, I was an assistant manager at Patty's Platter."

"And did your parents also work?" Keene asked.

"Yes sir, my father was a plumber and my mother cleaned houses."

"And what about your brother, Timmy?"

"Timmy didn't have a full time job, but he was working odd jobs here and there."

"And how would you describe your family relationship," Keene asked.

The young man leaned into the microphone again. "We were very close. I always thought I had the best parents in the world. They would have done anything for me and I would have done anything for them."

"Did you love them?"

Lawson paused and looked away. His face contorted into a grimace and his eyes began to blink rapidly as he tried to keep the tears back. After a moment, he finally leaned ahead and choked out, "Yes sir. I loved them very much."

A female juror in the front row pulled a handkerchief from her purse and dabbed at the corner of her eye.

"Where were you on the night of April Eleventh of this year?" Keene continued.

"I was in Richmond at a concert."

"And when did you return home?"

"I didn't get home until the next night, Monday, the Twelfth."

"Where were you until then?" Keene asked.

"I stayed in Richmond on the night of the concert, and the next day I was with a friend, Johnny Randolph, all day."

"I know this may be difficult for you, but please tell us what you found when you finally got home."

"Well, I knew there was something wrong the minute I got home. All of the lights were off in the house and the door was locked. I just knew something wasn't right. And when I opened the door . . . ." He stopped there and grimaced again. Squeezing his eyes with his fingers, he began to sob.

"Take your time," the judge said. "There's a tissue there if you need it."

The young man reached ahead and pulled a tissue from the box. He held his head down and wiped at his face. Finally, after several moments, he looked up with puppy dog eyes and blurted out through sobs, "They were all dead!"

The school teacher made an audible sniffle and began to cry openly, wiping the tears away as they rolled down her cheeks. Several other female jurors began to cry as well.

"What did you do then?" Keene continued in a comforting tone.

"I remember seeing my brother first," he sobbed. "He was on the floor in our bedroom and there was blood all over. And I touched him and knew that he was dead." He paused again to collect himself. His voice turned into a high pitched whine as he continued. "And then I found my dad on the floor at the end of the hallway and he had blood all over him. And I touched him and he was cold too. And then I saw my mom in bed." He stopped again and cried into his hands.

"Take your time," the judge reminded him.

The young man continued to cry for several seconds. Finally he looked up again and blurted out, "He shot her right in the face! Right in the face!" he said again, shaking his head and crying.

Even the male jurors began to lose the battle with their emotions. Several men were blinking rapidly, trying hard not to cry. A few others were staring directly at the defendant, as if they wanted to kill him with their own hands.

"What did you do then?"

"I called 9-1-1," he sobbed.

CHAPTER 31

Nolan and Danny signed in at the front desk and a jailor escorted them to the visitation booth. Within a few moments, Larice Jones appeared on the other side of the glass.

"This is Danny Roberson," Nolan said. "He's an assistant lawyer in my office and he'll be helping me at your trial."

Larice nodded to Danny as he sat down in the chair on the other side of the glass.

"I've got good news," Nolan said. "We got the tape of the anonymous 9-1-1 call and we have an expert that says the voice pattern is consistent with Timmy Lawson."

Larice grinned. "That's going to help a lot, right?" he asked.

"It may," Nolan answered. "Right now we're going to need to know some background information about you," Nolan explained. "Danny here is going to ask you some questions about your family history and the sort, just in case there's something there that can help you at trial." Nolan didn't want to tell him that the information was for sentencing -- otherwise Larice would think that they had given up.

"Ask away," Larice responded.

"Were you born here?" Danny asked.

"Yeah, I've lived here all my life."

"And do you also have family here?" Danny asked.

"My mother lives here in town over on Second Street and my younger sister lives with her."

"What about your father?"

"I never knew my father. He died before I was old enough to know better."

Danny continued with other questions. Larice had gone to school in Big Shanty until he was in the tenth grade. He dropped out of school at that time because he wanted to work and help his mother with the bills. His first job was at the Mr. Suds Car Wash, where he worked for over a year. It was at that time that he was first introduced to crack cocaine.

His crack habit started out as recreational use on weekends, but it didn't take long for the addiction to take hold and consume his life. By the end of the year, he was spending most of his paycheck on the little white rocks, and eventually, he began to miss work because of it. Some time later he lost his job because he was taking every other day off to smoke crack.

Not having any income to buy the drugs that he needed, Larice began to sell everything that his mother had accumulated, and when he ran out of personal items, he began to steal things to sell, which eventually led to his first arrest for larceny. His second arrest was for possession of crack cocaine, and things worsened from there.

That's not exactly what Larice was saying in his own words, but Nolan could read between the lines enough to know what had happened to him. He'd seen it a hundred times before; the pattern of drug use and the downward spiral that always occurred as a result.

"Is there anything that we can present to the jury about your attempts to kick the crack?" Nolan interrupted.

"I tried so many times I lost count," Larice said. "My mom even got our preacher involved and he got me signed up for a one of those rehab programs. I was in it for two weeks and I was doing real good. Me and my pastor even went down to the Boys and Girls Club and talked to them about how bad drugs are and I told them how bad it is to be in jail. But then I had a court date on a distribution charge and they sent me to jail for it. When I got out, they didn't have room for me at the program and I just went right back into it."

Danny wrote down the preacher's name and continued.

"What about your girlfriend, would she be willing to testify on your behalf?" Danny asked.

Nolan already knew the answer to that.

"We broke up right before I was arrested. She aint' gonna have nothing good to say for me," Larice answered. "My momma says that she never did like me anyways -- all she wanted was the little bit of money that I made."

Danny continued with more questions about his family and work history, until he finally ran out of things to ask.

"Do you have anything to wear for the trial, like a suit?" Nolan asked.

"Everything I had was in the house where Monica and me was living. And she's already moved back with her mother. She probably threw everything out. Besides, I didn't have no suit, anyway."

"We can get you some decent clothes," Nolan said. "That's no problem. I'll come back up next week with some clothes that you can try on and at that time we can go over what your testimony is going to be at the trial."

"All right, man," Larice said.

"We'll see you next week," Nolan said as he got up to leave. As they were opening the door to the booth, Larice stopped them.

"Hey, Mr. Getty," he said.

Nolan and Danny turned to look at him.

"Thanks for what you're doing. I appreciate it."

"We're just doing our jobs," Nolan shrugged.

"No man, it's more than that. You're the first Public Defender I ever had that seems like he cares."

"No problem," Nolan felt embarrassed. He cared all right . . . about defeating Keene. "We'll see you next week."

CHAPTER 32

August 19th, Big Shanty Circuit Court

"Your witness Mr. Getty," the judge nodded.

Nolan stood up from the defense table and buttoned his suit jacket. The Lawson boy continued to sniffle and wipe tears with a tissue as he approached the podium.

For Nolan, the cross-examination of Lawson was going to be the turning point of the trial. Up until that point, the identity of the Lawson boy had not been challenged. Nobody -- not the jury, not the judge, and not even the prosecution had any idea that Tommy Lawson was dead and that Timmy Lawson was sitting on the stand, impersonating his dead brother. Nolan hadn't mentioned his theory in opening statements and he'd been careful not to give it away during the cross-examination of previous witnesses. But now, it was finally time to unveil the truth and Nolan hoped that with a series of well planned questions, Lawson would buckle under pressure and admit that he was really Timmy Lawson. Most of all, Nolan looked forward to seeing the look on Keene's face when he dropped the bomb.

"Mr. Lawson, I want to make sure the jury and the court reporter can hear your testimony clearly, so just let me know when you're done crying," Nolan said, glancing at his watch.

Several members of the jury glared at Nolan, as if he was inhuman. They didn't understand how an attorney could be so callous to a boy that had just lost his family. After all, they had no clue what Nolan was about to show them -- that the young man on the stand had slaughtered his own family.

After a few seconds, Lawson put his tissue down. "I'm ready," he said.

"Very good, Mr. Lawson. Is it true that you and your brother were identical twins?"

"Yes," he answered.

"And being identical twins, it follows that your appearance is identical to your brother's appearance, correct?"

"That's right," the young man answered. "We looked the same."

"And what you're telling us today is that your name is Tommy Lawson and your deceased brother is Timmy Lawson?"

The young man bristled. "Yeah, I'm Tommy Lawson."

"Isn't it true that you are in fact Timmy Lawson and you're pretending to be Tommy Lawson?"

Most of the jury members turned to Nolan with a quizzical expression on their faces. Nolan cocked his head and nodded to them -- silently reassuring them that what he was asking was true. Then Nolan glanced at John Keene, who appeared to be casually writing notes, as if he wasn't listening. But Nolan knew he was.

The young man leaned into the microphone. "No," he said firmly.

"Do you remember the preliminary hearing in General District Court? The one where you first testified back in June?" Nolan asked.

"Yes."

Nolan held up the sketch that Lawson had marked. "And do you remember when I had you mark the locations of the bodies on this rough outline of your house?"

Lawson looked at the sketch and nodded. "Yeah, I remember that."

Nolan reached into his jacket pocket and retrieved the plastic baggy with the marker inside of it. He held the plastic baggie up as he approached the witness.

"And do you remember how you used this big fat marker that I gave you to mark the location of the bodies?"

Lawson shrugged. "I don't remember what marker you gave me."

"I don't suppose you do," Nolan shot back. "But what if I told you that this is the exact same marker that you held in your hand at the preliminary hearing? Would it surprise you if I told you that the fingerprints on this marker match the fingerprints of Timmy Lawson?"

For the first time, the young man appeared nervous instead of sad. But he quickly recovered. "You could have gotten that marker anywhere," he blinked rapidly.

Nolan shrugged, "That's true." And then he turned to the judge. "Excuse me, your Honor. At this time I would ask the deputy to retrieve a witness for identification purposes only."

"What are you talking about?" the judge asked.

"As part of my cross-examination, I would like to ask this witness a question about the identification of another witness," Nolan answered. "I've previously spoken with the deputy and he knows which witness to bring into the courtroom. It will only take a second."

"Very well," the judge answered. "Bring in the witness," he turned to the deputy.

The deputy exited the side door. A moment later he reentered the courtroom with a young man wearing a golf shirt and slacks. The deputy escorted the young man, who appeared to be in his late twenties, to the center of the courtroom in front of the witness box.

"Mr. Lawson, do you know the name of the gentleman standing before you?" Nolan asked.

Lawson thought for a few seconds. "No."

"Have you ever even seen this man before?" Nolan asked.

The Lawson boy shifted in his seat and squinted. "Not that I remember . . . no."

"Thank you," Nolan nodded to the deputy, who escorted the young man from the courtroom. When they had gone, Nolan continued his cross-examination.

"If you're Tommy Lawson, then you're the one who was an assistant manager at Patty's Platter, right?"

"Yeah, that's right."

"And you worked there for over a year?"

"Yeah, that sounds right."

"Tell us then, Mr. Lawson, who was your boss when you worked at the Platter for over a year?"

The young man paused for a few seconds. "My boss was the manager, and I was just an assistant," he answered.

"I mean his name. What was his name?" Nolan pressed.

The young man paused again. "I can't remember his name. So much has happened to me and I never went back there after my family was murdered."

"You worked there for over a year and you can't remember the name of your boss?"

Lawson's eyes blinked rapidly and shifted from side to side, as if he was watching a ping pong game in fast forward motion. "Like I said, it was a long time ago and I haven't been back."

"I see," Nolan glanced at the jury. "Would it surprise you if I told you that the supervisor you worked with for over a year was the gentleman who just came into the courtroom?"

Lawson flushed. With feigned casualness, he began to scratch the side of his face, but he couldn't stop his eyes from darting and blinking. "I don't remember ever talking with him."

"So if that gentleman comes into this courtroom later and tells the jury that he spent twenty hours a week with you every week for a year, and that you two had become good friends, he's lying?"

Lawson fidgeted in his chair. "I can't remember everything," he said. "But now that you mention it, I agree he was my manager. But we wasn't ever good friends."

Nolan paused to glance at the jury, noticing that most of their expressions had changed. The jury box that was once filled with sad, puppy dog faces had suddenly turned into a box full of suspicious looks. Pleased with the jury's reaction, Nolan continued.

"If you're Tommy, then you also went to a year of community college here in town, correct?" Nolan asked.

"That's right," he answered.

"And Tommy had finished his first year right before the murders occurred, correct?"

"That's right."

"Tell me then, what classes was he taking?" He purposely switched the pronouns from 'you' to 'he'.

"If I recall correctly, he had a math class, an English class, and a history class."

Nolan smiled and glanced at the jury. But it appeared that only a few jurors caught it.

"Did you just hear yourself, Mr. Lawson? You just said that *he* had a math class. You didn't say that *I* had a math class."

The witness flushed again. "Well, I was just saying it like you were saying it to me."

"What was the name of your math teacher, Mr. Lawson?" Nolan pressed.

Lawson shifted in his chair and looked at John Keene, as if he wanted him to help. But John Keene wasn't even looking up.

"What about your English teacher, Mr. Lawson? What about any teacher? Can you tell the jury the name of any teacher that you just spent a whole year with?"

The witness looked at John Keene one more time, but Keene's head was down, jotting notes on a pad of paper. He shifted in his chair again before leaning into the microphone. "I don't think I want to answer any more of your questions."

A collective murmur spread through the jury box. Nolan glanced at Keene, who appeared to be in a trance-like state.

"That's not for you to decide," Nolan responded.

The judge cut in before Nolan could continue his reprimand. "Mr. Lawson, you don't have a choice in the matter. You must answer Mr. Getty's questions," he barked.

The witness looked around in a panic, as if he wanted to run. But there was nothing he could do. There was nowhere to run.

"You're Timmy Lawson, aren't you?" Nolan asked one more time.

The young man shook his head. He leaned into the microphone and looked at the judge one more time. "I'm pleading the Fifth."

"No further questions," Nolan said, before the judge could react. He smiled at John Keene as he walked by the prosecution table.

* * * * * * *

In the beginning of Nolan Getty's cross-examination, when he had first started questioning the identity of Tommy Lawson, John Keene remained calm, assuming that it was just a desperate attempt to throw anything at the jury that might stick. But then as Getty progressed and the questions continued to whittle away, he began to feel as if his star witness had fallen on a mile long treadmill, which was whisking him far away. In his mind he tried to reach out; to save his witness from falling, but his arms were too heavy to move.

With each question, Keene's heart rate increased, pumping fresh loads of adrenalin through his body. When he felt the first rush of adrenalin and the panic welling up inside him, he tried to stop it. He reached for a pen and began to scribble notes on his notepad. But as the questions continued and the adrenalin began to flow faster than his body could absorb it, his hand began to shake and his notes degenerated into a series of senseless doodles.

Near the end of Getty's cross-examination, but only for a few moments, Keene's conscious thoughts slipped away from the reality of the proceedings, to a time and place far away from the drama that was enfolding before him. In those moments, he fell into his own pit of despair; one of great sadness and unimaginable grief.

At the same time, although he was not consciously aware of it, the pen fell from his trembling hand. And in between the random doodles that were left on the notepad, only one word stood out; one hastily scratched word that appeared to be from the hand of a broken child . . . MOTHER.

The judge quickly brought Keene back to reality. "Mr. Keene, do you have any re-direct on this witness?"

John Keene slowly stood up. "May we have a conference outside of the jury, your honor?"

"That's probably a good idea," the judge said. He turned to the jury and dismissed them to the deliberation room. While they were filing out of the box, Keene regained his composure. He walked over to the defense table and leaned down to speak to Nolan.

"If you don't mind, I'd like to get to the bottom of this. Do you have any objection to me speaking privately with Mr. Lawson during the recess?" he asked.

"Knock yourself out," Nolan nodded.

After the jury was gone, Keene addressed the court.

"With your permission, and of course with the permission of the defense, I'd like to have a private conversation with this witness. I think we need to straighten a few things out."

"Any objection to that, Mr. Getty?" the judge asked.

"No objection, your honor," Nolan smiled.

"Good luck, Mr. Keene," the judge said. He banged his gavel. "This court will reconvene in fifteen minutes."

John Keene leaned into Mutz's ear. "Bring him into the conference room at the end of the hall."

Keene pulled a manila envelope from his briefcase before turning to leave. He walked down the main aisle of the courtroom, not making eye contact with any of the spectators. Just outside the courtroom doors, Keene took a quick right in the corridor and entered a door with a sign that read, 'Lawyers Only.' It was the only restroom in the courthouse that had a locking door.

Once inside, he locked the door behind him. Placing the envelope on the counter beside the sink, he loosened his tie and turned on the cold water tap. With both hands he cupped the cold, flowing water and splashed it into his face repeatedly.

It was plainly obvious to him that the young man on the stand was indeed, Timmy Lawson. He was angry at himself more than anyone for not seeing it earlier. If he would've spent more time with him, he probably would've figured it out. But instead, he had let his victim witness advocates and Mutz deal with him.

Never again. Never again will I make such a mistake.

When he was done splashing cold water, he grabbed a paper towel and held it to his face. With his eyes closed, he slowly rubbed his face with the towel, as if he could somehow wipe away the past half hour of time. When he was done, he lowered the towel and opened his eyes.

In the mirror, he saw a grown man; a lawyer who was the Chief Commonwealth's Attorney for the City of Big Shanty; a man respected by the community and responsible for its safety.

You can't let him get away with this. It's up to you . . . and only you.

He looked at the manila envelope then, as if it was something that had been left behind by someone else. After a few moments, he finally grasped it and held it in his hand. As he held the envelope, he looked into the mirror again.

You fucking coward. See what you did. It's all your fault.

He wanted to punish himself. He wanted to feel the pain. Like a confused teenager that engages in self-mutilation, he wanted to remind himself that he was alive and that his mother was dead.

He turned the envelope over, pinched the tiny metal clasps that fastened the flap, and opened it. Reaching inside, he squeezed his eyes shut and slowly began to withdraw the photograph. When the photograph was free of the envelope, he opened his eyes and looked upon the ghastly image of his mother in death.

Much like Cleo Lawson, her face was frozen in terror. Gone were the compassionate eyes that had looked upon him with love throughout his childhood. In their place were bulging black orbs that protruded from her eye sockets. But unlike Cleo Lawson, there was a wound on the side of her head and her beautiful auburn hair was matted with blood where Richard, his stepfather, had dealt the final death blow.

There were two tendrils of blood from each nostril that separated and trailed down opposite sides of her mouth, which was agape in horror, as if she was still screaming out to him; begging for him to help her.

As he gazed into the photograph, he could still hear her screams from that night over twenty years ago. And once again, he was overwhelmed with guilt, knowing that he had done nothing to save his own mother; the only person who had ever loved him. Instead, he hid in his closet and listened to her scream until the screams finally ended.

Oh God, Mother . . . I'm sorry. I'm so sorry.

Keene's eyes welled up with tears as he thought of his defenseless mother dying at the hands of his stepfather. He was the one to blame. He knew that he if he had done something . . . anything, she may have not died that night. But he had been a coward, too afraid to do anything.

The tears spilled down his face as the sounds of that horrific night echoed in his mind. What started as an argument between her and Richard, quickly escalated into a fight. There were loud voices, accusations . . . then shouting. He had heard his mother running and the heavy footsteps of Richard chasing her. He had heard her slam the bedroom door, but less than a second later, he also heard it crash open. When he heard the violent crash, he slipped out of his bed and ran to his closet, where he buried himself under a pile of clothes and stuffed animals.

Then came the screams . . . the horrible screams that had stayed with Keene for more than twenty years. And finally, there was silence, followed by his step-father's heavy footsteps. He could still hear the loud foot stomping from room to room; the enraged man, shouting for him, searching for him, and what seemed like an eternity later, the evil man giving up his search and leaving the house.

After replaying the events in his mind, Keene began to slowly pull himself from the darkness, grasping onto the only thing that kept him sane -- the rationalization that his mother did not die in vain. There was a purpose to her death. It was all part of God's plan.

God had allowed his mother to die. God wanted him to feel the pain of losing a loved one. But at the same time, God had spared his own life that night. God had covered him in a protective cloak so that his stepfather could not find him and kill him too. And there was a reason for all of it.

In Keene's mind, it was God's plan for him to survive and to pursue a life of law enforcement. God wanted him to spend his life fighting evil doers and bringing them to justice. That's why he was given an evil stepfather. That's why his mother was taken from him. And that's why he had been saved.

As Keene rationalized his existence and all that had happened to him, he began to consciously replace his feelings of guilt and despair with anger. He was angry with the Lawson boy. He was angry with Nolan Getty. And he was angry with himself.

He brushed away his tears and quickly pushed the photograph back into the envelope. Looking into the mirror one more time, he began to whisper to himself, so quietly that it was almost inaudible.

"You did not die in vain, Mother. I promise. No killer will ever go free under my watch."

* * * * * * *

When Keene entered the conference room where Mutz and Lawson were waiting, he had a different look on his face; one of determination and resolve. Mutz looked up and noticed that Keene's eyes were bloodshot and filled with rage.

"All right, you better give it to me straight, boy," Keene said. "It's obvious that you're Timmy Lawson."

The young man sat silently, biting his lip and looking at the floor. He shook his head from side to side. "This can't be happening," he muttered. "I can't believe this is happening."

"You better start talking, son, cause you're in one big heap of trouble here!" Keene shouted.

"Fuck you!" the boy screamed with tears in his eyes. He stared at Keene with a look of pure anguish on his face. "You don't know what it's like!"

Keene exploded in anger, reaching out and grabbing the boy by the collar. "Like hell I don't! You killed your mother! So stop with the lies!" he screamed, shaking the boy.

Mutz instinctively reached out and put his arms between his boss and the witness. "Mr. Keene! Mr. Keene!" Mutz yelled.

Keene continued shaking the boy until Mutz yelled one more time. "Stop it Mr. Keene!"

Keene finally stopped shaking the boy and looked at Mutz, as if he was seeing him for the first time. Mutz's face wrinkled into a worried grimace and his voice trembled with fear. "Please . . . you're hurting him," he begged.

Keene released his grip on the boy's collar. "He's a murderer. And you want to sit here and coddle him?"

"I am not! That son of a bitch killed my family!" the boy yelled, pointing to the door. "If he knew that I was still alive, he would never stop coming after me. That's why I told everyone that I was Tommy. Because I was afraid of him!"

"Nice try," Keene said coldly. "I'm pretty sure the defense has a different theory. And that theory is going to be that you killed your own family and framed Larice Jones for it."

"You're wrong!" Timmy yelled. "I would never hurt my family. I loved them."

"You've been lying to us since the beginning. Now why should we suddenly believe anything you have to say?"

"Because I'm telling you the truth!" Timmy whined. "I didn't kill my family. And I can prove it!"

CHAPTER 33

During the recess, while Keene was questioning his star witness in private, Nolan and Danny exited the courtroom and walked down the corridor to the steel door at the end. After knocking, a small panel slid open and a deputy peered at them.

"We need to see Jones," Nolan stated.

The deputy nodded and slid the panel closed. The electronic lock beeped and the deputy opened the door for them.

Just inside the lockup door, there was a small open area with a table and chairs. Looking down the corridor, the right side was the wall shared between the lockup and the courtroom, and the left side was lined with seven cells, each of them only about eight feet by eight feet. The cells were separated from the corridor by steel mesh that ran from floor to ceiling. At the end of the corridor on the right, there was another steel door that led directly into the courtroom.

"He's down at that end," the deputy said. "You want to get inside?"

"Yeah, that would be great," Nolan answered.

Nolan and Danny emptied their pockets, placing their personal items in small plastic trays that were on the table just inside the door. When they finished, the deputy gestured for them to go down the corridor. On their way to Larice's cell, neither of them noticed the inmate in the first cell on the left, who was lying on the bench against the back wall of the cell, sleeping soundly.

As they approached the last cell, Nolan saw that Larice was pressed against the cage with his fingers poking through the metal mesh.

"Move away from the door," the deputy ordered.

Larice grinned. "Yes sir."

After Larice had backed up to the wall, the deputy opened the cage door and waved them inside. "Holler when y'all are done," he closed and locked the door behind them.

Larice came forward to greet them. "You did real good in there," he gushed, patting Nolan on the shoulder. "Did you see the look on T's face when you started asking him those questions? That was something!"

"Sometimes things work out," Nolan said. "Let's sit down."

"Are they gonna drop the charges against me now?" Larice asked.

Nolan wanted to say that they would. But after dealing with Keene and the gang for so many years, he didn't trust them to ever make the right decision. "I'm not sure. We'll see what they have to say after the recess."

"He lied to everyone!" Larice exclaimed. "He can't get away with that."

"I know," Nolan consoled him. "We'll just have to play it by ear and see what they do next."

"How about that judge? He seemed like he didn't like T lying very much."

"No he didn't," Nolan commented. "Even he could see what was happening."

They spent the rest of the time during the recess talking about the jurors and their apparent reactions. Ten minutes later, when Larice ran out of things to ask about, Nolan excused himself. "I'm going to go see what's going on," he said. "Danny will stay with you until they call us back."

Nolan hollered to the deputy, who promptly appeared and opened the cage door. After retrieving his personal items, Nolan exited the lockup just as Keene was approaching in the corridor.

"What's the deal?" Nolan asked. "Are you dropping the charges?"

Keene smiled. "I don't think so. Let's go see the judge." He turned and began to walk in the opposite direction, down the hallway towards the judge's chambers.

Nolan shook his head and followed. "You just don't know when to quit, do you?"

Keene walked without making eye contact. "I know exactly when to quit," he quipped. "After I win."

When they reached the end of the hallway, Keene rapped on the door and opened it. The judge's secretary greeted them as they entered.

"Can we see the judge?"

She pushed a button on the telephone. "The lawyers are here to see you," she said. And then she hung up the receiver. "Go ahead," she nodded to Keene.

They walked past the secretary's desk and Keene tapped on the judge's chamber door before entering his office. The judge looked up from behind his desk. "What's going on Mr. Keene?"

"It's my duty to inform you that my witness has perpetrated a fraud upon the court," he explained. "I've talked to the boy and he's admitted to me that he is really Timmy Lawson."

The judge turned to Nolan. "Why didn't you say something before the trial began, we could've saved everyone a lot of time."

Nolan shrugged. "Hey, I've tried to reason with the prosecution in the past, but it never worked, so I gave up. Besides, I'm under no obligation to reveal my defense before trial."

The judge grunted and turned to Keene. "Are you going to nolle prosequi the charges?" he asked.

"No sir."

"See what I mean?" Nolan interjected.

"We're ready to go forward," Keene explained. "I'd like to start with the redirect of Timmy Lawson."

The judge rolled his eyes. "Your main witness lied to the jury, Mr. Keene. And now you want to go forward with this?"

"That's correct, your honor. If you would allow me to redirect, I think we'll be able to clear this whole thing up."

"Suit yourself," the judge replied. "Let's get in there and get this over with."

Nolan and Keene turned and walked out of the judge's office. As they were heading back to the courtroom, Nolan couldn't help himself. He just had to get in another dig. "Whatever you're planning, it's not going to work."

"We'll see about that," Keene answered. "You played your card and now I get to play mine."

CHAPTER 34

Before court reconvened, the deputies retrieved Larice Jones from the lockup and escorted him to the courtroom. As he was being brought in, Danny joined Nolan at the table.

"What's going on?" Danny asked.

"Keene is going to redirect Timmy and continue with the trial."

"Damn," Danny shook his head.

Larice took his seat at the defense table. "What's happening?"

Nolan glanced at Larice. "You're still in a murder trial."

"They ain't droppin' the charges?" Larice practically yelled. "Why can't you do something?"

"Just relax," Nolan said. "We still have our evidence to put on."

As they waited for the jury to enter the courtroom, Nolan thought about the confession that Timmy Lawson was about to make and the implications to his case. Nolan knew that if Timmy Lawson came into the courtroom and admitted who he was, then there would be no need to bring up the fingerprint analysis on the marker and no need for him to call the restaurant manager back to testify.

When the jury returned to the courtroom and settled into the box, Keene stood up and spoke first.

"I call *Timmy* Lawson to the stand," he said as he turned to look at the jury.

Another murmur spread through the jury box.

The deputy opened the side door of the courtroom and yelled out for Timmy Lawson.

When Timmy appeared in the doorway, he did not make eye contact with anyone. With his head down, he stepped up to the witness stand and took his seat. Once he was situated, the judge leaned over. "You are still under oath," he said. "You may proceed Mr. Keene."

"Is it true what Mr. Getty has suggested? Are you really Timmy Lawson?" Keene began.

The young man leaned into the microphone. "It's true." His voice was soft and timid.

The woman in the front row of the jury box who had been quick to cry, now had a stern look on her face.

"Before today, have you ever told me that you were Timmy Lawson?" Keene asked.

"No sir, I never have. Until now."

"And do you realize that because you did not tell us the truth today, that you can and will be charged with perjury, which could possibly result in a five year prison sentence?"

"Yes sir, that's what you told me during the recess."

"Are you going to tell the truth from here on out so that you don't get any more charges?"

"I promise, I'll tell you exactly what happened."

"Thank you, Mr. Lawson," Keene continued. "Now let me take you back to the night that your family was murdered. Were you really in Richmond at a concert?"

"No sir. I made that up because that's where I thought Tommy was going to be that night. He told me he was going to that concert."

"Well, if you weren't at the concert, then where were you?" Keene glanced at Getty.

"I was in jail," Timmy answered. "In Albermarle County."

A murmur swept through the gallery.

"When did you go to jail in Albermarle County?"

"On Saturday night, April Tenth. And I didn't bond out until Monday afternoon, on April Twelfth," he answered.

As Timmy was answering, Fred Mutz entered the courtroom from the main door and nodded to Keene before sitting down at the prosecution table.

"May I have one second, your honor?" Keene asked.

The judge nodded as Keene left the podium and walked to the prosecution table where Mutz was seated. Mutz whispered into Keene's ear and then handed him two pieces of paper. Keene glanced at the papers and then smiled.

"What were you doing in Albermarle County and how did you end up in jail?" Keene asked as he returned to the podium.

"I was up in Charlottesville visiting a friend, and we were driving around town when we got pulled over by the police. They found cocaine in my car and arrested me."

"When you returned home on Monday, is everything that you told the jury earlier true? Did you really find your family murdered?"

"Yes sir, that part is true."

"So why did you lie to me and the police and tell us that you were Tommy?"

"Well, when I saw that my family had been killed, I knew right away who had done it. And I was just scared," Timmy answered. "I didn't think about it right away, but sometime between when I called 9-1-1 and when the police came, I realized that Ice probably thought that he had killed me . . . ."

"Objection," Nolan stood.

"Sustained," the judge turned to the jury. "You must disregard what the witness just said. He has no personal knowledge of who killed his family."

Keene nodded. "Mr. Lawson, just tell us why you pretended to be Tommy."

"Because I feared for my life and I wanted the killer to think that he had killed me. So I just told the police that I was Tommy. I was going to tell them the truth later, but nobody ever questioned me and so I never changed my story."

"Who were you afraid of?" Keene asked.

"Ice," Timmy answered.

"Why were you afraid of Ice?" Keene asked.

"Because I heard he was out to get me for setting him up."

"Objection, hearsay," Nolan said as he stood up.

"Sustained," the judge quickly said. "You are to disregard the last statement of the witness," he said to the jury.

"Who is Ice?" Keene asked.

Timmy pointed to the defendant. "That guy right there. Larice Jones."

"Your honor, at this time I would like to introduce two exhibits, which I have marked for identification as Commonwealth Exhibit Seventeen and Eighteen." As he talked, he approached the defense table and handed the documents to Nolan for his review.

Nolan took the documents from Keene and held them between him and Larice so that they could both review them. They were fax sheets with a date and time that indicated transmission to the Commonwealth Attorney's office just minutes earlier. The first page was Timmy Lawson's arrest warrant, which indicated that he had been arrested at 6:40 p.m. on April 10th by the Charlottesville Police Department -- the evening before the murders had taken place. The second page was the discharge record from Albermarle County Adult Detention Facility, and it showed that Timmy Lawson had been released in the late afternoon of April 12th.

Danny leaned into Nolan's ear and whispered, "This is bad . . . this is real bad."

Nolan turned and looked Danny in the eye. "Just calm down and relax," he said. "And keep your mind clear. For all we know, Keene had his secretary type this crap up and fax it over."

Nolan handed the documents back to Keene.

"May I approach the witness, your honor?" Keene asked. The judge nodded and Keene approached the witness stand.

As Keene was approaching the witness stand, Nolan stood up. "Your honor, I object to those exhibits. Lack of authentication."

Before the judge could respond, Keene cut in. "Your honor, I'm going to have the witness authenticate the records."

"I request argument outside the presence of the jury and the testifying witness," Nolan responded.

"Very well," the judge said. He turned to the jury. "Please follow the bailiff to the deliberation room while we discuss some evidentiary matters." And then he turned to Mr. Lawson. "Please wait in the conference room while we discuss the evidence."

After Lawson and the jury had filed out, the judge continued. "What's your argument, Mr. Getty?"

"I don't believe that this witness has the ability to authenticate the second document that Mr. Keene is attempting to admit."

"Give me those documents, Mr. Keene," the judge ordered. Keene walked to the bench and handed the judge the papers.

"As you can see, your Honor, the second page purports to be a jail record. Unlike an arrest warrant, which must be given to the defendant, the jail record is a record which is not given to the defendant. Therefore, there is no way that he can possibly authenticate a document that he never received."

"Your Honor," Keene cut in. "First of all, this is a government record. Secondly, if you look at the bottom of the document, you will see that there is a certification and it says, 'I, Mark Jeffries, am the custodian of records at the Albermarle Adult Detention Facility and I certify that this document is a true and accurate copy of such records.' Therefore, it is self-authenticating."

"What do you say to that, Mr. Getty?" the judge asked.

"There is no statute that allows this type of authentication in a criminal matter such as this. And there's a reason for that. For all I know, Mark Jeffries could be Mr. Keene's dead brother-in-law and this could be a fake document because nobody present in this courtroom can swear to its authenticity."

"What statute are you relying on for self-authentication, Mr. Keene?" the judge asked.

Keene glared at Nolan. "I'll have to look it up, your honor. He quickly pulled a code book from his briefcase and paged through it. After a few seconds, he read from a specific statute. According to the statute he cited, certified copies of government records were self-authenticating and allowed to be submitted into evidence. Nolan opened his own code book and paged to the statute that Keene cited.

"Your Honor, this statute is listed under the rules of civil procedure," Nolan argued. "And this is obviously criminal procedure. Therefore it does not apply in this criminal trial."

The judge reviewed his own code book and then looked to Keene. "I believe Mr. Getty is correct on this one. Unless you can cite a criminal procedure rule on point, I'm afraid that this exhibit is not self-authenticating."

Keene sat down in defeat. "Please note my objection."

It was a small, but important win for Nolan. Although Timmy testified that he was released on April 12th, the jury would not see any corroborating proof of the matter. Therefore, Nolan could still argue that Timmy was lying about his release date and that he got out of jail and returned to Big Shanty in time to commit the murders.

"How do you come up with this stuff?" Danny whispered as Nolan took his seat.

Nolan leaned into Danny's ear. "RTFS," he whispered.

Danny nodded, then paused. "What's that?"

"My professor in law school taught me that you can't win cases unless you RTFS."

Danny looked confused.

"Read the fucking statutes," Nolan whispered.

When everyone had returned to the courtroom, Keene handed the arrest warrant to Timmy, who authenticated the document. He ended his redirect examination there.

"Any further cross-examination?" the judge asked.

Nolan stood up and approached the podium.

"So it's true that you lied to the jury today, correct?" Nolan nodded to the jury box.

"Yeah," Timmy answered. "But I just told you why."

"So even though you've been under oath and you've sworn to tell the truth, it's okay to lie if it suits your own interests?" Nolan asked.

Timmy shrugged. "I told you, I was afraid. That guy is a killer," he pointed to Larice.

"But now that I've exposed your lies, it suddenly suits your own interests to attempt to create an alibi, doesn't it?" Nolan prodded.

"I'm telling you how it is, that's all."

"Mr. Lawson, do you remember the preliminary hearing where you testified under oath?"

"Yeah."

"Isn't it true that you stated, under oath, that you stayed over night in Richmond after going to a concert on Saturday, April Tenth?"

Timmy hesitated. "Yeah, that's what I said, but it wasn't true."

"So you lied under oath at the preliminary hearing as well, right?"

"Yeah, that's right."

"You say you were with a friend when you were arrested. Did you bring that friend here today to testify to that fact?"

"I didn't know that I would have . . . ." Before he could finish his sentence, Nolan interrupted him.

"It's a yes or no question, Mr. Lawson. Is there any person here today to corroborate your version, yes or no?"

"No," he shifted in his chair.

"And is there any person here today who can verify when you were supposedly released from jail?"

"No."

"Isn't it true that since your family was murdered, you have purchased a brand new car?"

Timmy fidgeted in his chair before answering. "Yeah, I needed a new car, so I bought one."

"Where have you been working since the murders?"

"Just odd jobs, here and there."

"Odd jobs?" Nolan asked. "Like what kind of odd jobs?"

"Like yard work and landscaping labor."

"Who employs you in these odd jobs?"

"No one in particular, I just go down to the corner on weekends and people show up and ask if I want a job."

"And how much do they usually pay per hour?"

"Ten bucks or more."

"If you make ten bucks an hour on weekends, and you work maybe twenty hours a week, that's two hundred a week, then wouldn't it take you over a year to buy a twenty thousand dollar car?"

Timmy shrugged. "I don't know, I'm not so good with math. Besides, I had other money."

"Other money from what? Selling crack cocaine?"

"My dad had life insurance."

Nolan felt the surge of excitement rush through him, as if he had just scratched off a winning lotto ticket. He was only trying to show the jury that Timmy had other sources of money. He didn't really expect Timmy to reveal the true source. His plan was to fill in the blanks during closing argument; perhaps suggest that it was either drug money or insurance money. But Timmy had just done it for him.

"How much life insurance?" Nolan asked.

"Ten thousand," Timmy answered.

Nolan glanced at the jury with a raised eyebrow before continuing his cross-examination.

"Let me take you back to the night that you worked for the cops and set Larice up for an arrest. That's not the first time that you had purchased drugs from him, was it?"

"No it wasn't."

"You've known Larice Jones for quite awhile now, haven't you?"

"Yes, for a few years now."

"And you claim that during the last few years, Larice has been supplying you with drugs to resell to other people, correct?"

"That's true."

"So tell me, Mr. Lawson, if you know so much about selling drugs, what is a tenth of a gram of crack cocaine worth?"

Timmy answered without hesitation. "Twenty dollars."

"That's it, twenty dollars?"

"That's it."

"And just how big is a tenth of a gram of crack cocaine?"

"Like in size?" Timmy asked.

"Yeah, is it like the size of a marble?"

"No, it's small. Like the eraser on the end of a pencil," Timmy answered, showing the jury by holding his index finger and thumb close together.

"So if you know the value of a tenth of a gram of crack and you know the size of it, then how is it that on the night that you set up Larice, you paid him two hundred dollars for forty dollars worth of crack?"

"I don't remember the exact amounts, it was a long time ago."

"Well if I tell you that I have the records that show it was about two-tenths of a gram of crack cocaine, and also that Agent Calhoun has testified today that you gave Larice two hundred dollars, you couldn't argue with those facts, could you?"

"I guess not, if that's what it was, then that's what it was."

"So I'll ask you again, why did you pay two hundred dollars for forty dollars worth of crack?" Nolan prodded.

"If I remember right, I think I was paying him for something that he had given me previously."

Another surge of excitement hit Nolan. Timmy was becoming a real fountain of truth, bubbling out honest answers and trickling life into Nolan's defense with each response. Perhaps he will eventually just admit that he killed his family, Nolan thought.

"So Larice fronted you drugs on a previous occasion and you were paying him back for something that you already sold, correct?"

"Yeah, I think that's what the deal was," Timmy responded.

"But you didn't tell the officers that did you? Because according to Agent Calhoun's testimony today, you told him that you were buying two hundred dollars of crack cocaine from Larice that night, correct?"

"That's probably true. I probably left out the background details. I mean, I wouldn't have wanted to tell Agent Calhoun that I had been buying and selling drugs before that."

"So once again, when it suited your purpose, you lied, didn't you?"

Lawson shrugged.

"I need a yes or no answer, Mr. Lawson. You lied, didn't you?"

"Yes."

"And isn't it also true that the gold watch found in my client's possession was the watch that you gave him as collateral for fronted drugs?"

Timmy glanced at Keene before answering. "Yes, that's true."

Nolan smiled. Timmy's answer was almost too good to be true. He was finally regaining some traction.

Nolan glanced at Keene, who was playing ignorant and doodling on his notepad.

"And on the night that you set up Larice on the drug exchange, isn't it true that you stole about 125 grams of crack cocaine from him?" Nolan continued.

Timmy looked surprised. "No," he answered, darting his eyes from side to side.

"Isn't it true that you scraped off the two crack rocks, the same two crack rocks that you later gave to the police, and then you hid the rest in your car?"

"No," Timmy shifted his eyes again.

"And isn't it true that after stealing the drugs and sending Larice to jail, you went to the house that he shared with his girlfriend and tried to get her to give you the other half of the drugs?"

"No," Timmy answered.

"But when she didn't give you the drugs, you came back and broke into the house, and you stole the drugs, as well as the gun that Larice owned, didn't you?" Nolan asked.

Timmy shook his head. "No."

"And then you used that gun to kill your own family, just so that you could frame Larice and send him to prison for life, didn't you?"

"No!" Timmy shouted. "I did not!"

"No further questions," Nolan stated.

CHAPTER 35

"I call Monica Lee," Keene stated loudly.

Nolan had seen her name on the Commonwealth's subpoena list that Danny had retrieved from the clerk's office, but he couldn't figure out why they wanted her to testify. He had asked Eric to contact her again in an attempt to find out if the police had talked to her but she never answered her door or returned his calls. He could only hope that her testimony would be just filler information regarding Larice's background.

After shouting her name through the side door, the deputy held it open and Monica Lee appeared in the courtroom. The first thing that Nolan noticed was her tall beehive hairdo which jutted up in the air like a cone. She was wearing a bright orange, velvet-looking sweater that went down below her waist, covering her large rear end. Her fat legs stuck out below the sweater, stuffed into black spandex pants. The combination of hair, orange top, and black pants made her appear as if she was dressed for Halloween, in a homemade pumpkin costume.

As she waddled to the stand, she glanced over to the defense table and made eye contact with Larice. Lifting her nose at Larice, she quickly broke eye contact and stepped up into the witness box, assisted by the deputy.

After Monica Lee was situated on the stand, Keene began his questioning.

"Please state your name for the jury."

"Monica Lee," she answered.

"What is your relationship with Larice Jones?" Keene asked.

"I was his girlfriend."

"And back in April of this year, where were you living?"

"I was living at Seventeen Sherman Street," she lisped.

"Was there anyone else living at that address?"

"Yes, Larice was also living there with me," she nodded towards Larice.

"Larice Jones, the defendant?"

"Yes."

"And how long had you been living together at that address?"

"About six months," she glanced at Larice.

"And what was your telephone number when you lived at that address?"

Monica Lee thought for a few seconds before answering. "It was 386-9642."

"Let me take you back to April Eleventh of this year, the night that the Lawson family was murdered. Do you remember that night?"

"Yes."

"Where were you that night?"

"I was staying at my mother's house."

"Were you with Larice Jones?"

"No, I was not," she shook her head. "We had a fight that day and I went to stay at my mother's house."

"What was the fight about?"

"Objection," Nolan interrupted. "Irrelevant."

"No problem," Keene didn't wait for the judge to rule. "And how did you get to your mother's house?"

"I walked."

"Why did you walk?" he asked. "Don't you have a car?"

"I have a car, but Larice had the keys to it and he wouldn't give them to me."

"What kind of car is it?"

"A 1997 Ford Thunderbird."

"And what color is it?"

"Blue."

"And so Larice had your 1997 Blue Thunderbird on April Eleventh?"

"That's right," she nodded.

"Did he ever bring it back to you?"

"No," she glared at Larice. "I had to go get it back. My mother had an extra set of keys, so I just went back over to Sherman Street later and took the car back without him knowing about it."

"When did you do that?" Keene glanced at the jury.

"It was definitely after April 11th, like the next day or so."

"By the way, Ms. Lee, what is the telephone number at your mother's house where you were staying?" Keene asked.

"It's 384-0021."

Thank you, Monica, that's all the questions I have," Keene ended.

Nolan found it interesting that Keene had called Monica Lee to the stand to talk about her car. Obviously, his line of questioning had something to do with Larice possessing the car on the night of the murders, but Nolan didn't have any other information that would allow him to connect the dots on Keene's picture. So he did the only thing he could do during cross examination -- he pursued his own interests.

"Do you remember when Larice was arrested for selling drugs to Timmy Lawson?" Nolan asked as he approached the podium.

"Yes."

"You and Larice were living together on Sherman Street at the time, correct?"

"That's correct."

"And shortly after Larice's arrest, when he was in jail, isn't it true that Timmy Lawson came to your house asking for drugs?"

"Yes. He showed up at my door and told me that I was supposed to give him drugs that Larice had."

"And did you give him any drugs?"

"No sir. I had no idea what he was talking about."

"If Larice had been storing illegal drugs in the house, would've you known about it?"

"No sir. I'm against drugs and I don't want nothing to do with them."

"And isn't it true that the very next day, your house was burglarized?"

"That's correct."

"Did you call the police about that burglary?"

"Yes sir, they came out to the house and took a report."

"Did the burglar take anything of value?"

"Just some money that was in my spice jar."

"Did you have a television, stereo and other electronics?"

"Yeah, I had all that," she crossed her arms.

"Were those items stolen?"

"No."

"And what condition did the burglar leave your house in?"

"It was a mess," she leaned ahead to the microphone. "The furniture was tipped over, the drawers in the kitchen were all pulled out. The pictures on the wall were pulled down. Everything was torn up."

"Were you aware that Larice had a gun in the house?"

"I don't know nothing about no gun," Monica shook her head.

So if Larice had a gun in the house, and it was stolen in the burglary, you wouldn't even know it, would you?"

"Nope," she answered, this time glancing at the jury as she shook her head.

"And if Larice had drugs in the house which were stolen during the burglary, you wouldn't know that either, right?"

"That's right."

"Thank you Ms. Lee, that's all the questions I have," Nolan finished.

CHAPTER 36

"Captain Wayne Danforth," Keene stated loudly.

The deputy opened the side door and retrieved the next witness. He was a slightly overweight, middle-aged man with a mop of red hair and black, horn-rimmed glasses. Unlike the other police officers that had taken the stand, he was wearing a white shirt with more colorful emblems on the shoulders and a large golden badge. His pants were royal blue with a gold stripe down the sides, and freshly pressed. He had no utility belt, no holster, and no weapon; just a very fancy uniform and a large badge. Without the belt and sidearm, he looked like a cheap impersonator, rather than a real police officer.

"What is your name and occupation?" Keene asked.

"I am Captain Wayne Danforth and I am the commanding officer at the Big Shanty Adult Detention Facility."

When Nolan had seen the captain of the jail on the subpoena list, he immediately questioned Larice about his activity at the jail. But Larice insisted that he had not done anything wrong since he had been arrested. He also claimed that he hadn't spoken to anyone about the case, either by telephone or by mail.

"Back in January of this year, did you have Larice Jones as an inmate in your facility?" Keene continued.

"Yes we did."

So that's it, Nolan thought. Larice did something when he was in jail for the distribution charge -- not during his current incarceration.

"And why was he in your facility at that time?" Keene asked.

"He was incarcerated pending trial on charges of distribution of crack cocaine."

"Is there a telephone system that inmates can use to make calls outside of the jail?"

"Yes sir. In each wing there is a telephone. Inmates are allowed to make collect calls only."

"And what is the procedure for making a collect call?"

"The inmate must first punch in his identification code, and then he is allowed to dial a telephone number. The call is connected only if the party answering the call agrees to accept the charges."

"Are the calls made by inmates recorded?"

"Yes, both the identification number of the inmate and the outside number that they are calling are stored in a database. In addition, the audio of every call is digitally recorded."

"Pursuant to my request, did you find any telephone calls made by Larice Jones while he was incarcerated at that time?"

"Yes I did," Danforth answered.

"And did Larice Jones enter your facility a second time?"

"Yes he did," Danforth looked at a notepad. "He returned to our facility on April 13th of this year when he was arrested on his current charges."

"And pursuant to my request, did you find any telephone calls made by Larice Jones while he has been incarcerated on the current murder charges?" Keene asked.

"Yes I did."

Nolan sighed as he glanced over at his client. Larice was shaking his head, as if he had no idea what the captain was talking about.

"And is the CD that you are holding the recorded telephone conversations of Larice Jones?" Keene asked.

"That's correct."

"How many calls are on the CD?"

"All together, there are three calls -- two from his incarceration in January, and one from his current incarceration."

Nolan looked at Larice again and shook his head. "I told you the phone calls are recorded," he whispered.

"What are the dates and times of these phone calls?" Keene asked.

The first Two. One was on January 12th at 3:40 p.m., the second and the other wwas on January 15th at 3:32 p.m., and the third was on April 16th, at 3:36 p.m."

"And what number did Larice Jones call?"

"On the first two calls, the number was The number was three eight six, nine six four two.386-9642. On the third call, the number was 384-0021."

"Your honor, at this time I would ask that the CD, which is Commonwealth's Exhibit Nineteen, be admitted into evidence."

Nolan had no legitimate objection to the recording. He knew that any statements made by a defendant could be used in court, regardless of any hearsay argument. He could only stare at Larice in disappointment.

"Any objection?" the judge asked.

Nolan shook his head. "No sir."

Keene popped the CD into his laptop computer and pushed a button to play it. An automated voice began the call.

"You have a collect call from the Big Shanty Adult Detention Facility. Press one to accept the charges."

There was a beep and the voice of Larice Jones followed.

"Hey baby, what's up?"

A female voice responded. "Where the fuck are you? They said this call is from the jail!"

"Yo, T set me up. He's a narc for the Five-O and he got me arrested."

"What?" the female voice yelled. "Arrested for what?"

"Distribution. And if you see that punk-ass bitch, you tell him he's a dead man when I get out."

"When are you getting out?" she asked.

"I don't know yet. Hopefully soon. I have a bond hearing Thursday."

"What are we going to do?" she asked. "What if you can't get out? How am I gonna cash your checks?"

"Don't worry about that. Look, I got to go now."

Keene reached over and pushed a button on the computer. He clicked a few more times before turning to Captain Danforth. "Was that the first call that was made on January 12th at 3:40 p.m.?"

"That's correct," Danforth nodded.

Several jurors eyed Larice with disapproval. Based on their expressions, it was as if Keene had just cleaned their glasses and they could finally see the evilness of the defendant.

Keene clicked a button on the computer again. There was a moment of silence followed by the automated voice which announced another collect call. A beep followed and Larice's voice came on again.

"Yo. How you doin'?"

"I'm not doing too damn good!" Monica shrieked.

"What's going on?" Larice asked.

"T was here the other day and he said that you told him that he was supposed to pick up the other stuff."

"I told you, that motherfucker is a narc!" Larice hissed. "He's a dead son of a bitch! Did you tell him what I told you? That he ain't gonna get away with it?" Larice yelled.

"I just told him that I didn't know what he was talking about," Monica answered.

Keene pushed another button on the computer to stop the audio. "And was that the second call made on January 15th at 3:36 p.m.?"

"That's correct," Danforth answered.

Reaching to his computer one more time, Keene pushed the button again. After the automated voice announced the collect call, a female voice accepted the charges and the conversation began.

"Stop making collect calls to my house!" the female voice yelled.

"Mrs. Lee!" Larice's voice whined. "I have to talk to your daughter. Just let me talk to her one time."

"She's done with you," the voice answered.

"Please, Mrs. Lee, it's very important. If you just let me talk to her one time, I'll stop calling."

There was a moment of silence before the female voice continued. "One time. That's it. Then you leave us alone, or I'm calling the cops."

The same female voice yelled out, "Monica! Come answer the God-damned telephone! There's some stupid-ass motherfucker want to talk to you!"

A few seconds later, Monica's voice came on the line.

"Hullo."

"I've been trying to call you at home -- where you been?" Larice asked angrily.

"I'm done with you. I cleared my stuff out and I ain't going back."

"Just listen to me," Larice whined. "They got me in jail for murdering T and his family. You got to tell them that you were with me the whole night and we were watching T.V. It was last Sunday. Find a T.V. schedule so you know what was on so you can tell them what we was watching."

"No fucking way!" Monica yelled. "I ain't about to lie for your sorry ass. It's over between us. And I ain't ever coming back. So don't you ever call back here again, or my mama's gonna call the cops!"

The phone clicked and the conversation ended.

Just so we're clear, those calls were made by Larice Jones?" Keene asked. and they were made to the number 386-9642, correct?"

"That's correct," Captain Danforth answered.

"No further questions," Keene finished. He pushed the eject button on his computer and the CD pushed out. As he returned to the prosecution table, he smiled and winked at Nolan.

"Hold on one minute, there," Nolan said. "Your honor, I may be mistaken, but it seems to me that there was more conversation that may have occurred in those telephone calls. And the defense has a right to hear the entire conversation, not just a little snippet."

The judge turned to Keene. "Mr. Keene, have you played the entire conversations from the telephone calls?"

"I played the relevant portions, but the defense is correct. There are further conversations that I didn't play because they have no relevance to these proceedings."

"Your honor, I'd ask for a short recess to review the recordings before we continue," Nolan said.

The judge ordered a short recess and the jury was sent to the deliberation room.

During the recess, Nolan played the CD on his own computer while listening to the audio with ear buds. When he was finished listening to the remainder of the telephone calls, he realized that Keene's interpretation of relevance was just a bit different than his own. More importantly, it was clear that Monica Lee had been lying about her knowledge regarding the drugs.

After the jury had returned to the courtroom following the recess, Nolan immediately worked the recordings into his cross-examination.

"Captain Danforth, what we just heard in the courtroom was not the full extent of the telephone recordings was it?"

"I believe there was more conversation on the first two calls, but that was the extent of the third call," No, the conversations continued," Danforth shifted in his chair.

"Is this the remainder of the first conversation?" Nolan asked, as he clicked to the end of the first callhe played the CD from where Keene had left off where Keene had stopped.

Larice's voice continued during the first call. "But I need you to do something for me. Call J and tell him that T is a narc and he stole the shit."

"What do you mean?" she asked. "He's got your stuff?"

"Yeah, tell J he stole everything."

"But you still got the other half here, right?" the female asked.

"Yeah, I only gave T half of it. But you tell J that T took the whole thing. That motherfucker wants to play games, we'll see how he likes my games."

"What should I do with the stuff that's here?"

"Just keep it in a safe place until I get out. I've got to go. Bye."

"Bye."

Nolan stopped the recording. "That's the extent of the first call, right?" he asked.

"That's right," Captain Danforth answered.

Nolan pushed a button on his computer to start the second conversation where Keene had stopped. . After the part that the jury had already heard, the remainder of the conversation played.

"You didn't give him the stuff, did you?" Larice asked.

"No. But it's gone," she answered.

"What?" Larice yelled. "What do you mean it's gone?"

"It's fucking gone!" she yelled. "Someone broke into the house and stole it!"

"When?"

"Yesterday."

"Did you talk to J?" Larice asked.

"Yeah, I called him a few days ago."

"What'd you tell him?"

"I told him what you said to tell him. I told him that you were in jail and that T is a narc and he stole the stuff."

"What did he say?" Larice asked.

"He said that's not what he heard from Timmy. He said that Timmy told him that you were the narc and that you were trying to steal the stuff without paying for it."

"That motherfucker!" Larice yelled.

"What have you got yourself into?" Monica whined. "J said he wants the money for the stuff or he's coming after you. What are we going to do?"

"I'll figure it out," Larice answered. "Just stick with me and we'll get out of this just fine." The phone clicked and the call ended without any goodbyes.

"I don't have any further questions for this witness," Nolan said, popping the CD from his computer and handing it back to Keene.

Although it was very bad that Larice had verbalized an intention to kill Timmy, Nolan gained some comfort in knowing that Larice had not lied to him about Timmy stealing his drugs and then showing up at the house to ask for the other half. Everything that was said on the recordings was consistent with their main theory that Timmy had a reason to kill his family and frame Larice for the murders.

CHAPTER 37

"I call Gamond Edwards," Keene stated loudly, while staring at Nolan.

Nolan raised an eyebrow and looked at Danny. "I don't remember that name on the subpoena list."

Danny opened a manila folder and began shuffling through papers. A moment later, he turned to Nolan. "He's not."

Nolan turned his attention to the door in the corner of the courtroom. The deputy was not there. But then he saw that the deputy was still at his desk. He was leaning forward, talking into a microphone. When he was done, he turned to the judge and said, "He's in the lockup. They're bringing him out."

A rush of panic welled up in Nolan's chest. The witness was not subpoena'd, and he was incarcerated. A feeling of impending doom began to sink in as Nolan realized that Keene's next witness was most likely a jailhouse snitch.

Nolan leaned over to Danny. "They must have used a transportation order instead of a subpoena," he said. "Did you see anything like that in the clerk's file?"

Danny shook his head. "I don't remember."

Nolan leaned into Larice's ear. "Do you know someone named Gamond Edwards?"

Larice shook his head. "Never heard of him."

Nolan sighed. Larice had already broken the golden rule. Although Nolan had warned him that the telephone calls were recorded, he had called Monica Lee and asked her to lie for him. And if he had ignored Nolan on that simple instruction, there was no telling who else he talked to and what else he had said.

The door opened and a tall African-American male in orange coveralls appeared with a deputy at his side. The deputy stayed by his side as they made their way across the courtroom to the witness stand. As they passed the defense table, the tall man turned his head and grinned slightly at Larice. As he did, Larice stiffened in his seat and breathed, "Son of a bitch!"

Nolan glanced at Danny before leaning into Larice. "What's up? Who is that?"

Larice turned to look at Nolan. Wide eyed and slack jawed, he had a stunned look on his face, as if his family doctor had just told him that he had cancer.

"What's the matter?" Nolan whispered impatiently.

"It's J," Larice answered in his zombie-like state. "It's fucking J."

CHAPTER 38

"Please state your name for the jury," Keene began.

"My name is Gamond Edwards," he said. When he stated his name, he used the "J" sound instead of a hard "G" sound.

Larice, still with his panicked look, leaned over to Nolan. "Whatever he has to say, he's fucking lying."

"Why would he lie?" Nolan asked, perturbed.

"Because Timmy told him that I was a narc and I was trying to steal the stuff!"

"Did you ever see him in jail?" Nolan asked.

"Nope," Larice answered. "Like I say, he's lying."

Nolan turned to stare at the witness as Keene questioned him. Historically, when a person on the stand was in orange coveralls, the prosecution viciously attacked them with slashing accusations and condescending remarks. But in this case, Keene was politely asking questions, which made the situation seem surreal.

"And you're currently incarcerated for a pending drug charge, is that correct?" Keene continued.

"That's true," Gamond answered, nodding his head.

The orange-clad witness had a mass of dreadlocks which were pulled back and tied in a bunch. But Nolan's attention was focused on the snitch's eyes, which were pools of gray steel, gleaming in the fluorescent lights of the courtroom.

"How long have you been incarcerated?" Keene asked.

"Since June of this year," Gamond stated.

"Before you went to jail, did you know Larice Jones?" Keene pointed to the defendant.

"Yes sir, I've known him for a few years now."

"And what is your relationship with him?" Keene asked.

"We're friends."

"How and when did you first meet Mr. Jones?" Keene crossed his arms.

"If I remember right, it was through a friend of a friend. He was hanging out with another friend of mine and we got to know each other over time, and eventually we became friends."

"Do you hang out with him often?" Keene asked.

"Yeah, sometimes. I mean, we're in the same circle of friends so we see each other a lot."

"And did there come a time when you saw him since you've been incarcerated?" Keene continued.

"Yeah. It was at General District Court. We were both in the lockup behind the courtroom. I don't know why he was there, but I was there for a bond hearing."

"And for the record, what was the date?"

"It was June 11th," Gamond answered.

"And you shared the same cell in the lockup on that day?"

"Yes sir, they put us in the same cell before our hearings."

Larice leaned into Nolan's ear. "He's fucking lying. He was never there."

"And while you were in the lockup together, did Larice Jones make any statements to you regarding the murder of the Lawson family?"

"Yes he did."

"What did he say?" Keene glanced at the jury.

Gamond Edwards stared directly at Larice when he answered. "He said he took care of Timmy Lawson, but he needed my help. He said he'd give me five thousand dollars if I helped him."

"And how exactly were you supposed to help him?"

"He wanted me to go get the gun that he used to kill that family when I got out of jail."

"And why did he want you to go get the gun?" Keene asked with feigned ignorance, as if he didn't know the answer.

"He wanted me to take the gun and put it in Tommy Lawson's car."

Keene looked at the jury, obviously enjoying their reaction. "And did he tell you where to find the gun?" he continued.

"Yes sir. He said it was under the seat of his car -- the blue T-bird."

"Did he explain to you how he was going to give you five thousand dollars if he was in jail?"

"He said that after I planted the gun, I should make an anonymous call to his lawyer and tell him where the gun was. And as soon as they found the gun in that kid's car, he would tell his girlfriend to bring me the five thousand."

"Do you know his girlfriend?" Keene asked.

"Yeah, I know her," he bobbed his dreadlocks. "They was living together."

"What's her name?"

"Monica."

"If you and Larice are friends, then why are you telling us about this?"

Gamond Edwards shook his head. "Friend or no friend. What he did to that family is just plain wrong. And I wasn't about to help him on it, either."

"Objection, opinion," Nolan interrupted.

"Sustained," the judge ruled without allowing Keene to argue. "You shall disregard the last statement of the witness," he said to the jury.

"Since that day when he spoke to you in the lockup behind General District Court, have you been incarcerated the entire time?" Keene asked.

"Yeah," he nodded. "I never did get a bond."

That's all of my questions," Keene finished.

Nolan felt Larice's hot, stinky breath on the side of his face. "You got to do something. He's lying!"

"Your witness, Mr. Getty," the judge prodded.

Nolan stood up. "Your Honor, at this time, I would ask the court for a short recess."

"Granted," the judge banged his gavel. "This court will be in recess for fifteen minutes."

CHAPTER 39

During the recess, the deputies took Gamond and Larice back to the lockup. As Nolan and Danny were leaving the courtroom, Nolan turned to Danny. "I need you to go over to General District Court and find out if this Gamond character was transported to the court on the same day that Larice was there for his preliminary hearing. If he wasn't, the only way we can prove it is if you can bring a clerk back to testify that there are no transportation orders for Gamond Edwards on that day. Talk to Carol over there. She owes me a favor or two."

"All right," Danny answered.

"And get his criminal record on the way back. They'll have it in the clerk's office at the end of the hall."

"How do I do that?" Danny asked.

"Just ask the clerk to look his name up on the computer. Ask her to print out the record and then have her sign and seal it as official," Nolan answered.

"Okay -- will do," Danny nodded as he turned to go.

Nolan went directly to the lock up door in the corridor outside of the courtroom. He knocked twice before a deputy opened it.

"I'll need to get in," Nolan said as he emptied his pockets.

After placing his belongings in a plastic tray, the deputy waved for Nolan to go ahead of him. "He's in the same cell."

Nolan glanced into the first cell, which was visible from where he was standing near the table. Gamond Edwards was standing in his cell with his hands pressed against the cage, staring at him with cold, gray eyes.

Nolan broke his gaze and proceeded to the end of the corridor. Seeing his attorney, Larice immediately backed up to the far wall. The deputy glanced into the cage before opening the door to let Nolan inside.

Once the door was shut, Larice sat down on the bench. He still had a panicked look on his face.

"This ain't right. They can't just bring in someone to lie like that," Larice whined.

"Well they just did, so we better get our heads together and try to figure this out," Nolan sat down beside him. In a quieter voice he continued. "Let me get this straight, Gamond is the person who you call J and he is the one who has been making you sell drugs?" Nolan asked.

"That's right. That's him."

"Tell me the truth right now. Was he with you in the lockup when you went for your preliminary hearing in General District Court?"

"I told you! He's lying. Can't you get the records or something?" Larice whined.

"Danny is over there checking as we speak."

"Good. That's good," he said again, as if he was trying to convince himself of the fact.

Nolan eyed him carefully. Although it may have been his paranoia, Nolan thought he saw a glimpse of apprehension in Larice's eyes.

"Listen," Nolan continued. "All they have is the word of Gamond Edwards -- that's it. If what he said was really true, then they would've tracked down Monica's blue T-bird and found the gun in it. But they didn't."

Larice nodded.

"So if we can show from the records that Gamond Edwards was not in General District Court when you were there, it's all over for them -- we can prove that he's lying."

"Yeah, I'm with you," Larice nodded. "That's what you have to do."

CHAPTER 40

When the court reconvened fifteen minutes later, only Nolan and Larice were at the defense table. Danny was still on his mission.

"Your witness, Mr. Getty," the judge began.

Nolan briefly shuffled through some papers and then slowly walked to the podium in an effort to stall for time.

"Mr. Edwards, your first name is spelled with a G at the beginning, correct?" Nolan asked.

"That's correct."

"But it is pronounced like a J, as in Jamond, correct?"

"That's right," he answered.

"And it's true that your friends and associates call you J, right?" Nolan asked.

"Some do."

"Well Larice Jones calls you J, right?"

"Yeah, he calls me J."

"And Larice's girlfriend Monica calls you J, correct?"

He shrugged. "I guess so."

"And you testified that you've been friends with Larice for quite awhile, right?"

"Right," he crossed his arms.

"But there's more to it than that, isn't there Mr. Edwards?" Nolan asked. "Isn't it true that you've been pushing drugs on Larice?"

Edwards shook his head. "I don't know what you're talking about."

"Mr. Edwards, you are a drug dealer aren't you?"

"No I am not," Edwards shook his head.

"Well, didn't you just testify that you're in jail on a drug charge?"

"That's true."

"And that's for distribution of drugs, which carries a maximum sentence of forty years in prison, correct?"

"Yeah, but it's a false charge. I don't deal drugs."

"If you don't deal drugs, then why did you give Larice Jones two large balls of crack cocaine to sell earlier this year?"

Gamond paused before answering. "I didn't."

"Mr. Edwards, you weren't in the courtroom when the prosecution played a recording of two telephone calls between Larice and his girlfriend, so you may not know this. But are you aware that they talked specifically about you?"

Edwards leaned into the microphone. "I am not aware of that, no."

Nolan stepped over to the prosecution table and picked up the CD. He placed it into his computer and played the telephone conversations again.

As the recording played, Gamond crossed his arms and looked up in the air, as if he was completely bored with the exercise. When the conversations were over, Nolan turned to the witness again.

"Did you hear that?" Nolan asked. "Isn't it true that you talked to Monica and she tried to tell you that Timmy was a narc and that he had stolen the stuff that you had fronted Larice?"

Edwards fidgeted in his chair before answering. "They must be talking about some other J."

"Some other J?" Nolan asked. "What other J is there who knows Timmy and Larice and Monica?"

Edwards paused for a second. "I don't know," he said. "How should I know?"

"I'm asking the questions here Mr. Edwards, not you. Isn't it true that you were also 'friends' with Timmy Lawson?" Nolan asked, putting quotes in the air with his fingers when he said the word.

"Not really, no."

"No? Why is he coming to you and telling you that Larice is a narc and that Larice was trying to steal your stuff, then?"

"Like I said, they must be talking about some other J."

"Some phantom J that nobody has ever heard of?"

Edwards shrugged.

Nolan glanced behind him, hoping that Danny would appear, but he didn't.

"Mr. Edwards, according to your testimony, Larice Jones gave you specific information about the location of the gun, correct?"

"That's right," Gamond nodded.

"If you were Larice Jones and you had such information, wouldn't you want to guard it very carefully because it would link you to the murders?"

"Yeah, I suppose."

"And if you were Larice Jones, wouldn't you want to get some kind of assurance from your friend that he would be willing to help you, before you told him the location of the gun?"

"I suppose."

"But according to you, Larice Jones just blurted out the location of the gun and offered you five thousand dollars to retrieve it."

Gamond Edwards thought for a second before answering. "He just didn't blurt it out. I mean, we talked about it first."

"So you worked out a deal with him. He said he would give you five thousand dollars if you retrieved the gun, correct?"

"Correct."

"And at the time that you parted ways in the lockup behind General District Court, all of the details had been worked out and the agreement had been made between you, correct?"

"That's what he thought. But like I say, I never got out of jail and besides, I was never going to do it anyway."

"But you didn't let him know that, did you?"

"No."

"So if everything had been worked out, where exactly were you supposed to find the gun?"

"I told you, under the seat of his car."

"What if I told you that he doesn't own a car? How could he tell you that the gun was under the seat of his car when he doesn't even own a car?"

"I know what he drives," Gamond quickly answered. "He's been driving a blue T-bird since I've known him. And that's where he said the gun would be."

Nolan looked down at the podium and began paging through his notes. Several moments went by as the judge and jury sat in silence. He continued to page through his notes, as everyone waited patiently for him to continue his cross-examination. Just as the judge was about to prod him, Nolan asked without looking up, "And where were you supposed to find the blue T-bird?"

Gamond paused for a moment. "At the house where he lived. On Sherman Street."

"And where were you supposed to find Tommy's car in order to plant the gun?" Nolan asked, still looking through his notes.

"Where Tommy lived . . . on Astor Street."

Nolan looked up, seemingly exasperated. "Do you even know what kind of car Tommy drove?"

Gamond thought for another moment before answering. "No, but that's something I could've easily found out. I mean, if I had gotten out of jail and I was actually going to do what Ice wanted me to do, then I would've found out what kind of car he was driving."

Just then, Nolan saw Danny out of the corner of his eye -- he was gesturing to him as he approached the defense table.

"Excuse me, your honor," Nolan said. "May I have just one second with co-counsel?"

"Make it quick," the judge ordered.

Nolan walked to the table and sat down beside Danny. "What do you got?"

Larice leaned in to hear the conversation.

"The transportation orders are there," Danny whispered. "Gamond Edwards was transported to General District Court for a bond hearing on the same morning that you were there for your preliminary hearing," he turned and stared at Larice.

"That's just great," Nolan whispered. Then he turned to Larice and shook his head. "You just can't be honest with me, can you?"

"I swear. I'm not lying. I never saw him there!" Larice whined.

"He could be telling the truth," Danny cut in. "There were lots of people transported to court that morning and so they would have been put in several different cells. The problem is that the deputies don't keep track of which inmates are put in each cell when they're in the lockup. They just write their names on a dry erase board on the door, and when court is done, the boards are erased."

Nolan shook his head, convinced that it was just too much of a coincidence anyway.

"He's got a long criminal record though, if that helps," Danny offered, pushing a sheaf of papers across the desk to Nolan.

"Mr. Getty, let's get this thing going here," the judge cut in.

Nolan stood up at the defense table. "At this time, I have no further questions for this witness. But I reserve the right to call him later."

Nolan wanted a chance to study Gamond's criminal record, which appeared lengthy. If there were particular crimes -- any felonies, or misdemeanors that involved lying, cheating, or stealing, he could always call Gamond to the stand again and impeach him with such crimes. Later, at the close of the trial, the judge would give the jury an instruction that they could consider such crimes when evaluating the truthfulness of the witness.

"Suit yourself," the judge stated. "Mr. Keene, call your next witness."

Keene grinned at Nolan. It was a devilish grin -- as if he was about to reveal another surprise.

CHAPTER 41

Much like a football game, there can be momentum changes in a trial where one side or the other is suddenly enveloped in an aura of invincibility in which nothing can or will go wrong. After the initial kickoff in the trial of Larice Jones, the prosecution had the momentum, driving the ball down the entire field, before Keene's star player, Timmy Lawson, fumbled the ball on the one yard line. For a brief moment, the momentum switched to the defense. But after a timeout, Keene got his team back on track and they began to methodically march down the field again.

It was the trick play that really turned the momentum -- the unveiling of the jail house snitch. With the defense caught on their heels, Keene marched closer to his goal as the jury cheered him on.

Unfortunately for Nolan, things were about to get even worse. Keene had a few more surprises in his playbook and he was about to punch the ball in for the game winning touchdown.

"I call Officer Brad Monahan," Keene stated loudly.

Nolan had seen the officer's name on the subpoena list, but it hadn't raised any red flags for him. He knew from the request letter to the state lab that the only damaging physical evidence found at the scene was the shell casings with Larice's fingerprints. Therefore, he assumed that Officer Brad Monahan was just another officer who was going to testify about the crime scene. After all, there was always a host of officers lined up to testify in such cases, most of whom the prosecutor put on just to corroborate findings. But this time, Nolan was wrong.

Like the previous police officers, Brad Monahan was wearing a regular uniform with a utility belt and a holstered sidearm. He was young;

perhaps in his late twenties with sandy hair cropped in a marine cut -- shaved on the sides and short on top.

"What is your name and occupation?" Keene asked.

"My name is Brad Monahan and I am a police officer with the Big Shanty Police Department."

"And what is your involvement with this case?"

"I was the evidence technician on a search warrant that was executed at the home of Monica Lee, at Twenty Four Jackson Street."

The officer's words were like alarm bells going off in Nolan's head -- the kind of alarm that blares obnoxiously in repeated, monotone blasts, as if the core of a nuclear reactor was about to explode. They found the gun, he thought. *They found the damned gun!*

A flood of adrenalin surged through his body with the realization that his case was about to fall apart. But he was a lawyer, and lawyers hide their feelings well. Except for a slight flush in his face, his outward appearance remained stone cold.

Nolan turned to Danny and whispered in his ear. "Did you see any search warrants, besides the one at Larice's house?"

"No," Danny shook his head.

"Did you check for additional warrants since the first time that you went up there?" Nolan asked.

"No, was I supposed to?"

Nolan shook his head. "It's my fault. I think I just told you to check the case file for subpoenas. They keep search warrants in a separate filing system in the clerk's storage room."

"And when was that search warrant executed?" Keene continued.

"July Eighteenth."

"Why did you execute a search warrant at that address?"

"Well, it was all based on information that we received from an informant named Gamond Edwards," the officer answered.

"And who was at the address when you executed the warrant?"

"Georgia Lee and her daughter, Monica Lee."

"And what did you find during the execution of that search warrant?"

"Based on information that we had obtained from an informant, we searched a 1997 Blue Thunderbird which was parked in the driveway. Under the passenger side front seat, we found a Smith & Wesson, nine millimeter semi-automatic pistol."

"Did you find any registration and insurance information in the car?"

"Yes. I found a registration card under the visor."

"And who was the registered owner of the car?"

"Monica Lee," the officer answered.

"What did you do with the gun?"

"I packaged it and sent it via certified mail to the West Virginia State Lab."

"Why did you send it to the West Virginia State Lab?"

"Well, we had less than three weeks until this trial and our lab had a lengthy backup. So we sent the gun to the West Virginia lab because we knew that they could give us a quicker turnaround."

Keene opened a cardboard box that was under his desk and pulled out the plastic baggy containing the gun. After the officer identified it, Keene had it admitted into evidence.

The sneaky sons of bitches, Nolan thought. Keene had reached a new low in trickery. Most prosecutors would have asked for a continuance, but Keene had his evidence sent out of state, where the defense could never track it. The worst case scenario had come true. Keene had found the weapon and obviously, all of the analyses were going to match Larice.

"This is bad," Danny whispered. "What are we gonna do now?"

Nolan looked at Danny. "Don't panic."

Glancing at Larice, Nolan saw that he was staring dumbly ahead with his mouth open.

"And what type of analyses did you request from the West Virginia State Lab?" Keene continued.

"Fingerprints and ballistics."

"Did you send anything else in the package?"

"Yes. I also submitted the bullets which had been recovered from the bodies of the Lawson family and the shell casings that had been recovered at the scene."

"No further questions," Keene finished.

"Your witness, Mr. Getty," the judge stated.

Still reeling from the surprise evidence, Nolan couldn't think of any way to attack him.

"No questions at this time, your honor. But I'd like to reserve my right to recall him later in trial, if necessary."

"You have that right," the judge said.

"Your next witness, Mr. Keene?"

"Doctor Larry Fitzgerald," Keene stated loudly.

Nolan turned and whispered to Danny. "He must be from the West Virginia lab -- another witness not on the subpoena list."

Danny sighed and nodded.

Nolan realized that Keene had not sent a subpoena to the doctor because he didn't want Nolan to know that the gun had been found. It was a huge gamble on his part. If the doctor had gotten sick or couldn't have made it to the trial for any other reason, Keene could not have obtained a continuance, because he hadn't sent the witness a subpoena. But knowing Keene, he probably had a contingency plan if the good doctor couldn't have made it -- some false pretense for a continuance.

For the first time, Nolan fully understood the extent of Keene's desire to win. Keene was using every little foot hold, every niche and crevasse that he could find to scale the mountain of conviction. And with the same sense of awareness, much like the panic that one feels upon realizing that the iron was left on at home, Nolan knew that Keene was about to deliver the coupe de grace.

Doctor Larry Fitzgerald was an elderly man with strands of gray hair combed sideways across the crown of his mostly bald head. With reading glasses perched near the end of his nose, he testified that he was the forensic scientist who had analyzed the gun that Officer Monahan had submitted to the West Virginia State Lab. He told the jury that two latent fingerprints were identified on the weapon, both of which matched Larice Jones. In addition, he testified that ballistics testing resulted in a match with the bullets and shell casings that had been sent to him by Officer Monahan.

Nolan stared at Keene, who was reveling in scientific glory. Keene continued to press the good doctor about the basics of firearms tool marking. The doctor told the jury that no two guns could leave the same impression on shell casings and bullets. He showed enlarged photos taken through his comparison microscope of the test round shell casings along side the crime scene shell casings. He pointed out the similarities in the breech marks, the firing pin impressions, and the extractor marks with a laser pointer as the junior scientists on the jury nodded in agreement. The jury continued to nod when he concluded that the marks left on the shell casings were perfectly identical. And according to the photos, Nolan had to agree that they appeared identical.

Unfortunately, there was nothing Nolan could do. There was no way he could effectively challenge the results without advance notice of the analyses. He leaned into Danny's ear and whispered, "Do you want to cross-examine him?"

Danny's eyes widened. "No! I have no idea what to ask him. Maybe we should ask for a continuance so that we can think about this."

Nolan shook his head and whispered. "The judge will never allow it, especially since we declined to file a discovery request."

Keene turned the doctor's attention to the bullet comparison. Enlarged photos appeared again and the doctor pointed out the striations left by the barrel of the pistol. And then after walking the jury through the analysis, Keene prompted him for the magic words.

"Based on a reasonable degree of scientific certainty, this is the gun that fired the bullets at the crime scene," the doctor stated. With the magic words on the record, Keene had finished his examination of the doctor. Nodding to the defense table, he grinned. "No further questions."

Although Nolan knew that he couldn't effectively cross-examine the doctor, there were some things that he could pick at. He had a vague recollection of reading an article written in a law review regarding tool mark identification.

Approaching the podium without any notes, Nolan put one hand in his pocket and rubbed his chin with the other. "Isn't it true that the shell casings and bullets fired from two different firearms can have many similarities?" Nolan asked.

"That is true to some extent, but when comparing all of the markings, one can identify the firearm from which it came," the doctor answered.

"Just so the jury's clear on this, let me use an analogy. Although two oak leaves are never alike, if you were to take one small part of the oak leaf and compare it to another small part of a different oak leaf, they may appear identical. Isn't that also true for the identification of marks left on bullets and shell casings?"

"That's correct," he answered.

"And when you tested the gun at your lab, you fired test bullets into a water tank or some other medium so that the test bullets remained fully intact, correct?" Nolan asked.

"That's correct. What we have is a large water tank that's about, oh, four feet . . ."

Nolan cut him off by holding up his hand. "Doctor, it's a simple yes or no question. This will go a lot quicker if you just answer my questions.

You fire it into water, correct?" Nolan asked, looking at the jury, instead of the witness.

"Correct," the doctor answered, adjusting his glasses.

"And the bullets that you recover from the water are undamaged, correct?"

"For the most part, yes."

"But the bullets that purportedly came from the crime scene were damaged -- they were warped and broken so that you could not examine the entire bullet for marks, correct?"

"That's correct."

"So isn't it possible that we have my oak leaf analogy here. That only the small portion of the bullets that you examined match, but the remainder of the bullets, the part that you can't see because of damage, does not match?"

"Anything's possible, but that is highly unlikely. There were enough undamaged portions of the bullets to make a match," the doctor explained.

"But you wouldn't know what striations and marks are on the damaged portions of the bullets, therefore, you cannot say, with one hundred percent certainty, that these bullets were fired from the same gun, can you?"

"I can say that within a reasonable degree of scientific certainty," he answered.

"That's not my question. My question is one hundred percent certainty. Yes or no."

"No."

"Thank you doctor. No further questions."

"Can he be excused?" the judge asked.

"Yes sir," Nolan answered.

"Mr. Keene, call your next witness," the judge nodded.

Keene flashed a quick smile to Nolan as he stood up.

"The prosecution rests," he announced.

About friggin' time, Nolan thought. One more witness and he would've taped a piece of white paper to his pen and raised it in surrender.

"Very well," the judge said. "Do you need a quick recess before we continue?" he turned to Nolan.

"Yes sir, thank you."

CHAPTER 42

"We'll meet you in the lockup," Nolan said to Larice as the deputy tugged at his arm.

"What's our next step, boss?" Danny asked as they sat at the defense table.

Nolan shrugged. "I don't have a damned clue. If we took off running now, we'd be long gone by the time the judge comes back."

Danny chuckled.

"Or we can go see what Larice has to offer."

Larice appeared shell-shocked when Nolan and Danny entered his cell. He was sitting on the bench against the back wall with a distant look upon his face. Only after the jailor slammed the door behind them did he look up at Nolan. Shaking his head, he mumbled something unintelligible. And then he whined like a puppy dog, "Now what are we going to do?"

"Let's just start from the beginning," Nolan sat down beside him.

Danny sat down on the other side of Larice. "Yeah, let's just think this whole thing through," he offered.

"This is what we know. You've been selling drugs for J, who is actually Gamond Edwards. Timmy steals the drugs from you and sets you up with the cops. I think we can prove that through the facts of the case and the telephone recordings."

"Yeah, that's what happened," Larice said, rubbing his hands over his face.

"Then, when you're in jail, Timmy shows up at your house and tries to get the other half from Monica, which is corroborated by the telephone recordings from the jail. And Monica also claims that she told Gamond that Timmy took the drugs, which is also corroborated in the telephone calls. But she also says that Gamond talked to Timmy and Timmy told him that *you* were the narc and that you were trying to steal the drugs. Are we on the same page so far?" Nolan asked.

"Yeah, all that's right," Larice nodded with a thousand yard stare.

"Then we have Gamond testifying that you told him where to get the gun. The records from General District Court show that he was there at the same time as you, but let's just assume that he wasn't in the same cell and you never talked to him."

"That's true," Larice whined. "I never saw him."

"That's fine," Nolan continued. "But if he is lying about his conversation with you -- then how did he know that the gun would be in the T-bird?"

"I have no idea," Larice said. "Timmy's the one who stole it from me. Maybe Timmy told him."

Nolan thought about the theory. It made sense. Timmy broke into the house and stole the gun. Timmy killed his family and then planted the gun in Larice's car, assuming that the police would find it. He then made the anonymous call to complete the frame job. Later, when Timmy realized that the gun had never been found, he had to find a way to ensure that Larice would be convicted. So he contacted Gamond and paid him to lie. Timmy was the one who told Gamond where the gun would be found, not Larice.

Nolan turned to Danny. "That actually makes sense. We can show the jury through the telephone recordings that Gamond and Timmy know each other. And we can also show through those recordings that Timmy was trying to set Gamond against you. But we still need some way to prove that Timmy hired Gamond to lie."

"How we going to do that?" Larice asked.

"Well, in order for Timmy to do such a thing, he would've had to contact Gamond Edwards while he was in jail."

Almost immediately, Nolan and Danny came to the same conclusion. Before Nolan could say anything, Danny popped up from the bench. "How can I find out if Timmy Lawson has visited Gamond Edwards at the jail?" he asked.

"There's a visitation log book right at the front desk. They'll let you look through it."

Danny nodded and ran to the cell door. "Deputy!" he yelled.

The deputy came to the door and unlocked it.

"If he was there, he would've signed in under the name of Tommy Lawson," Nolan added. "And make sure you check every day that Edwards has been there."

"Yes sir," Danny said. "I'll check it."

"Text me "yes" if it's there, or "no" if it's not. That way I don't have to wait for your return."

"Okay," Danny answered, before departing.

CHAPTER 43

With Danny's five minute head start before court reconvened, Nolan knew that he could keep the judge occupied until Danny texted him with the answer. After the judge returned to the bench, but before the jury was brought out, Nolan stood up to address the court.

"I have a motion, your honor."

The judge nodded. "I suppose you do."

The motion that Nolan was about to make was one that every defense attorney made at the close of the prosecution's case. In effect, it was a request to dismiss the charges on the basis that the prosecution had not proven its case. The motions were usually baseless, but every once in awhile they had teeth.

"Go ahead, Mr. Getty. State your motion."

"I have a motion to strike the evidence with respect to the indictment for the murder of Timmy Lawson. As has been proven by the prosecution, Timmy Lawson is still alive. Therefore, the defendant cannot be convicted for his murder."

Keene stood in protest. "I have a motion to amend the indictment so that it reflects the actual name of the victim -- Tommy Lawson."

"The prosecution can't amend the indictment in the middle of the trial, your honor," Nolan countered. "The defendant must be given prior notice of the charges against him. That's basic Constitutional law."

"He's right, Mr. Keene," the judge responded. "You can't amend an indictment after resting your case. Do you agree that Timmy Lawson is still alive?"

Keene paused before answering. There was only one answer which he could give. "Yes, your honor."

"Then I have no choice but to sustain the motion to strike. The indictment shall be dismissed with prejudice."

"Thank you, your honor," Nolan smiled.

"Anything else?" the judge asked.

"Well, the associated robbery and firearm charges must be dismissed as well."

"That's right," the judge nodded. "I am also dismissing the associated charges of robbery and using a firearm in the commission of a felony, but only those charges that involved Timmy Lawson."

"Thank you," Nolan responded.

"Are you ready to proceed with your case, Mr. Getty?" the judge asked.

"Yes sir," Nolan didn't give away his mounting anxiety.

"Very well," the judge said as he turned to the deputy. Bring in the jury."

As the jury was filing into the courtroom, Nolan sat down and poured himself a glass of water at the defense table. Taking a long drink, he set the glass down and leaned over to Larice. "One down -- two to go."

"What's that mean?" Larice asked.

"The judge dismissed one of your murder charges -- the charge that said you killed Timmy Lawson," Nolan explained.

Larice's eyes lit up. "That's good, right?"

"Yeah, that's a good thing, but don't forget -- you still have two other murder charges, the breaking and entering, the firearm charges, and the robberies against the parents."

Larice frowned.

After the jury was situated, the judge nodded. "Go ahead Mr. Getty."

Nolan glanced at the entrance to the courtroom before standing to address the court. "I would like to recall Gamond Edwards."

The deputy leaned into the microphone at his desk -- calling for his staff to bring Gamond Edwards from the lockup. A few moments later, the door in the corner made a beeping sound before it opened. Then the deputy appeared with Gamond Edwards. As the deputy escorted him past the defense table, Larice glared at him and cursed under his breath.

Gamond returned Larice's stare and then lifted his arms out to the side as he walked by. Although he didn't say anything, Nolan knew what he was thinking by his gesture. *You want a piece of me? Bring it on!!*

"Keep moving Edwards," the deputy prodded.

When Gamond returned to the stand, the judge nodded to Nolan. "Go ahead."

Before he went to the podium, Nolan put his cell phone in the breast pocket of his suit. That way, when Danny texted him, he could open his suit jacket and look at the message while keeping the phone hidden from the judge and the jury. All cell phones were supposed to be turned off while in the courtroom, but as long as he had it on vibrate mode, no one would know the difference.

"Permission to treat him as a hostile witness, your Honor," Nolan stated as he stepped up to the podium. He knew that the judge didn't really have a choice in the matter. Because Gamond Edwards had already testified as a witness for the prosecution, he was legally presumed to be hostile to the defense. Most importantly, unlike other witnesses called by an attorney, a hostile witness could be examined with leading questions.

"Granted."

Nolan placed Gamond's criminal record on the podium and then put his finger on the first impeachable crime.

"You're a thief, aren't you Mr. Edwards?"

Edwards shook his dreadlocks. "No sir."

"Are you denying the fact that you have a larceny conviction on your criminal record?"

"What's that got to do with anything?" Edwards bristled.

"I'll tell you what it has to do with, Mr. Edwards," Nolan fired back. "Thieves can't be trusted -- and according to your criminal record, you are a thief, aren't you?"

"That was a misunderstanding between me and a pawn shop," Edwards looked away.

"A misunderstanding?" Nolan prodded. "It says here that you had a trial, and then you were found guilty of larceny. You were convicted, Mr. Edwards. Is that what you call a misunderstanding?"

Edwards shrugged. "That doesn't mean I'm a thief. I mean, that was a long time ago."

Nolan laughed. "It says here that you were convicted of this larceny charge less than eighteen months ago, isn't that correct?"

"Yeah, that sounds about right."

"And Mr. Edwards, you are not only a thief, but you are also a convicted felon, aren't you?"

"Yeah, I got a felony on my record. So what?"

The judge cut in. "Mr. Edwards, the attorneys ask the questions, not the witnesses."

Edwards rolled his eyes.

"You've got more than a felony, Mr. Edwards," Nolan continued. "One . . . two . . . three," Nolan counted. "You are a three time convicted felon, isn't that true?"

"Whatever you say," Edwards answered.

"It's not what I say, it's what the records say. So are the records true or not?"

"True," Edwards rolled his eyes.

"What kind of deal did you make with Mr. Keene for your false testimony here today?"

Gamond glanced at Keene before he shook his head. "We don't have no deal."

"Oh, come on Mr. Edwards, do you expect this jury to believe that a thief and a three-time convicted felon such as yourself is testifying out of the goodness of his own heart?"

Gamond shrugged. "That's right."

"Mr. Edwards, isn't it true that you're facing a possible forty year prison sentence on your current drug charge?"

"I guess," Gamond answered.

"You don't want to go to jail for forty years, do you Mr. Edwards?"

"No, would you?"

Nolan ignored his question. "And you know that Mr. Keene is the Chief Commonwealth's Attorney here and that he's the one that's going to prosecute you on that charge, don't you?"

"Yeah, I know that."

"And whether Mr. Keene promised you anything or not, you're hoping that because of your testimony here today -- he's not going to send you to prison for forty years, right?"

Gamond glanced at the prosecution table. "I told you before -- we ain't got no deal."

"That's not my question, Mr. Edwards," Nolan reprimanded him. "You're hoping that if you testify, Mr. Keene's not going to send you away for forty years, correct?"

Gamond shrugged. "I never get my hopes up about anything."

Nolan felt his phone vibrate inside his pocket. Opening the left side of his suit coat, he reached in with his right hand and retrieved it, but at the same time keeping it concealed from the judge and jury. It was the text that he had been waiting for, but not what he wanted to hear.

No record. But wat about tel or mail?

Nolan sighed and shook his head. The doomed feeling that he had had earlier fell down upon him like a cold, wet blanket. It was all over -- his latest theory was a flop. Timmy had not been to the jail to visit Gamond. Although it was possible that he had called or written -- it was highly improbable. They wouldn't have been that dumb to leave a record. Besides, even if he wanted to subpoena the telephone and mail records, he knew that the judge would never give him a continuance.

"Mr. Getty, we're waiting," the judge prodded.

Nolan let the phone drop back into his pocket. He couldn't bring himself to accept the obvious. Worse yet, he couldn't see himself losing to Keene again. In his desperate situation, there was only one other question he could ask Edwards.

"Mr. Edwards, isn't it true that you've been in contact with Timmy Lawson since the night of the murders?" He didn't really expect an affirmative answer, he just wanted to see his reaction. He wanted to know if Gamond Edwards knew that Timmy was still alive.

Edwards cocked his head with a quizzical expression. "How could I be in contact with Timmy Lawson? He's dead."

Gamond's reaction was the final confirmation. Assuming that Edwards was not an academy award winning actor, it appeared that Gamond really didn't know that Timmy Lawson was alive. And if he didn't know that Timmy was alive, that meant that Timmy had never contacted him. And if Timmy had never contacted him, then he couldn't have told him where the gun was located.

"No further questions," Nolan said, giving up the fight.

"Anything, Mr. Keene?" the judge asked.

"No questions, your Honor," Keene smiled.

"Take him back," the judge said to the deputy. "Call your next witness."

With no viable theory to win the case, Nolan felt as though he was lost at sea without a sail. Despite all of his efforts, his situation was helpless. He was being swept away in the tide of Keene's case and there was nothing that he could do to stop it.

"Your Honor, may I have a short recess?" Nolan asked.

The judge frowned. "Mr. Getty, we just got started with your case."

"I know, but I just need ten minutes."

"Very well, let's take a recess. Take the jurors into the deliberation room," the judge nodded to the deputy.

Nolan glanced at the jury. One of the female jurors in the front row rolled her eyes.

Returning to the defense table, Nolan sat down beside Larice.

"Have you heard from the other lawyer?" Larice whispered.

Nolan nodded. "Bad news -- there's no record of Timmy or Tommy visiting him at the jail."

Larice twisted his face into a worried grimace. "What are we going to do now?" he whined.

"I don't know," Nolan answered honestly.

"Come on Mr. Jones," the deputy cut in. "Let's go back to the lockup during the recess."

"Come talk to me," Larice insisted.

"I'll come back to see you in a few minutes. Right now I need some time to think."

The deputy escorted Larice to the lockup door.

As he watched Larice disappear, Nolan didn't want to believe Gamond Edwards. But his mind raced ahead like a runaway train, chugging away with the undisputed facts which were leading to only one destination; only one conclusion. Larice was guilty.

Gamond was in General District Court while Larice was there, Nolan thought. The court records proved that. Gamond and Larice knew each other well. At the time of the alleged conversation between Larice and Gamond in the lockup, the only theory that they had come up with was that Tommy Lawson had killed his own family. And at that time, Larice didn't know that Timmy was alive and impersonating his twin brother. Therefore, it made sense that Larice told Gamond to plant the gun in Tommy Lawson's car. In addition, the gun was found in the blue T-bird, exactly where Gamond said it would be. And Larice was in control of the blue T-bird at the time of the murders.

Nolan made a conscious effort to stop his mind there, not wanting to believe that Larice was guilty. After months of gathering evidence, interviewing witnesses and analyzing evidence; after the countless hours of preparations, he couldn't bear the thought of it all being a waste of time. He especially couldn't stand the thought of losing in such a way to John Keene -- being outsmarted and outflanked by a lunatic.

With the judge and jury gone, Nolan sat at the defense table, forcing himself to review the evidence in a logical manner. He knew that his search for a theory had to involve Gamond Edwards. Edwards was the glue that held Keene's case together. And the only way to win the case was to somehow prove that Edwards was lying. But first, he needed to sort out the plethora of contradictory evidence that had been fed to him.

He knew that the root of truth was imbedded somewhere in the undisputed evidence, the hard facts that both sides agreed upon. His first task was to build a foundation from all of the undisputed facts. From there, he would try to piece together a theory favorable to Larice Jones. The problem was that just about every player in the trial had either held back evidence or had outright lied to him, including Larice himself. And now, he only had ten minutes to separate the lies, or at least use them to his advantage.

Going back to the beginning, Nolan examined each piece of evidence in his mind. Gamond claimed that Larice had told him the location of the gun. The gun was found in the blue T-bird, right where he said it would be. Larice was in possession of the blue T-bird on the night of the murders . . . .

In that moment, Nolan's thoughts came to a stand still. The lies and false debris that had previously clouded his mind began to fade away. It was as if he stepped into the eye of a storm and could suddenly see everything with absolute clarity. And in that burst of clarity, the facts quickly fell into place before him; one by one, like paving stones being plopped down in a divine path of enlightenment to the truth.

Grabbing his notebook, he flipped through the yellow legal pad until he found the notes that he had taken during the cross-examination of Gamond -- the first time that he had taken the stand. He vaguely remembered his line of cross-examination, but he wasn't sure if he had asked the specific question -- a question that would have been innocuous at the time, but now was more important than ever. Scanning through his notes, he saw that there was nothing there.

As he looked up from the pad, his eyes came across the court reporter, who was seated at a small table in front of the judge's bench. She was his last hope.

Nolan stood up and quickly walked over to the court reporter's table. She was reloading a spool of paper in her stenotype machine.

"Excuse me," Nolan said. "Could I bother you for a second?"

"Sure," she said, brushing her bangs away from her eyes. "What do you need?"

"Is it possible for you to look back to the testimony of Gamond Edwards when Mr. Keene called him to the stand?"

"Yeah, sure," she said. "I can bring it right up on the screen here. What are you looking for?"

"I think what I'm looking for is at the very end of my cross-examination. If you just go to the end, I'll be able to pick it out."

"No problem," she said, pushing a few buttons. A stream of words began to scroll across the small LCD screen on her machine. A few moments later, the last few lines of Nolan's cross-examination appeared on the screen. Bending over the machine, Nolan eyes fell upon the question and answer that he was looking for.

He had asked the question! And Gamond had given the wrong answer!

"Can you print that out for me?"

"Sure," she nodded. "No problem."

"What's going on? Did you get my message?" Danny's voice came from behind him.

Nolan turned around. "Yeah, I got it. But it's not over yet -- we still have a chance."

CHAPTER 44

Nolan didn't have time to visit Larice in the lockup during the recess. Just as he was about to explain his new theory to Danny, the deputy appeared, escorting Larice to the defense table.

"Everyone get ready," the deputy said. "The judge is on his way in."

Nolan and Danny walked to the defense table and sat down beside Larice.

"Why didn't you come see me?" his putrid breath wafted into Nolan's face.

"I didn't have time." Nolan heard the judge's door open behind the bench.

"Remain seated. This court is now in session," the deputy announced, as the judge appeared on the bench.

"You finally ready?" the judge asked.

"Yes sir," Nolan responded.

"Bring in the jury," the judge nodded to the deputy.

When the jury was back in place, the judge turned to Nolan.

"Call your next witness."

Nolan stood up. "I call Monica Lee."

The deputy went to the corner door and shouted her name. A few moments later, Monica Lee entered the courtroom for the second time. When she was seated on the witness stand, the judge reminded her that she was still under oath.

"Your honor, I ask permission to treat her as a hostile witness," Nolan said.

"Granted," the judge ruled without argument.

"Ms. Lee," Nolan began, "you haven't been completely truthful with the jury today, have you?"

"About what?" she asked defensively.

"Well, let's start with the drugs. Did you know that the jail records every telephone call made by every inmate and that we've heard recorded telephone conversations between you and Larice Jones when he was in jail on the drug charge earlier this year?"

"No."

"In those conversations, Larice told you that T stole his stuff, and the stuff that he was talking about was drugs, isn't that right?"

"I don't recall the conversation," she crossed her arms.

Nolan retrieved the CD and put it in his computer. "Maybe hearing it will refresh your recollection," Nolan said as he pushed the play button.

When Monica heard her voice on the recording, she appeared surprised. As the recording played, she fidgeted in her seat and pretended to pick invisible pieces of lint off of her sweater. When the recording had ended, Nolan continued with the questions.

"Ms. Lee, I'm going to remind you that you are under oath, subject to felony perjury. Now please be honest. Everyone here today in this courtroom already knows that the stuff you are talking about is drugs, so will you now tell us the truth -- you knew about the drugs, didn't you?"

Monica Lee gyrated her big bottom in the chair. "What I meant was that I had nothing to do with those drugs. I never used them, I never touched them, nothing. I had nothing to do with them."

"But you knew about the drugs, didn't you?" Nolan prodded.

"Yeah," she said nodding her head. "I knew about them."

"You even knew where they were hidden in the house. Because if you didn't know, you would not have asked Larice what to do with them, correct?"

"I knew that he kept them in the bathroom closet," she answered. "But I never touched them."

"And what you said in that telephone conversation is also correct. You did as Larice told you to do -- you passed on the message to J that Timmy was a narc and that he stole the drugs, didn't you?"

Monica thought for a few seconds. "Yeah, that's what I told him."

"But at the time that you told J that, you knew that at least half of the drug stash was still in your house, correct?" Nolan asked.

"Yes," she answered.

What is the real name of J?"

"I don't know. I just know him as J."

"Your Honor, at this time, I'd ask that Gamond Edwards be brought into the courtroom for identification purposes," Nolan stated.

The judge shrugged. "I don't have a problem with that, do you Mr. Keene?"

Keene couldn't think of a valid objection. "No sir."

The judge turned to the deputy. "Please bring Gamond Edwards into the courtroom."

The deputy went to the lockup to retrieve Mr. Edwards. A few moments later, the lockup door opened and the deputy escorted the witness to the center of the courtroom. Mr. Edwards looked around the courtroom, confused as to why he was there again.

"This man is who you call J, correct?" Nolan asked.

Monica glanced at him briefly before turning her attention back to Nolan. "That's him."

"Thank you, deputy," Nolan nodded. The deputy tugged at Gamond's arm and they returned to the lockup. When they had exited the courtroom, Nolan continued.

"And that person is the same J who you were talking about in the telephone conversation, correct?"

"That's right," Monica answered.

And it's true what you said in the telephone conversation, the drug stash was stolen in a burglary, correct?"

"Yes."

"And the gun was stolen too, correct?" Nolan asked, hoping that she would change her mind about that too.

Monica didn't answer immediately. After a few seconds of what appeared to be deep thought, she finally responded. "I don't know nothing about the gun. I had no idea there was a gun in my car either."

"What day was it that you got in a fight with Larice and you left to go stay with your mother?"

"It was the same day. On the same day that that family was murdered."

"When you lived with Larice on Sherman Street, where did you usually park your car?"

"Right in the driveway," she answered.

"And when you walked away that day, to go stay with your mother, where was the car parked?"

"In the driveway," she repeated.

"And when you came back with the extra set of keys to retrieve the car, where was it parked?"

"It was still in the driveway."

"And when you retrieved the car, that was the day or two after the murders occurred, correct?"

"That sounds about right."

"That's all the questions I have."

Keene declined to cross-examine his own witness.

"Call your next witness," the judge said.

"I would like to call Officer James Huber," Nolan stated.

When Officer Huber was situated on the witness stand, Nolan began.

"Officer Huber, you are the officer who conducted surveillance at the home of Larice Jones on the night that he was arrested, correct?"

"That's correct."

"And the place we're talking about here is the house on Sherman Street, correct?"

"That's correct."

"And did there come a time when you saw Larice Jones exit the house?"

"Yes, we saw the lights go out in the house and then we saw him exit the front door."

"And did there come a time when it appeared that he saw you?"

"Yes, he looked right at us," the officer answered.

"Where was he standing when he looked at you?"

"He was in the driveway, right in front of the house."

"And how was your line of observation? Was there anything blocking your view of Mr. Jones?"

"No, nothing. I could see him clearly."

"What about a car, was there any car in the driveway?"

The officer shook his head. "No, the driveway was empty, except for Larice, who was standing there in plain sight."

"Thank you officer, no further questions."

"Mr. Keene?" the judge asked.

"No questions," Keene stated.

"Your honor, I would like to ask for another short recess to confer with my client before we continue."

"Mr. Getty, you've had more recesses than an elementary school child. It's time to finish this thing."

"Just one more, your Honor. I just need one more, and then I'll finish my case."

"One more, that's it," the judge scolded him. "And when we come back -- you better be ready to get this thing over with."

"Yes sir," Nolan stated.

The judge banged his gavel. "This court is in recess for ten minutes."

Nolan returned to the defense table and sat down. As the jury was filing into the deliberation room, a deputy came to the table. "It's only a ten minute recess -- he can stay here, or do you want to talk to him in the back?"

"That's all right," Nolan responded. "We're fine right here."

Larice turned to Nolan. "What's going on? Am I going to testify?"

"Just give me a minute," Nolan said. "I need to think this thing through."

As Nolan thought about the evidence, he realized that he had a choice between two paths. He could continue down his original path by continuing to call witnesses, which included a list of several people: the operator who answered the anonymous call at the Big Shanty Communications Department; the voice expert who would testify that the anonymous caller's voice was consistent with Timmy Lawson's; the fingerprint expert who would say that Timmy Lawson's fingerprints were on the marker; Eric his investigator; Larice's sister, Larice's mother, and possibly Larice himself. Or, he could follow another path that would end the charade immediately -- one that was in the complete opposite direction of his original intentions.

Weighing the evidence, Nolan thought about his obsession with beating Keene and he wondered if that desire was clouding his judgment. He also thought about the implications involved in his decision, and he knew that the safe bet was to go through the motions of his original plan -- calling every witness that he had subpoena'd, so that his own client could not later claim that he had ineffective assistance of counsel. But none of those witnesses had anything to add to his new theory.

After a few minutes of intense analysis, Nolan finally turned to Larice. "Our theory that Timmy had paid Gamond to lie just isn't going to work," he said.

"What do you mean?" Larice asked. "Just because there's no record, doesn't mean that Timmy didn't contact him. Maybe he called him."

"Gamond didn't know that Timmy was alive," Nolan responded. "I could tell by his reaction when I accused him of having contact with Timmy after the night of the murders. Therefore, Timmy didn't tell him where the gun was. So that means there's only one person who could've done it," Nolan smiled as he stared at Larice.

Larice's eyes widened and his eyebrows creased with worry as the panicked look spread across his face once again. He swallowed hard before lashing out. "I didn't do it!" he said, louder than he should have.

"You can stop denying it," Nolan said as he reached out to pat him on the back. "I understand."

"Fuck you, man!" Larice hissed. "I knew you was against me. You didn't get Discovery and you didn't get that evidence excluded, like you should've. And I aint' going down cuz of you," he shook his head. "I want a new fucking lawyer!"

"Take it easy," Nolan said, holding up his hand.

For the next seven minutes, Nolan, Danny and Larice huddled at the table, whispering back and forth. They were still talking when the deputy interrupted them.

"The judge is coming out -- everyone ready?"

Nolan nodded.

After the judge entered, he called for the jury. When everyone was in their place, the judge turned to Nolan.

"Call your next witness, Mr. Getty."

Nolan stood up.

"The defense rests," he stated loudly.

Nolan heard a murmur spread through the jury box. He glanced over to the prosecution table and saw that Keene and Mutz were smiling at each other. They appeared confident in their win.

"Mr. Getty, please have your client stand up," the judge ordered.

Larice stood up.

"Mr. Jones, do you agree with your attorney's decision to rest your case?"

Larice glanced at Nolan. "Just answer his questions," Nolan whispered.

"Yeah, I guess."

"Have you been informed that you have a right to testify, but if you don't the jury cannot hold it against you?"

Larice nodded.

"I need a verbal answer, Mr. Jones."

"Yes sir."

"And is your decision based on your own free will, without any coercion, whatsoever?" the judge asked. Obviously he had seen too many defendants base their appeals on a claim that they weren't given an opportunity to testify.

"Yes sir," Larice answered.

"Very well then." Turning to the jury, the judge told them that they had just heard all of the evidence that would be presented. After a few preliminary instructions regarding the closing arguments, he turned to the deputy. "Release all of the witnesses and let them know that they may return to the courtroom to hear closing arguments."

CHAPTER 45

When Keene stood up to address the jury, many of them smiled as he approached. And Keene smiled back.

"I would like to first apologize to you for not discovering the truth earlier," Keene began. "And the truth is that Timmy Lawson was so afraid of Larice Jones, that he thought he had to lie about his own identity. He thought he had to lie to save his own life. But please don't hold that against him. Can any one of us say for sure that we wouldn't do the same thing if we thought our lives were truly in danger?"

After pausing briefly, Keene continued with his closing argument. He started with the motive and the fact that Larice had a reason to kill Timmy for setting him up with the police.

"If you see that punk ass bitch, you tell him he's a dead man when I get out," Keene stated loudly. "And those words came from the mouth of this man!" Keene raised his voice as he pointed to Larice, who fidgeted in his chair. "Those are the words of the defendant, Larice Jones."

Some of the jurors nodded in agreement.

Keene reviewed the evidence regarding the telephone calls from the jail. He reminded the jury that Monica Lee's phone number on Sherman Street was 386-9642, and that the telephone call came from Larice Jones at the jail. Besides the threats that Larice had made against Timmy Lawson, Keene also talked about his desperate attempt to get Monica to lie for him.

"You heard it from the defendant's own mouth. After he was arrested on these charges, he attempted to get Monica Lee to fabricate an alibi -- to lie for him. He said, and I quote, *They got me in jail for murdering T and his family. You got to tell them that you were with me the whole night and we were watching T.V.'* And what was Monica's response?" Keene asked. "She did the right thing -- she said she wasn't going to lie for him."

"Monica Lee told you under oath in this courtroom that she was not with Larice Jones on the night of the murders -- she was at her mother's house. But she also told you that Larice Jones had possession of her car during the time of the murders. And there has not been one iota of evidence to refute that."

Keene continued with his argument, reminding the jury that Larice had run from the police and then lied to them during his initial interview. From there, he began to weave each exhibit into his argument. He started with the photographs at the scene, parading each gruesome image in front of the jury. He talked about the physical evidence, including the fingerprints on the shell casings, the fingerprints on the gun, and the fact that the bullets and shell casings matched the gun that was found in Monica Lee's car.

"The only fingerprints on the shell casings and the only fingerprints on the gun, were those of Larice Jones," he said. "No other fingerprints were present."

"That's enough right there folks," Keene continued. "That's all you need to know to convict Larice Jones. But there's more. We also have the testimony of a third party. Someone who has no connection to the case and no reason to lie. And that is Gamond Edwards."

Keene built up Gamond Edwards to saint-like status, telling the jury how courageous he was to testify in court. He told the jury that despite the fact that Larice had befriended him and offered him a large sum of money, Gamond Edwards did the right thing.

"In the end, it was a friend of Larice Jones, a man who is facing criminal charges himself, who recognized the difference between right and wrong . . . between good and evil, and who acted upon that inherent knowledge to prevent evil from winning the day."

"Now the defense wants you to believe that Timmy Lawson killed his own family, that young Timmy Lawson killed his own flesh and blood. But the idea is not only ridiculous, it's not supported by any physical evidence, whatsoever," Keene stated. "Not one shred of physical evidence points to Timmy Lawson. It all points to the defendant, Larice Jones."

"I have shown you the motive. I have shown you the circumstantial and physical evidence. And as promised in my opening statement, I have shown you the smoking gun," Keene continued as he began to move closer to the defense table. "And now it is time to do your job. It is time for you to convict this man . . . Larice Jones!" Keene bellowed, pointing directly at the defendant. "And show him that he cannot get away with murder in this town!"

Keene walked back to the prosecution table. "Thank you," he said to the jury.

The judge nodded to Nolan.

The jury furrowed their eyebrows and fidgeted in their seats. They had heard enough. As far as they were concerned, Larice Jones was guilty. And everything else was going to be a waste of their time, including the defense attorney's argument.

Some of the jurors crossed their arms as Nolan approached the jury box.

"I was wrong," Nolan said, staring directly at the school teacher in the front row. "And Mr. Keene was right all along. Timmy Lawson did not kill his own family." Nolan paused for several moments, enjoying the confused look that each juror was giving him.

"There is only one person who could have killed the Lawson family," Nolan said as he turned to face Larice. "And it is most definitely not Larice Jones."

Larice smiled.

"I told you in my opening statement that Mr. Keene was going to help me with my case, but at the time, I had no idea that he was actually going to solve it for me," Nolan said, glancing at the prosecution table. "And I must say, without his help, we would've never known the true identity of the killer."

"You see, Mr. Keene called the killer to the stand. You know who he is. You've seen him with your own eyes," Nolan said as he faced the jury. "And that person is Gamond Edwards."

A loud murmur swept through the gallery and the jurors began to look at each other in confusion. Even the judge looked surprised.

At the prosecution table, Keene made an audible grunt and shook his head; then he and Mutz began whispering back and forth.

Nolan waited until the courtroom became absolutely silent again.

"Gamond Edwards," Nolan said again, this time louder. "Mr. Keene claims that he is a third party, unconnected to the case, but that couldn't be farther from the truth. Gamond Edwards is the guy who supplied Larice Jones with drugs. You heard the telephone recordings. Monica Lee told Gamond that Timmy stole the drugs. And when Larice asked

Monica what Gamond had said in response, she told him that Gamond wanted the money or he was going to come after him. Only a drug supplier would say that. Only a drug dealer would be in jail on charges of drug distribution," Nolan added.

"Gamond Edwards is a big time drug dealer who doesn't have patience for lies, and even less patience for people who steal drugs from him. First, he hears from Timmy Lawson that Larice stole his drugs. Then he hears from Monica Lee that Timmy stole his drugs. So what does he do?" Nolan asked. "He finds the truth himself. He breaks into the house where he knows Larice is living. He finds half of the stash that he had fronted to Larice. And when he finds only half the stash, he knows two things. He knows that Monica and Larice were lying to him about Timmy stealing everything. And he knows that Timmy must have the other half of the drugs -- so Timmy has lied to him too." Nolan paused, giving the jury time to absorb the information.

"When Gamond Edwards breaks into Larice's house, he also finds Larice's gun. And when he finds that gun, he comes up with a plan to take care of both Timmy and Larice. He can't kill Larice, because Larice was in jail at the time. But he can kill Timmy Lawson and he can do the next best thing for Larice -- he can frame him for the murder. So he takes that gun and keeps it . . . waiting until Larice is released from jail. And when Larice is released, he takes that gun to the Lawson home. And he uses that gun to kill the person who he thinks is Timmy Lawson. And in the process, he kills Timmy's parents as well. Thank the Lord that Monica Lee was not at home when the break-in at her house occurred. And thank the Lord that Larice was in jail at the time that Gamond Edwards discovered the truth. Otherwise they would probably be dead too."

"You heard from the police officers. Timmy Lawson's bedroom had been completely turned upside down, as if someone had been looking for something. That someone was Gamond Edwards, and that something was the other half of the stash that Timmy had stolen."

"When he had retrieved his drugs and killed the people involved, he went over to Sherman Street -- to the home of Larice Jones and put the gun under the seat of the car that he knew Larice drove," Nolan continued. "You heard Gamond Edwards when he testified. He said, *I know what kind of car he drives'.*"

"In the beginning, the extent of Gamond Edward's plan was to kill Timmy and then plant the gun to frame Larice. But then after the murders took place, Gamond was arrested on drug distribution charges himself. And while he was sitting in jail, worried that he may spend up to forty years in prison for dealing drugs, he came up with a second phase for his plan. And that plan was to give the police information about the location of the gun in hopes of getting a good deal, while at the same time, sealing the fate of Larice Jones."

"Gamond Edwards thought he had it all figured out, but he made a huge mistake -- an error that exposes him as the killer. During my cross-examination I asked him about the location of the gun, and he told us that it was in the blue T-bird. But when I asked him where he was supposed to find the blue T-bird, he gave the wrong answer." Nolan held up a piece of paper as he continued. "This is a printout of Gamond's testimony that the court reporter gave me during the recess," he explained. "When I asked Gamond where he was supposed to find the blue T-bird, he testified, and I quote, *'At the house where Ice lived. On Sherman Street.'* But he was mistaken."

"What Gamond didn't know is that some time after he stashed the gun in the blue T-bird, Monica Lee retrieved the car and took it to her mother's house. This must have happened sometime after the gun was stashed, but before Larice was arrested. We know that because Monica told us that when she walked to her mother's house, the car was in the driveway at Sherman Street, and when she returned to get it, the car was still in the driveway. In addition, you heard from Officer Huber that the driveway was empty when Larice came out of the house on the night that he was arrested."

"If Larice had really confessed to Gamond Edwards in the lockup at General District Court, Larice would've told Gamond that Monica had taken the car to her mother's house, over on Jackson Street. Because at the time of the preliminary hearing, the evidence shows that Larice knew that Monica had taken the blue T-bird back to her mother's house on Jackson Street. When he stood in the empty driveway on the night that he was arrested, he could not have possibly missed the fact that the car was gone, which is why he stood there for a few seconds, looking around, before he ran. In addition, the telephone call that Larice made from the jail on April 16th proves that he knew the T-bird was not at Sherman Street. In that telephone call, which was made to Monica's mother's house, Larice told her that he had been trying to call her at home, but she had never answered. And Monica told Larice that she was done with him -- she had cleared out her stuff and she wasn't going back."

"So if the car was gone on the night that Larice was arrested and he knew that Monica was at her mother's house and had no intention of going back to live with him, then why would Larice tell Gamond that the car was on Sherman Street?" Nolan asked the jury. "The answer is simple -- he would not have said such a thing. He would have told Gamond that the car was on Jackson Street. And that proves that Gamond Edwards is fabricating the whole story about his conversation with Larice Jones."

Nolan smiled and paused. "If the conversation didn't happen, then how did Edwards know the gun would be in the blue T-bird?" Nolan asked. "The only logical reason; the one supported by all of the evidence; is that Edwards put the gun there himself. Fortunately for Larice, Edwards made the mistake of assuming that the car would still be on Sherman Street."

"Now, the prosecution talks about fingerprints, but we all know that if Gamond Edwards wore gloves when he killed that family, his fingerprints would not be on that gun. And because it was Larice's gun, of course Larice's fingerprints are still on it. So forget about the fingerprints -- they don't prove one way or the other who fired the gun that night," Nolan explained.

"In fact, if you look at the prosecution's case, there is not one single piece of evidence that can exclude Gamond Edwards as the killer. Edwards is a drug-dealer, a thief, and a three-time convicted felon. On top of that, he had the gall to come in here today and lie to you. He lied about his conversations with Monica Lee, he lied about his associations with Larice, and he lied about his conversation with Larice at the jail.

"If you have questions, go back and review the evidence. The evidence reveals that Gamond Edwards is guilty of these crimes. And Larice Jones is an innocent pawn in his chess game."

"Now it's time to do your job. Larice is counting on your verdict of acquittal. Thank you."

The way Nolan told it to the jury, the evidence was clear and obvious -- Gamond Edwards was the killer. But Keene still had his rebuttal argument and one last crack at the jury. And Nolan knew from experience that Keene did not easily surrender. He also knew there was another possible theory that could be supported by the evidence. The only question for Nolan was whether Keene had the vision to see it.

CHAPTER 46

Keene stood up and buttoned his suit coat for his final rebuttal argument. He casually strolled to the jury box as if he was in control of the situation and not panicking from the last minute defense theory.

"It always amazes me how defense attorneys can just throw stuff at a jury and hope that something sticks. Now, I suppose if I were a defense attorney, I'd do the same thing. But Mr. Getty acts like this theory that he just came up with is the only scenario that could've taken place. And he is wrong."

Well, here it comes, Nolan thought as he doodled on a notepad, trying his best to look disinterested. I guess he's smarter than I thought.

"There is no physical evidence to show that Larice Jones knew that the blue T-bird had been retrieved by Monica Lee. Mr. Getty, in his attempt to twist the evidence, can only suggest that Larice Jones was aware of that. For all we know, Larice came out that front door of his house, saw the police officers, and ran away -- never once ever consciously thinking that the car was gone."

"Even if we take Mr. Getty's fantastic leap and assume that Larice saw that the car was gone, that doesn't change anything. In real life, in stressful situations, people make mistakes and forget things all the time. And that's probably what happened here. When Larice tried to get Gamond Edwards to be his accomplice, he forgot that Monica Lee had retrieved the car. They only had a short time together in the lockup behind the courtroom. And Larice quickly hatched his plan for Gamond to retrieve the gun, but he forgot that Monica had taken the car or perhaps he just didn't have time to tell him."

"Folks, don't fall for the stuff that defense lawyers throw at you. Just look at the cold, hard evidence. And the cold, hard evidence shows that

Larice is the only one that threatened to kill Timmy Lawson; Larice is the only one who left his fingerprints on the shell casings that were found at the scene; Larice is the only one who left his fingerprints on the gun; and we have proven that the gun matches the bullets that killed the Lawson family."

"Now, there are always some fantastic theories that if you stretch your imagination to the limits, may be somehow possible. That's why your job is not to decide if the defendant is guilty beyond *any* doubt. It's your job to decide beyond a *reasonable* doubt. And we have proven here today, that Larice Jones is guilty beyond a reasonable doubt."

As Keene took his seat at the prosecution table, Nolan smiled. Keene wasn't like Mutz or the other minions that worked for him. Keene was, as his name implied, a very keen person who was hard to fool. But sometimes, the desire to win overshadowed everything else and the truth got left behind in the dark. And that's what had just happened to Keene. If he hadn't been so desperate for a conviction, perhaps Keene would've had a better chance to nail Larice. But in his zealousness, Keene couldn't see the other scenario; the one that Nolan had not mentioned to the jury - - the one that could've sealed his client's fate.

After Keene's rebuttal, the judge read from a book of jury instructions that covered general trial issues and those specific to murder. He also read the instructions that the lawyers submitted pertaining to the case. Before he was done, he reminded them that the lawyers' closing arguments were not evidence and that they should look at all of the evidence when making their decision on guilt or innocence. When he finished with the instructions, he excused them to deliberate.

Nolan turned to Larice. "We'll meet you in the lockup."

Larice nodded as the deputy escorted him out.

Once he was gone, Danny turned to Nolan. "That was awesome! How did you see that tree in the forest?" he asked.

"I guess when you're living in the forest for several months, you eventually see them all."

"Wow," Danny said again. "How long do you think they'll deliberate before they find him not guilty?"

Nolan shook his head. "If I've learned one thing, it's never to expect the jury to do anything. They could be done in an hour with a guilty verdict for all I know."

"I don't think so," Danny said, as if he had any experience with juries. "There's no way he's guilty."

Nolan smiled. He didn't bring up the other theory; the one that Keene failed to see.

"Let's go back and see our boy," Nolan said. They left the courtroom together and walked down the hall to the lockup door. The deputy opened the door on the first knock and let them into the secured area.

"We don't need to get inside -- we can talk to him through the cage," Nolan said. The deputy shrugged, "Suit yourself, you know where he is."

As they began to walk down the corridor, Nolan glanced into the first cell on the left, where Gamond Edwards was sitting. His head was leaning back against the wall and his eyes were closed.

At the end of the corridor, Larice was pressed against the steel mesh.

"Son of a bitch!" Larice yelled out with a big grin on his face. "That was fucking mad dogs, man! Just fucking mad dogs!" he said as slapped the cage with his hands.

"Don't get too excited yet," Nolan said. "The jury's still out."

"Man, they got to find me not guilty after what you said. They just got to!" Larice exclaimed.

"I'm with you, Larice," Danny chimed in. "I'd be shocked if they didn't."

"We'll see," Nolan said. "The deputy will bring you out when the jury has a decision. We'll see you in the courtroom when that happens. But right now Danny and I need to work on other things," Nolan said. He didn't want to tell Larice that they had to prepare for sentencing if Larice was found guilty.

"How long will it take for them to decide?" Larice asked.

"Who knows?" Nolan answered. "It could be in the next second or the next two days."

"All right. Thanks man --you did one hell of a job in there. And I appreciate it."

"No problem," Nolan said. "Like I told you before, I'm just doing my job."

CHAPTER 47

Two hours and ten minutes after they began their deliberation, the foreman of the jury pushed the electronic button near the door of the deliberation room. A loud buzzer sounded and a light above the room lit up. The deputy immediately went to the door and opened it. "Is there a verdict?" he asked.

There was.

From there, the deputy alerted the judge, who entered the courtroom and took his place on the bench. The deputy also retrieved the defendant from the lockup and escorted him to the defense table. When the lawyers and the defendant were in their places, the judge told the deputy to bring in the jury.

As the jury filed into the courtroom, Nolan stared at each person. He was looking to see if any of them would make eye contact with him. His theory was that if one or two of them made eye contact with him, the verdict would be for acquittal. If not one person had the guts to look him in the eye, then the verdict would be guilty. He continued to watch after they were seated. Not one juror glanced his way, but several were staring at Keene.

"Members of the jury, have you reached a verdict?" the judge asked.

"Yes we have," the foreman answered.

"Please hand it to the deputy," the judge ordered.

The deputy took the piece of paper from the jury and walked it to the judge. The judge looked at it briefly, before handing it back to the deputy. The deputy then walked it over to the clerk, who was standing in her clerk box next to the judge's bench.

"Have the defendant stand," the judge ordered.

Larice stood up between Nolan and Danny at the defense table.

"Ladies and gentlemen in the courtroom, the verdict is about to be read. Let me remind you that this has been a fair trial and that both sides have had an opportunity to present their evidence. When the verdict is read, I don't want to hear any outbursts of any kind either in support of or against the verdict." He nodded to the clerk.

Nolan glanced at Larice. Although he was standing, his arms were in front of him and his hands were pressed against the top of the table, as if he needed the support to stand. Nolan could see that the cuffs on his suit jacket were shaking.

The courtroom was completely silent as the clerk began to read the paper.

"The jury of Big Shanty Circuit Court has rendered a verdict in the case of Commonwealth of Virginia versus Larice Jones. On the charge that you, Larice Jones, willfully and deliberately, and with premeditation, did kill Cleo Lawson, the jury finds you . . . not guilty."

Larice let out a rush of air from his lungs, as if he had been holding his breath since the beginning of the trial. He dropped his head and clasped his hands together and muttered, "Thank you Jesus, thank you Jesus."

"On the charge that you, Larice Jones, willfully and deliberately, and with premeditation, did kill Frank Lawson, the jury finds you . . . not guilty."

Larice continued to thank the Lord as a big grin began to spread on his face.

The clerk continued reading the verdicts of the other crimes that Larice was facing, including the weapons and robbery charges. At the end of each charge, the clerk read the words "not guilty."

Despite the judge's warnings, Larice could not help himself. He turned to face the prosecution table and raised his arms above his head, as if he had just scored the winning touchdown of the Super Bowl. "Yes!" he shouted with his arms raised. And then he held his arms out and turned to Keene. "What's up! What's up, bitch?"

The judge banged his gavel and shouted at Larice. "Shut your mouth or you'll be thrown in jail on contempt!"

Larice turned his hands up. "My bad," he said. "My bad."

Nolan pushed Larice back down into his seat and whispered. "Just let the judge wrap this up and you'll be out of here in no time."

"Thank you," Larice said, pumping Nolan's hand again. "Thank you for everything."

"You're welcome," Nolan said. "I'll come back to the lockup before they take you back to the jail and process you out."

After a quick thanks to the jury for their time, the judge dismissed them and ended the court session. Keene and Mutz headed straight for the door without so much as a glance at Nolan.

Danny turned to Nolan. "Congratulations," he said, holding out his hand. "I knew he was not guilty."

Nolan shook his hand and shrugged. "Well, only the jury decides that and until then, everybody's guilty."

Danny followed Nolan to the lockup one more time. This time, Gamond Edwards was standing with his hands on the cage, staring at Nolan.

"Hey lawyer," he said as they were passing. "The deputy told me what happened in there. You think you know everything, don't you?"

Nolan shrugged. "I don't have to know everything . . . just more than the prosecutor." He turned and continued down the corridor.

"Lawyer!" Gamond Edwards yelled again.

Nolan stopped and glanced back.

"Tell Ice I was just doing what I had to do. It's all good."

Without saying anything, Nolan turned and continued to Larice's cell at the end of the corridor, with Danny following at his heels. Nolan didn't bother to enter Larice's cell, he peered through the mesh instead. "Gamond wants me to give you a message. He says he was just doing what he had to do . . . it's all good."

Larice grinned. "Will they charge him with the murders?"

"I doubt it," Nolan shrugged. "The prosecutor made his bed and now he has to lie in it. Besides, he probably still thinks that Gamond is telling the truth."

"That prosecutor ain't none too smart, is he?" Larice asked.

"Oh he's smart . . . it just may be that you're the luckiest man on the planet today."

Larice smiled.

"One more thing," Nolan said. "If I were you, I'd get the hell out of this town as soon as you're released from jail. Don't even stop to look back."

Larice shrugged. "I'll bring you the suit when I get out. Where's your office?"

"Keep it," Nolan said. "It may remind you to stay out of trouble."

Without saying goodbye, Nolan turned and marched back down the hallway to the exit door. Danny followed closely behind him. "Why did you tell him to leave town?" Danny asked.

"Don't worry about it. I'll tell you later."

CHAPTER 48

After the jury's verdict, Fred Mutz did not return to the office with his mentor. Keene stopped him in the corridor just outside the courtroom and said two words to him: "You're fired."

Mutz didn't immediately respond. Instead, he stared in silence, appearing completely dumbfounded.

"Hello!" Keene said, snapping his fingers in front of Mutz's face. "Give me your office key!"

Mutz reached in his pocket. Still in shock, he fumbled at his key ring until the office key came off. Without saying anything, he held the key out for Keene, who snatched it quickly from his hand.

"You can come back tomorrow morning after nine to pick up your personal belongings," Keene said, turning to leave. "I'll have them in a box."

Before he could leave, Mutz managed to get out one word . . . "Why?"

Keene turned to face him. "You're not a prosecutor . . . and you'll never be one."

Keene's words were like a hard slap to Mutz's face, waking him from his semi-delirium state of denial.

"You're wrong!" Mutz yelled.

Keene shrugged and walked away.

Most people in Mutz's situation would've either lashed out in anger, or succumbed to self-pity. But Mutz apparently wasn't like most people. Instead of turning to walk towards the nearest bar to drown his sorrows, he turned the opposite way; the direction in which he thought he could obtain justice, and at the same time, save his career.

Exiting the main doors of the courthouse, Mutz quickly made his way down the sidewalk. As he walked at a brisk pace, he muttered under his breath and jabbed at the air with his hands. He was obviously angry at the outcome of the trial and even more so at the outcome of his career as a Big Shanty assistant prosecutor. But any prosecutor in his position would have reacted the same way. And there was something else that any good prosecutor would have done. A really keen prosecutor would have made a special visit to the magistrate, which is exactly what Mutz did next.

Walking past the building in which the Commonwealth's Attorney's office was located, Mutz turned left at the corner and proceeded towards the jail, which was two blocks away. He was on his way to see the magistrate, who sat behind a thick panel of bullet proof glass in a small office space just inside the entrance of the jail.

Just like most towns in Virginia, the magistrate was on duty twenty four hours a day, seven days a week. The magistrate's primary duty was to issue arrest warrants and search warrants. When the police arrested anyone, they had to take the arrestee to the magistrate, who issued a formal arrest warrant and set bail. When the police wanted a search warrant, they also had to apply to the magistrate. And in Virginia, when a citizen had a valid criminal complaint against someone, they could also go to the magistrate's office and get an arrest warrant issued.

When he arrived at the magistrate's office, Mutz told the officer of the court exactly what had happened, why it happened, and how it happened. He also described the perpetrator and where he could be found. The magistrate listened intently to what Mutz had to say, and after a few questions, issued an arrest warrant.

The magistrate made a call to the police station and an officer was immediately sent over to pick up the warrant. Mutz stayed at the magistrate's office until the police officer arrived. Once the police officer had the warrant in hand and he was on his way to arrest the defendant, Mutz grinned and nodded to the magistrate. "Thank you," he said. "You did the right thing."

* * * * * * *

"How did it go?" Keene's secretary asked as he approached her cubicle.

Keene didn't answer her question. "Hold all my calls and don't disturb me," he said, without making eye contact. He slammed the door behind him as he entered his office and then flipped the lock.

In a not so gentle manner, he slung his briefcase onto his desk and then kicked his chair, sending it wildly spinning into the corner. Instead of sitting, he paced back and forth like a zoo animal, rubbing his hands through his hair and swearing under his breath.

How could this happen to me? There must be something I can do. Think . . . Think.

His thoughts were centered on revenge, more than justice. And they raced at a wicked pace, back and forth from Larice Jones to Nolan Getty.

Larice Jones is a murderer. I'll indict the bastard for the murder of Tommy Lawson, and this time, I'll make him pay. No more surprises. Now I know their fucked up theories and how to stop them.

Getty cheated. He had to have cheated. I'll call the bar and make a complaint. I'll have his fucking license and he'll never practice in this town again!

As he was pacing and plotting his vengeance, his cell phone vibrated. He looked at the caller identification and saw that it was Scotty, from the Big Shanty Gazette. In a fit of rage, he threw his cell phone into the couch.

Damned vultures! Go ahead, write your stories against me. I'll sue you for slander and take every penny you have!

In Keene's mind, everyone had turned against him; first the judge, then the jury, now the reporters.

The judge had not upheld the law, Keene thought. He had favored Getty throughout the trial and went out of his way to rule against him.

I'll teach that arrogant bastard a lesson. I'll file a complaint with the Judiciary Department. I'll call our representatives. When they hear what he's done, they'll think twice about re-appointing him when his term ends.

The jury -- the very citizens that he had been working so hard to protect -- had also betrayed him. But it couldn't have been all of them, Keene thought. The school teacher must have tried to make a stand on his behalf. Perhaps she was unlawfully coerced into following the others, Keene thought. He knew their addresses -- he could track every one of them down and interrogate them until he found out who was responsible. Perhaps he could even bring charges against one or more jurors for obstruction of justice.

Keene continued to plot his vengeance on everyone who had betrayed him. But his mind was too clouded with anger to see the truth.

Getty had not cheated; he had merely represented his client zealously. The judge had not favored either side; he had followed the law to the letter, making sure that the defendant had been provided a fair trial. Not one juror had acted inappropriately; every one of them, including the school teacher, had found reasonable doubt in Keene's case. And they too followed the law.

In reality, there was only one person who had betrayed Keene. And he never saw it coming.

Keene's thoughts of revenge were interrupted by a knock at his door. He spun on his heels and yelled out, "I told you. No interruptions!"

"Mr. Keene, open the door," a voice said. There were three more loud knocks.

God-damned insolent bitch! You want a piece of me? I'll send you packing too!

Keene stomped over to the door, and flipped the lock. He swung the door open, ready to lay into his secretary, but she was not there.

"Mr. Keene," the police officer said. "You're under arrest."

Keene shook his head and blinked at the police officer, unable to comprehend who he was and why he was there.

"What?" he blinked rapidly.

"Turn around and face the wall, sir," the officer said. "You're under arrest for assault and battery on Timmy Lawson."

A surge of panic coursed through Keene's body as he finally realized what was happening. "You can't arrest me!" Keene yelled. "I'm the Chief Commonwealth's Attorney!"

"I understand who you are, sir. But I have an arrest warrant signed by the magistrate, and that means I have to arrest you and take you in for booking."

"What did I do?" Keene whined. "You have to tell me what crime I've committed!"

"It says here on the affidavit from Fred Mutz that you grabbed someone named Timmy Lawson by the collar and shook him violently, which is an assault and battery."

"No," Keene said, taking a step backwards. "You can't do this. He's lied to the magistrate. Let me call down there and straighten this out," Keene said, stepping over to his desk and picking up the telephone.

"I'm going to tell you one more time," the officer raised his voice and placed his hand on the pepper spray attached to his utility belt. "Turn around and face the wall!"

Keene flinched and dropped the phone. He realized that he couldn't talk his way out of it. Due to fear more than anything, he slowly turned and put his hands behind him.

The officer snapped handcuffs on his wrists and patted him down. He pulled a pen knife from his left front pants pocket and a laser pointer from his right pocket. After turning his pockets inside out, he pulled at Keene's arm and said, "Come with me."

As Keene was led down the corridor in handcuffs, almost all of his employees began to filter out of their cubicles and offices. They all lined up to watch the single float parade. But not one of them offered any words of encouragement.

CHAPTER 49

Rick shook the bottle of beer and then opened the top as Nolan and Danny reached the bottom of the steps to the basement of the chateau.

"Yah Boss!" he shouted, placing his thumb over the opening and spraying it wildly upon them.

"Keep it off the felt," Nolan yelled as he ran through the shower and grabbed the bottle, turning it on Rick and spraying him back. They struggled for a few moments, until the bottle finally spewed its entire contents onto both of them. Nolan released his grip and held his hand up, giving Rick a high five.

"A B C," Nolan said with a grin, as the beer ran down his neck. "Always be closing!"

"I heard everything -- I was up there for the closing arguments," Rick laughed. "Is second place a set of steak knives, or does Keene get fired?"

Nolan laughed with him.

"Tell me the details," Rick begged. "How did Keene look when the verdict came in?"

"He didn't look none too good," Nolan answered in a fake, southern drawl.

They continued to discuss the details of the case. Danny did most of the talking, telling Rick how Timmy Lawson had fallen apart on the stand and how Keene had to come groveling back into court with the truth.

"And just when Keene had everyone back on board, Nolan dropped the Gamond Edwards bomb. Even I didn't see that coming," Danny exclaimed.

"No shit," Rick said. "What a shocker that our boss thought that up without your help."

Danny gave Rick a friendly push. "Yeah, well who was the one who was afraid of sitting second chair?"

Rick laughed and changed the subject. "How does it feel to finally be done with it?"

"I'm just glad it's over," Danny shook his head.

"It's over for us, anyway," Nolan commented. "But not for somebody."

"Do you think they'll indict Gamond Edwards for the murders?" Danny asked.

Nolan smiled. "I'm not talking about Edwards. I'm talking about Larice."

"Larice?" Danny asked. "What do you mean? He was acquitted."

"At the end, the only two murder charges that he faced were against Frank and Cleo Lawson. Keene could still go after him for the murder of Tommy Lawson," Nolan explained.

"But isn't that double jeopardy?"

"You're forgetting one thing," Nolan responded. "Larice was never indicted for the murder of Tommy Lawson -- he was indicted for the murder of Timmy Lawson. Therefore, there is no double jeopardy because he hasn't faced trial for that . . . yet."

"Keene wouldn't do that, would he? I mean, we've already proven that Gamond Edwards is the killer, so why would he go after Larice again?"

Nolan smiled. "There's one more theory that fits the evidence -- one that even Keene didn't see."

Danny cocked his head and raised an eyebrow. "And what would that be?"

"What Keene failed to recognize is that Gamond Edwards could have known the location of the gun, not because Larice told him at the lockup, and not because Gamond planted the gun himself, but because he was with Larice Jones on the night that they killed the Lawson family."

"Whoa!" Danny said, taken aback. "I never thought of that."

"Think about it," Nolan continued. "I told the jury that Gamond broke into Larice's house, but it's just as possible that Timmy broke in and stole the drugs. When he discovers that his family was murdered, of course he thinks that Larice killed them. And he's afraid that Larice will come after him, so he comes up with the lie that he's Tommy. And maybe he even calls 9-1-1 and tells them that Larice did it -- to ensure that Larice goes to jail. But if Larice kept his gun in the blue T-bird, Timmy couldn't have stolen it when he burglarized the house. In fact, maybe the gun was never stolen at all."

"Interesting," Danny nodded.

"Think about this. Gamond confronts Larice about the drugs. Larice tells Gamond that Timmy has stolen the drugs. Then Gamond and Larice make a plan to go get them back. Maybe they drive together over to Astor Street that night. Maybe one of them is the driver, the other is the killer, either way they are both guilty of murder one. They get the drugs back though, which is the important thing."

"Wow," Danny said. "You really think so?"

Nolan shrugged. "Not really. I'm just saying that Keene could've argued that. In fact, he could be thinking about it right now, and getting ready to bring down indictments for both of them. And because Larice was never indicted for the murder of Tommy Lawson, his lawyer wouldn't have a leg to stand on as far as double jeopardy."

"Well, wouldn't that lawyer be you?" Danny asked.

"Not me," Nolan said, "or any one of us in this office. I'll claim conflict of interest in any further murder trials. And that goes for Gamond Edwards, too. No matter what happens, we're done with those yahoos."

Rick reached into a paper sack and handed Nolan and Danny bottles of beer. They clinked the bottles together and drank.

"You've just won your first jury trial, riding on the coat-tails of a master," Rick said after he gulped down the beer. "I hope you finally learned something so you can start pulling your own weight around here."

Danny thought for a second. "I guess there's one thing I've learned." Taking a sip of beer, he smiled at Rick. "As you said . . . the truth is in the lies of the beholder."

EPILOGUE

When the mayor of Big Shanty heard what had happened, he called a special meeting of the city council. During that meeting, the council heard testimony from both Fred Mutz and Timmy Lawson, both of whom testified that Keene had committed an assault and battery against Timmy by grabbing his collar and shaking him like a rag doll. Timmy told the council that Keene had not only physically injured him, but that he was also suffering emotionally due to Keene's attack upon him.

At the conclusion of the meeting, the council voted to suspend John Keene without pay, at least and until the criminal charge against him could be resolved. In his place, they appointed Fred Mutz as the interim Chief.

When John Keene went to trial on the charge, the judge agreed to take the matter under advisement for a year and to dismiss the charge completely if Keene remained on good behavior during that time. Keene was happy with that decision because his official term as Chief Commonwealth Attorney ended within that same time period and there would be no criminal conviction on his record which could prevent him from running for re-election.

Nonetheless, during the election campaign against his mentor, Fred Mutz pointed to the Lawson murder trial as evidence that John Keene was soft on crime and incompetent at bringing criminals to justice, not to mention the fact that he had pending criminal charges as well. In addition, Mutz vowed to bring the Lawson killer's to justice and to protect the community from future criminals.

In the end, it was the rhetoric of Fred Mutz that won the day. He defeated John Keene, becoming the youngest Chief Commonwealth Attorney ever elected.

One month later, after reviewing the evidence in the Lawson murder case, Mutz made a special presentation to the Grand Jury of Big Shanty. The Grand Jury subsequently returned indictments against Gamond Edwards for the murder of Frank, Cleo, and Tommy Lawson.

But unlike his predecessor, Mutz had a different game plan for the trial of Gamond Edwards. Now that he was calling the shots, he was going to prosecute the defendant for capital murder. And later, if any of his assistants questioned him about their game plan, he already knew what he was going to say.

We're going to fry the bastard.

The author may be contacted at:
liesofbeholder@comcast.net

CPSIA information can be obtained at www.ICGtesting.com
Printed in the USA
LVOW080726280412

279522LV00001B/163/P